Medieval
LORDS & LADIES
COLLECTION

*When courageous knights risked all
to win the hand of their lady!*

Don't miss any of this stunning collection!

July 2007 – Volume 1
Conquest Brides
He took her lands – but can he capture her heart?

August 2007 – Volume 2
Blackmail & Betrayal
Forgive and forget…or take her revenge?

September 2007 – Volume 3
The War of the Roses
Brought together by passion, torn apart by war!

October 2007 – Volume 4
Christmas Knights
Spend a medieval Yuletide with a perfect knight!

November 2007 – Volume 5
Exotic East
All the heat and spice of the desert…

December
Mediterr
These men have a
their

Medieval
LORDS & LADIES
COLLECTION

Christmas Knights

Joanna Makepeace & Elaine Knighton

*M&B™ and M&B™ with the Rose Device
are trademarks of the publisher.
Harlequin Mills & Boon Limited, Eton House,
18-24 Paradise Road, Richmond, Surrey TW9 1SR*

MEDIEVAL LORDS & LADIES COLLECTION
© Harlequin Books S.A. 2007

The publisher acknowledges the copyright holders of the
individual works as follows:

King's Pawn © Joanna Makepeace 1996
The Alchemist's Daughter © Elaine Knighton 2005

ISBN: 978 0 263 85884 6

53-1007

*Printed and bound in Spain
by Litografía Rosés S.A., Barcelona*

King's Pawn

by

Joanna Makepeace

Joanna Makepeace taught as head of English in a comprehensive, before leaving full-time work to write. She lives in Leicester with her mother and Jack Russell terrier called Jeffrey, and has written over thirty books under different pseudonyms. She loves the old romantic historical films, which she finds more exciting and relaxing than the newer ones.

Chapter One

Peter Fairley paused with his hand on the door of his master's bedchamber. He looked down the stair to the winter parlour where their illustrious guest was waiting. Recently the Earl of Wroxeter had been given to retiring to his own chamber with strict instructions to his household not to disturb him for any reason whatever.

Peter knew, to his cost, that any disobedience was likely to receive dire punishment and he gritted his teeth determinedly. Whatever his master's reaction to this disturbance this morning, his wrath must be faced squarely. Such a visitor could not be kept waiting and certainly not sent away from the house without seeing its master. He lifted his hand again and knocked loudly.

There came no order to enter, nor any surly call to take himself off. Peter sighed, irresolute, but knocked again and pushed open the heavy oak door. He advanced nervously into the room.

Martyn Telford, Earl of Wroxeter, sat, legs stretched out before the sea-coal fire in his padded armchair. It was a chilly November morning in this year of Our Lord, 1484, and the mist from the river seemed to penetrate all the rooms of this fine town house in the Strand.

A book lay discarded upon the carpet near the Earl's chair as if it had slipped unheeded from his knee. He was staring through the glazed window over the secluded garden which backed up towards the river but Peter thought he was not seeing the mist-shrouded pleasance or the herb beds.

He turned suddenly as the squire's footsteps halted some paces from the chair and snapped out ungraciously, "Well, is the house on fire?"

"No, sir." Peter did not dare to smile and nervously glanced down at the polished boards of the chamber floor.

"I told you earlier that you were not to disturb me unless there was an emergency. Since the house appears to be intact, is there a riot in the streets? I confess I have been aware of no outcry."

"No, sir." Peter's acute nervousness was growing by the moment.

"Then will you inform me of what dire need causes you to so flagrantly disobey me?"

The boy's brown eyes implored him for understanding.

"You have a visitor, my lord."

Dark brows rose in sarcastic enquiry. "Have I not taught you to deal with importunate visitors, boy?"

Peter swallowed and glanced uncomfortably back towards the chamber door as if he feared he might be overheard.

"The visitor will not give his name, my lord..."

"Then send him about his business."

"Sir, I cannot. He is from Court and I believe... He is muffled against the weather, my lord, and two men-at-arms are waiting in the street as escort for him, but," he finished in a rush, "I could not refuse him, my lord. I believe him to be on the King's business. He demands to see you urgently, sir, says he is aware of your need to seclude yourself from the world at large but—it is imperative he see you at once.''

The Earl's slumberous dark eyes stared into the boy's anxious brown ones. His lips tightened then he sighed, stooped and picked up the precious book and replaced it on the small table near him, stood up and stretched his tall frame. ''Very well. See that our important guest is plied with wine and offered what other refreshment he might require and say I will be with him in moments. I take it you showed him into the winter parlour?''

''Master Rawlings did, my lord. Like me, he thought...''

''Quite. Go down, boy, and see our guest is well served.'' The Earl smiled a trifle grimly. ''I'll put to rights my dishevelled appearance since you are so keen to stress our unknown visitor's importance. All is well, lad; I'll not keep him waiting long nor...'' he hesitated with a wintry smile ''...nor will I prove too disagreeable despite my unamiable mood.''

The boy scurried out and the Earl moved towards a mirror on his dressing chest. He was still dressed in mourning black, unrelieved by ornamental chain. He wore no jewellery save two rings, one a cabochon-cut emerald deeply prized.

He hesitated after running an ivory comb through his ruffled dark hair then, sighing, slipped the golden chain with its gleaming Yorkist suns and roses, which had been lying, discarded, on the chest before him, over his shoulders, smoothed down the fine-cut velvet of his doublet and prepared to confront this court visitor whom Peter had considered so important.

As he entered the winter parlour, he saw that the man was seated before the fire still wrapped in his cloak. If he had come from Westminster, as Peter supposed, he must have got very cold indeed seated within the ferry boat which had brought him downriver.

Wroxeter spoke from the doorway. "I see my servants have provided you with refreshment. I'm sorry to have kept you waiting. Recently I've lived a hermit's life but my squire tells me your business is urgent."

The man in the chair rose and turned. He was wearing a low-crowned velvet chaperon with an enveloping scarf which swept round the throat and over one shoulder. Wroxeter saw the ruby glimmering sombrely in its grey velvet depths as its wearer put back the scarf and faced him squarely. He gave a great gasp of recognition and came on into the room at a run and dropped to one knee.

"Your Grace, you honour this house. Why did you not summon me immediately to Westminster if you had need of me? You had no need to suffer the inconvenience of travelling in this bitterly cold weather."

King Richard smiled down at his friend and held out a hand to signal to the Earl to rise. He divested himself of chaperon, cloak and gloves, laying them by on a stool near him.

"Martyn," he said, gently reproving, "you have been hard to reach these last weeks. I know you had no taste for court ceremonial. To tell the truth, I have little heart for it myself, but I did wish to speak to you on a purely personal but important matter, one on which I did not wish to be overheard. It seemed appropriate that I should call on you without ceremony and, I hope, without undue notice from others."

The King was gesturing for Martyn to seat himself in the second chair drawn up in front of the fire.

"No, don't summon your servant again. This burgundy is excellent. Take wine with me, Martyn."

A table had been drawn up beside the King's chair and

the Earl was relieved to see that Peter had provided the King's favourite wine in a silver flagon and two silver goblets, beside a platter of meats and fine white manchet bread. The King appeared not to have touched the food but was drinking appreciatively.

Martyn Telford smiled as he poured out wine for himself, as ordered, and took his seat beside his sovereign.

"I think Peter guessed your identity, Your Grace, and knew your fondness for burgundy. He was at pains to impress upon me the importance of my visitor but did not dare actually name you."

The King chuckled. "You are fortunate in that boy, Martyn. I hear he shapes up well in the tilt-yard, but his discretion is worth his weight in pure gold."

"He is a good lad," Martyn conceded, "and he has had much to put up with lately."

The King eyed him steadily. His shrewd grey eyes took in the dark shadows round his friend's eyes, the strained air and tight, hard line of the usually mobile mouth. Wroxeter was not handsome but personable. His tall, lean length was well proportioned and strong-muscled. The long-featured face, formerly good-humoured and sleepily attractive, with the strong, dominant nose and heavily lidded, dark eyes, marked by black, well-arched brows, had proved a favourite with the Queen's ladies.

The King knew that that sleepy, half-bored expression hid a mind both quick to grasp essentials and as shrewd as his own when needed to grasp the intricacies of court intrigue. His brother, the late King Edward, had instituted a system of scurriers and spy networks which had kept him well informed as to the propensities of those about him at court, within the realm at large and overseas.

When Richard had been offered the throne by Parliament, after the discovery of the bastardy of King Edward's children, Richard had found the need to continue that very useful organisation and had discovered in the young Martyn Telford a superior intelligence to oversee its work. He had come to rely on Wroxeter to make him aware of what his normal military scurriers failed to discover by usual means. Lately he had missed the presence of so clever and discreet an adviser by his side at Westminster.

He said quietly, "I know what a terrible blow Elinor Maudsley's death has been to you, Martyn. I've suffered a similar crushing pain myself."

Martyn turned his grief-ravaged face full upon his sovereign and, for a moment, a hint of tears glimmered in his dark eyes. He too saw marks of intense suffering upon that narrow, clever countenance which he had come to love and admire.

The King had had much to face during this first year of his reign: the rebellion of his trusted, much loved cousin, George of Buckingham, intrigue at home and abroad, problems upon the Scots border where the thieving reivers were set to take advantage of the King's absence from the territories he had kept secure during the previous eleven years, as the late King's ruler in the north, from his fastness of Middleham Castle in Wensleydale.

He had also had to deal with more immediate concerns, not least the scheming of the French King, ever his enemy, determined to keep the presence of the last Lancastrian heir on French soil as a dependant, constantly a thorn in the English King's flesh.

Henry Tudor was scheming quietly and determinedly, surrounded by disaffected Lancastrian gentlemen who had fled the realm following the Yorkist victory at Tewkesbury, the principal supporter being his uncle, Jasper Tudor, the exiled Earl of Pembroke. It had been Martyn's work to keep a careful eye on any courtier or country squire who might be tempted to change allegiance and offer support to the Tudors.

All this as well as the King's most personal tragedy—the death of his only son and heir, young Edward, Prince of Wales, on March the ninth last, when the King and his Queen had been on progress. They had received the dread news at Nottingham and Richard had declared the fortress his "Castle of Care".

Only too well, Martyn was aware that the gentle Queen Anne was ailing and unlikely ever to be able to give the King a second child. He sighed, recognising his weakness in allowing his own loss to take him from his loyal attendance and duties at the King's side.

He said, chokingly, "Your Grace, you must forgive me. What can be my loss compared to yours?"

The King shook his head. "Every man's sorrow is as great to him as another. You have known Mistress Elinor Maudsley since you were both children, yet it is only a short time since you became reacquainted and your affection for her grew. You had great hopes of a happy life together stretching long into the future. It has been a terrible blow to you for her to become so ill so suddenly this summer and die with so little warning."

Martyn said slowly, "I could not believe it. She had a pain, she said, on her right side, and she was dreadfully sick. At first I thought of poison yet no one who knew Elinor could wish to harm her. The physicians could do nothing. She became worse by the evening and died early the next day in excruciating pain. I could do nothing... Thank the Virgin I was there with her—"

He broke off suddenly, noting the haggard expression which had deepened upon the King's countenance. "Dear God, forgive me again, Your Grace, for my crass insensitivity. I know you were unable to be with the Lord Edward…''

"It was that which has gnawed at the Queen's peace," the King said soberly. "It was days afterward before we knew. She had missed him so much and then—to lose him like that…" His voice had become hoarse with emotion and, abruptly, he cleared his throat and began again. "From what you tell me his symptoms were similar to those of the Lady Elinor. He too died in great pain and his illness developed as suddenly."

They were both silent for moments, then Martyn said, "If you have need of me, of course I will come to Westminster this very day."

"That will not be necessary, Martyn. Your clerk, Master Standish, is managing well, John Kendall, my secretary, informs me, though it is essential that a good watch is kept continually, particularly upon the Welsh Marches. It is on that very matter which I wish to consult with you."

"Some insurrection, sire?"

"No, not yet, but some of the Marcher barons could be open to temptation. I know the Tudor's agents are constantly on the move, gathering information as to our strengths and weaknesses and offering promises of preferment should Henry gain his desire and ascend my throne."

"We all pray that may never happen, my lord."

Richard's lips twisted wryly. "No more determinedly than I do, my friend." His eyes were showing grim amusement now, the grey-green irises dancing in the firelight.

"Rumours are continually put about concerning the fate of my nephews. You know well enough that such deliberate mongering is false. The boys are safe enough where I have placed them and young Edward of Warwick is, at last, making some considerable progress in his arrested development under careful tutelage at Sheriff Hutton, but all this adds to the fuel of men's resentment.

"These southern lords have never been as ready to give me their trust and devotion so readily granted to my brother Edward. They do not know me well, or my officers from the north. Besides these, there are still men disaffected since Tewkesbury, men who did not flee abroad like Pembroke and Oxford but who still hanker for the old Lancastrian cause, men like Daniel Gretton."

Martyn's eyebrows rose and the King leaned forward in his chair. "He is a close neighbour. You know Gretton?"

"I have met him," Martyn said cautiously. "I had not thought his allegiance in question. He is married happily, I understand, and appears thoroughly contented with his lot."

"I have received information that he has harboured men suspected to have been sent by Pembroke."

Martyn frowned. "You wish me to have him arrested?"

"No, nothing so drastic. The man is wealthy and influential on the Welsh border. He has a manor near Ludlow. Naturally he must have seen something of the young Lord Edward when his household was there with Rivers as his tutor."

"Yes, sir."

"Gretton and his father fought for Margaret of Anjou at Tewkesbury. Old Sir John Gretton was killed in the retreat. Daniel took refuge with Somerset and the other Lancastrian knights in Tewkesbury Abbey, and was released and allowed to disperse the day following the battle, after Somerset surrendered and he and the ringleaders were brought before me for judgement. As you will know, those ringleaders were executed in Tewkesbury market-place. Sir Daniel Gretton must still recall those grim days, as I do myself."

He gave a brief sigh and gazed into the fire, as if remembering the terrible slaughter in the pursuit after
Tewkesbury and his harsh task as Lord Constable of England, as he had been then, at only eighteen years of age.

Acting on his brother's orders, he had seen to it that
Margaret of Anjou's principal captains had not lived to
challenge the new Yorkist dynasty under Edward and
soon after Edward's return to London with his brothers,
Gloucester and Clarence, the confused, pathetic King
Henry VI had died in the Tower.

Martyn thought there must have been many mourning
the victims of that battle, Gretton amongst them, and that
resentment could have festered. Would that man now risk
his life and fortune by allying himself with some rebel
force, devoted to the exiled young Lancastrian claimant,
Henry Tudor? Martyn pursed his lips. Surely not—and yet
he knew only too well that ambitious men were like to
risk anything for the hope of preferment.

The King turned to face him again, his lips curving into
a rueful smile. "Gretton has, as you said, made a happy
marriage, or so I hear, but he has no heir and is unlikely
to get one now. He has a daughter, Cressida, almost sixteen
and ripe for the marriage bed."

Martyn stared back at him, astonished.

The King smiled again regretfully.

"I see you find it hard to accept that you know what I
am saying."

"Your Grace, you cannot mean that—that you wish me
to consider marriage with this—child?"

"Yes, Martyn, that is exactly what I am saying."

"But…"

"I ask too much, even from one so loyal as you are?"

Martyn had risen from his chair, half in surprise, half in
anger, then, finding his sovereign's eyes on him, com-

manding his attention, he sat down again, drew a hard breath and subsided into sullen acquiescence.

"Believe me, I know what a hard sacrifice I ask of you." The King turned away for a moment and his fingers drummed awkwardly upon the chair arm. "Martyn, my Queen is sick. My physicians inform me she cannot improve, at least not permanently. I may soon be compelled to make this same sacrifice—for the good of the realm."

"Your Grace, I confess I am confused. My brain addles with the newness of this suggestion, but I need to have it spelled out to me what you intend and how you think it will achieve your ends."

"You are an earl, wealthy, Gretton's neighbour. Despite his wealth and standing amongst the Marcher knights and lords he could not aspire so high for his daughter and, I am informed, she is everything to him. If I could dangle before him the hope of so important a match I can bring him here waiting attendance upon me, under my eye, at least for the next months when the crisis is looming."

Martyn was still silent, but the King could see that the thoughts were ticking over in that clever, astute mind.

"You need an heir, Martyn. The girl is young, malleable. I have it on good authority that she is more than presentable, but, that aside, I know men have different attitudes to beauty. By this marriage I would see you did not lose."

"My lord, you have been more than generous. I would not wish—"

"Continue to hear me out patiently, Martyn. As I said, it is unlikely Gretton will have an heir. The girl will inherit extensive estates which will march well with yours. By all standards it will be an excellent alliance. Allow me one personal question, my friend. Is there amongst the ladies— are your affections in any way engaged elsewhere?"

Martyn gave one small, anguished cry of protest. "By the Saints, no, Your Grace. I still can think of little else but Elinor. This is why I cannot concentrate on reports brought in by your scurriers."

The King nodded serenely. "It is as I thought. Will you consider this, Martyn? All I wished to do for the present was invite Sir Daniel with his wife and daughter to the Christmas festivities and the crown-wearing ceremony. I shall suggest to him that it would be my pleasure to try to arrange an advantageous marriage for his daughter. He will not dare refuse. We shall have opportunity to see the girl and assess her suitability. Should you still object to the match—" he shrugged "—then I will have to look elsewhere."

Martyn had buried his face in his hands. He sat leaning forward, his body rocking slightly in the chair. The King touched his shoulder in a light, affectionate movement then rose to his feet.

"I must leave you, Martyn. I have a council meeting at the Tower. I do not demand an immediate answer. Think over what I've said. You will be present at Court over the Holy Season? You must begin to put grief aside, man. It is God's will that our loved ones are taken and we cannot—*must* not allow ourselves to become bitter or neglect our duties."

Martyn had stumbled to his feet as the King had risen and he gritted his teeth against the justice of the gentle reproof. He bowed deeply.

"Your Grace does right to remind me of my loyalties at this uncertain time. If you have need of me, you have but to command my service…" He hesitated for a second, then added, "In all matters, both official—and personal."

Richard smiled. "Thank you. Some of my southern lords may be tardy in their allegiance, but I know I can always rely on my very special friends.'' His lips twitched slightly. ''Unfortunately, none but you is available for this very special service.''

Martyn lowered his head again in courteous acceptance of his King's command. ''I understand, Your Grace.''

He rang a small hand-bell for service and Peter Fairley came running.

''Peter, please escort our illustrious guest to the door. I take it you do not wish to be seen openly with me just at this moment, sir?''

''You have it exactly, my lord earl. It would be unwise, yet, for my intentions to be guessed at—by anyone.'' The King assumed his chaperon and pulled the velvet scarf across the lower part of his face. ''Farewell, Martyn. I hope to see you soon at Westminster.''

Martyn bent to kiss the bejewelled hand and watched as the King left with his squire. He moved to the carved oak fireplace and, placing his two hands on the overmantel, leaned down, staring once more into the flames.

He was twenty-three. In these unsettled times it was only sensible that he beget an heir. He had served as squire in the household of Sir Francis, now Viscount Lovell, until he had been knighted by Duke Richard of Gloucester, as the King had been then, for service with him on the Scottish border.

He had been then almost twenty and so busy with martial affairs that he had not thought to take a wife. His father had not pressed him and he had not been betrothed in childhood, a circumstance which he had come to believe fortunate, when faced with the evidence of mismatches he had seen in others of his acquaintance. Then Lord Wroxeter had died suddenly of an inflammation of the lungs and his heir had been hastily summoned south to be invested with his title.

The hasty necessity of his former duke ascending the throne in the past year, and the intrigues and rebellions which had followed, had demanded his loyalty and complete attention, and rendered him impervious to the bright eyes of suitable court ladies until Elinor Maudsley had arrived at Westminster to serve Queen Anne.

They had known each other in childhood and been close friends. That pleasure in each other's company had ripened into love. They had become betrothed with the King's gracious approval. Martyn had looked forward eagerly to an autumn wedding, then the cruel fates had struck without warning. Elinor had sickened suddenly and died four months ago.

He would not have believed that he could suffer so terribly from his loss. She had been gentle, yet intelligent and competent, an entertaining companion, and he had known she would make an excellent chatelaine for his castle and manors. He missed her constantly. She had come like a bright star onto his horizon and like a meteor had left it as suddenly. He felt unmanned by the depth of his grief.

Now the King was requesting that he face the possibility of marrying some child bride, a stranger, chosen for him simply by the necessity of welding an alliance in the Welsh Marcher lands. He tasted salt blood as his teeth bit down savagely onto his nether lip.

So be it. The King had need of him. He would not— *could* not love again. Why not this unknown girl? If by marrying her he could solidify Gretton's allegiance to the Crown, and achieve some measure of gain in lands and standing in his king's affections, then surely he would be a fool to refuse?

He straightened up in sudden determination and glanced down ruefully at his mourning black.

He would present himself this very afternoon at his of-

fice at the Palace of Westminster, then, perhaps tomorrow,
he would summon his tailor to consult with him about
more suitable attire in which to greet the youthful Mistress
Gretton at the coming Christmas feast.

Cressida had watched the arrival of the messenger from
the window of her bedchamber. Over this last year she had
seen men arriving, sometimes clandestinely, being received by her father privately, then going off hurriedly
about their business. She could not understand now why
the arrival of this particular courier should arouse in her a
feeling of vague unease.

The man had been dressed in the usual leathern jack,
salet and breastplate, but she had glimpsed beneath the
martial accoutrements the murrey and blue livery of the
royal house of York. So the courier came from Westminster.

The doubt which had assailed her grew stronger. Was
her father under suspicion? Yet surely if he was to be
arrested there would have been an armed escort, not a solitary messenger?

She called to her nurse, Alice, now serving her as maid,
to bring her a warm hooded cloak and to send down to the
stables for a groom to saddle up and bring into the courtyard her favourite jennet.

Alice grumbled as usual. "It's very cold this afternoon.
Why do you want to ride out? I imagine you'll go alone
as usual. You know I don't approve. Anything can happen
to a young lady alone these days. You are too old now to
risk insults from any peasant who might be around, or even
worse…"

"Alice, not many months ago you were insisting I was
too young. I'm only going into the copse. I shan't even

leave our own desmesne land. What harm has ever come to me there? You know I hate to be watched over.''

''Aye, I know you've always had your own way in everything,'' the nurse said tartly. ''One of these days you won't.''

Cressida was adjusting the fur-lined hood over the plain linen cap she preferred to wear about the manor, rather than the elaborate headdresses her father had recently ordered for her from the embroidress in Ludlow. She pulled on her riding gloves and looked up into her nurse's face, her brows pulled together into a frown of concern.

''Now, what ever can you mean by that?''

''You know what I mean right enough. Your father is already looking for a suitable husband for you, and husbands, let me tell you, do not expect or allow their wives to get their own way. They require them to be patient and obedient.''

''You are always issuing me deadly warnings like that. Father does not treat Mother as a slave. He loves her and often defers to her wishes.''

Alice gave an expressive sniff. ''And very fortunate she is, but there are times when she keeps silent about his declared plans, especially when she disapproves of them, and you'd best learn a trick or two from her—and soon.''

''Perhaps I shall learn the knack of leading a man by the nose without allowing him to be aware of it.''

''Aye, that depends on the man, my lady. Pray you'll get one as considerate as your sire.''

Cressida's amused smile vanished. ''I trust my father to find a man who will love me and be considerate of my wishes.''

Alice was silent as Cressida continued to stare at her challengingly, then she said, ''Your father will make the best match for you he can. His considerations as to that will hardly take in your prejudices. Fathers' wishes seldom do. You'll be a wealthy heiress, mistress. He looks high for you.''

''A royal duke, think you, or an earl?'' Cressida bubbled over with laughter. ''I should be quite satisfied with a plain country knight or squire, thank you.''

''Will you?'' Alice moved away to close the heavy lid of the clothes chest. She said over her shoulder, ''Just take care while you're out and about, that's all I ask. Your father would have the skin off my back and half kill all the grooms in the household if anything were to happen to you because we allowed you to wander at will, but there, you'll do what you want, whatever I say.''

''I promise I will be careful.'' Cressida touched the older woman's hand reassuringly. ''I shall be back within the hour. It is just that I feel stifled indoors today.''

Her jennet was ready as requested. The elderly groom who lifted her into the saddle murmured the same warnings as Alice had done. Cressida dimpled at him prettily and uttered the same reassuring platitudes. The old man was genuinely fond of her.

Cressida was aware that the household servants indulged her as much as her parents did. She felt a little guilty sometimes for using their affection to obtain her own ends but her natural youthful spirits always returned quickly after such conscience-stricken moments and she found herself repeating the charms she had used previously to entice submission to her will.

She rode hard at first through the copse along the ride which led towards the ancient town of Ludlow and finally drew rein within a small clearing where a charcoal burner's hut had been built some years earlier and was now abandoned. From here, through the bare canopy of tree branches, she had a distant view of Ludlow Castle. It had been a favourite place since early childhood when her father had brought her here, and later when she had ventured even nearer and been delighted to observe the household of the young former Prince of Wales issue forth on hawking expeditions.

Cressida dismounted onto a convenient flat-topped boulder which made a useful mounting block, tied her jennent's reins to the low branch of an oak and walked up the small rise facing her for a better view.

She had never been near enough to see the young Prince clearly. He would now be almost her age, she thought regretfully. How life had changed for him! The disclosure of his father's, the late King's, secret marriage, first to the Lady Eleanor Butler, daughter of the great Talbot, Earl of Shrewsbury, then bigamously to the Dowager Queen, Elizabeth, formerly the widow of Lord Grey of Groby, had resulted in the loss of all his hopes. He and his brother and sisters had been declared illegitimate and his uncle, the new King Richard III, had ascended the throne.

Cressida knew that her father bitterly resented what he considered a usurpation of the throne. He had never discussed it openly, but had received the news tight-lipped. Her father was not Yorkist in sympathy. He had fought for Lancaster at Tewkesbury, but the Queen had been Lancastrian before her marriage and for the past years the young Lord Edward had lived amongst them, here, at Ludlow, and his supplanting had been a bitter blow. Now a King's courier had arrived at Gretton Manor.

Cressida leaned against the bole of a larch and frowned in concentration. Surely her father had not been foolish enough to speak openly of his reservations concerning the new King? If so, it could bring disaster to them all.

A familiar voice hailed her and she turned eagerly to greet the newcomer who had ridden into the clearing.

Howell Prosser, the son of their nearest neighbour, was ascending the rise. He was of middle height, a square-made, brown-haired young man with an open, good-natured countenance.

"Little Mistress Gretton. What are you doing out in such inclement weather?"

Cressida had been so deep in thought that she had not really considered the icy chill which blew down the length of the ride. She was reminded of it now and drew her enveloping brown frieze cloak well around her.

"I am not so little, Master Prosser," she said, tossing back her head. "I shall be full sixteen next month."

Howell Prosser laughed as he joined her, throwing back his own hood to reveal curling brown hair. She was not disturbed by his presence. Howell was only three years her senior. She had become used to his teasing over the years and often encountered him on her rides. He was a frequent visitor to her home and she knew that her father trusted both him and his father implicitly.

"It is cold," she admitted, "but I needed the air. Mother was busy checking the linen and father engaged with his steward. I just felt in need…"

"Of pleasant company," he finished and she laughed.

"And you consider yourself worthy?"

"I always consider myself worthy. As for describing you as 'little', you will always be so to me and quite perfect."

"Stop teasing me, Howell. You know my father would disapprove of such talk."

"Because you will be sixteen next month?"

Her face clouded and her expression grew grave.

"Is there talk of a betrothal?" Howell Prosser was merely an esquire and he was aware that, despite the easy camaraderie which existed between his own father and Sir

Daniel Gretton, Gretton was wealthy and looked much higher for his daughter than the son of his friend, however well Howell was liked.

She shook her head. "Oh, no, nothing like that. I suppose you are right; up till now I have really not thought of myself as really grown-up, but now Alice keeps warning me that…" Her voice tailed off uncertainly.

"I suppose it must come soon and I shall have to leave the Marches. Oh, I love it so, Howell; I have been so happy here and that could all change, just as the Prince's fortunes changed so abruptly. Whenever I see the castle I think of him and wonder how he and his brother are faring."

Howell's countenance darkened. "If they are faring at all."

"You mean they might have been—murdered?" The distressed note in her voice was obvious and he gave her a regretful smile.

"You must not let my gloomy talk alarm you, Cressida. Who knows what has happened to the Princes?"

He shrugged. "There have been rumours, some emanating from the French Court, that the boys were done to death soon after the new King's coronation. Certainly they have not been seen in public since that time, but there is no proof that the boys are dead, certainly none that could involve their uncle in any *accident*." He stressed the last word ruefully.

"But you are inclined to believe the talk?"

He looked hurriedly round the clearing to assure himself that they were alone together, then lowered his head and said softly, "The fate of overthrown kings has never been good. King Edward II died a tragic death; so did King Richard II. Is it sensible to believe that King Edward V will fare any better at the hands of a usurper?

"Come, Cressida, you must not even think of these

things. It is unwise to talk openly of these rumours even amongst friends. You cannot know who could be nearby and overhear. Do not question your father on the subject. Keep your own counsel.''

Cressida nodded thoughtfully. His grave words had not allayed her fears. She said hesitantly, ''A courier arrived at the manor house just before I left. I could swear he was wearing royal livery.''

Howell Prosser's brown eyes darkened and his brows drew together. ''He was alone?''

''Yes, there was no escort of men-at-arms.''

It seemed that Howell relaxed his tense stance slightly. ''I should not think there is any cause for alarm. The King fears armed insurrection since the Earl of Buckingham's rising of 1483. Richmond sailed for England and was almost trapped on that occasion. The King sends his minions to see that all is well about the realm, especially here on the Marches and on the Scottish borders.''

She nodded again, her blue eyes widening, lips pursed. ''I am sure my father has committed no foolish act...''

''Of course not.'' He offered her his arm to lead her back to her jennet. ''I think you should return to the house. These November days are short. It will be dark soon.''

He lifted her into the saddle and sprang into the saddle of his own mount. She was glad that he was riding beside her for part of the way. She had always felt safe with Howell.

He pulled up his horse within sight of the Gretton manor house.

''You should be perfectly safe from here. I should not ride too much alone these days, Cressida. If there are King's men in the vicinity—'' He broke off awkwardly. ''You might not be safe, even on your own land.''

She held out her gloved hand to him and he grasped it.

A year ago he would have accompanied her right into the courtyard. She had noticed lately that he did not appear to wish to be seen with her alone, especially by her father. It was a tacit reminder that Alice's words were meaningful. She was no longer a child and should not be seen in the company of any man without a chaperon.

She lifted her ornamental riding whip in salute and he drew off slightly as she rode on ahead.

It was always a pleasure for her to come home to the manor house. It was constructed in honey-coloured stone, sturdy and welcoming against the background of fine pasture land with the vague shape of the Clee Hills in the distance. Her father owned several manors here on the Welsh border, but she loved this one the most and the family spent much of their time here.

As she entered her chamber, Alice rose hastily from the window-seat where she had been repairing a small tear in one of Cressida's gowns.

''Your father is asking for you. He's in the solar with your mother. Best make yourself presentable.''

Cressida tugged at the strings of her cloak and Alice hastened to help her.

''I saw a courier arrive. There is no bad news, is there?''

Alice clucked impatiently as she drew off the cloak and stood back to eye her young mistress critically. The dark blue woollen gown was plain, but did not appear to be muddied or too crumpled. It would do rather than keep Sir Daniel waiting longer than need be. When he'd come up an hour ago he had seemed excited and more than a trifle impatient.

''How am I to know what news your father has had? He wasn't like to take me into his confidence. If you hurry, you'll probably find out.''

Cressida's parents were seated close to the roaring fire

in the new side fireplace. The solar was luxuriously furnished, with tapestries on the lime-washed painted walls, even two fine carpets upon the floor. Even on this cold November afternoon it was warm and inviting.

Lady Gretton looked up, smiling, to greet her daughter as she paused in the doorway to give a quick curtsey. Cressida's mother was small, as Cressida herself was, but, in middle age, her figure had developed pleasantly rounded curves. Her features were less fine drawn than her daughter's but as yet unlined, possibly because her expression showed her nature to be generally serene and kindly and she frowned less than any other woman Cressida knew.

She wore a slightly outmoded gown in heavy cranberry velvet and, like Cressida, she had put off her veiled hennin in favour of a more comfortable embroidered linen cap, from which her still fair hair curled at the front and sides.

No one could have doubted that they were mother and daughter or that Sir Daniel Gretton, who towered over both of them, his arm around his wife's shoulder, loved both of them exceedingly and, unlike many of his contemporaries and equals, was not ashamed to display that deep affection openly.

He opened his arms now to greet his daughter and she hastened into them to be hugged to his muscular chest.

He put her aside gently. "I have been worried. You have been from the house too long unescorted."

"I met Howell in the clearing near the charcoal burner's hut." Cressida dimpled up at him and came to seat herself on a small stool at her mother's feet.

Sir Daniel Gretton came from behind his wife's chair and seated himself opposite, his eyes regarding his daughter steadily. Even dressed as she was in that plain, unfashionable house gown she was exceedingly lovely, so tiny and yet exquisitely fashioned, her glorious golden hair streaming to her shoulders beneath her cap.

"I have had a visitor," he announced without preamble.

Lady Gretton's hand rested lightly upon her daughter's bowed head.

"I saw a courier arrive." Cressida looked up at her father questioningly. "I feared there might be bad news, but you look quite happy, Father."

"Indeed I am. The man came from the King at Westminster. He honours me with an invitation to the crown-wearing ceremony at the Christmas feasting."

Cressida frowned slightly in doubt. "Could not that be dangerous? You have not been to Court since the late King's coronation and your sympathies were well known. You have said as much when you talked of the slaughter following the battle of Tewkesbury. You said you only went to Court for the coronation because you judged it politic to do so and you received a safe conduct on that occasion."

Sir Daniel smiled benignly. He was a big man, dark, square-featured, almost ugly compared with the beauty of his wife and daughter.

"I am convinced of his Grace's goodwill. He has instructed me to bring both my wife and daughter to Court. It seems he has heard of your coming sixteenth birthday, Cressida, and wishes you to be presented to his Queen, on the understanding that you might enter her household as a lady-in-waiting—until your marriage, that is."

Cressida sprang to her feet, almost falling in her haste as her unwary foot caught at her hem. She righted herself, faced her father squarely, and gave a little stamp of her foot.

"Father, we cannot be from Gretton over the Holy Season. Every year our people look forward eagerly to the celebrations. We always invite the Prossers and our other neighbours to join in and the household servants so enjoy the feasting…''

Sir Daniel rose and took his angry daughter's shoulders in his two large hands. "Child, I am sorry we shall miss the traditional celebrations, but our neighbours will understand. I swear you will not be disappointed. You cannot imagine the splendours of the royal festivities, and you will be able to wear your finest gowns…''

"Am I a doll to be dressed and displayed?'' she raged. "I do not wish to go. I want to be with my friends.'' Her face was flushed with angry colour and her taut young breasts rose in agitation.

"Father, you don't understand. I know my sixteenth birthday marks a milestone in my life, that you have plans for me. This may be my last Christmas at home. Please, you must let me share it with my friends.''

His smile had faded now and his expression became grave. "Daughter, you are the one who does not understand. The King has issued a command. He cannot be disobeyed. He wishes to see me at Court and you and your mother with me. He has made a point of stressing that. You, a mere knight's daughter, will be one of the Queen's ladies. He has also assured me that he has your interests at heart and will make it his business to find a suitable husband for you.''

She broke from him and turned passionately to face her mother.

"This cannot be. I am no heifer to be sold at market to the highest bidder. I know I must marry soon, but to a man of your choosing, Father, not some elderly courtier of the King's household. I had so hoped I might find a husband from amongst one of our neighbouring families. That I should not have to leave the Marches. I want to be near you both.''

Tears were spilling down her cheeks now and her father's embarrassment deepened. Cressida had that rare ability to weep without tears marring her beauty in the slightest. Those violet-blue eyes sparkled like the flowers they resembled in colour, bedewed by the crystal drops from the spring showers. He always felt totally awed by her beauty, he, a man completely practical in nature, never before given to poetical thought. He could never resist her pleading when she was so distressed.

He cleared his throat in an effort to hide his own discomfort. ''Cressida, the King is scarcely above thirty years of age. Those nobles who form his household are like to be of a similar age or younger. Trust me. I will not allow you to be given to some doddering old man nor yet some dandified lecher, no matter how wealthy or high-born he might be.''

''Then you will send some excuse? Please, Father, I beg of you. Say I am ill...''

''That cannot be, Cressida. I have already accepted the King's invitation.'' Sir Daniel looked pleadingly towards his wife for support. ''It would be unwise, indeed dangerous, to refuse. Such a refusal would be considered grave insult and I could come under suspicion—''

He broke off and looked into the fire. ''It is impossible, child. We have been commanded to Westminster and we must go with all speed before worsening weather makes it difficult to travel.''

His daughter's bleak expression of desperation made him soften his tone as again he reached out and squeezed her shoulder reassuringly.

''I promise you will find this journey a great adventure. Cressida, other girls in your position would be delighted at this opportunity. I have heard Queen Anne is a gentle mistress, beloved by her attendants, and we promise we will remain with you in London until—'' he cleared his throat again ''—until your future is determined.''

Cressida rushed to her mother's side. Mildred Gretton sighed heavily and enfolded this one beloved child in her arms. Too well she knew what Cressida was feeling. She had experienced the same doubts and fears, only to find delight and fulfilment in her husband's arms. She prayed that Cressida would discover a like joy.

''Nothing is determined yet, but your father must obey the King. You would not wish to put him into danger by your foolish fears?''

Cressida shook her head vehemently.

''No, of course not. Go and inform Alice Croft and tell her to look out your finest gowns. She will go with us, naturally.'' She cupped her daughter's chin in her hands. ''You are so lovely, child. The world will be at your feet. There will be so much to do and see in the capital that you will forget your disappointment at not spending Christmas here at Gretton.''

She bent close so that her words were hardly more than a whisper. ''It is the lot of us all, child. You must make the best you can of life. Your father has high hopes for a noble match for you. The King has hinted at it. He needs your father's support.''

''And I am to be the price to be paid for the King's favour?''

Mildred Gretton sighed again. ''We are all little more than chattels, child, however highly prized.'' She forced a smile. ''You have a gift, Cressida, of getting others to do what you wish. See that you use it well on your future husband. It is more priceless than jewels or land. Think about what I say. We'll talk again before we ride east.''

Cressida turned and faced her father. She forced a brave smile.

"I am sorry, Father. I am being foolish and childish. Of course you must obey the King. I'll go now and make some preparations for our coming journey."

He nodded, relieved by her apparent compliance, and shot his wife a grateful glance.

At the door, Cressida said softly, "Will you send to inform the Prossers of our imminent departure? I would not have them think us ungracious."

"Aye." He nodded again. "There will be several neighbours to be informed. Be assured that Howell will know why you leave in such haste without formal farewell."

She crimsoned and he grinned back at her. "Don't worry, lass. He'll understand. He's been a good playmate over these years, but he is not for you. He knows that well."

Her violet eyes clouded again. She had never seriously considered… She drew a hard breath. Yes, if she was honest with herself she knew that she had vaguely considered the possibility of marriage with Howell Prosser. It would have been highly convenient. She would have continued to live here, near to her loving, indulgent parents.

She had never asked herself what her true feelings were for Howell. She knew she liked him, was always happy in his company. Yes, such an alliance would have suited well.

And now the King, that shadowy, sinisterly menacing figure, so far away in Westminster, had declared his wishes concerning her and the whole pattern of her life had changed disastrously. She would never forgive this unwelcome interference in her affairs.

Chapter Two

Fortunately, the weather did remain fair for their journey to Westminster. Despite her earlier forebodings, Cressida was excited by the new sights and experiences, though Alice grumbled almost every step of the way.

Like her charge Alice had not wished to leave Gretton so near to the Holy Season of Christmas. She had promised herself visits to her kinfolk, who lived close to the manor; now she faced arduous days of travelling and the prospect of dealing with a recalcitrant young mistress when they reached their destination, for Cressida had been in a foul temper when she had ordered her nurse to make preparations for their departure.

"As if it is not enough that we must make this journey at the worst time of the year and miss Christmas here at the manor, my father is already planning to wed me to some doddering old lord chosen for me by the King," she had announced disgustedly. "It is insupportable that someone who does not know me should have the power to so interfere in my concerns."

"The King is the King," Alice had returned stolidly, as if this explained everything, whereas, in fact, it had merely emphasised Cressida's growing sense of resentment against this man living so far from them, yet who exercised such dominance over her.

She determined not to allow her parents to know that she did actually begin to enjoy the adventure of this first long journey of her life. She had had a tearful parting with Howell, and her father in particular, whom she held totally responsible for giving way too easily to the commands of his sovereign, was made to suffer her constant show of displeasure.

Loving her dearly as he did, and suffering her deliberate rejection of his displays of affection, Sir Daniel found the travelling uncomfortable and tedious, and the problems facing him when they arrived in Westminster alarming. Lady Gretton accepted her daughter's tantrums with her usual equanimity, though she did scold her on one or two occasions for making Alice's life difficult.

"Really, Cressida, you are behaving like a spoilt child, which I fear you are. My father would have taken a whip to my buttocks if I'd behaved as you are doing, and there is simply no excuse for acting so churlishly towards those who are only trying to do their best to serve you."

It was no help to Cressida's wounded sensibilities to acknowledge to herself that her mother was speaking the simple truth. They were all in the King's hands and she must accept her lot more patiently. Often she castigated herself for such shows of childishness, but Cressida was no "Patient Griselda" however often she promised herself that she would make an effort to curb this tendency towards waspishness.

She was an excellent horsewoman and did not find the long hours in the saddle too trying. The roads were hard-rutted and the weather chilly without excessive frost, the sun watery on most days and low in the sky, but, despite the barrenness of the brown earth fields, and the stark, skeletal branches of trees arching over their heads, Cressida rejoiced in the sights of the rolling English country they passed through.

The towns were a special delight for she had considered Ludlow important until they passed through Hereford and Gloucester, with their towering cathedrals and bustling streets.

They broke their journey for several days near Witney, visiting her mother's brother, Sir John Paynton, and it was here that Cressida celebrated her sixteenth birthday on the twenty-eighth of November. It was a joyous occasion and she was made much of by her burly uncle, who had longed for a daughter, his wife having given him four sturdy sons, two of whom were older than Cressida and the two remaining still too young to be sent into the households of neighbouring gentry to be trained as pages.

Cressida received fine presents of rich silks and brocades as well as jewellery from her devoted kinfolk. She forced herself to accept them with cries of delight, though they reminded her again of how she was to be displayed and sold in the marriage market at their journey's end.

Sir John escorted them into Oxford where Cressida stared entranced at the spires and walls of the magnificent, finely endowed colleges and marvelled at the unfamiliar sight of black-clad clerks and scholars scurrying about their business.

The weather broke at last as they were approaching the capital, and, with it, Cressida's bubble of optimism which had sustained her throughout the days of travelling. Her mother now began to exhibit signs of exhaustion and the six men-at-arms who had escorted them began to grumble amongst themselves and look eagerly ahead to their destination, which now seemed almost within reach.

Alice, riding pillion behind one of the men, expressed

her profound relief when they clattered finally into the stinking, crowded streets of London.

"Thank the Virgin. I think my aching bones can endure no more of this junketing about. I can only pray we find comfortable accommodation, for I hear it is in short supply in palaces."

Alice's forebodings proved unjustified, for Sir Daniel found that the rooms set aside for his use in the Palace of Westminster were far more commodious than he had dared to hope, considering the fact that many other of the country's greatest nobles had arrived to witness the age-old custom of the Christmas crown-wearing ceremony and the rambling old palace, with its outbuildings and extensions, was solidly packed to the rafters.

Cressida and Alice were to share a small chamber off that of her parents and Alice clucked her satisfaction at the sight of it. Cressida was not so pleased. Her own apartment at Gretton was far finer. She had no experience of the cramped conditions under which most of the Court lived and did not realise that to be granted private rooms within the palace at this time was a signal mark of the King's favour to her family.

She was astonished by the size and frantic hubbub of the place and wrinkled her nose against the river stinks which assailed her nostrils when she thrust open the small glazed window of her bedchamber to look down upon the bustling activity of the King's steps below, beyond the small pleasance, then to the brown depths of the Thames, crowded with barges carrying sea coal and market goods, and the ferries which constantly conveyed nobles and officials to and from the city downriver.

"Oh, Alice," she said despairingly, "how long do you think we shall have to remain here in this dreadful place?"

Alice looked up from a travelling chest from which she

was lifting Cressida's finest gowns to shake out their creases. Somehow she must find one which would be suitable for her mistress to wear during supper tonight in the great hall.

"This is Westminster," she said flatly. "The city itself near the great bridge and the Tower is much more crowded and insalubrious. Your father brought your mother to the capital when he came to pay his respects to the late King Edward. We lodged then near the Chepe and I thought I could scarce breathe for the stink from the open kennels, but, there, it was summer then. We were all glad to get back to the clean fresh air of the Marches."

Cressida plumped down upon the narrow bed. "Did you see the King, Alice? They say he was the handsomest man in Europe—quite unlike his brother, the new King, who is said to be dark and small and not in the least attractive."

"Aye, Edward was bonny, tall and huge and fair. 'The Rose of Rouen', they called him. He was born there, you know, and I saw young Gloucester, as the King was then. He was certainly smaller and darker, less impressive, I suppose, but I thought him personable enough. He was little more than eighteen then." She sighed. "He's seen a mort o' trouble since. I reckon he'll have aged considerably."

"Some of the trouble he brought on himself," Cressida snapped. "He should not have usurped the young Prince of Wales's throne."

Alice rose, rushed to her charge and caught her fiercely by the wrist. "Hush, you foolish child! Would you put us all in danger by such parlous treasonable talk? The King is the Lord's anointed and when you are presented you will behave with true humility, do ye hear me? Have I taught you no respect for your elders and betters?"

Cressida smiled ruefully. "Alice, I'm sorry. I'm just

tired and over-excited. Mother has explained over and over how I must be respectful and grateful—though for what I cannot say.''

''Well, plenty of girls would give their eye-teeth for the privileges offered to you. I suppose the King must be in great need of your father's support to honour him like this.''

Cressida leaned down to whisper mischievously in Alice's ear, ''Now who is talking treason?''

Alice's round red face expressed almost comical alarm and she covered her mouth with her hand, but Cressida laughed, shaking her head in real amusement at sight of her nurse's discomfiture.

Lady Gretton dispatched her maid, Bronwen, to fetch Cressida to her. Sir Daniel had gone from their chamber on some errand of his own, possibly to see that his men-at-arms were suitably lodged.

''Well,'' she said, smiling, ''it seems all has been done to ensure our comfort. Now, Alice, find a suitable gown for Cressida. Sir Daniel was informed that the King will sup privately tonight so she will not be formally presented. Keep her finest gown for the feasting, but we must not be outshone by these court nobles. Do your best.''

She eyed her daughter critically. ''You should lie down and rest for an hour or two. It wants some time before supper is served and you need to look your best.''

Cressida curtsied formally, then impulsively hugged her mother and returned to her own chamber. Already the excitement of their arrival was leaving her, yet she was still too wrought up to sleep at this hour in the afternoon.

Restlessly she watched from the window while Alice pulled out the truckle after laying out a blue velvet gown for the evening's first appearance in the great hall. The older woman then thankfully removed her shoes and lay down on the truckle, patting Cressida's bed invitingly.

"Your lady mother talks sense, child, as ever. You are over-tired and excited still. I can read the signs in your heightened colour. Great ladies do not behave like children. Rest and calm yourself. Your father will wish to be proud of you when he takes you down."

Reluctantly Cressida left her post of vantage where, at least, she could watch the novel sights below, and came to remove her travelling gown and lie down, as her mother had recommended.

Alice had already settled to rest and Cressida did not want to bother her with the back lacing of her gown, but she experienced some difficulty in trying to manage it unaided. Worn out by the journey and flurry of arrival, Alice was already snoring softly, lulled by the warmth of the two braziers set for safety, one near the window and the other near the door.

Cressida paused, undecided. She hated to disturb Alice, whom she loved dearly for all the care the older woman had bestowed on her since her babyhood, but, at the same time, Alice's strictures and continual murmurings against Cressida's natural need for independence as she grew older had developed a mild sense of resentment too.

She did not want Alice to wake and begin reminiscing about her former visit to Court, or to listen to her admonitions about Cressida's behaviour and how fortunate she was that some noble husband was shortly to be found for her.

She looked longingly towards the outer door. This palace would be a wonderful source of new discoveries and experiences. Tonight she would be escorted by her parents to the great hall. They would not take their eyes from her for a moment. She felt stifled by their protectiveness. She had a little time before supper. She would explore for a short time alone.

The corridor outside her chamber was deserted. Cressida could hear voices in the distance, laughing, shrill—women's voices? Possibly pages, too, had opportunity now to go about their own pursuits before they were summoned to wait upon their masters and mistresses at table.

She had slipped on her travelling cloak and pulled up the hood. It was cold in the unheated passages and she shivered, yet the freshness of the air after the brazier-scented atmosphere of her chamber was welcome and she made for a passage she thought would lead outside. The river terrace had appeared infinitely interesting and she had seen from her window that both men and women seemed to be walking there unchallenged. She would not be noticed, she felt sure.

The palace was a veritable warren of passages. She passed rooms, some deserted, some where clerks pored over rolls of parchment, some inhabited by finely dressed courtiers chatting together near the huge hearth fires. Cressida did not enter but hastened on, seeking for a doorway to the courtyard outside.

When at last she saw the great oaken door open before her, granting her a vista of cobbled courtyard, she had to pass a small guard chamber where men-at-arms were drinking ale and dicing. As she tried to emerge into the open air she was challenged abruptly by two guards who crossed their bills before her face, pulling her up sharply, winded and frightened.

She tried to stutter some excuse for leaving the palace, but one of the men saw that she was young and a woman, and thought perhaps that she was some maid on an errand for her mistress. He signalled for his comrade to lower his bill and nodded for her to proceed, grinning broadly and making some lewd comment which brought a bright flush to her cheek. Cressida scrambled by the men, thankful that she had not been forced to identify herself.

The broad courtyard was bordered on two sides by long, low outbuildings which Cressida judged to be stables and mews. She could hear men whistling inside one of them, and the fluttering of hawks on their perches and their shrill, angry cries. There was no one to whom she could ask directions, but she made for a gateway and turned to where she was sure she would find a path leading to the pleasance she had seen from her window and, ultimately, a way to the river quay.

Obviously the many corridors within the palace had confused her, for she found herself in another courtyard, where the sound of hammering and sawing from the buildings contained within it told her that this was the quarter of the smiths, armourers and carpenters.

The cold was intensifying now that darkness was approaching and no one lingered here, outside. Cressida was in two minds about proceeding further but she disliked the idea of returning to her chamber and the enforced rest she must take there. She was too restless in spirit for that, so she forged on, hoping to come across another way which would eventually lead back to the palace pleasance.

As she passed through the second entrance she heard the sound of laughter and the clatter of horses' hooves. She paused for a moment, hesitating, then she recognised the place as the tilt-yard.

Her father had no squire and there was not one at Gretton, but she had heard her father and Howell's father discuss often how they had been trained to arms in their youth. A mounted knight had to control his mount by knees alone, handling either a lance or other weapon in one hand while he protected his body by his shield in the other. He learned to aim well for jousting by striking a wooden shield mounted upon one arm of a quintain and riding forward steadily.

She saw the wooden structure now some yards from her across the courtyard. Two mounted men prepared to try their skill and Cressida's blue eyes widened in astonishment as she saw a heavy weighted bag on the second arm of the structure. One unbalanced thrust would cause the crudely painted shield to swing wildly and, if the knight riding beneath was not skilful, the full weight of the bag would strike him and thrust him from the saddle.

Cressida was utterly fascinated. She had never seen a tournament, had imagined the colour and splendour of the occasion, the thrill of watching, breathless, as a gallant knight charged down the lists towards his antagonist and their lances splintered in the impact. How exciting it would have been to have some knight wear her favour bound around his sleeve and ride to risk himself, his aim to achieve victory for her delectation!

These men were practising, she knew that; both wore armour and the visors were lowered so that neither could be injured in the passes. They were clearly not rivals, for their laughter and friendly banter proclaimed them companions.

The destriers pawed the ground impatiently and Cressida saw that the men needed all their skill to control the powerful beasts. Cressida's lips parted in sheer delight at the sight of these glossy-coated creatures.

Neither man appeared to see her and, with a warning shout, the taller man rode towards the swinging quintain. He struck the centre of the shield unerringly, dead centre, and rode through as the weighted bag swung harmlessly over his head and he skilfully reined in his mount for the turn.

The second man prepared to follow, but Cressida must have made some sound or movement for he turned sharply in her direction. The brief break in his concentration brought him to the shield too soon. He had no time to strike it clear and as he rode on, in the impetus of the practice charge, the bag struck him full on the shoulder. He gave a startled shout and fell heavily from the saddle.

Cressida stood transfixed with horror as his mount charged on riderless, then neighed shrilly and reared. It seemed that the frightened horse would turn and come crashing back to trample his helpless master. Without waiting to consider the second knight and the probability of his coming hastily to the rescue, she gathered her skirts and dashed to the fallen man. She must either drag him clear or try to snatch the reins of his frenzied mount.

She crouched by him, horrified by the sounds of frantic hooves pounding inexorably towards her. There came an infuriated shout, and the neighing and screaming of the riderless courser. Too late she realised that her intervention had merely served to frighten the beast further. She could hear it snorting and scrabbling and stamping in fury.

There came several more shouted commands and what sounded like war-like oaths muffled by the helmet's visor, then, abruptly, she found herself lifted from the ground and swung across the second knight's saddle bow as he rode clear to the end of the courtyard.

Cressida struggled wildly. She was lying ignominiously, like a sack of grain, face down, with a powerful male hand holding her firmly in position and resisting every effort she made to lift her head. She was finally forced to give up her frantic fighting through sheer loss of breath and, equally, was unable to make any protest when she was as unceremoniously dumped upon the ground, upright, when the far end of the courtyard was reached.

Her stance was precarious indeed, and she waddled in-elegantly a few steps forward in order to keep her footing. Her rescuer's destrier was snorting and prancing as fiercely as the other courser and only superb horsemanship on the part of the rider successfully held him in.

Head held down and panting, Cressida could do nothing but try to regain her breath. Even so, she was aware, though furious with the knight who had seized her so pre-cipitately, that she was in no danger from his mount. The mailed hands forced the beast to stand compliantly while he swung himself out of the saddle.

He thrust up his visor. His voice was low-pitched, de-liberate, but with the bite of hard steel.

"Children are not allowed in the tilt-yard. Where is your nurse?"

He stood, one hand on hip, a tall, dominating figure, looming over Cressida.

She lifted her head and glared back at him. The light was fading now and she could not see his features clearly, shadowed as they were by his helmet. She was painfully conscious that her hood had fallen back and her tangled hair was streaming free of its pins. Desperately she hoped that he had as little a clear view of her as she had of him.

She must not be identified. Her mother would be furious if the tale of this misadventure were to be repeated within the court circle. She knew well enough that it would be politic to apologise quickly and make her escape before this man took further note of her appearance, but such a cowardly retreat was foreign to her nature. She shook back her cloud of hair with an impatient hand.

"I am no child, sir," she said frigidly. "It is long since I needed the care of a nurse. I regret that my sudden ap-pearance frightened one of the horses. I was afraid the rider would be hurt and tried to go to his help."

"I'm not so sure you should be without a keeper," he retorted grimly. "Anyone with sense would know better than to interfere when men are practising at the quintain. It needs full attention. Destriers are valuable. Your foolish intervention could have caused the animal to damage itself."

She was stung by his implication that she was less valuable than the horse. Throughout the course of her short life Cressida had come to believe that she was quite the most valuable creature within her parents' vicinity, and all the servants on the manor had treated her with the care they accorded the priceless Venetian glass which her father had imported to glaze the solar windows at Gretton.

No one had dared to afford her less respect than would have been offered to her father. The rudeness of this stranger was not to be borne without retaliation!

"I'm sorry that you should consider the horse more valuable than that of a mere human life," she said haughtily. "I repeat, I acted merely in an attempt to save the rider from being trampled."

"Destriers are trained to command, but a stranger arriving on the scene so abruptly could have spelled disaster. Don't you know they are also trained to trample and bite enemies underfoot? You could have been killed."

He was leaning forward slightly now and staring at her. He was puzzled. At first he had thought the intruder one of the palace pages, but the cumbersome skirts had told him that his first surmise was incorrect and he had wrongly assessed the sex of the newcomer.

It was dusk now and he could not see the girl clearly, but her voice was cultured, so she was not one of the serving maids. Her dignified bearing, despite her terrifying ordeal, showed him that she was not the child he had thought her, yet she was quite small of stature, very young still, although the softness of her curvaceous young body as he had held her close momentarily before setting her down revealed the fact that she would soon ripen into womanhood.

By God's wounds, what was she doing unattended in the palace environs? Wasn't she aware that she could be molested, even here, so close to the palace buildings?

He called imperiously, "Peter, see this young person safely into the palace."

His squire hastened to his side. He had been momentarily shaken by the heavy fall but was now quite recovered. He'd listened, not without an awareness of concealed humour, for he would not have dared to laugh outright, to the exchange between the Earl, his master, and this youthful but insolent stranger.

"Certainly, sir."

She flashed an instant answer. "Must I repeat myself yet again? I do not need a keeper and am perfectly used to looking to my own safety."

"Mistress, I have seen little evidence of that ability this even." He turned his back on her and gave his attention to his mount. "Peter, regardless of this young maid's assurances, do as I order."

Gently the squire offered his mailed arm to the rebellious stranger. "Truly, mistress, you would be wise to take care, especially at this hour of the day. There are rogues and beggars nearby, some emerging from the sanctuary at Westminster Abbey, who would cut your throat simply to acquire the good cloak on your back. Allow me to escort you into the palace."

She turned once to stare after the retreating back of her erstwhile rescuer, then turned and placed a hand, now somewhat grubby after her encounter with the dust of the ground and the knight's horse, upon his proffered arm.

''Thank you, sir,'' she said quietly, mollified by his courtesy. ''I shall be glad to accept your offer, for I fear I am new to this palace and have missed my direction.''

The knight took the reins of both destriers and moved towards the stable-block. Cressida was further irritated by his decision to relinquish care of her to his inferior, for his mode of address to the second rider had suggested that he was the master and this more kindly and considerate escort his man.

She sniffed her displeasure. Once more he had shown a preference for his so valuable horses over his more obvious duty of courtesy to her. She bestowed upon her escort her brightest smile and allowed him to lead her towards the courtyard entrance archway.

Alice was awake and already panicking when Cressida reached her bedchamber. It had been difficult to find again. The corridors of the palace seemed all alike and now that the light had almost gone serving men were hastening to light the sconces, their air of urgency indicating that preparations were being made for the evening's supper in the great hall.

Cressida began to unfasten the strings of her cloak as Alice hurried forward, her eyes widening in alarm as she saw her charge's state of dishevelment.

Cressida did not wait to hear her complaints but said sharply, ''Have you informed my mother that I have been absent from the chamber?''

''No, of course not,'' Alice said in a horrified whisper. Even now she was afraid that Lady Gretton would be made aware that her charge had been out of her sight for some time.

''Good,'' Cressida replied crisply. ''Come, prepare me for this supper tonight.''

''Where have you been and—'' Alice hesitated almost

fearfully ''—what ever have you been about? Your parents will be furious…''

''If they find out, undoubtedly,'' Cressida replied imperturbably, ''and it would be unfortunate for you, Alice, were they to do so, so let us get on. My mother will demand to see how I look any moment now.''

Alice had been Cressida's deeply loved nurse and attendant and she was too sure of herself to be truly rebuffed by her charge's sharpness; nor was she to be deflected by Cressida's evasions. If anything untoward had occurred during her excursion, unescorted, into the palace environs, she must know about it, and at once. She stood, arms akimbo, facing Cressida, who was struggling with the refractory laces of her travelling gown.

''Now, mistress, I want to know, now, just what mischief you have been at and, I warn you, trouble or no, I shall inform your lady mother if I think there is need.''

Cressida bit her lip uncertainly. On the one hand she did not want to tell anyone of her mortifying and embarrassing encounter with the stranger knight in the tilt-yard; on the other hand she did not wish Alice to magnify the possible consequences of any adventure which had befallen her. She sighed briefly.

''Alice, I was just restless and anxious to explore. I wanted to go to the river terrace but lost my way.''

''And?''

''I found myself in the tilt-yard by mistake and—and almost got trampled…''

''What?'' Alice was almost incoherent with alarm.

''No, no, I came to no harm, as you can see. A knight snatched me up on his horse and got me safely out of danger.''

''He knows who you are?'' Alice was scandalised.

''No, certainly not. We exchanged few words. His—

squire, I think, showed me the way back to the palace door.
I doubt either of them would know me again were they to
see me at Court.'' She gave a little stamp of her foot,
though her manner was pleading rather than imperious.
''Please, Alice, come and help me or my mother will suspect something is wrong.''

''I shall want to know more about this man and what
was said, mistress,'' Alice said tartly. ''For now we must
hasten to get you ready. Really, child, I turn my back for
just one moment and you do something foolish—and dangerous. I am responsible for you, Cressida. Don't you care
about what might happen to me should your parents cast
me out?''

Cressida smiled winningly and placed her arms fondly
round her maid's neck. ''Silly Alice, as though I should
let them do such a thing—ever. I love you, you old tyrant,
and you know it. Besides, soon I shall have a household
of my own and you will be the most valued member of
it.''

''Not if you carry on like this and earn a reputation for
yourself,'' Alice chided, but her homely face flushed with
pleasure and she was already weakening from her concerned anger.

By the time Cressida was ready to be viewed by her
anxious mother Alice had accomplished a total transfor-
mation. From the girlish, untidy hoyden, Cressida now
stood revealed as an elegant court lady. To complement
her eyes, Lady Gretton had insisted on a gown of deep
blue velvet, edged with grey fur both round the hem and
the cuffs of the modishly tight sleeves, as well as the deep
V of the neckline. The modesty vest and covering of the
small truncated hennin was of blue and silver brocade.

One single band of smoothly combed golden hair
showed at Cressida's forehead, for Lady Gretton had de-

creed that the fashion of shaving the front hair to enhance
the depth of the forehead was unsuitable for so young a
girl and, besides, Cressida's unusual, bright burnished hair
colouring was so lovely that she felt it should be glimpsed.

The complicated folds of the wired butterfly veiling
shaded the youthful features and gave merely a hint of the
beauty of her unblemished complexion. Lady Gretton
grunted her satisfaction that her daughter's pale skin was
not wont to freckle in the summer's sun, for no amount of
warnings persuaded Cressida to anoint herself with fards
and creams before venturing out in it.

She herself wore a gown of deep burgundy velvet and
was convinced that it would not be discovered to be far
from the present fashion. Sir Daniel joined them, fussing
with his ornamental gold neck-chain over his green velvet
doublet. He opened his eyes in astonishment at the sight
of his daughter.

"Well, well, you look very fine indeed. See that you
behave with decorum, daughter, for at Court, believe me,
every foible is noted and remarked on."

Cressida ate very little at supper, although she had not
eaten since mid-morning, but she found the hubbub, colour
and confusion in the great hall completely absorbing.

They were conducted to their seats near the high table
by an officious, elderly steward, splendidly dressed and
flourishing his white wand of office. Her father did not
appear to be recognised by any of the nobles, knights and
their ladies seated near them, though their presence was
acknowledged by nods and half-bows of greeting.

It was obvious that their presence here was expected by
the steward and places had been laid for them. Cressida
was seated between her parents and, for once in her life,
was almost nervous of peering too closely around her.

The moment they were seated the noise around them

began again, as servants appeared at their side to provide them with plates and cutlery and two youthful pages also came with a bowl of rose-scented water for the rinsing of fingers, a ewer and clean napkins.

Cressida watched as her mother dipped her fingertips into the water and took the napkin from the boy who proffered it, kneeling on one knee. They wore the Yorkist colours of murrey and blue, ornamented with the King's personal device of the white boar.

Sir Daniel and Cressida followed Lady Gretton's example, and Cressida peered cautiously from beneath her shadowing gossamer veil to see if any other lady was watching closely, ready to laugh if she was clumsy or made a mistake.

There were no homely bread trenchers here and gingerly Cressida handled the newfangled two-pronged fork provided. Since she was not squired by husband or attentive suitor she was content to be served by her father with various delicacies and shared his cup with her mother.

The removes of food were many and varied, but too rich and heavily spiced for Cressida's taste. She ate sparingly and found the malmsey wine over-sweet, so drank little. The places of the King and Queen in the centre of the high table beneath the richly embroidered cloth of estate were unoccupied, though several other lords with their ladies were seated in their places on either side of the royal chairs.

Her father pointed out to her the King's chamberlain, Viscount Lovell, whom, he said, had been the King's friend since boyhood and had served him loyally for many years on the Scottish border and on the Council of the North. The haughty lady beside him, whom Cressida thought to be his lady, appeared to have more time for her neighbour than her lord, for she constantly engaged him in conversation.

Lady Gretton was soon chatting with a lady beside her and Sir Daniel tucked heartily into his food, oblivious of what was going on around him.

Cressida looked round anxiously in case any man in the hall was regarding her with too much attention, but surely the knight she had encountered in the tilt-yard would not be able to recognise her, dressed so totally differently, and it had been half-dark then—yet she continued to look covertly into the faces of those men near her to see if she might notice anything in manner or demeanour which would convince her of his identity.

No one appeared to give her the slightest notice after the first curious glances and after a while she sat back with a little sigh of relief. Alice was seated with her mother's maid at the far end of the hall with other servants, so she was free for a while of her constant vigilance.

The gossip was continual but subdued, as if the courtiers were conscious that they could be overheard and their remarks noted and informed on. The palace must be a hot bed of intrigue, she thought ruefully. Her father would have to be constantly on his guard here and watch his tongue. So must she.

She was more than a little startled when the steward appeared at their table near the close of the meal to summon them to the King's chamber of presence.

"If you will follow me, Sir Daniel, with your wife and daughter, the King wishes to greet you personally."

Cressida's father rose at once, dabbing hastily at his mouth with his napkin. There was an instant hush in the talk near them and they found themselves the focus of all eyes.

Sir Daniel uttered some conventional polite response

and offered his arm to his lady. Cressida half stumbled in rising, stared resentfully at the long-nosed elegant lady opposite whose lips were curved in a contemptuous smile, then swept after the retreating backs of her parents, who were too bemused by the signal honour afforded them to even look round to see if their daughter was following.

The King's private chamber was guarded by two men-at-arms in Yorkist livery with crossed bills. They stood aside as the steward fussily gestured for them to do so. The doors were flung open and the steward marched before them, announcing their identities in loud, ringing tones. At first Cressida was too concerned that she might fall over her own feet to look curiously around her.

Her father was dropping to his knees and her mother stooping in a deep curtsey. Cressida approached and curtsied low, as she had been instructed so many times during the course of their journey. She had been instructed repeatedly on how to behave, what to say and what not to say, how to look modestly down at the ground until she was commanded otherwise, so that she ought to have felt fully confident about this moment, but she found that that was not to be.

She was so terrified of disgracing herself before this man, who was the cause of this sudden, frightening alteration in the course of her life, that she found her limbs trembling and had to tighten her leg muscles lest she collapse before his feet.

A kindly, mellow voice greeted the visitors.

"Ah, Sir Daniel, my lady, Mistress Cressida, please rise. I regret I was unable to greet you earlier in hall, but it was necessary to consult with officials over supper tonight so we ate apart. My Queen and I wish you heartily welcome to Westminster. I trust apartments have been placed at your disposal and you are relatively comfortable? Palaces are so crowded, I find, and often less pleasant than one would wish, and at this, the Holy Season, more uncomfortable and thronged with visitors than usual.''

Cressida's father rose and bowed, then stepped forward slightly to kiss the beringed hand offered to him.

''Your Grace, I am honoured by your invitation and assure you that everything is to our complete satisfaction.''

Cressida rose from her curtsey to see that the King had risen from his high-backed chair and was offering his hand to her mother. Lady Gretton kissed the King's fingers and stood back to allow her daughter to approach.

Sir Daniel said quickly, ''May I present my daughter, Your Grace? She is overwhelmed by your kindness in offering to arrange a suitable marriage for her.''

The King's voice sounded almost teasing. ''Perhaps she is, Sir Daniel, or would Mistress Cressida prefer to speak for herself in this matter?''

Cressida kissed the strong brown fingers, her eyes dutifully lowered. There was a slight silence while her anxious parents waited for her to make some dreaded outburst.

She could not see the King's features clearly yet. She was too concerned by her need to obey protocol correctly.

She said in a hurried half-whisper, ''Your Grace honours my father by this interest in our concerns, sir, and I must be duly grateful.''

There was a faintly ironic note in the mellow-voiced answer. ''Well spoken, mistress. I see you have been suitably schooled.''

She looked up then sharply, straight into a pair of mocking grey-green eyes which were dancing with amusement. She tightened her lips and shook back threatening tears of embarrassment. Had she, in spite of all her care to be dutiful, said the wrong thing?

He was gesturing to her mother to take a stool nearby and turning to the woman seated in a chair near him.

"Anne, this is the young lady whose future we have been discussing recently. I trust she will prove a loyal and trustworthy attendant."

A gentle voice bade Cressida approach the chair and quickly she curtsied low once more, this time to the Queen.

"Your Grace, I will strive to please you in every way I can, but I am a country mouse and unaccustomed to court ways."

"Come, child, we shall not expect too much of you. You must not be timid. Come and stand by me."

Cressida gazed helplessly towards her mother, who nodded imperceptibly for her to obey the Queen.

She went to the Queen's side, while her father took up his stance behind her mother's stool. Now, at last, when the King began to enquire about affairs in the Marches and the Queen engaged her mother in talk about the suitability of their Westminster apartment, Cressida was able to really look about her.

This presence chamber was not unduly large, though comfortably, almost luxuriously furnished. There were glowingly colourful tapestries on the painted walls—one depicting Christ as a child before the elders in the Temple, the other some pastoral, Classical subject, showing in the foreground a beautiful woman carrying a bow and arrow sheaf—possibly the Greek goddess Artemis.

A bright fire blazed in the hearth and the polished oak floor was strewn with fine carpets from the East. Wax candles in sconces on the wall and set in silver candlesticks on a low table near the Queen's chair gave a rich, comforting glow to the room. There were two high-backed, cushioned chairs for the King and Queen's comfort, fald stools and, in one corner, a cushioned prie-dieu.

Cressida's quick eye glimpsed signs of the interests of
the pair. There were printed books upon the table, several
devotional and one on hunting, and a rush velvet-lined
basket containing embroidery silks and wools. A tambour
containing what Cressida thought to be a half-completed
altar cloth in white silk had been laid aside by the Queen
at their entrance.

There was a movement near the shuttered window and
an elderly brachet hound emerged from the shadows to
flop down heavily beside the King's chair. Cressida was
surprised to see the royal pair unattended. Even in this
private chamber Cressida had expected to see courtiers and
ladies-in-waiting. Evidently the King and Queen preferred
to spend their quiet hours together in an atmosphere of
pleasant domesticity. Cressida thought these hours must be
few in number and valued the more for that.

The Queen had never been beautiful, Cressida decided.
Her features were regular, her complexion pale and unblemished, though there were high spots of colour upon
her cheekbones. She must be little more than thirty, Cressida supposed, but she looked older, ill. Once or twice in
her talk she broke off to cough and apologised.

She was dressed in a dove-grey gown trimmed with sa-
ble and Cressida recalled that this last year she had lost
her only child, Prince Edward. Her hair, beneath the black
velvet frontal to her simple cap hennin, was fair and looking faded. Despite the gentleness of her demeanour, Queen
Anne had a determined chin and Cressida believed that
she would not allow sloppiness in her attendants.

She was aware suddenly that the King had paused in his
talk and was regarding her sardonically. She coloured hotly
and lowered her gaze in an attempt to evade the cool ap-
praisal in his grey eyes.

"Your father assures me you have been well schooled

in household management, though you love the Marches and like to be about country pursuits. Do you ride well, mistress?''

Cressida swallowed nervously. "I am told I do, Your Grace."

"So you enjoy hawking and the chase?"

Cressida considered. "I enjoy the challenge and the thrill of the hunt, sire, but not the kill."

He nodded, as if approving her answer. "Can you read?"

"Yes, Your Grace. Our local parson was sent to tutor me."

"Good. I like to see a woman who is educated to think and know her own mind. My own nieces are well read. I like to discuss literary matters with the Lady Elizabeth."

Cressida thought, fleetingly, that the two princes had been well schooled by their other uncle, Anthony, Lord Rivers. He lay now in a cold grave after his execution at Pontefract. Where were his charges now? This domestic scene had momentarily diverted her from her natural wariness towards the King.

He was, as Alice had said, of middle height, spare of build but well muscled. He had been a doughty warrior, she knew. He was not unattractive, with a clever, narrow face, the Plantagenet nose dominating the even features. His eyes were fine and luminous, but his mouth rather thin. She thought he held it in too tightly when struggling to control moments of tension or inner pain.

Like the Queen, he appeared older than his thirty-two years and Cressida considered that the problems and suffering over these last months had left their marks. For all that, there was something very winning about this man when he smiled, as he was doing now, inviting openness in her and without the suspicion of tantalising humour at her discomfort that she had noted earlier.

Like the Queen, he was dressed soberly in a doublet of very dark blue, but the jewels in his ornamental shoulder-chain and on his long brown fingers glowed richly.

Her parents had remained silent throughout this questioning and Cressida blushed hotly as she realised she was being assessed as a suitable bride.

There came a respectful knock upon the door and the King called permission for the newcomer to enter. A young page appeared, behind him a noble, for Cressida's shrewd eyes summed up the worth of his fine violet velvet doublet and well-fitting grey hose. He remained just within the doorway and bowed low.

"Your Grace requested that I present myself at this hour."

The King rose at once, smiling.

"Come in, my lord. You come well in time. I was talking to you recently about my intention to invite Sir Daniel Gretton to our Christmas revels this year, knowing him to be a neighbour of yours. Allow me to present also his wife, Lady Gretton, and their charming daughter, Mistress Cressida, whose father informs me she has only days ago, during their journey to Westminster, turned sixteen."

He addressed Sir Daniel, who also had risen. "My Lord Earl of Wroxeter, a trusted member of my council and one whom I rejoice to acknowledge as friend."

Sir Daniel bowed to the newcomer deferentially as his title required. He glanced swiftly back towards the King, who smiled almost conspiratorially. With a tremendous shock, Cressida understood that this man had been commanded to the King's presence especially to view her. She watched, bemused, as her father and the Earl clasped hands and the Earl bowed low to the ladies. Feeling her mother's anxious eyes upon her, she too sank low in a curtsey.

The Earl turned to acknowledge her and, for a fraction of a second, stood perfectly still, his lips slightly parted in astonishment.

He had never encountered before a creature quite so divinely lovely as this girl. She was small in stature, almost diminutive, a fairy child, yet he knew instinctively that when she moved it would be with the natural grace and regality of a queen. Though she was so young, he could glimpse the budding curves of her high, rounded breasts and sweetly swelling hips and belly outlined against the soft blue velvet of her gown.

He started abruptly, aware that huge, luminous blue eyes shaded by dark golden lashes were regarding him curiously, almost hostilely. Her face was heart-shaped, her complexion and features flawless. Her nose was well shaped, with the slightest tendency to tilt upwards at the tip, and he could not resist a faint smile at the delightful air of impudence it gave her features, for her mouth was unsmiling, the full, sensuous underlip held in tightly, as if in an effort to prevent her thoughts from revealing themselves too readily.

Only one small band of hair showed demurely from beneath her hennin, but he almost gasped at the splendour of its colouring. Golden was a totally inadequate description; it was the deep, dark gold of the most precious Welsh metal prized above all other gold, the colour of ripe corn shining in the sun's full glory.

He was stunned and felt sharp desire stab at his loins. Immediately he was ashamed. How could he be so stirred by this child, and so soon after the loss of his adored Elinor?

He forced himself to bow again, stiffly, and lowered his gaze from that intense blue stare of hers.

"Mistress Cressida," he murmured formally. "Your parents I have had the good fortune to meet before. This is the first time I have set eyes on their lovely daughter. I trust and hope you will enjoy the Christmas festivities to the full."

"Thank you, sir." Her voice was lower than he had expected, pleasantly pitched and clear without being in the least strident. "The King honours us and, though I shall miss the revelries we enjoy at home at Gretton, I'm sure I shall find the feasting here at Court very splendid and not a little overwhelming."

His lips twitched slightly. "I cannot believe you would be overwhelmed by anything, mistress."

The small pointed chin jutted faintly, as if she was conscious that he was teasingly addressing her as if she were a child and resented it.

That movement, slight as it was, and the earlier suggestion of a rebuke for his assumption that she would be blinded by the unusual glitter and pageantry of court procedure, stirred his memory and he turned once more and stared full at her.

It was unbelievable—yet undeniably true, for all that. This fashionably attired creature, who behaved with as much confidence as if she had been present at Court since babyhood, was the same young woman whom he had snatched from impending death in the palace tilt-yard. She did not appear to recognise him, though he could not be sure.

He glanced enquiringly at her father and thought better of any prior acknowledgement of having met his daughter. More than likely the parents were unaware of her pecca-

dillo. She would undoubtedly be angered if he were tactless enough to let such a secret slip.

Queen Anne was addressing him warmly. It was clear
to Cressida that the Earl was a favoured friend to both
monarchs. He was stooping over her chair, flattering her
shamelessly, and Cressida saw the tired eyes light up in
pleasure.

When, at last, they were graciously dismissed, Cressida
was silent as they returned to their allotted quarters. Her
father was clearly overjoyed by what had transpired at the
interview.

The King had made it plain enough. He would be
pleased to approve a match between herself and the Earl.
Why? She was totally astounded. This man was so far
above her in station. Why, she would become a countess!
The understanding was no sweetener for her acute resentment.

Sir Daniel embraced her and her mother smiled her very
real pleasure. Cressida knew she should be grateful. The
Earl was young, personable, she supposed, wealthy and
powerful within the King's Council.

She stood docilely while Alice prepared her for bed. Her
maid must, in some way, have got wind of the honour soon
to be afforded her charge for she chatted incessantly about
how wonderful life would be for Cressida as the wife of
so important a noble.

Cressida made no tart rejoinders. She was too busy considering her next move. How could she convince her parents, and, most important of all, the King, that she had no
desire to be a countess and live so far from her beloved
Marches?

As she lay in the darkness, Alice sleeping contentedly
nearby on the truckle, she reviewed her first opinion of the
Earl.

He was quite young, younger than the King, perhaps twenty-five or -six? He was so tall that he towered over her, making her feel a veritable manikin. She had not liked to stare, though he had at her. He had dark hair worn to his shoulders, slightly wavy and brushed back from his long, high-cheek-boned face. The eyes had been heavy lidded, almost sleepy, she thought, when he had not been so intent on appraising her.

No, he was not handsome, though well formed, his body slim but muscular, highly presentable. Why, she wondered, had he not already married? Was he a widower? If so, they had not informed her. She considered those eyes. At parting they had displayed a distinct twinkle. An angry flush dyed her cheeks. If he thought her a child to be mollified and managed he was decidedly mistaken.

Then, suddenly, she shot to a sitting position, her heart thudding wildly. Those eyes—and that voice—Sweet Virgin, he had been laughing at her because—because he had only hours before rescued her from the hooves of a frightened horse in the tilt-yard. So he knew! And she had been pert with him—would he continue to keep such an amusing and titillating tale to himself?

More and more it was going to be difficult coping with her father's desire to wed her to this man. Perhaps it was just possible that he had conceived a dislike for her? Her behaviour had certainly not been appropriate to one who aspired to become his countess. She sank back, breathing heavily. Matters might well be left in the Earl's hands and prove quite satisfactory to Cressida herself, after all.

Chapter Three

It was not to be as she had hoped. In the middle of December, Cressida was summoned into the King's presence once more to formally give her consent to a betrothal between herself and Martyn, Earl of Wroxeter. During the intervening weeks negotiations had been put in hand concerning the terms of the wedding contract. Sir Daniel appeared to be in excellent humour and had agreed, with good heart, to all the proposals.

He was prepared to give his daughter a fine dowry in exchange for the happiness of knowing that she was soon to be a countess and the privileges she would obtain by this exalted position, not to mention the advantage he himself would gain by pleasing his sovereign with this match which the King appeared to favour.

Cressida had hardly been consulted. Her mother had chatted on happily about how proud they were of her and it would have been pointless to object. Though he loved her dearly and had greatly indulged her, Cressida had known only too well that her father would insist on her consent.

The Earl, it seemed, had no apparent objection to the match. She'd seen him rarely over the days following the

unpleasantness in the tilt-yard and, when she had, it had
been in the company of her parents, and on several occasions in the presence of the King and Queen. Her parents
had made no reference to the matter and Cressida judged
that the Earl had decided to keep the knowledge to himself.
Only once had she referred to it, when they were momentarily alone together on the river terrace, Alice walking
some paces to the rear, ever watchful.

"My lord," Cressida said, a trifle stiffly and more than
a little nervous, "I trust neither of the horses took hurt
from my unfortunate sudden arrival in the tilt-yard the
other afternoon?"

He checked slightly in his walk, his sleepy eyes regarding her coolly. "Ah, I see you have recognised me as the
knight who snatched you up so unceremoniously. I regret
that I may have hurt your feelings, but, you know, you
were in grave danger."

She lowered her gaze. "I think, my lord, that you have
made no mention of this to—my parents—or the King."

"Indeed not." His long lips were twitching at the corners in amusement. "It shall be our secret, Mistress Cressida. You would prefer it so?"

"Yes—oh, yes," she said hastily. "I mean—I think my
mother might be distressed…"

"Hardly distressed, surely? Nothing untoward took
place regarding your honour."

She shot him a challenging glance. She was sure he was
laughing at her, but his expression was perfectly grave
again now.

"Nothing whatever," she snapped. "Surely you cannot
believe my presence in the yard was to…?"

"To observe the men at their martial play?" His lips
twitched again. "No, no, of course not, mistress. As you

explained, you lost your way in the unfamiliar environs of the palace.''

She was strangely uncomfortable in his presence. Though she had been informed that he was but twenty-three years of age, she was aware that there seemed aeons of difference between them in maturity. He had been trained in the houses of the great, served the present King as household knight and lived constantly both at his northern court and here in the intrigue-ridden atmosphere of Westminster.

He was ever courteous, even when alone with her, exaggeratedly so, as if she were a child to be cherished rather than a woman of flesh and blood. That, she thought, venomously, would most likely change when they were wedded and bedded.

It would probably suit him, once he had pleased the King by this match, to return her to his principal estates near Shrewsbury, where she would see him but rarely. She thought that in many ways she would prefer such an existence. She would, at least, be where her heart was, in her beloved Welsh border land.

She said hastily, looking away from him, ''I thank you for your discretion, sir. I—I am unused to court life and do not know how such an innocent adventure would be received here.''

He laughed out loud then. ''I assure you, no one would think ill of you…''

''But they would laugh,'' she said bitterly.

He shook his head slowly. ''They will not have the opportunity, though, Mistress Cressida, I have judged you not incapable of dealing squarely with any man, woman or child who dared to laugh at you.''

There it was again, that note of humour at her expense.

She ground her teeth in impotent fury and made him a curtsey when she took her leave of him.

They were betrothed on the seventeenth day of December in St Stephen's chapel in the presence of the King and Queen. Cressida wore a gown of rose-coloured velvet and was glad of its warmth, for the day was icy cold.

Before he took her hand the Earl said quietly, "I would ask Mistress Cressida two questions, please, Sir Daniel."

"Certainly, sir, but my daughter—"

"Is ever dutiful. I am quite sure of that, sir, but please allow me this boon."

Sir Daniel glanced uneasily at his wife, who smiled to reassure him. She had already spoken with Cressida this very morning, early, and had obtained from her a promise that she would behave well during the ceremony.

Cressida looked up at the Earl, who was towering above her and so very close, a little uncertainly. He had not so much as broached the subject of this arrangement to her and she had assumed that he was completely satisfied. Now she was not so sure.

"First, Mistress Cressida, is your heart engaged elsewhere?"

"My lord, my daughter is very young. She would never be foolish enough…"

Again the Earl silenced Sir Daniel's bluster with an upraised hand. "Let her answer for herself. Though she is but sixteen she may well have developed a closeness to someone she has known well for some time. I would not have her forced."

Cressida's thoughts flew, fleetingly, to Howell Prosser. She liked him well enough. He would have proved a convenient partner to keep her where her heart lay, but she had never really considered him as a possible husband. She blushed slightly. Indeed, only now was she thinking of any man in that light, sharing hearth and board—and bed. Soon this man would be beside her, determining her way of life.

She shook her head and said firmly, "There is no one, my lord."

Behind her she heard her father utter a deep sigh of relief, only to give a slight gasp of alarm again as the Earl asked his second question.

"Have you, Mistress Cressida, developed any real antipathy for me?"

Cressida, too, gave a little startled gulp and looked up again sharply into his face. The usually hooded eyes were looking into hers intently and there was no sign of sleepiness or humour in them.

Her lips trembled a little as she said softly, "Why, no, my lord. Why should I? You have offered me no discourtesy."

He gave her a little bow, took her chilled hand in his, and turned back to the waiting priest.

"Then we will proceed."

Afterwards, as they moved towards the door of the chapel and she felt the unfamiliar weight of the betrothal ring upon her finger, he said clearly, "I shall wait impatiently for the marriage ceremony which will truly bind us together, Cressida, and I know you need some weeks, at least, to get to know me, but Lent will come all too soon, forbidding all unions, so we should marry before that."

She nodded hurriedly and withdrew her hand from his grasp. As ever, she felt uncomfortable in his presence, his fingers conveying to hers a faint tingle at contact, his eyes now sleepily hooded again, dominating her gaze as a stoat did a rabbit, forcing it to stand completely still for the kill. Why did such a thought occur to her now? She had told him she had no dislike for him, nor distrust—but fear, that was something quite different.

Yet he had never, by the slightest word or gesture, given her reason to be afraid of him, not even in the tilt-yard. No, this fear came of herself—fear that her life was changing inexorably, that childhood had gone for ever, and that, in her plighting of her troth to this man, she had accepted her own fate, for she knew instinctively that he would not have allowed her to go through with the ceremony if she had given a positive answer to either of his questions.

At the feast which followed he plied her with delicacies attentively, and she found herself drinking more of the sweet malmsey than she had ever previously consumed. Once she gave him an uncertain glance and found a strange, sad expression upon his features which caused her some misgivings. Was he, too, being forced into this match against his will for some political reason?

But the Earl of Wroxeter was a decisive man, powerful in the King's Councils. She had already discovered that, despite her newness to court circles. No man would force his hand had he determined otherwise. Her dowry was considerable. Had he embarked on this marriage to enrich his coffers? Yet she knew that his own holdings and estates were great enough to cause her own father some envy.

The King was smiling genially upon them. She was aware that he was now utterly triumphant and a little spasm of anger surged up in her that all of these noble persons seated at the table should be governed by his whim.

Despite her anger towards the King, Cressida enjoyed her work in attendance upon Queen Anne. There was nothing onerous about her duties and Anne was gentle though firm. Cressida soon saw that she was, indeed, quite sick.

The Queen tired easily and suffered bouts of coughing which left her even more exhausted.

It was obvious, too, that she adored her husband. Cressida often saw her gaze across at him yearningly when he was busied about his court duties and sit disconsolate when he was absent from her side. Her older ladies loved her dearly, but some of the younger ones sometimes gossiped about her lack of energy behind her back and her seeming inability to bear the King another child.

"She must have another son," Cressida heard Lady Mary Bolton say to her companion the day after Cressida's betrothal. The three of them were in one of the garde rooms, engaged in sorting out and airing the Queen's most elaborate gowns, ready for the coming Christmas feasting. Cressida had left the other two for moments to take out one of the gowns and shake it in the open air. Her companions were momentarily hidden from her by the half-open door to the garde room as she returned and they did not hear her approach.

"She'll not do that," Lady Joanna Scrope whispered back. "I heard Dr Hobbes talking to the King the other day and both their faces were very grave. It's my belief she won't live very long, poor lady, though, truth to say, her passing would leave the King free to marry again and sire an heir."

"My uncle insists he loves her now, even after her beauty has faded. If she dies I think it will nigh break the King's heart. He'll not wish to replace her, even for the good of the realm."

"People marry for other things than love, as you should know," Lady Joanna asserted waspishly. "Yesterday's ceremony showed us all that. Wroxeter has soon put aside his feelings for Lady Elinor to marry that chit with the sing-song Welsh accent and everyone knows he cannot love her. She's still just a child and they have only just met. It's being said it is to please the King and she has a considerable dowry, I'm told.''

Cressida gave a little gasp of hurt surprise. Until now she had not realised there was any resentment levelled against her for gaining the Queen's favour, though she might well have understood that, as she was so newly come to Court, yet the real spite in Lady Joanna's voice was only too obvious. She drew back a little, unwilling to face the pair until she was sure she had regained her air of tranquility.

A clear, authoritative voice spoke from the corridor behind her so that Cressida turned, startled.

''I should have thought you two would know better than to stand and gossip when Her Grace has need of your services. As to accents, Lady Joanna, your vowels are broad enough, clearly revealing your upbringing in the wastes of the north. You would know that well enough, if you paused in your own foolish prattling long enough to hear the sound of your own voice. Hurry, both of you. The Queen needs you in her chamber.''

The speaker was tall and slim, her stance regal, despite the fact that her purple gown, which had once been splendid, was now slightly rubbed and worn and the braid tarnished.

The two ladies addressed hastily put down the garments they were holding, turned and made low curtseys.

''Lady Elizabeth, we—we had no idea...'' Lady Joanna stammered. ''The Queen instructed us to do this...''

''She is not feeling well now and is anxious to lie down for an hour. Lady Mary, go for a towel and scented water to bathe her forehead and you, Joanna, turn down the bed in her chamber.''

Again the two curtsied low, with hurried glances at

Cressida, before hastening about their designated duties. Cressida was about to join them when the Lady Elizabeth placed a restraining hand on her arm.

"Mistress Gretton, you stay with me and help finish hanging these gowns. They can manage perfectly well without you."

Cressida had seen the newcomer once or twice about the Court, had heard her father's whisper to her mother concerning her identity. This was the Lady Elizabeth Plantagenet, the King's eldest niece, sister of the deposed King Edward V. Cressida curtsied a trifle nervously as she advanced into the garde room in the Princess's wake to place the heavy gown upon the waiting press.

Elizabeth, like her celebrated mother, the Dowager Queen, who had been first Elizabeth Woodville, then Lady Grey, and lately King Edward IV's Queen, was a decided beauty. Her face was heart-shaped, her features good, though she did have the slightly over-large Plantagenet nose.

Cressida caught only a glimpse of her hair, smoothed decorously back behind her velvet frontal, and judged it fair, almost silver fair. Her mother was famed for that hair and men said, unkindly, that she had spun with it a web to catch the late King. The Princess turned large grey eyes upon Cressida and the full mouth widened into a smile.

"Do not let their malice disturb you. You have won the prize that all the young ladies at Court desired—Martyn of Wroxeter."

"Oh." Cressida was a trifle winded by the discovery that she had carried off the most eligible bachelor knight. "I—I did not know my voice was so…"

"Liltingly Welsh?" The Princess said, smiling. "I assure you it is very pretty. Since it speaks directly to Wroxeter of his own border lands, he must find it so too."

"Your Grace…"

"I am Lady Elizabeth now, since the bastardy of my father's children was confirmed. Those who know me well call me Lady Bessy."

Cressida was even more embarrassed, but the Princess had spoken so simply and without any trace of rancour for her changed status that it was hard to know what to say in reply.

Lady Elizabeth said quietly, "I have accepted my new position and since we left sanctuary and came to Court life has become again much pleasanter, but I do know the ladies gossip behind my back as I found them doing about you. Court is a hard place to learn the lessons of assuming indifference. You will manage it in time and soon you will be Wroxeter's bride and immune from such malice."

"They—they spoke of Lady Elinor. Is she—is she Lord Wroxeter's mistress?"

"She was his betrothed. She died," the Princess explained bluntly. "Lady Elinor Maudsley and Martyn, Earl of Wroxeter, had planned to marry this last autumn, but she developed some internal disorder and the doctors could not save her. He has been absent from Court for some months during his time of mourning."

Cressida's brow creased in an alarmed frown. A discarded mistress she could have dealt with, accepted, but a promised bride whose memory might continue to haunt her betrothed husband was a more serious matter altogether.

"No one told me," she said slowly. "I saw at the feast last night how sad he looked when he thought himself unobserved. He must have loved her very much."

The Princess sighed. "Indeed, I think he did. They had been childhood companions. She would have made an excellent chatelaine, I'm sure, though who is to know how deep his passion for her was? At all events, we cannot live with the dead. Their passing changes all our circumstances.''

Her voice was calm, but conveyed to Cressida the sadness she was still feeling for her own father's death and the terrible change it had wrought in her life.

''Wroxeter has chosen you and I am not surprised. You are very lovely, Cressida Gretton, which is cause enough for those foolish girls to be jealous of you. He is a wealthy man, and generous. I have always had respect for him. You are fortunate. All we womenfolk must accept the fate chosen for us and make the best of it.''

Cressida nodded. ''My mother has said as much.''

The Princess laughed merrily. ''If I am beginning to talk like a mother, things are come to a sore pass indeed.''

Preparations for the Christmas festivities soon began in earnest and Cressida found herself fully engaged. She was delighted to discover that many of the traditions she had enjoyed at Gretton were kept up here at Westminster.

The festive yule logs were dragged into the palace and holly and laurel boughs were appearing in all the state and presence rooms. The Queen's ladies giggled over the mistletoe hanging conveniently from many boughs, an open invitation for kissing. The chaplains frowned on such pagan customs but on these joyous occasions were totally ignored. Even the King and Queen, known to be pious in their religious observances, much more so than the late King Edward, turned blind eyes to the general merriment.

Everywhere courtiers and ladies were refurbishing their finest clothes for the several feasts of the twelve-day season. Cressida was thankful that her mother had insisted on the careful packing of her own gowns, for she was confident that her wardrobe would prove more than adequate.

Her friendship with Lady Elizabeth prospered. Her feelings had been deeply hurt by the malicious gossip she had overheard and the Princess's kindness was balm to her soul. From Elizabeth's information she came to recognise some of the most important nobles of the realm and, though the subject of the recent usurpation was never mentioned, Cressida was aware of the undercurrents of treasonable talk rife in the chambers and corridors of the palace.

In her discussions with the Lady Elizabeth she never once dared to refer to the fate of the two young Princes, Elizabeth's brothers. It occurred to her that the princess's ease of manner in the King's presence was strange, but also reassuring.

The Court and common folk were known to be concerned about the health of the Queen. Anne herself knew it and was determined to lay some of the worst rumours to rest by appearing at her most splendid and radiant over the days of the feasting.

She enlisted the Lady Elizabeth to help her choose her finest gowns and jewels. Elizabeth was constantly at her aunt's side and Cressida was struck by the shocking contrast the two made when together. Both had inherited the Neville fairness of hair and complexion but in Elizabeth they shone like a beacon and, despite her brave efforts to appear youthful and lively, the Queen's faded looks and lack of energy were only too evident.

Once Cressida caught the Earl of Wroxeter watching the two bent heads close together while Queen Anne was purchasing new velvets with the advice and help of her niece. His expression was thunderous; for once those sleepy dark eyes of his were hard with disapproval.

Cressida said nervously, ''The Lady Elizabeth is a great comfort to the Queen, always attentive and kindly.''

''Is she?'' he said almost brusquely. ''Yes, I imagine it

is good for the Lady Elizabeth to be about in court circles again after her long months in seclusion.''

''The King constantly shows his gratitude to her for her devoted care of the Queen.''

The Earl turned his hard gaze on Cressida. ''Yes, I have noticed it. It would be better if he were to find a husband for her—and soon.''

Cressida considered that thoughtfully. Yes, the Princess was past the age when most girls were given in marriage. She knew Elizabeth had once been promised to the French dauphin, but the alliance had come to nothing. Now she was a penniless dependant of her uncle.

Despite the fact that the Queen, her mother, had taken sanctuary in Westminster and resisted all persuasion to give her second son, Richard of York, into his uncle's care until forced to do so, an obvious declaration of her fear and distrust of the new King, she had finally emerged with her daughters, apparently reconciled, and Richard had treated her well, promised her suitable marriage arrangements for the young Princesses, and Elizabeth, the eldest, had been made most welcome at Court.

No wonder she was glad to wait upon her aunt and show her devoted gratitude to the King. Yet Wroxeter seemed suspicious of her motives. Why? In what way could a defenceless girl possibly hurt the King's cause?

Cressida had not prepared herself for the actual splendour of Christmas 1484. The palace had throbbed with excitement for days before, but the reality was beyond all expectation.

Cressida sat with her parents and Wroxeter, very close to the royal table where Richard and Anne sat below the cloth of estate. Both monarchs wore their most elaborate, fur-trimmed and jewel-encrusted garments, and Anne had forced herself to an outward display of gaiety, despite the fact that her heart was aching still for her dead son.

Remove followed remove each day at table, throughout the twelve days of feasting, as no expense was spared. It seemed that the King was determined to show his Court and the common people that no rumours from France concerning Henry Tudor's intention to contest the English throne could destroy his peace.

Cressida found herself being helped to rich delicacies by her betrothed; pike in rich sauces, roast haunches of venison, tench served in jelly, rabbit, larks' tongues and, following, an assortment of sweetmeats. The subtleties, composed of spun sugar and marzipan, were magnificent sculptures of castles and carracks, birds and animals, the King's personal device of the white boar taking pride of place on the high table. Though she was becoming used to the richness of spiced dishes served at Court, this over-abundance was too much for Cressida and the prolonged festivities gradually made her wish for simpler food.

Throughout, the minstrels played from the gallery on flute, flagelot and vielles. The King had declared his intention to be patron of the arts and kept a company of musicians by him constantly. When the trestles were removed the hurdy-gurdies, trumpets and sackbuts played for dancing.

Cressida was intrigued to see that the King rose to lead the Princess Elizabeth onto the floor. They danced well, moving with grace through the complicated patterns, and there was hearty applause at the conclusion of the dance. Elizabeth was laughing happily, flushed and rosy from the exertion.

Cressida had once heard that the King was slightly deformed—malicious rumour had said, unkindly, that he was downright crippled—but she had seen for herself, long before this, that that was all nonsense. He was crook-backed, they said, but she saw no sign of it. If he had one shoulder higher than another, the discrepancy was very slight indeed, and no greater than that of many men who practised hard with sword and axe and developed the muscles of one arm and shoulder more greatly than the other.

Now she saw that he was very skilled in the dance, nimble-footed and able to lift his partner high into the air, which set to naught all such foolish speculation. The Queen applauded with the others, but took no part in the dancing. Cressida, who had seen her coughing and panting, exhausted in her chamber, well understood that she was not fit for such a show, but Anne had proudly accompanied Richard onto the balcony of the palace at the crown-wearing and received much good-humoured clapping and bantering advice from the crowd as to her duty in setting about providing another heir. Only too well did Cressida know that to be unlikely.

She glanced now sharply towards her betrothed, who had been watching the Lady Elizabeth with the King.

"The King dances very well," she said softly. "It is good to see him enjoy himself so much—a respite from the many cares of State."

Wroxeter nodded. He did not seem so concerned tonight with the Princess's closeness to the royal pair, or, if he was, was disinclined to show it.

He turned to her father. "Have I your permission, Sir Daniel, to dance with my betrothed?"

Cressida's hand trembled upon the stem of her wine cup. She had danced at court but never so publicly. She was not sure she would acquit herself well.

Sir Daniel was smiling expansively and readily gave his permission, and Lady Gretton smiled at her daughter fondly.

"Certainly, my dear. Go and enjoy yourself."

Cressida rose and took the Earl's proffered hand. She noticed in passing that her two former tormentors were watching her progress with avid interest.

He danced well, as she had expected. She had learned, from the talk about her over recent days, that he did all things well. He was popular with the Queen's attendants for his courtesy and good humour. Cressida thought wryly that apparently no one but she had seen glimpses of him when really angry, as she had seen him in the tilt-yard and when he had commented adversely on the Princess Elizabeth's constant presence at Court.

He was skilled in the joust, she had heard. That did not surprise her. He practised hard for that, she thought with some asperity. What did amaze her was his known prowess on the battlefield. The King's favour had been won during combat on the Scottish border.

Somehow, Cressida had not seen her betrothed as a doughty warrior. That sleepy expression had lulled her into a false understanding of his nature. She had thought him too fond of luxurious living to face the rigours of a battle camp, let alone the actual danger of face-to-face encounters, when more was at stake than the possible loss of horse and accoutrements.

The Lady Elizabeth had told her that her fellow ladies were envious of her good fortune in winning the hand of the wealthiest and most admired bachelor at Court. Now she felt many pairs of eyes fixed upon her, willing her to perform clumsily or even trip over her gown. She was, after all, the country maid, come but recently to town.

As in all things, he guided her with expert skill, smiling down at her encouragingly as the minstrels struck up a merry tune. Her fingers felt icy cold in his grasp and her heart was beating so fast with nervousness that she felt he must see her agitation, but the steps of the dance were fast and furious and she was forced to give all her concentration to them.

He drew her along the lines of dancers, swinging her expertly, then his hands were about her waist, strong and supportive, as he lifted her high into the air and brought her down safely, laughing and gasping. The great hall, with its colourful throng, moved madly round her as again she was swung into the elaborate patterns, till the music stopped and they halted at last, out of breath but triumphant.

He bowed and led her from the group of dancers to a side bench beneath a flaming flambeau.

"Wait while I fetch you wine. The room is growing over-hot from the throng of revellers—" he glanced round with some amusement "—getting drunker and more bawdy by the moment. I fear your lady mother will soon be withdrawing you from the company."

Her breathing had slowed by the time he returned with a goblet of wine and she sipped at it gratefully.

"Thank you, but I think I, too, am taking more than I should tonight."

"To give you courage?"

She glanced up, startled by his half-amused challenge, then lowered her gaze hastily. "Yes, you might well be right, sir."

"You seem over-anxious tonight. Why, Cressida? I assure you you are the object of admiration from all quarters."

"I do not think that is true. Many of my companions think me very boorish. They comment often upon my accent."

He glanced down at her fairy-like beauty. She was dressed tonight in a gown of softest blue brocade and tendrils of that extraordinary fair hair had broken free from the confines of her veiled butterfly hennin and brushed the rosy glow on her delicate cheek. He was not surprised that she faced spiteful criticism. What girl in the room could hope to match her ethereal beauty?

"I was not thinking of the ladies present," he returned drily.

"Oh?" She was surprised by her own state of confusion. She had never felt so downright stupid and churlish in Howell's company, but then, he did not pay her fulsome compliments which put her out of countenance.

"Do not avoid my gaze. You are my betrothed and I am proud to lead you in the dance, to show the world you will soon be mine indeed."

The half-veiled reference to what would follow the marriage ceremony caused her to colour again hotly and she turned away to look anxiously for sight of her parents.

He gave a good-humoured laugh. "You will have no need to fear me, Cressida, I promise you."

"I fear no-one, sir," she snapped, riled into a return to the spirited responses she had given him at their earlier encounters.

He laughed again. "No, I do not think you do fear any man or woman—except, perhaps, yourself."

"What ever do you mean, sir?" Her startlingly blue eyes were very wide now, challenging his dark ones.

"I think all maids look with apprehension—to what is unknown." His words were very gently uttered and the hard line left her mouth and she smiled so sweetly that his heart almost turned over. How childishly vulnerable she was, and determined that no one should know it.

She was again looking towards her parents and he took her fingers prisoner for a moment, concerned to reassure her, as he would any child looking to him for succour.

"I will treat you kindly, allow you to get to know me better before pressing my demands. I think it best if you remain for a while here at Court in attendance upon the Queen. I have duties in the Council, but later, if you wish, we can go for a while to the Marches and I shall take you frequently to see your parents."

She gave a little relieved gasp. Many women, she knew, were totally separated from all kith and kin once the marriage knot was tied, a future she had secretly feared. She loved Gretton so much that she knew her heart would be broken if she rarely saw it.

He seemed kind, this man who would soon command her obedience. They all insisted that she was fortunate, from the King to the Lady Elizabeth. Why, then, did she feel this strange presentiment that he was not as he seemed outwardly; that, if she were not compliant, he could prove a tyrant? She had felt a wild excitement when he had placed his hands about her waist and again when their fingers had touched as he had handed her the wine.

She forced a brave smile. "You are kind, sir. Your words convince me of your goodwill. I hope—I shall be able to please you, as you deserve."

The corners of his mouth quirked oddly. "Why do I feel that that is a more politic answer than an entirely sincere one?"

"I know my duties and—"

"Will perform them with punctilious regard for my approval. I think not, my Cressida. I do not wish for a mouse of a wife."

He took the empty wine goblet from her nerveless fingers and drew her to her feet. Within moments he had restored her to the care of her mother and strode off to lean attentively upon the arm of the chair in which the now exhausted-looking Queen sat.

*   *   *

The Christmas festivities continued until Twelfth Night, with all the traditional games and entertainments.

One evening a company of mummers performed the play of Sir Gawain and the Green Knight. Seated between her father and the Earl of Wroxeter, Cressida shivered with premonitory fear when Sir Gawain cut off the Green Knight's head with one savage stroke. The Earl turned to her, his amused expression, as the actor stooped to recover the stuffed head from the floor where it had fallen from its high woven supports upon his shoulders, changing quickly to one of alarm as he noted her unwonted paleness.

"Cressida, you are upset? I thought you must have heard the tale many times before and would be prepared for this scene. The Green Knight represents the dying winter while Gawain represents the burgeoning powers of spring."

She shook her head. "No, no, of course I know the tale, but have never seen it actually performed before. It—it made me think of real executions. My blood ran cold for the moment."

Her father tutted his disapproval of her unconsidered words. "Hush, Cressida. Westminster is no place to speak of executions." His voice was cautiously lowered as he regarded the King, seated some paces from them, laughing uproariously at the bawdy adventures of the hero, Gawain, as he attempted to find the sinister Green Knight and, true to his sworn oath, stand firm while the Knight took a retaliatory blow at his own head.

Cressida shivered again as she thought how frightening a place the Court was, despite its assumed atmosphere of merriment this Christmas. Collingbourne had died horribly not so many months ago at Tyburn for daring to write a scurrilous verse concerning the King and his closest councillors, and the King's cousin, George of Buckingham, had lost his head in Salisbury market-place after his failed rising of 1483.

She had seemed so very far from these terrifying events at home at Gretton. Soon, as Wroxeter's bride, she would be forced to live far closer to these men who waited attendance on their sovereign with murder in their hearts and smiling lips.

She wondered if Martyn of Wroxeter was as truly loyal to the King as he seemed. Could she innocently find herself embroiled in such a plot? The thought appalled her. Again she longed with all her heart to return safely to Gretton after these festivities and to remain there safe and protected from all poisonous intrigue and danger.

Twelfth Night was to be the culmination of all the Christmas activities. The Queen dressed with special care and showed a forced jollity as her ladies fussed around her for this final state occasion of the season. Privately Cressida thought that Anne would be glad to rest for a while in her own apartments after all this, when many of the summoned lords and their ladies had returned to their own manors.

As Cressida stepped back with her companion ladies to view their handiwork, she felt that their efforts had been fully justified. The Queen looked magnificent. The material of the undergown of purple cloth of gold, with its woven design of suns and roses, was the King's Christmas gift. Over this Anne wore an ermine-trimmed white velvet overgown sewn with seed-pearls.

She wore her golden hair unbound to her waist beneath her golden crown, and when the King came gallantly to her chamber to escort her to the great hall Cressida saw his grey-green eyes light up with the glory of his love for his wife. Truly, tonight, she looked like a bride adorned for her husband.

He stooped and kissed the palm of her hand.

"You are so beautiful. No woman will outshine you tonight, my Anne." He seemed totally unconcerned that his open adoration was observed and noted by all his wife's ladies.

She laughed gently. "You look very fine yourself, my lord."

He too was attired for the splendour of the occasion, in a scarlet velvet doublet over which his golden Yorkist collar gleamed beneath the candlelight, setting the ruby eyes of the pendant boar device glinting with artificial life.

The great hall was more crowded than ever tonight, and Cressida felt quite suffocated by all the noise and the greasy, spiced smell of the rich dishes. She had had more than a surfeit of such food over these last days and would have been grateful for more simple fare. Wroxeter, it seemed, was of a like mind, for he ate but sparely, though he was assiduous in placing the choicest morsels upon her plate.

The merriment seemed more bawdy and forced, as if the general company was making the best of this last chance to feast at the King's expense. Throughout it all the Queen sat resplendent beside Richard's side as a host of courtiers paid them both a wealth of fawning attention.

It was almost at the close of the banquet when the chamberlain announced the arrival of the Lady Elizabeth Plantagenet. Cressida craned her neck to see her friend approach the high table. Elizabeth had not been present in the Queen's chambers over the last few days and, only three days ago, Cressida had had only a hasty conversation with her on the river terrace before rushing back to serve the Queen.

There was a sudden silence which cut across the high-pitched laughter and chat in the hall. For a moment Cressida's view of the King's niece was obscured by taller people between her and the chairs of State. She felt Wroxeter give a little gasp beside her and turned to see an expression of pure fury etched upon his features.

Then Elizabeth moved into view and Cressida herself gave vent to a half-suppressed cry of shocked surprise.

The Lady Elizabeth was curtseying before her aunt and uncle, and when she rose Cressida saw immediately what had caused that sudden hush to fall upon the packed company.

Elizabeth's gown was almost a copy of the Queen's. The purple brocade undergown was not so fine, true, as Queen Anne's, but the cut of that and the white velvet overgown with its ermine trim was almost an exact facsimile. Whereas Anne's was starred with pearls, Elizabeth's was scattered with crystal drops which sparkled in the torchlight.

More shocking than the similarity of the gowns chosen by these two royal ladies was the fact that Elizabeth's youth and air of eager enthusiasm contrasted so starkly with the Queen's sudden pallor and wearied posture in her chair. It was as if a shaft of sunlight had appeared and totally eclipsed the moon's beauty.

As soon as it had hushed the company hastily resumed its assumed gaiety again as the King bent over the table to welcome his fair young niece and place her near to him at the high table, where, again, her position next to the tiring queen showed only too clearly the differences between them, despite the similarity of garb.

Cressida stole a hasty glance at her betrothed and found him watching the by-play at the high table with intense interest. Soon the trestles were cleared and the dancing began. Cressida sensed rather than heard the gossiping innuendo of talk as the King led his lovely young niece onto

the floor, while Anne remained quietly in her chair, outwardly engaged in watching the dancers, sipping occasionally from her bejewelled wine goblet, while, even from
a distance, Cressida saw her free hand tighten upon the
carved arm-rest of her chair.

Suddenly Wroxeter appeared before Cressida holding
out an imperious hand to lead her into the dance. His expression was grim. He did not even stop to ask permission
from her father as he usually did.

Tonight she was too concerned about the grimness of
her betrothed's expression to be worried about any inept-
ness on her part in the dance. They moved through the
complicated patterns without problems, largely due to the
Earl's expert guidance. Cressida was not surprised, nor in
the least relieved, when at the dance's end he led her from
the floor towards one of the doors into the corridor.

She glanced back anxiously to where her parents were
seated and then back to a little knot of superior attendants
where Alice was gossiping with a middle-aged, over-
dressed lady of considerable girth.

Wroxeter was tugging at her wrist impatiently, urging
her onward, and she thought she would have a bruise to
show for it later.

"Where are we going?" she panted. "We cannot leave
the company without a chaperon. I'll call Alice…"

"No need," he said calmly. "You are my betrothed. No
one will comment. We shall be gone only a short time. I
wish to talk to you and with no third person present."

She was pulled, willy-nilly, along the corridor and into
a small chamber some yards further on. Wroxeter passed
inside, still holding Cressida's wrist firmly. The light from
the sconce opposite the door showed her a small room,
furnished with a desk or table, two chairs and a stool. The
place was bare of comforts, with no fine rugs on the floor

or arras on the walls. It was clear that this was used only
for business, possibly by one of the King's clerks or a
secretary.

Wroxeter slammed the door to after lighting two candles
with tinder and flint placed ready. He shot across the heavy
bolt. He had released her wrist and she was rubbing at it
angrily. Then he indicated a chair facing the desk.

"Sit down, Cressida."

She obeyed him sulkily, glancing round the office with
a little shiver of unease. She could not rid herself of the
notion that this place was used for interrogation purposes,
and though there was no indication of any sinister means
of compulsion she was further uneasy.

Wroxeter appeared perfectly at home here. He sat back
in the chair opposite and eyed her gravely. For once the
hooded lids were drawn back clear of the dark, compelling
eyes.

"The Lady Elizabeth," he said coldly. "When did you
last speak with her?"

"What?" Cressida stared up at him in amazement. Was
this what had aroused his temper? He did not like the Lady
Elizabeth for some reason, and had stated that he would
rather she was far from Court, yet he had no means to
influence so important a lady as the Princess Elizabeth, nor
to object to Cressida's association with her. She set her
lips and jutted her chin angrily.

"I don't understand all this. Why have you withdrawn
me from the company? My mother will be alarmed…"

"I think not. She saw you were with me. Now, do not
fence with me, Cressida. When did you speak with the
Lady Elizabeth and talk about what the Queen intended to
wear tonight?"

Cressida's lips parted in shock. "You hold me responsible for... I know it was unfortunate that she—the Princess arrived in a gown so like the Queen's, but—''

"It was not unfortunate, it was deliberate," he said harshly, "and I wish to know if you informed the lady of what the Queen intended to wear. Answer me."

Cressida's blue eyes widened. "Deliberate? Oh, no, no one would..." Then she blazed, "This is nonsense. How dare you question me so...?"

He leaned across the desk again and once more gripped her injured wrist so that she winced sharply.

"Cressida, did you or did you not describe for the Lady Elizabeth exactly what the Queen was to wear for this Twelfth Night feasting?"

Her heart was now thudding against her ribs. That genial, good-natured expression had completely vanished from his features and she recognised the fact that this man could prove a very dangerous enemy indeed.

"Yes," she confessed at last, in a subdued voice. "The material was so very beautiful and we had all enthused about it. The undergown was the King's Christmas gift, but..."

"Did she question you about it?"

"Yes..."

"When and where?"

"She—she has been away from the Queen's apartments for some days. I—I wondered if she was ill and then I saw her walking on the river terrace and we talked..."

She swallowed uncomfortably, vaguely disturbed by the cold opacity of those dark eyes fixed intently on hers. "Yes, we did talk of the plans for this last Christmas feast. She asked what I was to wear and—and did ask after the Queen's health and—and which gown she..."

Cressida's voice trailed off miserably. "I did not think it a secret. The Princess is the Queen's niece and—"

He released her wrist abruptly and sat back in the chair, frowning, the fingers of one hand drumming upon the polished oak of the desktop.

She waited uncertainly. Gradually her sense of pique eclipsed her previous vague fear. What right had he to tell her what she should say and what she should not? She had said nothing unwise, voiced no criticism of the King…

She said suddenly, "Is that all you wish to say to me? If so, I would like to return to my parents. All this has been a great pother about nothing, if you ask me. It is embarrassing if one lady appears at a feast in attire like another's, but no great matter." Her lips closed together tightly, revealing her anger at his unjust attack on her. "The Queen did not swear us to secrecy."

"She would think there would be no need," he said wearily. "No one but Elizabeth would dare to do such a thing."

"Why are you so angry? The Queen has a right to be upset, I suppose, but—"

"No matter," he said hurriedly. "As you say, I must return you to the great hall, but—" he had risen from his chair and was now leaning down over the desk, his weight supported upon his two arms "—hear me well. You are soon to be my wife and I expect you to obey me. You will associate no more in private with the Lady Elizabeth."

Cressida went pale with fury. "The Lady Elizabeth has been undue kind to me when other ladies have not. I value her friendship. She honours me. You have no right…"

"I have every right," he said harshly. "I have an official position in the King's household—but, no matter, we will not speak of that. As your future husband I have authority to say with whom I do and do not wish you to associate. You will treat the Princess with courtesy, naturally, as you are bound to do, but you will offer no confidences. Do you understand me?''

She nodded unwillingly and rose from her chair as he took his hands from the desk and stood upright. He came round to her and took her hand, more gently this time.

''There are happenings at Court you do not understand, Cressida. This seems a small matter to you, but in reality actual harm has been done tonight and with your complicity—innocently, of course. Comply with my wishes. See as little of the Lady Elizabeth as possible. You have been used—and that could spell danger for you—and for others.''

She released a hard-held breath, her eyes widening again. She looked up into his eyes, seeking his understanding.

''I would not have willingly hurt the Queen,'' she murmured at last. ''I know it looked—I mean, when we all saw them together...''

''Exactly,'' he said grimly. ''Now you are beginning to understand. The Queen is unwell. She needs all our love and care. She should not be open to unkind speculation or rumour. You must respect all her confidences.'' He sighed. ''You are such a child. I must learn to be more patient.''

He unbolted the door and turned to extinguish the candles. Cressida experienced an overwhelming relief that she was to leave this chamber, not unmixed with growing irritation that he regarded her so slightingly. She tossed her head resentfully as he bowed to her, once more the courteous suitor, and allowed him to lead her back along the corridor towards the babble of talk and loud laughter issuing from the great hall.

Chapter Four

"I cannot marry him. I will not marry him." Cressida stood before her parents in her own small apartment, her voice shrill with unshed tears, almost hysterical.

Sir Daniel and Lady Gretton turned helplessly towards Alice who stood stolidly by the door. They had been hastily summoned to their daughter's chamber by her and had come at once. Alice shrugged equally helplessly. Her gaze went to her young mistress, standing there, looking so vulnerable, a child still but chin jutting rebelliously, determinedly defiant.

"You cannot tell us of anything alarming which has happened?" Lady Gretton sounded totally bewildered.

"No, my lady. Mistress Cressida seemed somewhat edgy when we left the great hall, then when we got back here I started to undress her but she suddenly began to cry. I could get nothing out of her and I thought at last I should send for you."

Sir Daniel waved testily to the two women to be silent. He seated himself on the edge of Cressida's bed and folded his arms.

"Now, child, what is this nonsense? You say you can't

marry Wroxeter? Why ever not? You went out of the hall with him. Did he attack you, offer you insult?''

Lady Gretton started forward angrily but again he waved her back.

Cressida gulped back tears. ''No,'' she said, so softly that he had to lean forward to hear her answer.

''Then, in the Virgin's name, what is all this pother? Come, Cressida, I thought you had more spirit than to be taken by a fit of foolish womanly vapourings.''

Cressida turned away, plucking restlessly at the fine silk of her gown.

''I tell you I will not marry him. He—he frightens me.''

''Frightens you?'' Sir Daniel looked even more bewildered. ''You tell me he did not touch you nor offer you insult, now you tell me he frightens you. The man appears courteous and considerate. The King thinks highly of him…''

''Oh, yes, the King,'' Cressida snapped. ''The King must be right, and obeyed whatever the consequences…''

''Of course the King must be obeyed, Cressida,'' Lady Gretton said worriedly. ''I cannot understand all this. Before the betrothal ceremony Lord Wroxeter asked if you had any misgivings. You told him you had none. Do you tell us now that you have become attached to someone here at Court…?''

''Of course not,'' Cressida said desperately. ''I would do nothing to make you ashamed of me. There is no one, but—but Lord Wroxeter is such a powerful Lord, with a position of authority here at Court, and he overwhelms me. He—he has already given me commands as to whom I am to befriend and whom to avoid…''

''You are his betrothed wife,'' Lady Gretton said quietly. ''He is well within his right. If there is some man…''

''There is no man. I have said as much.'' Cressida found

herself childishly stamping her foot. She stopped the moment she realised how foolish she was being as she caught Alice biting her lip in disapproval. "There are—ladies—one lady in particular—with whom he does not wish me to be associated. I will not be so commanded. He will not tell me to deny affections. He will want me to dispense with Alice's services next."

Lady Gretton pursed her lips. Only too well she was aware that many bridegrooms indeed preferred to dismiss their young wives' attendants. She herself had been ever fortunate in that her husband had willingly accepted her beloved elderly servants and welcomed them into his household. She had hoped that such would be the case for Cressida.

Sir Daniel grated, "Of whom do we speak? Wroxeter must have some reason for misliking one of your companions. Mayhap she talks immoderately of married life and frightens you. If this so, you must accept Wroxeter's ruling. Soon enough you will be wed and away from Court."

Cressida was about to speak of her interview with her betrothed, then something froze the intended words on her lips. "You have been used," he had said, "and that could spell danger for you—and for others." She could not forget her fears for her father's safety the very day the King's messenger had arrived at Gretton.

Why was Wroxeter the Lady Elizabeth's enemy? She had been kept from Court for some days. Had that been due to his orders? Cressida gave a little shudder. How powerful Wroxeter must be, indeed, if he could dictate to those about the Queen so that the King's royal niece was denied her presence at Anne's side.

She said stubbornly, "I do not wish to proceed with this marriage. Father, if you love me…"

Sir Daniel exploded into sudden, raw fury. "Have I bred

a rank fool? You are solemnly betrothed in the royal chapel. It would take a papal dispensation to break such a binding pledge. You are all but wed, but for the bedding—''

He broke off as he caught his wife's warning glance directed at him balefully. "Troth was plighted in the King's very presence. Do you think for a moment that he would countenance such a plea on my part to apply to the Curia? What excuse could I give but a maid's foolish premarriage fears? Make up your mind to it, Cressida. The match is made, contracts signed. You will go to the altar with Wroxeter and that is an end to it.''

Sir Daniel stood up decisively and her mother moved to embrace her. Cressida stood docilely, but withdrew a little stiffly as soon as she decently could. She curtsied dutifully as her parents withdrew to their own apartment, then said through clenched teeth, "Alice, go fetch a warmed brick. I am frozen to the marrow.''

Alice hesitated only a moment, then hurried off about her errand. Cressida stood, hands clenched into small fists at her sides, then, slowly, she began to undress. Alice had already unhooked her elaborate gown and removed her hennin before summoning Sir Daniel and his lady, so Cressida found she could manage well enough. In fact she felt flushed, almost fevered, and her need of a warming device for the bed was merely a ruse to rid herself of Alice, if only for minutes.

She needed, desperately, to be alone. She was not really angered by her father's reaction to her plea. She had not expected him to behave in any other way, yet she had needed both her parents to understand her need.

Logic, however, told her that that was an impossibility, since she had been unable to explain to them just how she felt. She could not explain it to herself. She only knew she was experiencing a state of helpless panic. From the moment that messenger had arrived at her home her fate had been sealed, and she could not help but fear the fates of others she loved could be sealed also, yet she did not know how or why.

Her travelling mirror revealed her body in misty outline in the soft glow of the two dips in her chamber. She stared at herself critically for the very first time, turning this way and that to observe the features of her naked form. He had said she was but a child. Was that how she appeared to him? She did not feel like a child. Her doubts and fears were anything but childlike.

She was very small. Had Wroxeter's lost love been tall and stately? Cressida tossed her head, allowing the mass of her golden hair to fall free from its pins and cascade over her shoulders, down to her waist and beyond. She was slim—too boyishly slim for a man with sophisticated court tastes like Martyn, Earl of Wroxeter? Her breasts were small but firm, the tips rosy in the golden half-light. She stood on tiptoe, arching her back, lifting her breasts with her two hands.

He had said she was fairy-like, but that was the stuff of myths and dreams, tales told by the border folk and Celtic peasants. A man like Wroxeter would want something more substantial in his arms.

The false warm glow which had suffused her body during the exchanges with her betrothed and her father was fading. She shivered and reached for her fur-trimmed bedgown and by the time Alice returned her need for the heated brick had become a reality. She snuggled down at last beneath the fur covering of the bed, glad of the blanket-wrapped brick's retained heat.

Alice stood by the bed, arms akimbo, looking perplexed and somewhat alarmed still.

"You are angry that I sent for your mother? I did not think your father would come, but I was worried…"

Cressida reached out a hand towards her maid, patting the bedside welcomingly.

"I know why you did it. You are not used to seeing me in a bout of hysterical tears. Faith," she added disgustedly, "I am unused to the frightening sensations myself."

Alice sank down and enfolded her former charge in her arms. "You mustn't blame your father, chick. He does what he thinks is necessary for your well-being. You were not very explicit in telling him what you fear. Cannot you tell old Alice?"

Cressida gave a little laugh. "Do not try those old tricks on me. You are not old, Alice, neither are you a foolish countrywoman, but wise in the ways of the world—probably far more so than my mother, who has been adored and sheltered throughout her married life."

"Aye, well, won't you tell me what truly ails you?" Alice's eyes had narrowed shrewdly.

Cressida sighed. "I'm not sure I know. Part of it is having to grow up so suddenly, face the dread of this coming marriage and all it entails—but," she cut in quickly before Alice could hasten to reassure her with all the usual platitudes about women's lot in life, "it is the atmosphere here about the Court. I am concerned that my father could be drawn into danger—and I know Wroxeter's loyalty is to the King and only to the King. He would sacrifice us all, if needful, to that cause."

She told Alice what had taken place between her betrothed and herself and his final warning.

"I do not understand quite why he was so angry," she said thoughtfully. "Of course, it was a tactless thing for the Princess to do and I feel partly to blame for having divulged the secret of what the Queen was to wear, but the Earl was unnaturally disturbed—indeed, beside himself with fury, and he held me responsible." She paused for a moment, thinking the incident through again.

"Do you think the Princess was making some point of her own? Does she now believe her brothers to be truly dead—and, if so, considers herself the rightful heir, her father's eldest daughter, Queen in her own right, and so dressed herself accordingly to show the assembled nobles at this ritual crown-wearing?" Cressida's lips trembled. "If that were the case, Wroxeter would consider it a challenge to the King's right and it could encourage others to take sides…"

She gave another shiver, knowing as she did her father's Lancastrian sympathies. He must not ally himself openly with any faction at this intrigue-ridden Court which was avid for scandal.

Alice was silent, then she shook her head. "It seems more likely she was but making a bid for attention," she said at last, then, before Cressida could question her further about her opinion on this matter, she bent and tucked in her charge and rose to her feet to seek her own bed.

"Never you mind about your betrothed. Like most men, he'll have got well over his temper in the morning." She was frowning, though, as she turned away, having noticed the darkening bruise on her nurseling's wrist. The man was more of an enigma than she had taken him for, and she gave a heavy sigh at the thought of Cressida's coming dependence on her future husband's moods.

Cressida dreaded to see her betrothed after their quarrel, but, as Alice had promised, when she did encounter him within the Queen's apartments the following day he greeted her courteously, as if nothing had happened to cause him annoyance.

"How is Her Grace today?" he enquired quietly.

Cressida glanced hurriedly back to the open door of the Queen's bedchamber. "She—she is exceptionally tired." She had noted with concern the dark shadows beneath Anne's eyes and her seeming reluctance to rouse and face the day.

"That is to be expected after the gruelling pace of all these past celebrations." His tone was normal, without any hint of anger, but Cressida could see that he was frowning. The Queen's condition concerned him deeply.

They were standing quite close, the other ladies giving them an opportunity to talk in private. He looked down deliberately at her bruised wrist, which she was nervously holding in her other hand.

"Was I responsible for that mark?"

Cressida flushed somewhat miserably. "It is nothing. I'm sure you had no wish to hurt me. I suppose it happened when I was anxious to leave you."

He inclined his head gravely. "Certainly I had no intention of giving you pain. You will forgive me if I was attempting to make my point somewhat forcibly."

She nodded and looked down at her feet without comment.

"Be careful, Cressida, with whom you gossip at Court. Repeat nothing of a doubtful nature."

She looked back up at him quickly. His tone was regretful still but his dark eyes were unhooded and she knew he was anxious to impress upon her the gravity of her position.

She nodded again.

There was a little stir near the Queen's door and Cressida heard the cool, clear tones of the Lady Elizabeth cut across some polite murmur from one of the more senior ladies.

"If, as you say, Her Grace, my aunt, is unwell, then I should be admitted to her presence at once. I am sure His Grace the King would approve of my determination to wait upon her. She may well have need of my services."

Cressida gave Wroxeter a hasty glance to see what his reaction would be to this move, but he merely watched thoughtfully as the two ladies near the door were swept aside and the Lady Elizabeth entered the bedchamber. His eyes were once more hooded as he bowed to the attendant ladies and excused himself. Cressida watched him walk away somewhat relieved. She wondered if he had gone to the small, somehow daunting chamber where he had questioned her.

Over the next days the Queen's health continued to decline. The weather worsened and the cold, damp air from the river caused her to cough badly. The attacks were so prolonged and weakening that Cressida was often alarmed when on duty alone, but the Queen would frequently refuse to allow her physician to be sent for.

The King seemed busy once more with affairs of state, but when he did come to the Queen's side she forced herself to appear better for his benefit. In her presence he assumed a cheeriness which Cressida saw vanish when the Queen could not see his expression and, despite her reservations about the King's nature, Cressida was forced to acknowledge that he loved his wife dearly and was daily becoming more concerned about her.

The doctors were summoned and prescribed cough remedies and noxious potions which the Queen swallowed valiantly and without complaint, but nothing seemed to do her much good.

"I shall be better in the spring," she averred confidently, her eyes far too bright and the hectic pink flush darkening her cheeks. Privately Cressida wondered if the ailing Queen would live until the spring.

The Lady Elizabeth came daily to her aunt's apartments and Anne valued her ministrations. The King himself drew his niece aside on several occasions to thank her for her services. No one referred to the unfortunate incident on Twelfth Night, at least not in Cressida's hearing, and the Lady Elizabeth was once more ensconced in the small coterie of the Queen's attendants.

She continued to single out Cressida for confidences. Cressida was stoutly determined to ignore her betrothed's former strictures and was warmed by this display of royal friendship. The Princess talked of her younger sisters, their hopes of a rosy future, and that the King would provide for them handsomely and find them youthful and wealthy husbands. Rarely did she speak of her mother, the Dowager Queen, whom Cressida had never seen at Court, and never was any mention made of the Princess's younger brothers.

Mary Bolton was overheard to remark that she had heard her father say that the infamous pretender Henry Tudor, Earl of Richmond, skulking at the French Court, had dared to declare his intention of wedding the Princess Elizabeth when he came into his own and sat on the English throne, rightfully his as the true Lancastrian heir.

"My father told my mother he thinks the King should hasten and marry her off to some gentleman of his household, so there would be no more of this nonsensical talk circulating about the Courts of Europe."

"And what did your mother reply to that?" Her companion inclined her ear to gain the answer.

Instead of whispering, as might have been more sensible, Mary tossed back her head and declared so that Cressida, some yards away, could hear only too clearly, "She says the King will not do that since he loves his niece well and is chary of parting with her company.''

The other girl broke into a spasm of soft giggles and Cressida frowned her disapproval.

"Her Grace the Queen would miss the Princess sorely if she were to marry now," she said as she drew level with the gossiping pair.

Mary Bolton favoured her with a calculating smile. "You think so? Perhaps she would be relieved to have the Lady Elizabeth gone from the vicinity of the Court."

"The Queen always rallies when the Lady Elizabeth is present. I know she is glad of her company, which cheers her mightily."

Mary Bolton shrugged and flounced off, her companion in tow. Cressida looked after them uneasily. Wroxeter had warned her not to become embroiled in this scandalous, almost treasonable talk. If Richmond was offering openly for the Lady Elizabeth's hand, it could only be to put one more thorn beneath the saddle of the King's peace, and such talk, here at Westminster, was not to be encouraged. It could only further distress the Queen were she to hear of it inadvertently.

Cressida's parents had delayed their return to Gretton until after her marriage and had taken lodgings behind an apothecary's shop in the Chepe in the city while Cressida, with Alice in attendance, remained at Westminster in the Queen's service.

Cressida was glad of a respite from the poisonous air of the Court when, one morning in early February, the Queen excused her from duty in order to allow her to visit her parents, and she and Alice set off downriver in one of the barges used to transport members of the royal household into the city.

Cressida was always relieved when they alighted safely at the steps near London Bridge, since the current beneath the Bridge piers was known to be very strong and dangerous. A servant in the royal service wearing the device of the white boar escorted the two women to the shop in the Chepe. Cressida courteously dismissed the man at the door, knowing her father would see to it that she was safely accompanied back to the palace when the time came.

The apothecary, a dry little stick of a man in a dark gabardine gown, his sparse hair standing up wildly round his bald crown, greeted her obsequiously, rubbing his hands together as he stood back for Cressida to mount the stair to her father's lodging.

Alice knocked loudly. They were kept waiting for some moments. Cressida could hear the sound of two male voices, then the door was jerked open suddenly and she was startled to see Howell Prosser standing on the threshold.

He looked as surprised as she was, then he broke into a delighted smile.

"Sir Daniel, here is joy indeed; Mistress Cressida is here to see you."

Sir Daniel hastily joined him. He looked, Cressida thought, more than a bit startled, as if this sudden arrival of hers was not to be welcomed at this time, then he too smiled and opened his arms wide to embrace her.

"Daughter, come in, come in. I had not expected... Well, as you see, Howell is here in London and in good time for your wedding day."

Cressida moved into the private solar, her astonishment at the unexpected news preventing her, for the moment, from acknowledging the presence of her childhood companion. Her father, too, realised that he had babbled out the announcement too suddenly for he gave a forced laugh.

"There, what am I thinking, girl, breaking the news like that, before your mother has properly prepared you…? Wroxeter was here last evening, requesting that the ceremony be performed within the next month since he cannot tell when the King will require his services to travel, possibly to the north.

"I had intended to send for you and inform you, but here you are unexpectedly and I blurted it all out inadvisedly. Your mother will scold me, for sure. Sit down, child, near the fire; you must be chilled to the bone. Did you come by river?"

He was talking much too quickly, uncomfortable in her presence. Why? Had the occasion when she had argued against the marriage alarmed him so that he feared her reaction to the news? Yet she had known it must come soon, had prepared herself, while still hoping that it might be postponed for months yet.

"I see," she murmured awkwardly. "I saw the Earl at dinner yesterday, but he did not speak of this to me. Doubtless he wished to consult with you first." She was determined to keep her tone level, especially with Howell here. She would not have him know how she dreaded the final moment when she would become truly Wroxeter's bride. She looked round anxiously. "Where is Mother?"

"She went out into the Chepe, shopping for the final items for the wedding day. It is a wonder you did not see her on your way." Sir Daniel brought her a tankard of spiced ale which he had mulled for her by thrusting in the glowing iron from the hearth. "Drink, child, and warm the cockles of your heart."

Howell had moved in closer. She smiled at him and he lifted her free hand and raised it to his lips. "You cannot know how pleased I am to see you looking so well and happy, Cressida.''

She wondered that he thought she looked happy. She supposed she was rosy from the hasty walk in the cold air. Alice was fussing with her cloak and hood, and she sank down in the chair her father had vacated. Alice caught Sir Daniel's eye and slipped from the room. Downstairs there was a small back chamber where the few servants the Grettons had brought to the capital spent their waking hours until summoned.

Howell was anxious to question Cressida about her work at Court and she was glad to reassure him that she was happy under the benign rule of the Queen.

''We all worry so about her,'' she said sadly. ''She seems so listless these days and the doctors are present constantly. It's said…'' She hesitated, recollecting hurriedly that, perhaps, she should not complete the sentence, but, on seeing Howell's and her father's gaze fixed on her with interest and concern, she continued in a whisper, ''It's said that they are counselling the King to keep from her bed for fear of contagion.''

Howell frowned and Sir Daniel tutted in sympathetic concern. ''Poor gentle lady.''

''The Princess Elizabeth is by her side constantly and proves a great comfort to her.''

There was a sound of doors opening below and brisk exchanges between Lady Gretton and her maid. Cressida stood up eagerly to greet her mother as she bustled into the solar.

''My dear, we hadn't expected you for days.'' Lady Gretton embraced her daughter warmly. Her skin was icy cold from the frosty air outside and she beamed expansively upon the company. ''Isn't it wonderful that Howell is here and can carry tidings of your wedding back to the manor and to our neighbours?''

''Ye-es.'' Cressida was less enthusiastic and her eyes went to the numerous small linen-wrapped packages which her mother had brought upstairs with her, having dismissed her maid with the bulkier purchases to join the rest of the staff downstairs.

Lady Gretton appeared not to notice Cressida's lack of appreciation for her endeavours on her behalf. She gratefully accepted from Howell a tankard of spiced mulled ale after Sir Daniel had helped her remove her cloak and hood. She chatted brightly about the high prices in these London shops, though was delighted by the variety of goods on offer, and, at last, carried off Cressida to her chamber to show her the new materials and ribbons and called to her maid to bring the half-completed wedding gown that Cressida must try on and stand patiently while it was fitted.

It was Howell who offered to escort Cressida and Alice to Westminster and Sir Daniel smilingly agreed. As they walked to the Bridge landing stage Cressida waited nervously for Howell to question her about her betrothed. Other than asking her quickly, with a hurried glance at Alice, who was slightly behind them, if she was satisfied by her parents' choice, he made no more attempts to embarrass her. They both knew that had matters stood otherwise they would have now been discussing plans for a marriage between them.

Cressida said between her teeth, ''Wroxeter is young, personable and well thought of at Court. As for my parents' choice, that is beside the point. King Richard has chosen my husband for me and my parents are naturally flattered by his attentions.''

''But you are not,'' Howell said bluntly.

"I have to admit I wish it had been differently arranged," Cressida said quietly.

"Wroxeter will make you a countess," Howell whispered with some trace of bitterness.

Cressida did not add, *Far too soon now, it appears,* but she was thinking it as Howell summoned a ferryman.

Seated within the boat, she asked, "What does bring you to London—not my wedding, I'm sure?"

He grinned. "No, no, business for my father. He wishes to know firsthand the prices of wool, for one thing—believes he is being cheated by the Ludlow merchants—but, of course, he knew I would be delighted to contact your parents in the hope that I would catch at least one glimpse of you."

"Will you be long in London?"

"I go to Southampton tomorrow, but I shall be back within the week—and present for your marriage feast."

As Howell was assisting her from the ferry boat at the King's steps at Westminster, Cressida saw Wroxeter with Peter Fairley in attendance alighting from a second boat. Immediately he came to her side and she introduced Howell Prosser.

"Master Prosser is a good neighbour of ours near Gretton. Fortunately he is in London on business and was present at my father's lodging and available to escort me back to the palace," she explained. Her mouth was unaccountably dry. Though Howell's attentions were in no way excessive, she would have preferred her betrothed not to have seen her with him. Perhaps Howell's expression revealed all too clearly his opinion of this hastily arranged marriage.

Wroxeter bowed to him. "How fortunate that you are here so near to our wedding day. Will you be able to delay your return so that you might honour the occasion with your presence?"

Howell bowed in return. "Indeed, I may do so, my lord. Our friends on the Marches will be eager to know the details. Mistress Cressida is held in high esteem amongst our friends."

Wroxeter's lips curved in a smile. "I'm sure she is, as she is already here, at Westminster. Thank you for your care of my betrothed, sir, and now, if you have no business within the palace, I will take over my duty and escort her to the Queen's apartments."

Cressida turned for a last sight of Howell as he was so summarily dismissed, but Wroxeter's light grip upon her arm was imperative and she was unable to gauge Howell's reaction to the lordly manner of her betrothed. She stopped at last outside the doorway to the Queen's apartments, breathless and angry. Wroxeter nodded to dismiss Alice, who had followed stolidly behind them. The maid moved off some distance along the corridor, but kept her charge in view.

"Why did you have to be so rude?" Cressida demanded furiously. "I have not seen Howell for weeks and he was kind enough to escort me home."

"Rude?" Wroxeter's dark brows rose in surprise. "I do not think I was in the least rude. I invited the fellow to our wedding feast."

"He did not need your invitation," she snapped. "My parents had already invited him. Howell is a very dear friend and his father and our other neighbours will want to hear about the proceedings and—"

"A dear friend?"

"A childhood companion," Cressida reiterated. "Trusted by my father and—"

"Often alone with you?"

She stopped open-mouthed at the sharp question as she had been about to go once more into the attack.

"Certainly alone, though rarely," she snapped again. "I say again, we were children together. Howell has never once said anything out of place. He regards me as a sister."

"Indeed? Does he?" Wroxeter's brows drew together and his voice had resumed its habitual sleepy tone. "And you think of him as a brother, I suppose?"

Cressida was brought up short again by the perceptive awareness of his question.

"Yes, of course." She was somewhat embarrassed by his sleepy but steely suggestion that she felt more for Howell than she was prepared to admit. "I have never— thought…" Her voice trailed off awkwardly.

"I see." He was smiling now, but wryly, and she felt that he was not convinced.

She was goaded again into attack, feeling uncomfortably defensive.

"My lord, if you feel at all concerned about my former friendship with Master Prosser, perhaps you should seek a dispensation to allow you to withdraw from our betrothal and not go forward with the marriage arrangements."

He turned steadily to face her. "Cressida, we shall marry on the day appointed. Nothing will change that. Afterwards it will be for me to decide just what friendships I am prepared to allow you."

He was still holding her wrist and she jerked at it angrily to free herself, tears very near the surface and cheeks and throat reddening in frustration.

He smiled deliberately. "I trust your parents informed you of my wishes concerning the day?"

She nodded sullenly.

"The King will honour us with his presence. I expect you to behave circumspectly and not disgrace me or your parents."

"You continue to treat me like a child," she spat.

"You *are* a child still and a spoilt one into the bargain, but the contract is signed, and I am not entirely dissatisfied with the arrangement. There will be time in plenty for you to mature and come to terms with the outcome."

He released her and called to Alice, then turned and walked away. Cressida conquered the urge to give way to tears. She must resume her duties and at any moment a page or servant might come along the corridor. She had no wish to be the subject of gossip, particularly as some of her companion ladies continued to treat her with some disdain.

Cressida's marriage to Martyn, Earl of Wroxeter, took place on the very last day of February within the royal chapel. Her wedding gown was magnificent, of heavy cloth of silver and trimmed with white fur. It was early evening and the candlelight glimmered on her slight form so that she appeared a veritable frost-faery creature as her father led her forward to the altar where the Earl waited, attended by his squire, Peter Fairley, the King by his side as sponsor.

Cressida's mother waited near the door of the chapel with the Queen and the Lady Elizabeth. Alice, her eyes shining with pride, stood behind them.

There was a little gasp as Sir Daniel appeared at the door of the chapel with his daughter. For the first time courtiers outside in the corridor had the opportunity to glimpse the unbelievable gold of her hair, which hung loose to her waist. There were few flowers at this winter season and she wore a simple circlet of silver adorned with pearls—the Queen's gift.

It was very cold. Even in the corridors of Westminster, breath froze whitely in the air as men spoke and there were braziers set near the door of the chapel and close to the altar. They did little to dispel the icy chill within Cressida's heart, yet she felt one stab of pure triumph at the sight of the King's niece. Wroxeter had not dared to protest at her presence.

In this one thing, at least, she had had her own way. She had continued her association with the Lady Elizabeth, despite her betrothed's strictures. This was a very private ceremony and St Stephen's chapel very small, so only immediate family members were present beside the sovereigns, but she would see Howell soon at the wedding feast within the great hall and she doubted that afterwards she would have an opportunity to speak with him freely again.

The scent of incense was so overpowering that she feared she would faint, but she stiffened her spine and tilted her chin and unprotestingly allowed her father to place her numbed hand within the Earl's. She took little note of the priest's exhortation and only turned when the ring was placed upon her fingers and the Earl recited his vows in his clear, ringing tones.

She saw now, for she had not dared look fully at him before, that he was clad in saffron velvet over dark green hose and the colour suited his dark colouring well. His tall form looked spare and elegant. Beside him the King, in blue, appeared small of stature, yet no one could ever have deemed Richard Plantagenet insignificant. His very demeanour and stance revealed his military prowess and his innate air of royalty.

She spoke her own vows woodenly and, as she knelt before the altar to receive the nuptial mass, realised, wonderingly, that she had given herself to this man whom she both disliked and feared without outward protest.

At the chapel door, the Queen embraced her and the

King came to give her a hearty kiss upon the cheek. She forced herself not to recoil from his touch.

He was clearly delighted by the success of this match he had made.

"My lady," he said gently, "I wish you all happiness. I could not have found you a husband who pleased me more, for he is loyal and true of heart. I trust he will prove himself to you as he has to me."

She curtsied dutifully and was hugged by her mother while Sir Daniel looked on, grinning expansively. He was hugely relieved that it had all gone so smoothly. He knew he had always indulged this beloved daughter of his and had secretly feared that she might, even at the last moment, refuse to pledge herself and disgrace him before his sovereign. Now it was over. She looked so very beautiful beside this tall, personable man who was her husband.

For one second his heart misgave him. Would Wroxeter treat her well, his Cressida, to whom he had never taken a switch in all her youthful happy life at Gretton? She was all unprepared to deal with a demanding, dominating husband.

He stole a hasty glance at that sleepy, inscrutable countenance. Surely there was no cruelty revealed by that long, sensitive mouth, no wanton sensuality either, for all he could see, and he had heard no undue, bawdy gossip about the man. No, the match was a good one. He must believe that since he had little choice in the matter. The King had been so determined on it from the beginning.

Cressida was placed upon the King's right at the nuptial feast, her parents near the Queen. She sat at the high table, still half-bemused after the ceremony, above the salt, her new husband beside her. She looked down from the dais at the courtiers and their ladies who had come to do the Earl of Wroxeter honour. She saw Viscount Francis Lovell, the King's chamberlain and friend since childhood, in laughing talk with her father. He was a handsome man, witty and charming.

Her father had hinted once that the King's household, which had come south with him from Middleham, was not completely accepted at Court. There too were Sir Richard Ratcliffe, Sir Robert Percy and William Catesby, who had turned his allegiance from his former master, the executed Lord William Hastings, more recently.

She remembered with a frisson of horror that William Collingbourne had died horribly only months ago at Tower Hill for penning the satirical rhyme which epitomised the opinions of many southern lords.

The Cat, the Rat, and Lovell our dog,
Rule all England under a hog.

Was Martyn, Lord Wroxeter, one of their company? Yes, she believed so. Fortunate for him that his personal device of a silver saltire on a green field, since he was related by marriage to the great Neville family, had not lent itself to being so lampooned.

She caught her mother's eyes upon her. They were troubled, she could see even from this distance, and she smiled back reassuringly.

Her husband was addressing her and she turned back nervously to meet his gaze. He was smiling and for once those brooding dark eyes of his were not hooded.

"I was saying," he remarked pleasantly, "that all that joyous company are envying me my wondrously lovely bride."

Was he mocking her? Her fingers clumsily tilted the golden plate set before her and he put out a steadying hand.

"The page waits for you to rinse your fingers, my love."

The word jarred, but there appeared to be no mockery in his expression. She turned hastily to the kneeling page, dabbled her fingers in the rose-scented water he proffered in a golden bowl and dried them upon a fine linen napkin. The King had spared no expense to honour his friend and loyal servant. The finest of jewelled plate was arrayed upon the snowy white drapery of this festive board and the food was excellently served and delicious.

Cressida had become used now to the Court custom of allowing her partner to choose the choicest morsels for her, but she almost baulked at the traditional ceremony when she was handed the loving cup filled to the brim with malmsey. With the eyes of the full company upon her, she took a hasty sip and handed it to Wroxeter, who gallantly placed his own lips upon the place where hers had rested and drank deep.

A hearty cheer rang out as courtiers rose to pledge bride and groom with good red wine. Turning away slightly, Cressida encountered the gaze of Howell Prosser, who was seated some way down the lower table. Her own eyes brimmed with sudden tears as she saw the yearning sadness in his.

She was glad when her mother came to lead her from the hall, Alice anxiously hovering behind her. It had to be faced, the final trial of this terrible day. As she passed the smiling courtiers with their ladies Cressida knew there were several of their number who envied her this moment. One man, she knew, felt quite differently. Howell Prosser deliberately did not look her way as she passed him.

A luxurious chamber had been put at Lord Wroxeter's disposal for his wedding night. Tomorrow Cressida would leave for his fine town house in the Strand. She would continue to attend on the Queen for the present, though now, naturally, she would not take her place at night within the Queen's bedchamber.

A roaring fire in the great hearth filled the room with heat and light, but, like the braziers in the chapel, failed to warm Cressida. She felt icy cold as her mother and Alice helped her off with her finery and into the simple white gown of embroidered lawn. She prayed that the shaking of her limbs would not be put down to pure terror but to the chill of the night.

She looked round at the great bed, which was covered with furs and the scarlet velvet coverlet. She noted, surprised, that it bore the embroidered device of Wroxeter's house and must have been brought from the Strand.

There was a goblet of wine upon the bedstand and the candles were of the finest wax and scented. The linen of the bed smelt of sweet herbs, marjoram, rosemary and rose petals. The scarlet velvet draperies on the testered bed gave the impression of enclosing her within a scented prison and she tried not to shudder.

Her mother whispered in Alice's ear and her maid kissed her and left. Cressida thought her cheek was moist with tears and hoped her own were not also.

Lady Gretton said softly, ''You said—you were afraid of him. I—I have been gainsaid in this arrangement. Child, all has been ordered, so it was impossible for your father to object. You must forgive him if...''

Cressida impulsively hugged her mother. ''I do not blame either of you. I know how it is.''

''Your father was known to be formerly allied to the House of Lancaster. Now that rumours of treason abound in the land, especially in the Marches, he dare not be seen to oppose the King's will.''

Cressida smiled bravely. "I know. Tell him I understand."

Lady Gretton gave a great relieved gasp for her understanding of the difficulty of their position. "This man—he has not shown you violence?"

"No." Cressida's whisper was faint. "He is just so very—lordly. I am used to a less ordered life—and—and I wanted so much to come home." There, it had come out in a rush, the foolish childish words which could not be held back.

Lady Gretton caught her daughter close to her heart and smoothed back the luxuriant golden hair. There was a great lump in her own throat. It had all happened so suddenly. One moment this so dear child had been theirs completely, so much so that she had found it hard to contemplate her leaving them—and then the summons to Westminster had come and now this marriage had followed on so frighteningly fast.

She feared for Cressida—she could not help it. She drew back slightly, gave a little crooked smile and bent to kiss her daughter in gentle blessing.

"Be brave, my Cressida. You have been well prepared. Give your husband no reason to discipline you. I know," she said, with a little catch in her voice, "you will not find it easy to be obedient and biddable—but try. It is necessary for your own chance of happiness."

She rose, leaving Cressida seated on the bed, and hastened out of the chamber. She knew that if she stayed longer she would give way to tears and she must not.

At the door she encountered the Queen and two of her ladies with the royal chaplain come to bless the marriage bed. Lady Gretton curtsied low as Anne went in to smile down at her youthful attendant.

"Stand up and let me look at you. Yes, you are so very

lovely, and so young. I was scarce older than you when my lord took me to bed. I could not know then how happy he would make me, and after a terrible time in my life. I want you to be equally happy, Cressida. Martyn Telford is a good man and worthy of you.''

The Queen bent and kissed Cressida gently upon the forehead as her mother had done. ''Martyn cannot but be overcome with your beauty, my dear. I wish,'' she said brokenly, ''I had had a daughter to bless on her wedding night but, today, I look upon you in this light. Be blessed, my dear, as I am with my dear lord.''

She was not alone long. The King accompanied the groom to the chamber door and Cressida heard his laugh of pure pleasure, but did not catch his last, pleasant exhortation to his friend. The chamber door was jerked open, then she was alone with her husband.

She sank back into a half-crouched, half-sitting position on the side of the bed as he came towards her. His squire had disrobed him and he wore a brocaded green and silver bedgown. The garment was magnificent and in it he looked huge and almost menacing. She caught her nether lip in her teeth, determined not to break into tears and reveal her apprehension.

He stood for a moment, looking down at her, and, despite herself, she shrank back a little. He cupped her chin in his hands and smiled down at her. ''So, they left you alone. I hope it has not been for too long.''

She shook her head mutely.

He moved to the other side of the bed and drew back the covers.

''If you sit there much longer you will freeze in that flimsy gown, even in this firelit room.''

He averted his eyes as she obeyed him and slipped beneath the coverlet. She was so overwhelmingly lovely and so vulnerable. He felt a stab of hot desire in his loins. She was his and he had every right to take her—indeed he would be a fool not to do so—yet he must not.

He had agreed, reluctantly, to please his sovereign in this. In time she would learn to accept his rule, be less afraid, for he could feel like a palpable thing her abject desperation and fear of him. No, he must wait until he could bring her to a more receptive mood. To take her now would be a violation.

She heard the stiff brocade of the bedgown fall to the floor as he discarded it and slipped into bed beside her. Her heart was beating so fast that she was sure he must hear it and she took deep, steadying breaths to calm herself. His body was so close to hers. It felt warm and hard beside her unyieldingly chill form.

He said quietly, "You need have no fear, Lady Cressida. I have no intention of touching you at this time. You have a deal of growing up to do before you become truly my wife."

She could hardly believe the words, the relief had come so amazingly. She swallowed hard.

"My lord?"

"Learn to address me, in private at least, as Martyn."

"Yes, my lord—Martyn. I..."

"Now try to sleep. You must be very tired."

"Yes, my lord."

He smiled in the darkness for he had turned and extinguished the candle before settling beside her.

"I must, naturally, in order to avoid gossip, remain in your bed tonight. Later, at the Strand house, you will have your own chamber for the present. I have considerable pressure of work which brings me late to bed often and I would not disturb you at such hours."

She made no reply, thinking through his words and attempting to come to terms with the knowledge that her most desperate fears had been groundless. At last she said through gritted teeth, ''My lord, my maid, Alice, said—said that the sheets will be noted and—and—''

''No one,'' he said coldly, ''will dare to question or oppose my will. You may sleep easy on that, my wife. Nor will the validity of this marriage ever be doubted.''

She could find no words to answer him. She was deeply relieved that she would not yet be forced to give her body to him—yet she could not prevent a niggling disappointment from clouding her heartfelt gratitude for his forbearance.

She thought, resentfully, that he considered her a child still and this jibe hurt and thrust deep at her inner pride. Worse than that, she knew that the ghost of his former betrothed had once more come between them. He would not have been so restrained and considerate had Elinor Maudsley lain by his side.

She felt immediately guilty. How could she be jealous of a dead woman, especially since she had no love for her new husband?

Could she ever be a true wife to Martyn Telford, Earl of Wroxeter? She was his Countess, had seen evidence already of her new-found nobility in the way she had been treated at that splendid feast, even by those ladies who had formerly been seen to despise her. The Lady Elizabeth had not accompanied the Queen to her chamber. She would have liked to have her good wishes too, but perhaps Elizabeth knew of Wroxeter's dislike of her and had decided not to embarrass Cressida within his presence.

She moved restlessly beside him but he did not stir. She must prove herself worthy of the title, must learn to rule his household wisely, prove a welcoming and efficient hostess to his noble companions. It would not be easy. Would he always compare her best efforts with those of his lost love, so clearly better suited to be his bride? She gave a half-suppressed sigh in the darkness, turned on her side and tried to compose herself to sleep.

Chapter Five

Cressida had expected the Strand house to be more commodious than her father's lodging in the city, but she was totally unprepared for the luxurious splendour of her husband's town property. She was conveyed there from Westminster in the Earl's private river barge, rowed by four oarsmen wearing his livery. In the stern was a covered area to protect the noble travellers from the elements.

She sat by his side, warmly wrapped in a cloak lined with squirrel fur, his squire, Peter Fairley, facing them, while she watched the smooth muscle-play of the oarsmens' backs as they plied their oars against the salt-laden fierce wind. The water was pewter-grey and the sky leaden. Cressida thought that the weather reflected the depth of her spirits on this miserable day when she moved to her new home.

She had taken a tearful farewell of her parents, only slightly comforted by the knowledge that they intended to stay a while longer in the city. At all events, the bad weather would prevent them from making the long journey back to the Marches for some days yet. She had received from them a promise that they would visit her before leaving.

Alice was to travel with the sumpter mules and baggage wagons, which would convey Cressida's dowry in plate and linen, besides her chests of clothing and personal belongings, to the Strand. Her old nurse, at least, was to remain with her, a confidante and friend. Cressida could not have borne to be parted from everyone from her former life.

The Queen had given her leave to be absent from her duties at Court for two weeks or longer if the Earl should request that.

"My dear," she had said fondly, "you will take quite all of that time to make yourself acquainted with the house and its appointments, besides getting to know the staff. Enjoy the time Martyn can spare to be with you. I know he is particularly busied about the King's affairs, but this time is important for both of you. Use it well."

Cressida was by no means sure that she wanted any time free to spend in her husband's company, nor did she think that he was too anxious to spend time with her. They had breakfasted together almost in silence this first morning of their new life together.

Cressida had been unwilling to meet Alice's enquiring eyes when her maid had come to wake her. She had spent a wakeful night, lying still and straight beside her husband's muscular form, afraid to disturb him. Finally she had drifted off into an emotionally drained doze after the dawn had thrust spears of grey light through the gaps in the shuttered windows.

When she had roused at Alice's gentle but imperative shaking, it was to find her husband already risen and gone to dress in an adjoining chamber. Alice had brought warmed water for her toilet and helped her dress after sweeping up the used sheets and thrusting them into a

wicker basket to be collected by one of the palace's laun-
dry maids.

She had made no comment, nor had she questioned
Cressida, to her profound relief, but when Cressida had
turned and impulsively hugged her Alice had stroked her
hair gently as her mother had done the previous night and
the embrace had been sufficient to comfort the stricken
girl.

She turned now to look at the Earl's averted face as he
gazed abstractedly over the water. He did not appear angry,
but she saw that his brows were drawn together as if in
deep thought and she wondered what problem was trou-
bling him. Not, she thought, concern for his young wife's
injured feelings.

She told herself, irritatedly, that she was fortunate that
he would not prove importunate as she had feared, but she
would have liked some evidence of his attention to her at
this moment, when everything in her world was fast becoming so frighteningly strange.

The barge ground against the private landing stage and
the oarsmen lifted their oars in unison. A liveried servant,
waiting ready for their arrival, made haste to make fast the
barge and the Earl stepped out, then leant down, hand outstretched, to help Cressida from the barge. He hastened her
through the dank garden to the rear of the house and into
the hall.

The undercroft was of red brick, the upper storey of
timber and lath, but she saw in one hasty glance from the
outside that all the windows were glazed and the plaster-
work was newly maintained and bright with lime-wash. A
stately steward came to greet them, bowing low. He was
so impressive that Cressida almost felt inclined to answer
his greeting with a deep curtsey of her own. He had drawn
up the senior members of the household for her perusal,

but the Earl waved away his steward's anxiety to present them, murmuring hastily that the Countess was cold and wished only to have mulled ale and cakes served in her solar.

"Send up the Countess's maid, Mistress Croft, when she arrives, and see to the disposal of the Countess's baggage. There will be time in plenty for her ladyship to come to know the other members of the household. I wish a cold dinner served in my chamber. I am needed at a council meeting later this afternoon and shall need the barge ready at the steps prompt for two of the clock."

Cressida smiled at the steward, who bowed again and preceded them to the foot of the stair. The Earl himself divested her of her cloak and hood and handed them to Peter, attentive as ever, behind him.

The house seemed immense, even to her eyes, used to the comforts of Gretton. Through the screen door she had glimpsed a sight of the dining hall and, opposite the stair, another half-opened door which she presumed led to the winter parlour. Above stairs the Earl established her into the comfort of the solar, bright with firelight and luxurious, with finely painted plastered walls and carpets from the East upon polished floorboards. She gave a little gasp of wonder at the court cupboards laden with silver and the jewel-like colours of the wall tapestries.

Two cushioned chairs stood at either side of the hearth and the Earl smilingly indicated that she should seat herself.

"This will be your domain. I have a small study and office where I deal with household accounts and interview the servants. I will see to it that you are soon shown to your sleeping chamber. There is a smaller room adjoining for Alice.

"The house is well run. You will find Master Rawlings

most efficient. He needs to be. I am rarely at home these days. The King has need of my services and affairs in France keep me constantly occupied.

"I have given instructions that you are to be instantly obeyed and all your wishes granted. Eventually you will want to make some changes in household arrangements and you will find Master Rawlings amenable, but, for the present, allow yourself time to discover what is needful. Your mother has prepared you well, I know, for the management of a household, but do not be alarmed; I shall not expect too much of you too soon."

Cressida managed a half-smile. There it was again, this tacit reminder that he considered her too young and immature to cope with the usual tasks expected of a wife. Elinor Maudsley would have known immediately what was required of her.

A serving girl came in with a tray and a youthful page who had opened the door for the girl came forward hurriedly to pour ale for his master and lady. Cressida gave the boy a nervous glance. Was she expected to school him in music and song? She played the lute well enough and was told she possessed a pleasing enough voice, but she had never given those accomplishments a great deal of attention, preferring to be out of doors frequently when at Gretton.

The Earl was clearly in a great hurry to leave her and be about his own affairs. She felt a total stranger and at a loss in her own house. Tears were very near the surface again and she angrily controlled the pricking of her lashes. She had never been one to use such wiles to gain her attention. With or without her husband by her side she would take control of this grand house and, most likely, she would be better able to achieve that in his absence, which she believed would be frequent.

After noon when he had departed Cressida sat discon-solately staring into the fire. She was unused to inactivity. Always at Gretton she had been busied about the house or out riding.

She had examined her sleeping chamber with Alice and overseen the unpacking of her baggage. The room was as splendid as she had expected and newly prepared for her. Obviously the brocaded curtains round the bed and match-ing coverlet had been only recently purchased, though she had wondered fleetingly if indeed Lord Martyn had readied the chamber for his former love. She had cast that thought aside with the dour knowledge that Elinor would undoubt-edly have shared her husband's chamber.

No, all this, including the beautiful wall hanging de-picting an Attic hunting scene—French, and wickedly ex-pensive—beside the finely carved and upholstered prie-dieu which matched her bed-covering, had clearly been bought for her.

Wearily she had acknowledged that since everything was in such pristine order there was nothing she could set her hand to. She had never been an accomplished needle-woman, had often complained about the necessity to learn the art, which her mother had patiently taught her, but repairs to worn arras would have provided some occupa-tion and here none was needed.

Alice had gone off to stitch the hem of Cressida's bridal gown which had been torn, caught on her chair during the banquet, and Cressida had been somewhat relieved that that had necessitated a search for suitable thread. She was lonely, certainly, but did not wish to sit opposite her maid and try to conceal her sinking spirits from her. Alice was very shrewd. Already she must have divined that all was not well between her master and mistress.

Cressida tapped an impatient foot. This would not do.

She refused to be confined to her room like a refractory child. She summoned attendance by ringing a small silver hand-bell laid ready for her use upon the table. In seconds the same page who had waited on them earlier tapped and entered. She was sure he must have been waiting outside.

He bowed low. She smiled at him reassuringly for she thought she detected an anxious look on his youthful features. Was the Earl so fierce a taskmaster that his attendants feared physical punishment if they did not appear promptly at his command?

"What is your name, boy?"

"Philip, my lady. Philip Kenton."

She judged him to be about ten years old. He was small and almost skinny, a brown-haired, elfish child. He stood, moving his weight nervously from one foot to another.

"Come here, near to me. There is nothing to be frightened of. Have you been appointed to wait on me?"

"Yes, my lady. The Earl said I was not to leave your side for a moment."

"So you wait outside my door?"

"Yes, my lady. You only have to ring the bell."

"Yes, well, I do not think it will be necessary for you to dog my every footstep, not when I am used to the house. Take me on a tour of inspection, Philip. I have yet to see the winter parlour and the downstairs chambers."

He bowed again and waited until she rose, and then went to open the door for her.

"You resemble Peter Fairley," she said as she signalled for him to walk beside her. "Are you related?"

"Yes, my lady. Peter is my cousin. Our mothers are sisters. My father died last year and my lord Earl immediately took me into his service. My mother is most grateful."

Cressida nodded. Poor child, to lose both father and

home at one fell swoop and to be catapulted into the service of a demanding master who clearly terrified him.

She nodded her satisfaction at the condition of the winter parlour, acknowledging the hurried curtsies of two waiting maids who scurried by her in the corridor, then paused with her hand on the opposite door.

Philip said quickly, "That is my lord's study, my lady. He allows no one to enter without being specially commanded to do so."

She smiled thinly. "So you think he would not wish me to do so. Does he conceal Bluebeard's secret?"

The boy flushed darkly but looked blank. He was unacquainted with the tale, she thought, and did not understand her grim pleasantry. She did not insist upon her right to enter. Philip believed that he would be in dire trouble if she persisted and she had no desire to worry him further. She had seen her husband's study at Westminster. If this room was similarly dismal she had no wish to be further acquainted with it.

"Now take me to the kitchen—the most important room of the house, don't you agree, Philip? Perhaps we can coax the cook into providing us with honey cakes. You could do with some feeding up."

"I should request Master Rawlings..."

"Nonsense. Why should we trouble him? Surely I have right of entry into my own kitchens?"

"Master Wainwright is very fussy..."

"No doubt he is. So am I, Philip."

The boy's face fell, but obediently he led her to the back of the house.

Even before she reached the cavernous domain of the cook she could hear his voice lifted in furious admonition.

"You thieving, lying little toad. Do I take you into my

kitchen to laze away the hours? I set you to watch the spit and ye cannot even do that to my satisfaction."

The booming tone was accompanied by the sounds of blows falling on hapless shoulders and squeals of protest. Cressida lifted her skirts and forgot her dignity in her race into the overheated, frenzied activity of the principal kitchen.

The victim of abuse and summary punishment was cowering away from the biggest man Cressida had ever seen. He was a positive giant, barrel-chested, powerfully built, looming over his captive, whom he held down with one great paw on the thin shoulder, while with his other hand he rained down blow after blow on the boy's back with the long, flat wooden paddle he used to draw fresh-baked bread from the oven.

The recipient of his fury had slipped to his knees and, since the breath had been knocked from his body by the onslaught, had ceased to protest or cry out, but remained almost prone on the stone floor, making no further resistance.

The page tried to call out a warning, but Cressida ignored him as she did the startled glances of cooking maids and scullions as she erupted into the kitchen and called an imperative command for the cook to cease punishment.

"Stop it; stop it at once. You will kill the boy. Can't you see how frightened he is?"

"Aye, and will be more so when I've done with him," the cook boomed, and dealt yet another blow.

The boy collapsed on the floor, attempting to shield his head with his hands.

Cressida marched up to the pair, her blue eyes smouldering with rage. She could not bear to see cruelty to any creature. No one at Gretton, not even the youngest scullion or stable-boy, was treated so.

"I said stop it." Her voice was raised to a screech in an effort to make herself heard over the loud accents of the giant. "How dare you, sir, treat a child so, and so small a one, and you so great a bully?"

The cook, desisting from further punishment, straightened to face her, hand on hip. He had a big round face, perspiring from the heat of the huge fire in the hearth, from which spiky, dark, short hair was thrust back from his bulging forehead. "And who in the devil's name be you to give me orders in me own kitchen?"

"I am the Countess of Wroxeter," Cressida snapped, "and your mistress. You will obey me and refrain from bullying the boy."

"Boy, is it?" The giant put back his huge head and laughed until tears came to his eyes. "Aye, he's a boy in years and the devil incarnate in wickedness. Leave him to me, my lady, as his lordship would do. He'd tell you not to interfere and that's the truth of it."

"That's as may be," Cressida returned haughtily, "but now the kitchen and the well-being of the servants are my responsibility, and I tell you now I'll have no deliberate cruelty meted out to anyone in my service. Do you hear me?"

The cook lowered the paddle and stared back at her unblinking. He showed no deference but continued to stand, legs straddled, regarding her defiantly.

"Aye, my lady, I hear you right enough and I tell ye to ye're face, you're wrong to challenge me rule here. The lad deserves what he got."

Cressida was breathing hard. Her gaze went beyond him to the round-eyed onlookers. The kitchen showed signs of the usual frantic activity before supper was prepared, but was in good order like everything else in the house. She could not doubt that this hectoring fellow was well served. She turned back to him slowly and deliberately.

"My lord informs me that I am to be instantly and implicitly obeyed by all in this house," she said icily. "I repeat, I will have no cruelty, whatever the cause. Send the boy to his sleeping quarters. He'll need treatment for his bruises before he resumes his duties. Disobey me again and I will see to it that you are dismissed, Master Cook. I am mistress here and will brook no challenge to my authority."

There was a concerted gasp from the assembled wenches, who stood open-mouthed, paring-knives stilled in their chapped work-worn hands behind the chopping blocks. The cook expelled his breath in a little hiss and looked over her head towards the door.

The quiet, authoritative tones of the steward broke across the embarrassed silence.

"Is there trouble here, my lady? Please return to the solar and I will deal with this matter for you."

She said between gritted teeth, "I do not wish to have matters dealt with for me. I am capable of asserting my own authority. This boy is injured. See to it that he is tended." She swung on her heel. "I will take up this matter with his lordship on his return to the house. Philip, escort me back to the solar."

When Alice joined her later she had stopped shaking with anger and was poring over a printed book from Master Caxton's press at Westminster, reading a tale she had not encountered before about the knights of the legendary King Arthur. She recalled the night she had seen enacted the sinister story of the Green Knight and shivered again at the thought of that terrible beheading. She did not acquaint Alice with what had happened in the kitchens.

She ate alone in the hall. Lord Martyn had apparently

been kept late at Westminster. Cressida picked idly at her food, while Philip Kenton served her attentively. The fare was excellently cooked and served and she gave a little sniff as she thought of that odious man's reign in the kitchen. She must find out more about him, how long he had been in Lord Wroxeter's service.

At the close of the lonely meal she returned to the solar and, again, picked up the book. Alice, opposite, was busily engaged in sewing seed-pearls on a frontal. Cressida gave a little sigh. She would be relieved when she could return to attendance upon the Queen. She was bored and restless. She wondered what business in the city continued to occupy her father and how long it would be before Howell Prosser returned home to the Marches.

There came a tap at the door and Cressida called permission to enter. Peter Fairley came in and bowed.

"My lady, my lord Earl requests your presence in his study. He will not keep you long, since he is sure you will soon wish to retire."

Cressida glanced up at the squire sharply. Was she to be summoned to her husband's study like a naughty child? Why could he not have waited upon her in person here in the solar? She was about to snap out a refusal when she met Alice's warning glance and the hard words froze on her lips. Such a response could only bring down wrath upon poor Peter's head and she was becoming aware that retribution fell fast upon any recalcitrant servant in this house. She nodded and rose.

"Alice, will you go and prepare my bedchamber? I shall not be long."

It was no longer necessary for Alice to accompany her when alone in her husband's presence, yet she could not brush off the notion that she was not yet truly a wife.

Peter opened the study door for her respectfully then

withdrew. Her husband was seated at an oaken table strewn with unrolled parchment and held a quill. He wrote his own letters, then, and did not employ a secretary as many nobles did.

She advanced and he looked up and leaned back lazily in his chair. She was somewhat relieved. She had had the feeling he was angry with her and yet she could think of no reason—unless—She frowned. Surely he could not object to her exercising authority in her own household? She tilted her chin and tapped an impatient foot.

"Peter tells me you wish to speak to me. Why you could not have—"

"Please sit down." He had risen now courteously and was pointing to the chair opposite the table.

"Peter said the matter was urgent, but I was about to—"

"Please, Cressida, sit down. I asked you to come here since this study is absolutely private. No one will dare to approach, let alone enter, without specific instructions to do so, and I do not wish to be overheard."

She subsided sulkily into the chair. Again she had the helpless, lost feeling that a prisoner must have felt when facing an interrogator—or jailor. Now she was his possession, chattel; she considered herself a prisoner in this house, luxurious as the prison was.

"Rawlings has informed me about the contretemps in the kitchen. I thought we should talk about it quietly."

She stared back at him, her eyes sparking blue fire. "Do you take me to task for coming to the assistance of a badly used boy…?"

"I take no one to task. I said I wished to talk to you about it."

She was irritated by his easy, pleasant mien and the way those hooded eyes of his hid his true reaction from her. There was steel behind that slow, leisurely manner and perversely she wished he would come straight out with it and express anger if that was what he felt.

He was leaning back in the chair again. "I simply wish to put you in the picture. That 'badly used boy', as you term him, is a lazy, idle good-for-nothing I have brought with me from my Welsh manor because, for the third time, I have had to rescue him from being hanged for poaching and theft. I could wish to leave him to the fate he so richly deserves, but that his mother has wept and pleaded with me to save him. She was my wet nurse and I love her dearly.

"Wat Forrester is the last of her brood and she dotes on the rogue. Unfortunately he does not take after her or his brothers, my foster brothers, and constantly gets into trouble. I decided that the only thing I could do was to remove him from temptation and bring him here to the city and put him under Jack Wainwright's control. If anyone can discipline the lad, Jack's the fellow to do it."

"By harsh physical punishment?"

The lazy eyelids swept back and he regarded her steadily.

"You would prefer that I had left the boy to his fate?"

"I do not like cruelty to underlings. The man is a bully..."

"Jack Wainwright is a soldier and a very fine cook to boot. I'm sure you have no complaint to make about supper."

"Of course not, but it does not excuse the man from beating the scullions."

He smiled infuriatingly. "Cressida, I'm sure your father found it necessary now and then to discipline men on his own manor." His brown eyes twinkled. "Possibly his own daughter."

"My father has never once laid a hand upon me in anger."

He smiled and she thought angrily that he was considering that perhaps she would not have been so impetuous or difficult if he had. Again she would rather he had said it openly than play this tantalising game of reasoning with her.

"Jack has been on campaign with me over the last six years. He is a valued servant—and friend. I trust him with the boy. He could get service in any household he chose. If left to his own devices I suspect he would rather leave me to return to active service, but he knows I depend on him. I would be grateful, Cressida, if you do not impel him to do so."

She drew a hard breath. "In other words, I am not to interfere, not to be mistress in my own house?"

"I did not say that. I asked you to take time to become acquainted with the method of service here. No one will countermand your orders. Rawlings would not have told me of this affair, and Jack has not complained, but the boy has gone missing and Rawlings knows I am anxious to prevent his being taken by the Watch on some foolish expedition into the city.

"We can only hope he will return when his belly is empty and that he does not find other ways of filling it by more nefarious means. I simply wanted you to know the circumstances of this particular incident so that you can avoid open conflict over the lad in the future."

She felt considerably deflated and childish. Of course she should not have rushed into the situation without acquainting herself with the details. The steward would have settled the matter for her if she had consulted him. Her mother would have castigated her for undue haste in judgement. She swallowed hard to keep back a sudden rush of

tears. She had acted childishly, giving the household a picture of her as a spoilt, impetuous mistress too anxious to
have her own way.

"You wish me to speak with this man, Wainwright,
apologise for…?"

"Certainly not. You are mistress here. That would give
quite the wrong impression. Jack understands that perfectly
well. I shall not refer to the matter with him, now or at
any time. I can only hope damage has not been done to
young Wat's chance of survival. Frankly I do not give him
the possibility of a long life if he doesn't mend his ways,
and I see little hope of that at present."

She rose and curtsied. "I will consult with Master Rawlings before taking any further action or reproving any of
the servants. Now, with your permission, I will retire. I am
very tired."

It was the last thing she wished to do, but she had to
get out of his presence before he reduced her to useless
tears.

Smilingly, he rose to accompany her politely to the door
where Peter Fairley waited patiently to escort her to her
chamber.

Alice had prepared her bed and was waiting to help her
undress. Though she looked at Cressida curiously she
asked no questions. As she was preparing to go to her own
adjoining chamber Cressida said, "Alice, will you find that
young page, Philip Kenton, the one who attended me in
the hall this evening, and ask him to come to me?"

Alice gave a puzzled shrug and went about her errand.
She stood stoutly in the doorway when she brought the
boy back with her. As usual his expression was anxious
and Cressida quickly reassured him that he was in no trouble.

"Philip, I want you to find out if anything more has

been heard of that young scullion who was being beaten today. I understand he ran away.''

The boy's expression cleared. ''Oh, he's back, my lady. Master Wainwright—that's the cook—went out with two of my lord's men-at-arms to look for him. They found him in a tavern on the South Wark and it's said Master Wainwright cuffed him about the ear and dragged him back to Wroxeter House.''

''Oh.'' Cressida smiled thinly. ''I'm glad to know he's safe. Master Wainwright will not thrash him, do you think?''

The boy grinned. ''His bark is worse than his bite, my lady. He caught me stealing some tarts one day and I feared for my life, but he cuffed me and sent me off. He didn't tell my lord Earl, either. He's harsh, but he's fair, they say.''

''Good. Thank you, Philip. I thought the boy might have come to harm in one of the thieves' sanctuaries. You can go now, and goodnight.''

Alice said dourly, ''And what was that all about, if I dare ask?'' as the page scurried off.

Cressida said, a little breathlessly, ''Oh, I interfered in his punishment and I've discovered he's a decided rogue. My lord Earl is constantly trying to keep him from trouble.''

''Ah.'' Alice's single syllable summed up her opinion of Cressida's incursion into discipline at Wroxeter House.

Some twenty minutes later Cressida lay in her lonely bed, wondering wryly why she was finding it so. Most of her life she had slept alone and been glad of it. Now, strangely, she felt that she had been cheated. She had been as good as instructed to keep silent about household affairs and her husband kept from her bed; not a state of affairs her mother would have approved of.

Next morning, again in the solar, working with Alice upon the embroidering of another velvet frontal for her court headdress, Philip admitted master Rawlings.

The steward bowed low. "A Master Prosser has arrived, my lady, and asks if you will receive him."

She started up from her chair eagerly. "Oh, yes, at once, Master Rawlings. Master Howell Prosser is a family friend newly come to London. I shall be very glad to see him."

The steward nodded gravely. "And is there any matter on which I can render you assistance today, my lady?"

She flushed, recalling the man's presence at the undignified scene in the kitchen.

"No, no, thank you. The house appears to be run excellently in your hands, Master Rawlings."

Again he nodded gravely and withdrew, to return only moments later to admit Howell Prosser to the solar.

Cressida advanced to meet him, all smiles, her hands outstretched in welcome. "Howell, how good it is of you to call."

Alice withdrew to the window embrasure and Cressida could not miss the slight tightening of her maid's lips as she bent her head industriously over her needlework.

Howell's lips brushed Cressida's cheek as he murmured that he hoped he was allowed the privilege of kissing kin. For a moment the lips lingered longer than ever before when he had greeted her in company, and, blushing even more now, she led him to a chair near to the hearth and sat opposite.

"I hope this does not mean that you have come to say goodbye, Howell. You do not intend to leave the capital yet awhile?"

"I came to say farewell, but only for a short time. I must travel to Dover on an errand for my father." He grimaced. "Something to do with wool sales to Calais. You would not wish to know the boring details."

He thought how very beautiful she looked, flushed and rosy with her delight at seeing him. She wore a velvet gown in green, which brought out a hitherto unknown greenish tint in her irises, making those glorious eyes almost aquamarine in the light from the oriel window. The particular soft tint of green, the colour of elf land, made his heart race, adding as it did to her exquisite fairy beauty.

"I was afraid my lord Earl might refuse me permission to see you."

"He is not in the house. He is at Westminster or the Tower. There seem to be so many hastily convened council meetings held there these days."

"He leaves you alone so soon after marriage?"

She looked down at the priceless Eastern carpet, veiling her embarrassment from him. "He is very busied about the King's affairs. News from France is not good, I hear."

"No," he said grimly. "Not for the King, at all events. You have heard, I imagine, that Henry Tudor has made it plain that he wishes to wed the Lady Elizabeth?"

"I do not think that likely," Cressida laughed. "Not unless he usurps King Richard's throne."

"You would call that usurpation? He is King Henry of Lancaster's only surviving heir."

She looked round hurriedly, placing a warning finger upon her lip. "You speak treason, Howell. Henry Tudor has no strong claim, and that only from the illegitimate line of the Beauforts. In any case, the King's throne is firmly occupied."

"Not all are satisfied," he said softly. "Your father being one of them as mine is. I suppose you have heard about Sir Roger Clifford's execution?"

Cressida looked startled. ''Sir Roger Clifford? I do not think I have heard of him.''

''Aye, he was taken near Southampton, arraigned and tried.'' Howell shrugged. ''He could not hope for mercy. The Yorkist Princes have never forgiven the Cliffords for their support of the Lancastrian cause.

''When he was being drawn on the hurdle to Tower Hill, the escort had to pass through the sanctuary of St Martin le Grand. The common people were so incensed at his sentence, they tried to pull him from the hurdle and help him escape. His confessor was urging those about him to save him and the attempt almost succeeded—would have done so had not the sheriff's officers summoned assistance. They managed to hold him down till other men-at-arms arrived and dragged him off to his execution.''

Cressida shuddered. ''Did he—did he die the terrible traitor's death?''

''He was beheaded but it's said that afterwards his body was cloven in two.''

Cressida was appalled by such senseless brutality.

''Sweet Virgin, I would not have thought such malice to be in the King's nature.''

Howell nodded. ''He fears insurrection is in the very air. There is trouble in Hammes Castle, near Calais. The Earl of Oxford has been imprisoned there since soon after poor King Henry's death. He managed to suborn the governor, James Blount, to release him, and, to cap all, Blount has fled with his former prisoner to Henry Tudor and the castle is ready to withhold a siege by the King's forces.''

''But King Richard is powerful enough to break the siege and hold the castle?''

''Oh, I am sure of it, but these happenings show that even his own people are turning from him. Your father will welcome this news, I'm sure of it.''

"Hush." Cressida was really alarmed. "My father speaks well of the King. He has honoured him lately, arranged my marriage."

"Aye," Howell said bitterly. "I know that right enough. How did I manage to contain myself during the wedding feast? I cannot bear to think of you in that fellow's arms."

Taken off her guard, she said quickly, "You need not distress yourself over thoughts of that, Howell."

He stared at her dumbfounded, and she realised, too late, that she had betrayed her neglected state.

Hoarsely, he said, "He has not—does not—?" He was leaning very close to her and Cressida, frightened now that she had revealed so much, heard Alice stir restlessly on the window seat.

She lowered her head, flustered, and whispered, "He considers me a child still."

"By all the saints, the man is an arrant fool," Howell said fiercely. "Then I am to believe you are not yet a wife?"

She shook her head slowly, feeling the warmth well up from her breasts to her throat.

"Does your father know?"

"No, of course not—and is not to be told. Howell, you must not shame me. I should not have let you know…"

He was staring at her intently and she avoided his eyes. "There is no shame in your virgin state, Cressida. I, for one, thank God for it. Who knows? It may well be fortunate in the time to come that you are so."

"Howell," she stammered, thoroughly frightened now by the gritty determination of his tone, "these are early days of my marriage. The King would never consent to an annulment, whatever the circumstances."

"No, he would not," Howell agreed, "but affairs might not always stand as they do now."

She put out a hand and touched his fiercely beating heart. "Howell, watch yourself. There is danger in uttering such words, even to think such thoughts. My husband, the Earl, is a far more ruthless man than you suppose. Do not be fooled by his pliant manner."

He took her hand and turned the palm to kiss it. "Do not fear for me or your father, Cressida. Look to yourself and do not despair. When I return from Dover I'll visit you again if allowed. Do you wait attendance again on the Queen?"

"Yes, in a few days I shall return to my duties. I shall be glad to. Time hangs heavily upon my hands here. Everything is so well run I have nothing to do."

He nodded, smiling, and they rose together as he made his excuses to leave her.

"I need to be well on my way before dark."

She watched wistfully as he left her. He was a link with the old happy days at Gretton and she hated to see him go.

Chapter Six

Cressida had heard mass and was about to eat breakfast in her own chamber when her husband came unexpectedly into the room. He dismissed Alice curtly and flung himself down into a chair near the table.

Cressida asked quietly, "Have you breakfasted, my lord?"

"I have. Please make a start if you have not yet done so."

Cressida shook her head and sat back, waiting for him to speak.

He stirred restlessly. "I understand that fellow Prosser called on you yesterday in my absence."

"So Master Rawlings made his report."

"No, I was informed by—other means." He avoided her gaze. "Rawlings merely confirmed that report when I questioned him."

Cressida waited but since he remained silent for a moment she said mildly, "Am I to understand that I must have your permission to receive visitors, my lord?"

He said testily, "I wish you would not continue to address me in that fashion. When we are alone, please call me Martyn."

"It is strange to me."

"That can easily be remedied and will be soon enough."

"Yes, but that does not answer my question. You appear to be angered that I received Howell Prosser without consulting you. Would I have received permission?"

"No."

He was rarely so ill-tempered and Cressida found herself trembling inwardly, though she made a brave effort not to reveal her doubts.

"I think I explained that Master Prosser is a friend of long standing. He merely called on me to wish me well in my new life and to inform me that he was soon leaving London."

Wroxeter chewed his nether lip. "Yes, I am informed that he took the Canterbury road."

Cressida was astonished. "So your spy informed you of that too?"

He turned and regarded her deliberately. "I know you find my restrictions on your acquaintances hard to bear, Cressida, but I have good reason for making them. These are difficult times, as you know very well. It would be better for you not to associate with this man."

His eyes were hooded again and she knew she would get nowhere, if she protested or tried to question him further. She gave a little sigh.

He sat back in the chair, crossing one long leg over the other. "I trust everyone in the household has been attentive?"

"Yes, my—Martyn," she corrected herself tonelessly.

"I regret that events have forced me to be absent from your side so much during these early days of our marriage."

She had reached for manchet bread and was beginning

to spread clear honey on it. "I imagine dealing with condemned men has taken a great deal of your time," she said coldly. "I hear Sir Roger Clifford has suffered a barbaric traitor's death. Were you present, my lord, and did it please you to witness the agony of one of the King's enemies?"

He shot up in the chair and she saw his eyes flash dangerously. "No, I was not, but I am glad to hear you admit the man was a traitor. I imagine you heard of this from Prosser?"

"And if I did? He was merely informing me of the feelings of the common people. I understand there was a vain attempt to free Clifford?"

"Made by his own supporters, yes." One finger tapped an imperative tattoo upon the tabletop. "I'm sorry that such information distresses you, but the man was fairly judged and condemned. He was taken in Southampton in possession of treasonable correspondence."

"Fairly condemned to die, possibly, but was it necessary for the King's spite to extend to treating the man so barbarously?"

Wroxeter's brows drew together in a frown. "Not so barbarously. Clifford was beheaded as befitted his rank. The King is not a cruel antagonist."

"But his body was badly mistreated."

Again he frowned. "It is not unusual for the bodies of traitors to be quartered and displayed as a measure of deterring others, as you know well enough. Spite does not enter into the matter."

"But the Cliffords have always opposed the House of York, or so I—was told," she finished uneasily, aware of the source of that information.

"Did your informant also tell you that it was a Clifford who cut down the King's brother, young Edmund of Rutland, on Wakefield Bridge?" His tone was scathing. "The battle was well over, the Duke scarcely more than a boy and fighting his first battle. It would have cost nothing to spare him, but he was butchered for all that.''

Cressida was appalled. In her mind's eye she saw that terrible moment, the young Duke at bay, surrounded by his enemies, possibly pleading for his life.

She swallowed hard. Only too well she realised that family feuds grew from such battle-hardened occurrences. So the King could be understood to hold a grudge against such a family and, if Martyn was to be believed, had held his hand from condemning his enemy, caught in an act of dire treason, to suffer the agonies of the traitors' death of disembowelling.

''I—I feel for all men—so slain,'' she said uncomfortably.

''Indeed,'' he said tartly, ''and for that reason I spared you all talk of it.'' He rose to his feet and leaned both hands on the table to look down at her. ''Prosser has no business to discuss matters of policy with you and you would be wise not to repeat the fellow's opinions—to anyone,'' he asserted harshly. ''Do you understand what I say?''

''I am not a fool, sir.''

''No, you are not a fool,'' he said slowly. ''No one would excuse you for incautious talk on that premise. Particularly, you are not to talk of these matters within the Queen's hearing when you return to your duties. She is not well and is not to be distressed by talk of any antagonism to the King's will.''

He was holding her gaze with his brown eyes and she looked away at last and nodded in acceptance of his command. He sighed. She was determined to oppose him and it was essential that he keep her from all harmful influences. Later he would attempt to win her heart so that they

could dwell more comfortably together during the long
years ahead of them.

He was about to leave her when Peter Fairley knocked
urgently upon the door of the chamber. Martyn bade him
enter.

"Yes, Peter, what is it? I shall be down and ready to
leave soon."

Peter's eyes went anxiously from his master to his mistress. It was obvious to him that matters were tense between them.

"My lord, a messenger has just arrived in haste from
Westminster, sent from the Lady Elizabeth Plantagenet.
She begs my lady Countess to come quickly to attend on
the Queen whose condition has worsened." He lowered
his eyes, concerned at the ill news he brought. "The messenger said he understood the Queen, poor lady, to have
suffered a severe haemorrhage, and that the King's physicians have been summoned urgently to her bedside."

Cressida gave a little cry of pity. "Of course; I will
come at once. She will need all her ladies near her." She
challenged her husband to refuse his permission, but his
stern gaze had already softened and he nodded.

"Aye, Peter. My lady will be at the landing steps within
half an hour. Fortunately the barge is all ready for my
departure. Send a page to alert Mistress Alice and ask her
to prepare a single saddle-bag of belongings and linen to
accommodate both herself and her mistress for the next
few days." He turned hastily to Cressida. "Alice had best
accompany you."

"Yes, of course." Cressida had already left the table
and was turning to her clothing chest to look for a warm
cloak and more sensible outdoor footwear.

She heard Martyn say, "Has the King been informed?"

"I do not know, my lord, or even if he is present at Westminster or already at the Tower in Council."

Martyn dismissed Peter on his errand and turned to watch Cressida find her more serviceable garments, suitable for the river journey. He muttered uneasily, "God help Richard now, when he has most need of comfort."

Cressida sat huddled for warmth against Alice as the barge pulled out from the landing stage and stared miserably over the pewter-grey waters of the river. The Lady Elizabeth had sent for her directly, so, despite all efforts to part her from the Queen, she was still in attendance. If the Queen was spitting blood she was, indeed, very ill. All their forebodings were coming to fulfilment.

Cressida's eyes filled with sudden tears. Poor, gentle lady, who had had sorrows enough over these last months. She would do all in her power to serve and comfort Anne in her need, and Cressida tightened her lips and looked mutinously towards her husband, seated opposite her. The Lady Elizabeth had need of her friendship and services. Nothing was going to prevent her from working alongside the Queen's niece.

The palace seemed unaccountably silent when they arrived. It was thronged to bursting point as usual with officials, courtiers, men-at-arms and clerics and clerks, and they were all talking to each other, but very quietly, each turning to look over his or her shoulder as if what was said might be overheard and give offence.

Cressida shivered and Lord Martyn's grave expression deepened. If the Queen should die, there would be constant speculation about the King's future. The recent death of his only son had left him without heir and he would soon be advised to remarry. Cressida blanched at the very thought. How could these folk think of anyone but the

Queen at this moment? She shied from the thought that Lord Martyn had also been badgered to marry soon after the loss of his betrothed—and by the King himself.

At the entrance to the Queen's apartments Lord Martyn took his leave. He drew her close and kissed her full on the lips in full view of several ladies passing in the corridor. She drew away as quickly as she decently might, conscious that many of them envied her. If only they knew, she thought bitterly.

"I shall stay close in my own office. There is a settle there which I can call into service as a bed if need be. Send Alice if you have need of me."

She curtsied dutifully and waited while Alice went in search of the Lady Elizabeth, unsure whether she should immediately enter the Queen's bedchamber without being summoned.

The King's physician, Dr Hobbes, emerged from the double doors of the royal apartment, followed by his young apprentice carrying a bowl covered by a fair linen cloth. The physican's mouth was held in a tight line and he gathered his gaberdine robe close to his thin body as he acknowledged Cressida's presence with a jerky little nod of his head.

Behind him came Elizabeth of York. The physician paused for a moment, holding her in talk, then he bowed low, nodded to his apprentice, and turned and walked majestically off along the corridor.

Lady Elizabeth came at once to Cressida, her hand outstretched. "Thank you for coming. Things are difficult—and delicate. Her Grace's women try to be helpful but they gossip." Her lips tightened. "You are my friend, Cressida; I can be easy with you."

"How is the Queen?"

Elizabeth shook her head. "There has been no further

bleeding, but she coughs constantly and exhausts herself. As you saw, Dr Hobbes is concerned and—'' she shrugged helplessly ''—over-careful not to alarm the King too much, but...''

''Does he realise how gravely ill she is?''

''Richard?'' Elizabeth's blue eyes grew dark with pity. ''Oh, yes; how can he fail to? And Richard was never one to refuse to face up to reality. He has seen too much horror to deceive himself.''

''And the Queen?'' Cressida whispered pitifully. ''Does she know truly—how serious her condition is?''

Elizabeth's eyes were wet with tears. ''She knows well enough she is dying. She—she tries so hard to—keep from breaking down—lest—lest she distresses the King further. He is the light of her life.''

Cressida's lips parted soundlessly. ''Sweet Virgin help them both,'' she murmured softly.

''Come now. I told her I had sent for you and she is anxious to see you.''

The Queen was propped high up on the embroidered pillows. As the Lady Elizabeth advanced to the bed with Cressida in tow her attendants withdrew. Anne was deadly pale but for a hectic flush which darkened her cheeks and her lips were bloodless, but she was breathing more easily for the moment. She greeted Cressida with a roguish smile.

''Ah, our lovely child bride. How does married life suit you, little Cressida?''

Cressida curtsied low. She smiled bravely, determined that the Queen should not glimpse the alarm she felt at the drastic change she perceived in Anne's appearance, and after only a few short days.

''I am very well, Your Grace, and glad to see you resting. They tell me your cough has been giving you trouble.''

Anne's smile broadened. "It will give me less trouble soon. No," she said, putting out a gentle hand to Cressida's shoulder, "do not turn from me to hide your pity. Though you are very young, I realise you are practical and brave and honest—too honest to try to deceive me with useless comfort. I am glad to have you with me, though I would rather not have spoilt these early days of marriage for you."

"Your Grace knows that my lord Martyn loves you well and is ever willing to spare me for your need."

"He is a loyal friend," Anne said softly. "Richard will need more like him when—when the time comes. Thank the Sweet Virgin he has them—Frank Lovell, Dick Ratcliffe, Rob Percy—so many true companions. I shall not fear for him—whatever transpires. I know he is brave and stalwart. He will suffer, but—later—he will do what is best for the realm."

Cressida was accommodated in her old chamber and for the next few days worked alongside the Lady Elizabeth. Their duties were light since the Queen was too ill now to leave her bed. All they could do for her was to keep her comfortable and amuse her as best they might. The cough came and went, sometimes tearing the frail body almost apart.

At those times when she was seated beside the bed, Cressida felt a chill of fear. She had never nursed someone so close to death, had never felt that angel's icy breath on her cheek before. Her parents had remained healthy throughout her childhood and her only griefs had been for pet dogs. Certainly she had suffered then, deeply, for she had a sensitive and affectionate nature, but this long-drawn-out agony touched her to her very soul.

The King spent as much time with his dying Queen as

possible. He was gentle with her, tending her intimately when there was need. His eyes were deep-shadowed and his mouth close-held. It was impossible to gauge the depth of his suffering. He would draw apart with Dr Hobbes, nodding gravely at the physician's instructions, and his gratitude to the Lady Elizabeth was marked.

Once Cressida saw him, just outside the chamber, stoop and take Elizabeth's hands within his grasp and kiss them fiercely, then he strode off to his own apartments as if he could no longer linger in the vicinity of the chamber where his wife lay stricken.

Lord Martyn presented himself often at the sick room. Always the Queen would greet him cheerfully and he would remain by her side, joking with her, chatting about the old days at Middleham Castle.

On one occasion he drew Cressida outside when the Queen began to cough harshly and Dr Hobbes was summoned.

"You are very young to have this charge," he said, his voice harsh with emotion. "We shall all understand if you feel this is too much for you to bear, if you are afraid…"

She stared back at him, blue eyes wide and blazing. "Of course I am afraid. We all fear for her, the Lady Elizabeth most of all. That does not mean that we wish to run away."

He was looking intently into her eyes and bent to tilt up her chin with one gentle finger.

"You are having to grow up very fast, little Cressida. I am sorry for it, but I applaud your spirit. Do what you can for Anne. She deserves all our prayers and good service."

"She is not neglected for a moment; the Lady Elizabeth sees to that," Cressida said fiercely.

He turned from her for a moment and when he again looked full at her she saw that his eyes were troubled.

She was both disturbed and angry when he left her to return to his duties. Why did he continue to consider her a child? Why could he not acknowledge the fact that events had forced maturity and it was a true woman who attended the Queen and waited, though with inner trembling, for the foreshadowing of death which must come soon?

She was taking a hasty break from attendance in the sick chamber later that morning, sitting on a window seat within an oriel of the hall, when a page approached.

"My lady Countess, there is a man asking to speak with you on the river terrace. He says he is a family friend and has news…"

Cressida stared at the boy sharply. "He gave no name?"

"No, my lady; he is a young man, finely but plainly dressed, brown-haired…"

"Yes, I know the man." She rose at once, her heart beating fast. "If I am needed in the Queen's chamber come to the terrace and summon me immediately. Do not wait."

"Yes, my lady."

She had snatched up a cloak earlier, knowing she might need to slip from the overheated apartment for a while, and the rooms outside the Queen's chamber were still chilly. March had come, but there was little sign of approaching spring yet. Cressida sighed as she made her way through the courtyards towards the terrace. A cold wind was blowing hard from the river and the brown earth of the palace pleasance was still barren of shoots. The Queen would be unlikely to see the earth burgeon.

So Howell had returned from Dover. She hoped fervently that Lord Martyn was closeted with the King. He had forbidden her to see Howell Prosser without his permission, and Howell must have had some suspicion of this for he had begged word with her privately.

She had no need of news from her parents. They had called at the palace only two days ago. They had not been able to see the Queen—she had been sleeping—but Cressida had spent a hasty hour with them and received reassurance that all was well with them and matters were as usual at Gretton.

She had been almost relieved that her time with them was so short and there was no opportunity for them to question her about her relationship with Martyn. Her father had said little, but Cressida believed her mother had been more perceptive, though she had tightened her lips and had not pressed matters. Cressida hoped that her reserve with them had been put down to her concern for the Queen.

Howell was waiting in an angle of the river wall, his brown-hooded cloak pulled well up, hiding his features from passers-by who came and went between the landing steps and the palace. Cressida had pulled her own fur-lined cloak around her against the dank chill of the morning and her hood was drawn carefully over the intricate folds of the wired butterfly veiling of her court hennin.

"I needed to see you. The boy was not averse to taking coin and promised to approach you when you were alone."

She was somewhat breathless for she had hurried, but was aware that some of her fast breathing was due to the illicit nature of this meeting.

"I am glad to see you, Howell, naturally, but I do not think you should have risked coming here."

"Your lordly husband has forbidden all contact with me, eh?"

"Not exactly, but he insists on being present or at least that he gives his permission."

Howell was stooping to kiss her fingers, and so passionately that she began to move nervously away.

"We must be careful. We must not be seen."

He shrugged lightly. "There is so much coming and going in and out of the palace, no one will have time or interest in our doings."

Cressida looked up as two officials hurried by talking earnestly.

Howell said quietly, "How is the Queen? All this commotion and speculation is because of her illness. The citizens are anxious. The future of the dynasty is in doubt."

Cressida shook her head sadly. "My news would be hardly likely to reassure them. She is very poorly, my sweet lady."

His eyes narrowed. "You are in constant attendance? You do not eat anything within the royal chambers, do you? There is talk of poison."

Cressida's lips parted in soundless amazement. "Poison? Nonsense; the Queen is sick with lung rot, the wasting sickness. All know her own sister, Isabel, also died of it."

"Aye, that is well known, but she could take some time to die and it is thought the King might be impatient."

Cressida expelled her breath in a decided hiss. "What idle gossip abounds in the city? The Queen is tended lovingly, and particularly by her own husband. All who witness him with her would know that. Her own niece is constantly watchful…"

"The Lady Elizabeth?" His eyelids flickered oddly.

She stared back at him wonderingly. "What are you suggesting? The Lady Elizabeth loves her aunt dearly…"

"And her royal uncle?"

This time Cressida gave a decided gasp. "Howell, how dare you…? The Lady Elizabeth—wish to see her aunt die—because… That is scandalous—and utterly preposterous."

"Then there is nothing in the rumours that should the

Queen die he might wish to ally himself with the people's darling, Elizabeth; that he had already consulted the Queen Dowager, her mother, on the matter?''

Cressida's eyes were wide with shock. ''Wed his niece? It is forbidden by Holy church—incestuous…''

''In the case of kings' desires, we all know dispensations can be obtained.''

''She would never countenance it and…'' Cressida stared past him, shocked beyond measure, yet—she saw vividly once again the scene within the corridor—the King stooping to kiss Elizabeth's hand, his eyes filled with tears of emotional gratitude. Were they in truth tears of gratitude? She pushed away the unworthy thought and turned back to Howell.

''Is this really what the people are saying? But, Howell, that is terrible. You said yourself that Henry Tudor has declared himself willing to ask for the hand of the Princess.''

''And you said, 'Not unless he usurps King Richard's throne'.'' His expression was bland. ''She is her father's heiress and the beloved of the Londoners. A marriage with her could foil, once and for all, the Tudor's hopes.''

''But her brothers, the Princes?''

He gave a short, hollow laugh. ''Who really believes the Princes still live?''

She sucked in her breath. ''I cannot believe that the King would contemplate such a possibility. Nor would Elizabeth…''

''Yet all London talks of her appearance at the Twelfth Night feast in a gown resembling that of the Queen.''

Cressida bit her lip uncertainly as she recalled Wroxeter's undoubted fury on that occasion. Had he heard rumours? No, she dismissed the thought. He could not consider…

As if he read her very thoughts, Howell bent close and whispered, "It is also said she has written to the Duke of Norfolk, speaking of her love for the King and desire to do him service and begging the Duke to speak well of her to His Grace."

"A sentiment any good subject would express, and especially now that the King needs all our love and goodwill," Cressida said hotly. "Howell, you must not repeat these ugly rumours. Such talk could cost you your head."

"Only if it were proved to be untrue."

Howell gave a sudden muttered oath as a man, walking hurriedly down the path towards them, head down against the wind blowing from the river, stumbled awkwardly against him. The man stopped, lifted his head and made a fulsome apology.

"Sir, forgive me. I am clumsy this morning, have just stepped ashore. The river barges toss uncertainly on the rough waves today." He backed away as Howell acknowledged him with a stiff little nod.

Cressida stared after the man, her brows creased in doubt.

"I have seen him somewhere about the palace." She gnawed at her nether lip uncertainly. "I hope he did not overhear..."

"No, no." Howell forced a laugh. "You heard him. He said he had only just stepped ashore."

"Yes, he did." Cressida drew her gaze from the retreating figure back to Howell. "How long will you be in London now?"

"Several days. I wait for a business reply—concerning the wool clip." He made a little grimace. "After that I must return to the Marches—far too great a distance from you, Cressida."

She forced a smile. "I shall miss you all, Mother and

Father too, when you leave me. Howell, I should not stay here with you longer. I shall be missed and—and the Queen might call for me.''

He nodded. ''Be careful. Promise me you will be watchful of all about the Queen, but give no open sign of suspicion. That could bring you into further danger.''

She inclined her head. Despite her brave words of repudiation of his ugly fears, he had disturbed her. He bowed. This time he did not seek to take her hand for she had withdrawn some distance from him, as if she could put space between his horrifying words and her own beliefs. She forced a smile.

''Give my good wishes to all at home. God keep you, Howell, and—and keep yourself from all treasonable dealings, especially this foolish rumourmongering…''

''I swear I will, but I fear for you.''

''I am sure there is no need to do so,'' she assured him, yet her eyes were dark with concern as she turned and left him, her thoughts in turmoil.

Alice met her at the entrance to the Queen's apartments.

''The Lady Elizabeth has been asking for you.'' Alice eyed her doubtfully. ''I went to your chamber and into the hall. One of the pages said he had seen you heading for the river quay.''

''Did he?'' Cressida's tone was brittle-hard. ''And why should my movements interest him, I wonder? Was he set to spy upon me?''

Alice sniffed. She knew well enough that her mistress would not have adopted such an attitude had there been nothing to hide.

''I doubt that,'' she said mildly. ''Pages are notorious gossips. They gain favours by entertaining the ladies with any titbit of information they think might be scurrilous, a reason, perhaps, why it is best not to give them arrows for their suspicious bows. It is very cold by the river.''

Cressida gave a little laugh. That last remark had been made so lightly yet had achieved its purpose. Very little could be hidden from Alice, but she could be trusted implicitly.

Cressida said anxiously, ''Is the Queen worse? Have you heard?''

''I do not think so. Nothing has been said and there has been no racing about after physicians. His Grace has been sitting with her.''

Cressida suppressed the terrible doubts that Howell had aroused in her mind. So the King was still attentive to his sick wife, but—would he not wish to appear so—outwardly at least. Once sowed, that horrible suspicion would grow, however assiduously she attempted to dismiss it.

''Thank you, Alice. Where is the Lady Elizabeth now?''

''With the King and Queen, I believe.''

Cressida nodded and moved into the outer chamber. Some of the Queen's other attendants were seated here, some chatting, some working at embroidery or reading from illuminated Books of Hours. One or two looked up at Cressida curiously, but few smiled in welcome. Still she felt an outsider though no barbed taunts were thrown at her now that she was my lady, Countess of Wroxeter.

She undid the neckties of her cloak and seated herself some distance from the rest on a window seat. She could not enter the Queen's bedchamber now without invitation, since the King was present there. She must wait to discover if the Lady Elizabeth had particular need of her services.

The King emerged at last and stood close to his niece, once more in grave consultation with her. The attendant ladies rose and curtsied low. He acknowledged them courteously and took his leave. Cressida bit her lip doubtfully as she observed how wistfully Elizabeth followed the King's retreating back with her eyes. Then she caught sight of Cressida and nodded for her to approach.

"You wanted me, my lady?"

"The Queen asked for you earlier but she is asleep now. She tires so easily. This rest will be good for her. Lady Allard is watching by her. We should leave her to rest." She looked thoughtfully at Cressida's cloak. "You have been out?"

"Only to the river terrace for a breath of air. I felt suffocated."

Elizabeth nodded. "It is stifling within the chamber. Mind you, I am thankful to be warm. You cannot imagine how cold it was when we were all immured within the Sanctuary of Westminster; even on the warmest days of summer the chill seemed to come from the grey walls of the place."

It was the first time she had referred to the time when her mother, the Dowager Queen, had hastened them all into sanctuary, so quickly that a wall had had to be demolished to accommodate the royal baggage, soon after the death of King Edward and during the uncertain days of her elder son's brief reign.

Months later she had allowed herself to be convinced that she and her daughters would be safe under the protection offered by King Richard and—now—Elizabeth had been established at Court to wait upon her aunt—and her royal uncle. Had some sort of bargain been struck then? Howell had intimated that the Dowager Queen was willing to countenance a marriage between her eldest daughter and the King—should the Queen die…

Cressida shivered nervously. It was totally unthinkable. For the first time in their acquaintanceship she felt uncomfortable in the company of her friend.

The Earl did not call at her chamber that evening to ask after her well-being and the Queen's health as he usually did.

Cressida was thankful. She was aware that she would have found it difficult to hide her guilt from him. Not only had she disobeyed him in meeting Howell Prosser in private, but she was conscious that what had passed between them was of a treasonable nature, and she sensed that it would not only have displeased Lord Martyn, but possibly prompted him to take some action against Howell.

Over the next few days the Queen kept to her bed, sleeping exhaustedly most of the time, only rousing or showing interest when the King arrived at her bedside, which he did frequently.

Cressida found herself watching him covertly whenever the Lady Elizabeth was present, but saw that his attention was fixed only upon his sick wife. He was very gentle with her and though he continued to smile bravely in her presence Cressida saw how haggard he appeared when he emerged from the chamber. Deep lines of suffering etched his nose and mouth and his eyes were deep-shadowed.

When Cressida *did* see her husband, she realised that he too showed signs of strain. His brows were drawn together as if in deep concentration and his usually sleepy expression had been replaced by one of alarmed watchfulness. He spent long hours in his small office and Cressida wondered if news from abroad and the realm at large was worrying him unduly and, naturally, he would not wish to bother his sovereign with such disturbing matters at so sad a time.

Cressida was with the Lady Elizabeth in attendance in the sick chamber when the curious darkening of the sun occurred in the afternoon of March sixteenth. Cressida had gone to the window to gaze curiously at the crowd of servants, grooms and officials thronging the courtyard, gaping up into the lowering sky. She knew it was said to be an eclipse of the sun, but had never experienced such a phenomenon. Though it was still early the room darkened unnaturally and she knew a sudden frisson of fear, as if the world itself were about to come to an end.

The Queen had been sleeping and the Lady Elizabeth was seated by the bed. Anne's breathing had been laboured earlier and her cough had given her a sleepless night. Now Cressida and Elizabeth were relieved that it had eased for the moment and she had managed to rest for a while. Dr Hobbes had come and gone in the morning, had examined her, nodded sagely and taken his departure now that the troublesome cough had stopped.

Cressida leaned down from the casement, frowning, then began to relax as the sky started to lighten again and there was a concerted gasp of relief from the watchers below.

"It seems to be passing," she called to the Lady Elizabeth. "I confess it is quite frightening. No wonder superstitious people in the past have regarded these occurrences as dire warnings of some disaster."

Elizabeth gave no reply and Cressida turned abruptly as there came a strangled gasp from the bed. The Queen was struggling up onto her pillows. Elizabeth had risen and was trying to help her when the Queen coughed harshly and gouts of bright blood spurted from her pallid lips over the coverlet and pillows, staining both the fine linen of the Queen's night-shift and Elizabeth's hands and gown.

Elizabeth gave one sudden shrill cry of terror and Cressida, for the breath of one heartbeat, stood stock-still by the bed, too horrified to move.

The Queen's blue eyes were distended in terror and she was striving to speak, her fingers clawing at the bed coverlet as she struggled for breath. Still the frothy blood poured from her mouth and Elizabeth put a hand to her own to stifle her sobs.

One of the Queen's senior ladies burst into the chamber, alerted by Elizabeth's first cry. She took in the situation quickly and took charge.

"My Lady of Wroxeter, go at once; find a page to summon Dr Hobbes and the King must be informed." She turned to the Princess.

"We must try to lift her higher. We'll need men to put some supports beneath the bedstead and servants must go for water." She called to Cressida as she reached the door, her voice deadly calm now. "Summon the Queen's confessor. He should be here—just in case."

Cressida could hear her uttering soothing words to the frightened Queen. "There, there, my dear. This has happened before. It will be momentary. The doctor will come. All will be well." Lady Allard had attended upon the Queen for many years, even before she and the then Duke of Gloucester had wed. Her husband, Sir Dominick, was one of the Royal household knights and, like Lord Martyn, he had served the King with Lord Francis Lovell, Sir Richard Ratcliffe and the other known companions of Middleham.

Cressida's limbs were threatening to let her down, but she found a page and sent him off on his errand. Most of the household were out watching the eclipse and the boy seemed half-bemused, whether at her frightened expression or the fearful happening in the sky she could not tell.

She exhorted him to find his companions and send them off about the palace to find the King, the Queen's confessor and serving wenches to bring water and towels to the chamber. Though she was thoroughly alarmed, she returned to the bedside to help Lady Allard.

The older woman looked her up and down briefly, then

nodded briskly. She addressed the Princess. "My lady, you should return to your chamber to change your gown. Lady Wroxeter will help me strip and change the Queen until the other attendants arrive."

Cressida concentrated grimly on the task in hand, gently removing the sheets and coverings slimed with blood and hastening the white-faced maids, who entered with water and towels and fresh linen. The coughing had stopped now and with it the bleeding, but the Queen had ceased to struggle to speak and lay back, doll-like in their hands, as they carefully tended her.

Later, Cressida was thankful when the physician and his apprentice arrived and Lady Allard quietly dismissed her from the chamber.

"Thank you, my lady. We can manage now. Go and take some rest. We may need you later."

In the corridor Cressida passed the King. He was biting down so savagely upon his nether lip that bright drops of blood showed. His face was as white as the linen sheets Cressida had replaced upon the Queen's bed and his grey eyes looked tortured in his haggard face. Behind him his attendants drew back apace as if they could not bear to witness his grief.

Two hours later she was summoned with the other attendants and senior members of the royal household to the anteroom of the Queen's chamber while the King's chaplain said mass. She knelt beside her husband, hearing the solemn words through the open doorway, and smelt the acrid yet over-sweet smell of incense.

At last Dr Hobbes ordered them all from the chamber so that the King could be alone with his wife. Lady Allard was crying quietly and the King's friends were unashamedly wiping their eyes. Cressida could feel her own hot tears falling onto her cheeks as Martyn led her down the corridor towards her own chamber. The Lady Elizabeth stood, white-faced and tearless, near the door as Cressida looked back. The Princess's eyes were fixed wistfully on the King's back as he remained kneeling by the bedside.

Alice, as ever, was quietly efficient yet mercifully silent. Cressida had been in attendance for hours and Alice helped her from her gown and encouraged her to lie upon her bed. It seemed that hardly any time had passed before they heard the tolling of the bell that told them Anne, Queen of England, was dead.

Cressida sat up, her hands clasped around her drawn-up knees, and cried soft tears which relieved her overwhelmed heart. She had known the Queen for only four months and had learned to love her unreservedly. She wondered, half-afraid, if she would be expected to help lay out her mistress, but no one came to summon her to the death chamber and Alice said that she thought the Queen's oldest and dearest friends would do that final service for her. Would her niece be amongst them?

Cressida bit her lip uncertainly as she sat and thought about the outcome. The King must mourn his wife a little time and then—then he must remarry—and soon—but to the Lady Elizabeth? Would the scandalmongering tongues in the packed streets of the capital accept such a marriage? Would those courtiers who had loved the Queen ever forgive him?

Lord Martyn had left Cressida alone, gone about the very necessary business which the King's Council must put in hand, plans for the royal obsequies, proclamations which must be issued, instructions concerning royal mourning. Cressida thought dully that those superstitious folk who had warned of calamity after the darkening of the sun would consider themselves proved right. What greater disaster could afflict the realm at this time of uncertainty than the death of its Queen?

Alice came to her side as she stirred. She was carrying a silk gown in mourning black. She shook her head as Cressida stared at it and flinched.

"We all knew it must come soon," she said flatly. "I knew it was necessary to prepare. Let me help you to change."

"Lord Martyn will grieve. He loved the Queen well."

"Aye, for all I hear there was no one here who did not."

Cressida looked at her sharply. "There is no talk amongst the servants of…?" She bit back the dreadful doubts she could not frame into words.

Alice sighed heavily. "There will always be those who cast doubts on the probity of others."

"They are saying the King—wanted her to die?" Cressida whispered the question fearfully.

"All knew it must be soon and while there was uncertainty—" Alice shrugged. "She could not give him an heir. It will be said he wanted it over and who could blame him, poor man? The physicians have forbidden him to share her bed for the last few months."

"The Lady Elizabeth must be especially stricken. I should go to her." Cressida waited while Alice adjusted the black veiling over her truncated hennin.

"Aye, she will be glad of your comfort. I doubt she'll get much understanding from that mother of hers," Alice retorted laconically.

Cressida could not entirely repress an almost hysterical laugh as she considered what Howell had said—that the Dowager Queen had been most anxious to conclude a marriage contract between her daughter and the King.

"And what shall I tell my lord Earl if he asks where you are?" Alice was clearly not unaware that Lord Martyn was not entirely pleased about the friendship between his wife and the Princess.

Cressida bit her lip. "Tell him—tell him the truth. Surely he must realise that I am in duty bound to try and offer solace to the Lady Elizabeth at this time of her suffering."

She was informed that the Lady Elizabeth was not within her chamber. The young maid who told Cressida looked uncertain as to what she was to say concerning the whereabouts of her mistress. Cressida stood still for a moment outside the closed door of Elizabeth's chamber. Could she, even now, be with the King?

She dismissed that thought as unworthy. Even if it were so, it would be natural enough for a niece to be with her uncle to offer comfort. Cressida decided to seek her friend within the antechamber to the Queen's apartment where other of the Queen's ladies might be expected to gather.

She found the place deserted and was about to leave when a sudden sound from inside the death chamber alerted her attention. She drew near to the slightly open door and peered inside.

Richard of England knelt upon the floor by the bed. Terrible sobs racked his body as he leaned forward over the bed, his two hands outstretched imploringly over the coverlet. In all her young life Cressida had never heard a man cry. It was a dreadful, anguished flood of overwhelming emotional agony. She knew she should go. She should not witness this, yet she could not move.

Realisation struck her with full force. Howell had slandered the King. No man could suffer like that and dissemble. She was hearing the true expression of the man's despair. Richard had loved Anne truly. She could no longer be under any misapprehension and she stood transfixed, one hand to her mouth to keep back her own sobs. All this time he had watched her slowly draw away from him, had dreaded this moment, and now she was gone—and he could no longer hold back his grief.

A powerful hand caught Cressida, drawing her back, while another pressed hard against her lips lest she cry out in sudden fear. Inexorably she felt herself pulled to the outer door and into the corridor. The door was closed and she was dragged round to stare into her husband's furious face.

"What in the Sweet Virgin's name are you doing? Can you not see he needs to be alone? Dear God, can he have no privacy?"

She gave a terrible choking sob and collapsed against Martyn's shoulder.

"I'm sorry. I did not mean to spy upon his grief. I—I did not know—did not know he was there. I—I thought—people said he—he—Oh, Martyn, I did not understand how—how he loved her. If—if my father had lost my mother he—" she choked "—he could not grieve more—"

Lord Martyn's expression softened and he drew her back, his hands upon her shoulders, and smiled into her blue eyes, which were wet with tears. He shook his head gently.

"We who have known them all these years, we know how deeply he loved her and how he has suffered over these months and will suffer yet more. Little Cressida, you have been under great stress over these last hours. I told you, you must rest."

He cupped her chin in his hands and bent to kiss her gently upon the mouth. As he straightened his lips curved into an understanding smile.

"You have been very brave. Lady Allard told me how you helped to tend her when the bleeding came. That must have been very frightening. I am very proud of my wife. You will not be needed now until the burial ceremonies. We must go home to the Strand house for a while. I'll call for our barge and send word to Alice to come on later with your clothing and necessities.''

As if in a daze she allowed herself to be drawn along to his office, where he stopped briefly to give instructions to his assistant and collect his fur-lined cloak, which he wrapped around Cressida.

She sat in the stern of the barge, her head pressed against his shoulder, numb with grief and reaction and intense relief that he had so quickly changed from his fury against her to an attitude of loving sympathy. There was a great aching within her, as if she was wanting to cry inside herself.

She stole one look at his strained features as he looked out beyond her over the river. He too grieved for the loss of a dear friend. She gave a little sigh and pressed yet nearer to his strong body, at this moment needing only to feel the comforting warmth of him.

She was glad of the welcoming heat from the fire in the solar hearth. It seemed that already the servants in the house had heard of the Queen's death and they went soft-footed about their tasks, watching carefully their lord's grim demeanour.

Lord Martyn requested that a light supper be served to himself and his lady in the solar. Cressida was overwhelmingly glad that he had decided to join her. She could not have borne to be alone at this time. Philip Kenton served them at table and took his leave at the close of the meal, respectfully drawing the door to after him.

Cressida found herself crying softly again, unable to stop herself. Martyn turned and, seeing her, came to her chair and drew her upwards into his arms.

"I'm sorry," she gulped. "This is so foolish—I..."

"Not foolish at all. The death of the Queen is cause enough for you to weep, but the strain of court life, which is new to you, bring its own problems."

He sat down in the opposite chair, drawing her down onto his knee, cradling her against his heart. She could feel his own beating steadily against hers and felt suddenly, totally safe and protected. Her father had always been demonstratively affectionate, and she had known herself fortunate in this, but her feeling now, for her husband, was completely different. He was kissing her gently, wiping away her tears with a gentle thumb.

"I have been considering you a child still, my wife, and I am realising that is no longer true."

She felt a sudden surge of longing and, as if in answer to her unspoken thought, he bent and kissed her passionately upon the lips. She responded eagerly, pressing her body against him, willing him to caress her as she knew, instinctively, a man caressed his lover. She needed him now; they were alive, together, and she wanted to feel that release of emotion that proved to herself that she was needed as urgently as she needed him, so that as he drew away she looked up sharply into his face.

"You felt the King's grief so deeply because you had suffered so yourself—for—for the Lady Elinor," she whispered. "Do—do you still love her?"

His brows were drawn together in thought and he peered down at her lovely face, tear-stained yet unmarred. She was like that faery queen of legend, who had welcomed the dying Arthur into the barge to convey him to Avalon. Mourning black served only to intensify her beauty. She had the rare ability to weep without the swelling and reddening of lids which other women suffered.

His heart missed a beat. He needed her as he had never

needed a woman before, to convince himself that he was truly alive—yet this was not the time. She would respond, she desperately wanted comfort as he did, but it would be unfair to take her now when she had no real understanding of what she was doing.

He said gently, "Yes, I loved Elinor, will always hold a place for her in my heart, but she is gone, my darling. No one can live with the dead. She was sweet and gentle and dear to me, but you are my wife. When the time is right I will show you that my heart is not closed to love.

"For now you need a quiet time to recover. Let me take you to your chamber. I think your maid, Alice, should be here by now. You must try to sleep and in the morning we shall still be sad, for we have lost a dear friend to both of us, but we shall also accept God's will and rejoice that the Queen's suffering is over."

At her chamber door he stooped and kissed her again. She experienced a sudden, violent resentment, so strong that she almost pushed him away vehemently. He was her husband. He should be here tonight, within her chamber, offering her the solace of his body.

Despite his assurance, she was by no means convinced that he had put his love for Elinor aside. She came between them still, a lovely ghost—and one more worthy to share his bed than Cressida. Instantly she regretted her revulsion. He was grieving. There was nothing in his thoughts at this time but the need to support his sovereign. She made him a curtsey and turned to enter the chamber.

Chapter Seven

Lord Wroxeter stared incredulously at the Lord Chamberlain, Lord Lovell, seated opposite him in the chair near the roaring hearth fire of the winter parlour.

"My lord, what you say is totally impossible. I cannot believe my wife capable of what you suggest."

Lord Lovell shifted uncomfortably in his chair.

"Martyn, I was loath to come to you with this story but, after due consideration, taking into account your duties in the Council, I thought it imperative that you should know of it immediately. There can be little doubt about the matter. Dick Ratcliffe told me he had it from one of his grooms that the man heard Lady Wroxeter actually talk of the King's plans to marry his niece. He passed her on the river quay and could not fail to recognise her."

"God in heaven, does the King know of this?"

Lord Lovell looked away into the fire. "Dick went to the King and challenged him."

"What?"

"Well, you know Dick, the bluff Yorkshire knight personified. He loves Richard well but, as we all did, well-nigh worshipped the Queen. He told Richard bluntly that were he to proceed with this his loyal northerners would desert his cause.''

Martyn took a harsh breath. ''Were you present?''

''Fortunately or unfortunately, whichever way you look at it, yes.''

''What—what was his reaction?''

''Like you, he was at first dumbfounded. Dear God, Martyn, he's still raw from his loss. He simply sat there and stared at Dick Ratcliffe. I thought he might enter into a right royal rage. I hadn't the courage to move. All I could do was stand stock-still and stare at both of them. His hands were gripping his chair arms and white to the bone, then he said quietly—dangerously quietly—'I would like to know, Dick, just where you obtained this slanderous story.'

''I think Dick had recovered from his first shock by then and realised just what he'd done. He went first red, then white, and opened his mouth like a fish gasping for air, then it was he related the story his groom had told him. In the end he blustered, 'Do you tell me, my lord, it isn't true?' Richard just looked at him and Dick went down then on one knee and sobbed out a plea for pardon.''

Martyn was looking full at his visitor, not moving a muscle. It was clear to Lord Lovell that his host was taking some moments to digest the truth of his news. He said at last, evenly, ''Please, my lord, tell me exactly what Sir Richard Ratcliffe said concerning my wife.''

Lovell cleared his throat nervously. ''It's as I said earlier. Ratcliffe's groom had landed at the King's steps. He said he was walking up the quay when he saw Lady Wroxeter in talk with a man...''

''Did he describe this man?''

Lovell hesitated, then resumed his story. ''Naturally I demanded that this fellow be brought before me. The King insisted on being present, though I counselled him to withdraw from all knowledge of the affair until we had probed the source of the rumour completely. The groom was a new man. Dick says he had recently been taken into his household in London, not one of the known men from Yorkshire. I questioned him closely and warned him of the consequences of lying and, of course, he was in awe of the King.

"His story bore out what Dick had said. Apparently he had recognised Lady Wroxeter because he had seen her at her wedding feast, though both she and the man were well muffled against the cold. They were speaking quite loudly, he said, and he pricked up his ears when they spoke of the King's love for his niece and—and of the gossip that the King was in haste for the Queen to die—and the man cautioned her to beware of poison used in the sick chamber…"

Martyn rose and paced the room with long, impatient strides. Lovell was aware that his friend's hands were clenched into fists and winced at Martyn's harsh questioning.

"But the man? What did this groom say about the man?"

Lovell shrugged slightly. "As I said, he was wrapped up so he was not glimpsed too clearly; he was young, well set up; there was no chance to see his hair colouring."

"Prosser," Martyn gritted between his teeth. "Yes, I think I know the fellow."

Lovell said gently, "She was merely repeating what she had heard elsewhere, Martyn. Lady Cressida is very young, new to Court. She could not be entirely aware what damage has been done to the King's reputation. You must not be too harsh with her."

Martyn had come to halt before the Lord Chamberlain's chair. "What have you counselled the King to do?"

"Since the rumour is abroad, it will be necessary for him to make a public denial."

Martyn's jaw worked and his eyes bore the suspicion of moisture. "How did he take it?"

"I think he is still numb with shock. He listened very carefully. I don't think he could believe it—that anyone could think—You know him, Martyn; he never stoops to explain or deny any slur on his character.

"You'll recall the slanders which connected him with the death of young Edward of Lancaster and the murder of poor King Henry, when he was not even in London at the time, even the malicious talk that he wished his brother, George, dead. None of these he deigned to comment on, but this—this has to be answered. There must be no hint of scandal which could harm Anne's memory. He has charged me to arrange a place and time when he can make a public statement of intent."

Martyn sighed and nodded. "God knows how he will find the courage to do this, but he will, thank God. And—and did he speak of the Lady Elizabeth?"

"He saw the wisdom of removing her from Court immediately. She is to go to Sheriff Hutton."

"Good," Martyn breathed. "That should have been done months ago. I never dared broach the matter to him."

"You saw some grain of truth in this vile slander?" Lord Lovell half started up in his chair.

Martyn held up a hand to indicate that he needed to explain. "My lord, you know it is my duty to collate rumour and intelligence concerning any danger or threat of danger both to the King's personal safety and to his reputation. Those vile accusations concerning the death of his nephews, the Princes, emanated from the Tudor faction, as we know well. All this will aid Henry Tudor's cause. Any mud he can sling at Richard will be well received by his enemies and those petty lords who envy his position and gain nothing from his elevation to the throne.

''I have watched the Lady Elizabeth closely. It is clear she has a deep affection for her uncle, possibly innocent enough. She means well and she loved the Queen, I am sure, but her closeness to the King encourages gossip.''

He frowned. ''That unfortunate happening on Twelfth Night when she came dressed like the Queen was due to careless talk between herself and Cressida. It was Cressida who, unknowingly, she says, told the Princess what the Queen was to wear. She brushed it aside as merely women's talk of current fashion and I believed her...''

He passed a weary hand over his brow. ''The King was anxious to restore his brother's daughters to their rightful place at Court, to counteract evil rumours concerning their brothers. He danced with her, paid her avuncular interest in all innocence, but the Queen was ill and—and he cannot afford such insinuations as lewd folk will draw from the friendship.

''I forbade Cressida to associate with the Princess, but could not avoid their being thrown together during the last days of the Queen's illness—yet I still cannot believe that she would knowingly spread such filth.''

Lord Lovell rose. ''I should return to Richard. He may need me.''

''And my wife? She could find herself charged with treason for this.''

''Martyn, there could be no question of that. What happened was done in naïve innocence. Perhaps it might be wiser if she were to stay from Court for a while. Perhaps you could arrange for her to leave Westminster, return to the Marches.''

"I could not be absent from my duties at this critical time."

"I was not about to suggest that. I know you are newly married, but—" again Lovell shrugged "—the King might be happier if he were not to see Lady Cressida for a while. Could she travel with her parents? Gretton came to court today to offer his condolences and to beg to be excused so that he might return to his manor and attend to urgent business there."

Martyn nodded grimly. "I would prefer her not to return to Gretton at this time, but, as you say, I will think of it. Certainly I will keep her from the King's sight."

Lovell leaned forward and placed a hand on his friend's shoulder. "I counsel you not to be too hard on her, Martyn. She can have no conception of the harm that has been caused."

As Martyn escorted the Lord Chamberlain to the door and called for his steward to attend him and see him well served in the stables, he said through his teeth, "I must see that I make her well and truly aware of the facts."

Cressida addressed Alice from the comfort of the great bed as her maid prepared to curtsey and leave her for the night.

"Alice, what is it like to be—to be in love?" The last words came out in a little embarrassed rush.

Alice returned to the bedside and looked down at her former nursling.

"I suppose it differs from person to person but—well, the one in love almost always knows without being told." She was frowning a little.

It was not lost on Alice that all was not well between her master and mistress, and this probing question had her really and truly worried. She suspected that Cressida had met with someone while absent from the Queen's apartments. She had searched for her in vain in the usual haunts of the Queen's ladies.

Cressida had not been forthcoming about her absence and she rarely kept secrets from her maid. If Lord Wroxeter had failed to express his feelings adequately to his wife, had she, perhaps, turned to someone else more anxious to flatter her interest? That could spell disaster indeed.

Cressida sighed. She said wistfully, "I suppose I shall never know the ecstasy they talk of in the romances the troubadours sing. They say your heart beats madly and you feel strangely excited in the presence of the loved one and—"

"My lady," Alice said sternly, "you have not done something which would anger your husband or—even worse, shame your parents?"

Cressida's blue eyes widened in astonishment. "No, of course not, but—" her voice faltered uncertainly "—well, not exactly."

Alice sat down on the side of the bed. "I think you should tell me."

"Well..." Cressida eyed her guiltily "...when you were looking for me the other day—well, I was with Howell—on the river quay."

Alice took in a hasty breath. "You mean you met him by assignation?"

Cressida tilted her chin defiantly. "A page came to tell me he wanted to see me. I would never have done so there—like that—had not my lord ordered me not to receive him. We did nothing to be ashamed of. Howell is leaving London and merely wished to say goodbye, but— my lord would be angry if he discovered we had met clandestinely."

Alice was silent for a moment while she digested this

information, then she said slowly, "Were you talking about Howell just now?"

Again Cressida's eyes widened and darkened in shocked surprise. "Howell? That I might—love Howell? No, of course not. He is a friend, has always been so, and—"

"Praise the Virgin," Alice muttered fervently. "I feared—but no matter. What is all this, my lady? Why this talk of love and feelings?"

Cressida flushed darkly and clasped her hands round her bent knees.

"My lord, he—he treats me as if—as if I were a child still. Last night he was very kind. He knew I was very upset over—over the death of the Queen and he brought me home, as you know, and we supped together and..." Her voice trailed off awkwardly. "Then he brought me to my chamber door and—and he left me." She said flatly in a frightened whisper, "Alice, I want to be a true wife to him."

"So that is it?" Alice gave a heavy sigh. "Child, this marriage was one of arrangement and entered into hastily. You must be patient."

"I know." One of Cressida's hands stole out and seized that of her nurse. "I cannot confide in my mother. My father would be angered if he thought—"

She swallowed. "I do not know how to deal with my feelings, Alice. When he is near—my lord Martyn, I mean—I feel frightened and anxious and almost sick with excitement. I do not know why, for he has never flattered me as other men at Court have done, and he rarely touches me, except to give me a pat or kiss of comfort when I am distressed as you would to a pet dog. But—but he looks at me sometimes—Only I know that he cannot forget his former love who died.

"I want to love him, Alice, and—and for him to love

me, as Father loves Mother. Is that too much to ask?'' Her lip trembled. ''I often seem to anger him without knowing why. The first time we met I was doing something foolish and—and I think he despises me for a simpleton.''

Then she said, passionately, ''I am no longer a child, Alice. I know how I feel when he is near—that is not the response of a child. How can I make him see…?''

Alice gently stroked back the lovely fair hair. ''I say again, sweeting, you must be patient. If I am any judge of men, Lord Martyn is a true and honourable husband who waits lest he destroy too soon what he wishes to create between the two of you. Despite your protests you are still very young and new to this life. He is busied about the King's affairs and this is no time for him to be distracted.

''For all that, it was very foolish and disobedient of you to meet like that with Master Prosser. Promise me you will do nothing stupid like that again.''

Cressida nodded solemnly. ''I promise. To tell truth, I dare not, for all that I—I want my lord Martyn to—love me, he frightens me too. I dread him finding out about this last meeting.''

''Aye.'' Alice tightened her lips as she rose. ''Best keep all this to yourself. Your father would not be pleased with me if he thought you had behaved so thoughtlessly. Now try to sleep, child, and pray to St Catherine to give you your heart's desire.''

Cressida began to snuggle down beneath the coverlets. Already she was beginning to feel better. All day her thoughts had been confused and confession to Alice always helped her.

Alice had almost reached the door when it was flung open and Lord Martyn strode in. His face was black with fury.

''Leave us,'' he commanded harshly.

Alice shot one anxious glance at her mistress, then, stealing another hasty look at her master, curtsied and hastened from the chamber.

Martyn strode to the side of the bed. He reached down and tore back the coverlet. "Get up."

Cressida struggled up against the pillows and, seeing his furious expression, cowered back. She was not easily frightened, though had been vaguely excited in the past by Lord Martyn's anger, as she had told Alice, but the look in his eyes now terrified her.

"I said, get up."

She reached for her bedgown, laid across the fur covering, and he snatched it up and threw it towards her.

She stood up hastily, though her limbs were trembling, and fumbled to pull the furred bedgown around her to cover her nakedness. She dared not look at him, but was uneasily aware of his smouldering anger.

Impatiently he pulled her to face him as she struggled to tie the cord. "Look at me. Look at me, I say."

She obeyed unwillingly. He was standing, feet astride, his back to the hearth, fully dressed still, so something had kept him from retiring. A late visitor?

Suddenly she realised that he had discovered the truth about her secret meeting with Howell and her lips compressed in anger to match his own. How dared he berate her so, when, had he been fair, she could have met with Howell openly and there would have been no need for disobedience on her part? He had no right to forbid her to take farewell of her friends.

Taking the initiative, she said, "Well, what is all this pother, that you drag me so unceremoniously from my bed and alarm my maid? Whatever the matter is, could it not wait for the morning?"

His eyes flashed ominously and, despite her resolve, she drew back apace.

"Do you know what you have done?"

His tone was so venomous that she was becoming even more alarmed, but was determined to put a brave face on it.

"I don't know what you are talking about. If you would explain…?"

"Explain?" He gave a single harsh laugh. "Explain, when I discover my wife has committed an act of outright treason? Why in the name of all the saints should I *have* to explain? Surely that is your business, madam?"

Cressida was totally bewildered by the accusation. Was he mad? How could her innocent meeting with Howell be deemed treason?

She echoed the word. "Treason? I don't understand. Has the King commanded his attendants not to speak to people outside the Court…?"

"How dare you make light of it, madam? Not only have you endangered yourself but you could destroy His Grace's trust in me, one of his most loyal councillors." He came close again and took hold of her, shaking her so roughly that her hair fell about her shoulders in wild disorder and she scarce had ability to draw breath.

"Do you know what the penalty is for treason should a woman be found guilty? For a man it's disembowellment at Tyburn, but for a woman, madam, it is burning at the stake."

She went deadly cold, limp in his grasp. Whatever he was talking of, he was in deadly earnest. What had she done? Had Howell been arrested and had he, under torture, involved her in some nefarious scheme? But in what?

Her eyes implored Martyn for an explanation and, again,

he gave that short bark of a laugh. "You don't realise the harm you've done, do you?"

She shook her head, too afraid now to attempt to defend herself.

"You accuse the King of wishing to poison his wife and, God help us, commit incest by intending to marry his niece, and this before his sweet Queen has breathed her last; and, to cap it all, you do it in front of the world and his wife passing along the busy river quay! And you ask me for an explanation?"

Her eyes had darkened and grown huge in a face gone completely white, devoid of even the flush of previous anger.

"But," she whispered piteously "you don't understand. It was not like you say. The gossip was merely repeated, what had been said by others…"

He released her abruptly and began prowling the room, his hand gripping the ornamental dagger he wore at his belt. It seemed he was not even listening to her attempt at explaining herself.

"Sir Richard Ratcliffe has been forced to demand an explanation from the King. His northern men-at-arms are loyal to the Queen's memory. She was great Warwick's daughter, I remind you. Any implied insult to her could lose the King the support of his followers."

She gave a terrible gasp of understanding and clutched at the carved bedpost to keep from falling. Slowly, inexorably, the deadly truth of this matter was seeping into her bewildered brain.

"The King, the supreme sovereign, must now stoop to explain himself to his people, and at such a time when he needs to know the deepest sympathy and support from all of us. He must go to Clerkenwell, to the hall of the knights of St John, and publicly, humiliatingly declare that he has no intention whatever of marrying his niece.

"God knows how anyone could ever have believed such a possibility in the first place. The King marry a bastard, niece or no, when his own claim to the throne depended on that very bastardy of his brother's children? Did you consider that, or were you so besotted with your friendship with the Lady Elizabeth that you would accept anything she chose to say?"

Cressida now felt that she must exert all her strength to refrain from a cowardly faint. She forced her spine to remain rigid and stiffened her trembling limbs.

"My lord," she managed to whisper, "you cannot believe that I meant to harm the King's cause. If we were overheard…"

"'If we were overheard'," he mimicked cruelly. "I take it by that you mean you and Master Prosser?"

Unable to find her voice, she managed a tremulous nod.

He was very close to her again now, bending down, his wine-scented breath fanning her cheek. After Lord Lovell had left he had taken solace from a carafe of brandy wine.

"So you deliberately disobeyed my orders."

"I did not mean to. It was just that…"

"Your desires outran your fears?"

She stared at him incredulously. He could not believe that she had deep feelings for Howell Prosser—that she would cuckold her own husband?

He caught her by the shoulder again and she could hear the harshness of his rasping breath. "Well, you wanted to see Master Prosser again in spite of my strictures. Tell me what was so urgent that you risked discovery."

"He—he was going away and…"

"Ah, so you could not bear the thought of that. He didn't suggest you should go with him, I take it? Did his gallantry not extend so far, or was he afraid of the consequences?''

Her own breathing had quickened now and fear had turned to anger that he had so deeply misjudged her.

''What you suggest is obscene,'' she snapped. ''There has never been anything but friendship between us. My father would never have countenanced it. Howell knew that and respected me.''

''And, like a dutiful daughter, you were forced to a loveless marriage,'' he sneered. ''That did not stop your feelings running riot, though, did it? You see him again and cannot resist—''

She struck out at him then, catching him a glancing blow upon the cheek pressed so close to her own with her wedding band. He gave a slight hiss of pain, but did not loosen his grasp on her. She could feel the bite of his fingers through the brocade of her bedgown.

''How dare you?'' she stormed. ''Yes, I married you at my father's command as you wed me at the King's. It pleased neither of us, but I do not break my vows whatever the provocation and, in all events, I am not a true wife...''

He released her momentarily in his fury, then reached out and seized her by two flowing tresses of her hair which fell on either side of her face onto her shoulders. He tightened his grip so that she needed to control herself from giving a sudden cry of pain. His usual lazy, good-natured expression had left his features. She could see a pulse beating fast at his temple. His neck muscles bulged with strain and there was a frightening glitter to his eyes.

''So,'' he muttered thickly. ''That is what disturbs you, is it—that you are not a true wife? That I, thinking you a child still, spared you what I feared might be an ordeal? But I misjudged the situation, didn't I? You are not a child. Your behaviour proves that.

"In that case I need no longer consider your feelings. I can treat you like a wife, beat you as is my right, and, by God, you deserve it. Only by the good offices of the Lord Chamberlain and the magnanimity of the King will you escape the full consequences of your treasonable actions. They, thank God, still think of you as a child bride."

His grip on her hair, which he twisted tightly, was cruel and she gasped, but she found the courage to cry, "All right, then, beat me; whip me to within an inch of my life. It is your right, as you maintain, but do not dare to believe ill of me. I merely said farewell to Howell Prosser. I will swear it before the altar."

"What you did with Master Prosser or any other man can be discovered," he said thickly as he released her hair with one hand, cast the free hand around her shoulder then snatched her up into his arms. She gave a little scream as he dumped her unceremoniously down on her bed and began to tear at the fastening of her robe.

She was thoroughly alarmed now. He was drunk and so lost to reason that in his unthinking madness he might well strangle her where she lay.

She had wanted to lie in his arms, become a true woman, but not like this, taken in anger. Wife though she was, this would be more a rape than a bedding.

Her own temper had dissipated now in her terror of what he intended. He could not do this. If he did, they would never be able to live together in amity. She would never forgive him. Tears were streaming freely down her cheeks and she clawed frantically at his impatient hands, still occupied in the remorseless task of attempting to untie her girdle, trying to beat him off.

"No, please, my lord, you must not—not like this. I beg of you…"

Something of her desperation reached his clouded brain

and he checked. Her bedgown had fallen open and he stared down, bemused, at the ivory young body fully revealed to his view, touched with the gold of the fire-glow. Her proud young breasts stood taut as her body arched in terror.

It was as if someone had drenched him in icy cold water. He was kneeling above her, and he straightened on his two arms as she said softly, pleadingly, "Please, you must listen. Punish me if you must, but—not like this. If you do, you will regret it for ever."

He let out one terrible great sob and she reached up and wonderingly touched a sweat-dampened tendril of his hair.

"You must understand. I was foolish. You are right—I have had my own way too long and—and I do have feelings for Howell, but not as you suppose. He is a friend. As a friend, I went to meet him and bid him goodbye and—and as a friend I listened to the tale he told me as—as I had listened before to what he said of Clifford.

"I—I think now—he—he meant us to be overheard—to create a scandal. He—he used me. I would not have him come to harm for his part in this, for old times' sake, but there is nothing between us."

"Dear God," he murmured throatily. "What was I about?"

"You are not yourself, my lord, and you have every right to be angry. I have harmed your chances of preferment, come between you and your lord, but I swear to you I had no intention of doing so. Last night—when I saw the King in his access of grief—I knew—knew how he loved his wife. I do not know how—how I can ever be forgiven for—"

"So it was Prosser who spoke of the King's marital intentions?"

"Yes, but the listener must have misunderstood..."

"No," he said curtly. "There was no misunderstanding. The man deliberately spun the poisoned web and you were caught in it." His lips curled in a little cynical smile. "You, my wife. The plotters were very aware of my role in the King's household. To involve you was very clever indeed."

"And Howell was part of it?" The extent of the bitter hurt she felt was revealed in the wistfulness of her shocked tone.

"The King has many enemies," he said. "They are totally ruthless. You were to be used and discarded. Do not feel besmirched by this. It was not your fault."

How lovely she looked, with those great violet-blue eyes of hers staring at him appealingly, the tears glistening wetly on the sculptured smoothness of her cheeks.

"What will you do?" It was so soft a whisper that he was forced to bend yet closer to catch the words.

His lips curved into a smile of ineffable sweetness. "Well, I shall not ravish you, if that is your fear."

A rosy flush crept from her breasts to her throat, staining the curve of her cheek. "I—I do not fear that now, my lord."

He blinked incredulously and stared down at her in wonder.

"By all the saints, I was right. You *are* no child, are you?"

"No, my lord."

He gave a soft chuckle and bent to kiss her full on her mouth. "Then it is time I did make you truly mine."

She felt a rising sense of panic as she heard him moving softly near the bed, divesting himself of his clothing, then he was bending over her again, leaning down on extended arms.

"You aren't afraid?"

She shook her head. "Not now."

He bent to fondle her hair, twisting a tress of it gently, this time, round his finger.

"You are the most exquisitely beautiful creature I have ever seen. No, don't say anything." He silenced her objection with a loving kiss. "Lovely and lively and—disobedient, and I love that in you—when you don't threaten to bring down the whole of the Establishment on our heads."

"My lord, you will not be punished for...?"

"No, no, my sweet, and, if I were, it would be worth it."

His kisses were sweet on her mouth—honey-sweet—and butterfly-soft on her throat, breasts and the curve of her belly. She gave soft little murmurs of acute pleasure. She was completely ready when he took her at last, the momentary pain swiftly retreating and giving way to total ecstasy.

He found her more responsive than he had dared to hope. Since their marriage he had schooled himself to wait; now he knew she was as eager for the delights of love as he was to teach her.

He had remained celibate since Elinor's death, feeling that the taking of some wanton would be an insult to her memory. His desires had been quenched, only to be rekindled at the first sight of this fairy child. His anger had drained from him at the first realisation that he might have taken her in anger, destroyed for ever any hope of abiding love between them. Now he lay spent at her side, bathed in the health-giving sweat of contentment.

She stirred and he gathered her close to his heart. Her arms stole upwards, around his neck, to draw his head down so that he might kiss her again. She gave a faint sigh and he tilted her chin with one finger, stroking back the bright cloud of her hair that he might see her face more clearly.

"That was a sigh indeed. You have no regrets?"

She shook her head fiercely. "No, no. I wanted—" She turned from him, avoiding his gaze, and he gently turned her back to look fully at him.

"Tell me. What did you want that I have not given you?"

"No, you don't understand. I have what I want—now. My mother and father have always been in love. Even as a small child I was fully aware of that. I thought—feared that I would never know it. You always seemed so remote, sometimes kind and indulgent, but not—loving. I think had I been a favourite hound you would have given me the same kindly, affectionate care—and the same admonishments for wrongdoing.

"And I always seemed to be found to be in disgrace, always guilty of some childish prank, until—" her voice broke a little "—until tonight, when I knew I had made you really angry and I thought—feared—that in that anger you would hurt me beyond recompense. I could not have borne that for—" she felt shy now, and sought to avoid his gaze again "—for I think I am beginning to love you, my lord."

He chuckled, low in his throat. "I should hope so, sweet madam, else your conduct tonight would be deemed wanton indeed."

They lay silent for moments, then she said with a little catch to her voice, "Will they—force you to send me away?"

He considered. "I think it might be politic. You should be away from the King's sight for a while."

She struggled free of his encircling arm and half sat up.

"Martyn, you cannot send me from you, not now."

"Sweetheart, you know how things are at Court. I cannot leave the Council at this critical time. I have work to do—important work." His tone was grim and she closed her eyes as she thought what that deadly work would be.

"You will seek out those who wish to harm the King's cause."

"That is my duty. The King's need is great. I thought you should go to the Marches for a while."

"To your manor at Wroxeter?"

He frowned in the half-darkness of the firelit room. "I had considered that, but I would have wished to take you there personally. Unfortunately that is not possible at this time. I must think this out carefully and—and I must wait for the King's command in this matter."

She said softly, "What is to happen about—about the Lady Elizabeth?"

"She is to leave London for the north—Sheriff Hutton, one of the King's Yorkshire castles. She will join other members of the royal household there."

"I—I have done her great harm, for I do not think she was fully aware—of all this and the consequences. I should contact her, beg her to forgive me."

His voice, when he answered, was decidedly chilly. "Cressida, you must swear to me that you will not communicate with the Lady Elizabeth—that is a direct order. I should be truly angry with you if you were to disobey me in this grave matter."

He turned to look up at her and she inclined her chin in answer.

"Do you think I will be allowed to attend Her Grace's funeral? Oh, Martyn, I want to so much, to do her honour with the rest of her ladies."

He sighed heavily. "For that I must obtain the permission of His Grace."

She nodded sorrowfully. With this she must be content, for she knew that Martyn would need supreme care to so much as approach the King with such a request, considering the magnitude of the harm she had done him.

Whatever pleas Martyn made to the King Cressida was never to know, but she was granted permission to follow the Queen's body with her other attendants when she was laid to rest within Westminster Abbey. Later, as the coffin was lowered into the cavity prepared for it near the choir stalls, Cressida saw that the King was openly weeping.

She did not attempt to hold back her own tears, for the Queen had been so very kind to her, considering the short time she had remained in her service, and she found she was not alone, for the other ladies were declaring that there was none quite like the dead Queen and they would never find another mistress so forbearing, for all that she had been no fool and could hold her own in dispute with any like the great Earl, her father.

The funeral feast that followed afterwards in the palace hall was a subdued affair, no one of the guests taking opportunity from the abundance of good food and wine provided to overindulge.

The King sat apart beneath the cloth of estate and Cressida saw that he ate little and drank even more sparingly than usual. He was flanked by his two oldest friends, Lord Lovell and Sir Richard Ratcliffe, and Cressida was relieved that there appeared to be no coldness between the bluff Yorkshire knight and his sovereign.

Apparently no great harm had been done by the gossip engendered by Howell Prosser. She glanced uneasily at Martyn, who sat by her side, only too aware that the King must yet face the ordeal of open declaration of intent within the hall of the knights of St John at Clerkenwell, which occasion, Martyn had informed her, had already been arranged.

"His Grace has also written to the mayor and aldermen of York, informing them of their duty to scotch this baseless and ugly rumour, with orders to apprehend any person speaking dishonourably of the King in this matter," he had told her.

"But surely this cannot affect people outside the capital?" Cressida had said unhappily.

Martyn had shrugged. "This rumour was put about to blotch the King's reputation by those rebels who mean him harm," he'd replied, "and is as likely to have reached all parts of the realm as here in London and Westminster."

The King left the hall very early but issued a command to his courtiers to remain and continue to feast in honour of the Queen, but even after his departure the mood within the hall remained sombre.

Martyn leaned towards Cressida. "I must go to my office and attend to some pressing business but will only be gone for a short time. Will you remain in the hall until I return to you?"

"No," she said hastily. "I will come with you. I—I do not feel comfortable here in the hall—considering what has happened."

"It is unlikely that the other attendants are aware of your involvement," he assured her. "Lord Lovell has promised to keep your name out of this affair."

She swallowed hard and cast the Lord Chamberlain a glance of profound gratitude as she left the hall with Martyn.

"I will wait in the Queen's antechamber," she said, "until you have completed your business."

Martyn nodded and turned to Peter Fairley, who was in attendance and had followed them from the hall.

''Peter, find young Philip Kenton and tell him to attend his mistress in the Queen's antechamber.''

Peter bowed and hastened off on his errand.

Cressida found the room deserted and desolate. She seated herself in a window seat and looked round sadly at the evidence of happier times she had spent there: a discarded beribboned lute, several pieces of uncompleted embroidery, a tapestry frame. Would she be summoned again to attend a new queen when the King remarried, as she knew he must?

She blinked back bitter tears of grief and regret for the part she had unwittingly paid in deepening his anguish.

The place seemed so forlorn and cheerless, despite the fire burning in the hearth, that she could not bear to wait there until her young page joined her and rose to seek out Martyn's office.

The corridors seemed cheerless and almost deserted, reflecting the saddened mood of the palace inhabitants, and, without concentration, she took a wrong turn and found herself very close to the presence chamber where she had first been presented to the King and Queen and seen Martyn clearly and recognised him as a possible bridegroom.

The door had been left ajar and the pikeman who normally guarded it was not in position outside. Had the King dismissed him or sent him on some errand or was he in his own private chamber? But, even so, this door should not have been left unguarded. Cressida found that strange and alarming. Knowing what she now knew, she feared that some ill-wisher might have lured the guards away, though she could in no way account for such negligence.

She peered anxiously round the door as she had done that night when she had found the King in an access of grief at his dead Queen's bedside.

Gazing round somewhat apprehensively, she encountered the King's cool grey-green eyes as he sat slumped in the armchair near the hearth. He was totally alone and her eyes widened at the lack of attendance.

His lips curved into a slightly bitter smile. "Come in, Lady Cressida."

"Your Grace," she stammered uncertainly. "I would not dream of trespassing upon your privacy. It is just that I thought—feared that—"

"I might be lying slain upon the floor?" The smile deepened now, though she could see the ravages grief had made only too clearly graved upon his features. "No, I sent the guard to the outer corridor. I had no desire to be spied on, which is why I left the hall, and though he protested I needed to be rid of the fellow for an hour.

"Kings rarely have the luxury of being alone, Lady Cressida, and, to be honest, I have no need of a guard. If necessary, I can take care of myself, even should I be attacked by an intruder as beautiful and charming as yourself."

"Then I must take myself off immediately, Your Grace."

"Now that you are here, come in."

"Your Grace, I am sure that my husband would not approve of my intrusion, nor do I think he would—"

"Approve of my lack of care for my own life? No," he acknowledged. "It is his business, amongst others', to guard my back and I agree with you—he would censure me—oh, in the most respectful of terms, but roundly, and for my own good, for all that."

She curtsied low and approached as his signal bade her. There was so much she needed to say, but could not, and to her great shame she burst into tears. He waited until the storm subsided then gestured her to seat herself on a stool near him.

At last she whispered brokenly, ''Your Grace, how can you ever forgive me?''

He sighed deeply. ''I understand you were ill informed, Cressida, and cannot be blamed.''

''But the harm I have done...''

''That others have done. Oh, Cressida, you must put all this from you, as I must do. The Queen loved you and you served her well.''

''We would all have given our lives for her.''

''Yes, I believe that,'' he said quietly. ''You know, I understand what it is to be held to account for something I had not done.''

He was musing, gazing into the distance, and she waited courteously for him to explain himself.

''I loved Anne so deeply and when she was widowed I thought all would be well with us, for I knew she did not love Edward of Lancaster, so I had hopes she would turn willingly to me.''

''And she did not?'' Cressida said, unwilling to believe that there could ever have been ill feeling between the sovereigns. Anne had shown only too plainly how much she adored her husband.

He made a little rueful gesture with one ringed hand. ''Someone anxious to make mischief between us informed her I had murdered the Prince.'' He tapped one finger meditatively upon the arm of his chair. ''He was killed in the pursuit at Tewkesbury.''

''If—if you were not responsible, Your Grace, why did you not explain?''

He smiled down at her sadly. ''He was badly disfigured, trampled by horsemen and men-at-arms. I did not wish her to know the hard facts. It took some time for me to convince her of my love, but, despite interference from others, she came to me at last, and I have never regretted a moment of the precious time we have had together.

"Never forget that, Cressida. When you love, make the most of what you have. Swear to me you will do that, for in this uncertain world it might not be as long as you hope for."

"I will, Your Grace."

Fleetingly, he touched her mourning veil. "I trust Martyn was not too hard on you. Frank Lovell tells me he was furious when he was first told."

She bowed her head in shame. "He was, my lord, and I thought—feared—that—but all is well now, my lord."

He nodded, satisfied, as she raised her chin and looked steadily at him through a blurring of tears.

"I hoped he would find contentment in this marriage. I still have faith in my own judgement."

She blushed hotly. "I think I—we—I think I will learn to love him, my lord."

The tight line of his mouth relaxed momentarily. "Good. I need to believe that those I love can trust those about them as I need to do."

She knew she should leave now and waited for his dismissal, which he gave with a smiling nod, but at the door she said hesitatingly, "Your Grace, I—I am afraid for the Lady Elizabeth. She befriended me and I fear I have done her grave harm."

She waited in dread lest he would become angry with her for her temerity, but he sighed again and said gently, "The Lady Elizabeth knows I have deep affection for her and will always have her best interests at heart. You need not fear for her."

"My husband has forbidden me to try to contact her, Your Grace. If only I could express my regret that..."

"Can you write, Lady Cressida?"

"Oh, yes, Your Grace, I was well tutored."

"Then write to her telling her from your heart what you truly feel and I promise you it will be delivered into her hands and none other."

She ran back to him and stooped to kiss his fingers, resting still now on the chair arm. She was sobbing again. "Dear my lord, I do not know how to thank you. I feel so guilty…"

"Guilt is a useless and harmful emotion," he said ruefully. "I have learned many times to put it from me. Do not be too hard on yourself. Go now into the adjoining chamber and write your letter. I'll see to it that Lord Martyn does not know of it."

She rose, gathered up her skirts, and began to back from his presence, then a harsh voice behind her froze her in her tracks.

"My lord, why do I find you unattended and unguarded? I shall see to it that these tardy fellows pay for their negligence with their lives."

Lord Martyn stopped in his stride as he approached the King and caught sight of Cressida. His face darkened with fury.

"Your Grace, I cannot find words to apologise for this intrusion. What my wife is doing, daring to approach you, I cannot think."

"In truth, Martyn, I believe she was as concerned for my safety as you are yourself," the King said mildly. "She too was alarmed at the absence of my guard and came in to discover if anything untoward had occurred. I explained I had myself dismissed the fellow and kept her to talk further—of her love for the Queen."

The last words were spoken very softly and slightly hoarsely as if tears thickened his throat.

"You must not take her to task for this and must allow

my erring guard to keep his neck intact. Actually, I asked her to write out for me some words she herself has found comforting. Will you do that, Lady Cressida, and give them to me personally before you leave Westminster?''

Martyn blinked, bewildered, and Cressida gave her husband a frightened glance as she fled past him into the adjoining chamber.

When she returned the King was in earnest talk with Martyn and he held out his hand smilingly for the sealed missive.

''Thank you, Cressida. This will be a salve to both our hearts.''

She curtsied low again, knowing she owed him a great debt of gratitude. Martyn was bowing and led her outside.

''By all the saints,'' he fumed, ''cannot I leave you alone for moments without you getting into some dangerous venture? I think yours is the face the King must least wish to view at this time.''

Cressida flushed hotly, her fingers clutching tightly at the black silk folds of her skirt. They were wet with the sweat of guilt.

''My lord, I am sorry. I had no wish to embarrass you but it was as the King said. I mistook my way, saw the door unguarded and feared—feared the worst. After all, I above all others have seen evidence of malice directed towards the King. He was, as always, very gracious to me.''

Martyn drew a hard breath. ''As you say, he has been more forbearing than we could hope for or deserve. I trust now you will think more kindly of your sovereign than I believe you did formerly.''

She lifted her face to his. ''Martyn, I know now how deeply I have wronged the King in my thoughts and will pray continually to the Virgin to grant him comfort in his great grief.''

''Amen,'' he murmured fervently as he led her back towards the great hall where his squire and other attendants waited to escort the Earl and his Countess home to the Strand house.

Chapter Eight

Though her heart was still heavy, Cressida returned to the Strand house with her burden of guilt lightened by the King's understanding. She was grateful that he had not revealed to Martyn her plea to contact the Lady Elizabeth for she still feared his anger over their association.

That night he did not come to her chamber. She told herself that the King's business kept him working late, but could not quite convince herself of the fact. She had waited so long to become Martyn's true wife that it was a distinct blow to her pride that he did not also long for their time of privacy within the curtained bed.

She remembered, blushing darkly, the expression on Alice's face when she had hastily collected up the blood-smeared sheets that morning. She had flashed Cressida a glance of pure triumph. Now Cressida lay in the bed alone, praying that Martyn would come, however late—but he did not.

He did breakfast with her, however, and after the page had been dismissed she ventured to question him.

"My lord, you were working into the small hours last night?"

He nodded abstractedly, spreading honey on fine white manchet bread.

"There is still much to be done to prepare for the King's presence at Clerkenwell. The Lord Chamberlain has placed the responsibility for the King's personal safety in my hands."

Her lips trembled slightly. However much the King had declared his forgiveness, she was aware that those in the know would always consider her partly to blame and her guilt would rub off upon her husband's reputation.

"He will be well guarded?"

"I shall see to it. Be very sure of that."

Her hand shook as she moved her ale cup nervously. "I was afraid you were still angry with me last night since— since you did not come to me."

He was avoiding her eyes, frowning slightly. "It was, indeed, very late. The day had been a difficult one for you. I wanted you to sleep undisturbed."

She did not reply and he turned to face her, his dark eyes unhooded, looking directly into hers.

He hesitated, then reached across the table and took her hand within his. "Cressida, dark days lie ahead. I do not wish you to be burdened…"

Her own blue eyes widened. "You mean I might bear a child? But I want to bear you an heir, Martyn. That is my duty."

He sighed. "In time, when life is more settled." He looked away again. "Over the next months I think it might be better if you were away from the capital."

She had to hold back a cry of protest. It was what she feared—separation from Martyn now, when they should be getting to know each other—beginning to love each other—and because she had been foolishly naïve she must be exiled from Court, from her husband's side. It was a harsh punishment.

"I am an embarrassment to you." She swallowed back the tears. "I understand."

"No, you do not." His voice was almost harsh with pent-up emotion. "If it were simply that, we could live this down—together—but hard days lie ahead, dangerous days, and I want you safe out of harm's way."

She was alarmed now. "Is your life in danger? If so I should be at your side."

"Cressida, *all* our lives may well be endangered. The Tudor spies are everywhere. The King's reputation is at its lowest. The people are distraught over baseless rumours concerning the Queen's death. It is time for Henry Tudor to strike. He will not wish to wait another year."

"You mean he will invade?" She was incredulous.

"I think it will come—this summer. The King knows it too—and, I fear, at this time of anguish, is not so dismayed by the prospect as he should be. You should be well away from London and so should your father."

It was a bald statement of opinion that made her catch her breath again. Sir Daniel was a Marcher baron and many of the Welsh lords could well be under suspicion of supporting the Tudor.

A cold frisson of fear touched her heart and she nodded, but she would bide her time. Yes, her parents should leave the capital, but she had every intention of trying to persuade Martyn to allow her to remain with him. Now was not the time; she must wait for a better opportunity.

She watched him leave the house later and knew he would be beside his sovereign at this humiliating occasion within the hall of the knights of St John and was forced to hold back the sharp bile in her throat, knowing she was partly to blame for the necessity.

The following days were long and tedious. The Court was in mourning, there would be no place for her there, and the hours stretched before her endlessly. She was determined to get to know the household and one morning Master Rawlings escorted her on a tour of inspection. In the kitchen her encounter with Jack Wainwright passed without too much embarrassment on either side, though a quick glance towards the spit revealed that Wat Forrester was back at his duties.

Throughout this difficult time when Martyn was absent for long hours Cressida was thankful for the friendship of Alice and the assiduous attentions of young Philip Kenton, whom Martyn had assigned to wait on her.

She was delighted when Master Rawlings informed her that her father had called, three days after the Queen's funeral. She rose to greet him, hands outstretched, when the steward ushered him into the winter parlour.

"Father, it is good to see you. I had thought you might soon be travelling home and feared that I might be at Westminster when you came to bid me goodbye."

He embraced her warmly and she led him towards the hearth.

"It is still very cold, even for March, but we have promise of spring at last. There are shoots pushing through in the pleasance. If the weather continues to improve you should have a pleasant journey home." She was chattering away in her happiness at seeing him and did not, at first, notice his strained expression.

He looked deliberately at young Philip Kenton, who was preparing to replace his lute on its nail on the wall, for the boy had been strumming to Cressida while she sat at her embroidery.

"Can your page fetch me some ale from the buttery, daughter?"

Cressida had been about to offer him malmsey from the wine jug on the table and she followed his gaze towards Philip's back, a little bewildered, but instantly understanding that her father had need to talk to her without any other present.

"Of course. Wine can be cloying at this hour of the morning, and you will want the ale mulled. Go at once, Philip, and wait while one of the kitchen wenches gets it good and hot and well spiced."

Philip withdrew at once, ever anxious to be useful, and after the door closed behind him Cressida turned quickly towards her father.

"There is nothing wrong with Mother, is there?"

"No, no, child. As you say, we shall be off about our travels in a couple of days. Your mother believes I am here to tell you of our impending departure. I did not want her involved in this business."

Cressida was becoming alarmed. It was unlike her father to keep any matter from her mother and she now saw that he was very pale indeed and frowning.

"You are not ill...?"

"No, no. Child, is your husband in the house?"

"No, he left early for the Tower. He is often there these days and—"

"Has he a place of business here?"

"He has an office, yes, where he reads all his correspondence concerning the Council."

"Is there a secretary at work there?"

"No. Master Standish is with him at the Tower. I saw them go down to the river quay together."

"Can you gain admittance?"

Cressida paled. "To the office? Without Martyn's consent? I would not like to do that. He—"

"But if the matter was of paramount importance?"

She hesitated. "Well, probably. It may well be locked, but the servants here give me complete obedience."

She was growing pale now. It was obvious that her father was in some trouble and had come to her for help.

"What is it, Father?"

"Howell Prosser is in grave danger of arrest."

She started visibly. "I thought he had left the city."

"I wish to God he had." Her father paced the room, his hands locked behind his back. "Your husband has control of the ports. The situation is grave and the Council fears possibility of invasion. Any man wishing to leave the country is suspected of being a spy for the Tudor and is required to answer to strict questioning or to have licence to travel."

"I know," she said soberly. "Martyn thinks the invasion will come soon."

Sir Daniel nodded. "That fool Prosser has been in communication with the Tudor faction. He needs to be got clear of England. He could be arrested at any moment. He is convinced he is under suspicion and is in hiding at present—where, you had best not know.

"I need you to obtain a licence for him to travel. My Lord Wroxeter issues men with such documents. It is likely there are some forms within his office. If you could obtain one I could smuggle Howell, under an assumed name, of course, out of the capital and he could be well on his way to Dover or Lynn within the next few days."

Cressida drew a hard breath. "You ask me to commit treason, Father. The King has been good to me—and to you. I would not wish to take part in any action which might bring him to harm, however much I think of Howell Prosser as my friend."

"Aye." Sir Daniel sighed heavily. "The King has been

good to me and I swear to you I am his loyal subject—at least, I am now.''

Cressida's heart turned to ice and she came very close to him. ''Father, what have you done?''

''Before we were summoned to Court I—'' He licked dry lips. ''Long ago, I was true to the Lancastrian cause, Cressida. I was disturbed when King Richard took the throne and concerned for the fate of the boy Princes.''

He turned away, avoiding her eyes, his voice a little hoarse with shame. ''I toyed with the thought of offering allegiance to Henry—only thought of it. I wrote letters, encouraged by the Prossers—and received replies from some exiled Lancastrian lords.''

''Sweet Virgin,'' Cressida said fervently. ''Don't you realise that it is my lord's special responsibility to ensure the safety of the King's Grace and to prosecute anyone suspected of treason or harbouring any man so accused?''

''I know that, or rather I suspected it. The truth is, if Howell Prosser is caught and interrogated, I could be in direct danger of arrest, and at this critical time, when every man's motives are questioned, there is little doubt I would be charged with treason—yes, and more than likely found guilty.''

Cressida went white to the lips. She recalled Martyn's account of what had happened to Sir Roger Clifford only weeks ago. Her heart was racing.

''And you think such blank documents are kept by Martyn and handled by his secretary?''

Sir Daniel nodded. ''These licences to travel are issued and unchallenged at the ports. Armed with one, Howell could reach Henry's court in safety. We have to help him, Cressida. If he is caught he will talk of his fellow conspirators.''

He swallowed nervously.

"However brave he thinks he is, he will be made to talk and I would be doomed by any such disclosure."

She nodded. "The document would need to be signed?"

"Probably not. Your husband's secretary may well issue them under Wroxeter's seal. There must be many of the King's officers who need to go to Calais on business frequently and in a hurry without need to consult the Earl personally. It is a chance, daughter. Will you go and search for any such blank licences—for Howell—and for me?"

She compressed her lips. "I will go for you, Father, but only on your sworn word that you will enter into no more conspiracies with the Tudor. I will not betray my husband's honour in this underhand fashion—except for your most pressing need."

He caught her to him and kissed her fiercely. "I would not ask you if the need were not desperate, Cressida. If I go down it could harm your husband's reputation and bring him down with me."

Her eyes widened in horror but, as Philip knocked at the door requesting permission to enter with the mulled ale, she nodded, and turned immediately to call to the boy.

Philip served the ale and Cressida dismissed him once more.

"Philip, will you go to the stables and make sure my mare has been exercised? I shall not be able to ride today but she should be taken out."

As the boy moved to go Sir Daniel said softly, "Could he not go first to the office and fetch the document for you?"

Cressida shook her head vehemently. "No, I prefer to go myself. Go and do what I ask, Philip."

The page looked at her curiously but she waved him off and he hastened out.

"Surely the boy could not be blamed if he were seen and it might be better so."

"No, Father," she said quietly but firmly. "I would not have young Philip blamed for what we must do." She gave a faint shudder as she thought how the boy might well be punished.

She rose at once and gestured to her father to remain seated. "Wait here for me. I should not be long."

He nodded, though his expression was still anxious.

As she suspected, Cressida found the door to her husband's office locked. Fortunately Master Rawlings was approaching down the corridor and she summoned him to provide the key.

"Lord Martyn promised to show me a letter which had arrived from the Wroxeter manor. He must have left in a hurry and forgotten it. It will be on his desk, I dare say. Give me the key, Master Rawlings."

The steward hesitated, but his mistress was clearly showing signs of impatience, and he produced the key from a bunch at his belt and opened the door.

Cressida explained as she entered. "My father is here, as you know, and would like to see the report."

Master Rawlings appeared to be waiting for her to re-emerge with her letter so that he might lock up once more, but firmly she sent him off to the kitchens.

"Tell Master Wainwright that supper should be delayed tonight as my lord might be kept late at the Tower."

He went reluctantly, looking backwards towards the office door, and she waited in the doorway, obviously determined to see him go on the errand. She smiled to herself inwardly. Master Rawlings's dignity must have been ruffled. He was unused to being sent off to give instructions to underlings as if he were a page or serving wench, but she had no wish to see him blamed either, if anything should go wrong and the loss of the travel licence were discovered. She alone, should it come to it, must shoulder the responsibility.

There were several rolls of parchment upon the desk, together with quills, penknives for sharpening and bottles of ink. One parchment lay open, a knife discarded by it as if either the Earl himself or Master Standish had been employed in scraping it clear for further correspondence. Cressida examined the rolled ones feverishly, but they appeared to be household accounts and a letter awaiting Lord Martyn's attention giving orders for the setting to rights of the Wroxeter manor for the possible arrival of the lord and his bride later in the year.

Cressida bit her lip and straightened. She had been optimistic indeed to expect travel licences to be left in full view of anyone who entered.

There were two small chests and she pulled at the lid of the left one impatiently. It was locked and she could see no small key in evidence. Obviously the Earl or his secretary carried those pertaining to private correspondence upon his person, and it would be useless to recall Master Rawlings and demand such keys from him. He would be unlikely to have access to such an item. Was she to be frustrated? If so, she would find it almost a relief—yet her father would remain in danger.

She pulled experimentally at the lid of the other chest and, to her astonishment, it came open. Either there was nothing of importance inside or Master Standish had been summoned to attend the Earl so precipitately that he had forgotten to secure it. Careful not to disturb the contents unduly and reveal the search, she sifted cautiously through them. To her joy, she discovered four small pieces of parchment sealed but unsigned, granting the bearer—and here there was space for the insertion of a name—permission to travel outside the realm.

She caught up one, returned the rest hastily to the chest and slammed it shut. Her heart was pounding erratically as she stood upright and listened to hear if Master Rawlings was about to return. He had not left the key with her, so undoubtedly he would do so very soon.

Her brows drew together as she realised he would report her presence there to his master. She would have to make some excuse for entering. That she must consider later but first she must get this to her father immediately.

It was then that she heard voices in the corridor and froze where she stood. She could not mistake her husband's peremptory tone. Why had he unexpectedly returned from the Tower? She stood irresolute as she heard Master Rawlings explaining himself.

"I was just checking that my lady the Countess had left your office, my lord. I know well your orders that the room is to be kept locked at all times when you or Master Standish are absent."

The door was jerked open abruptly and Martyn stood on the threshold staring across at her. She looked beyond him to the anxious countenance of the steward and tried to smile reassuringly.

"That is quite all right, Master Rawlings. I would have sent a page to tell you when I had finished in the room and you could lock the door again."

"You can go." Martyn dismissed his steward curtly.

He advanced further into the room, firmly shutting the door and enclosing them together, apart from prying eyes. Cressida waited, dry-mouthed, for him to demand an explanation. At last it came, coldly uttered and without any attempt at courteous preamble.

"Suppose you give me what you took from the desk."

She still remained silent, her eyes imploring, one hand behind her, resting on the desktop as if for support.

He said harshly, "Come, Cressida, obey me. I know that nonsense you talked to Rawlings about wishing to examine the Wroxeter manor accounts to be totally false. Obviously you came here to read my private correspondence, not out of curiosity but for some more dangerous purpose. Give me what you took or copied—now."

She gave a little apprehensive shudder then took the small scrap of parchment from the modesty vest of her gown where she had placed it and handed it to him without a word.

He scrutinised it quickly then sighed.

"I imagine you are not willing to tell me for whom you obtained this but I can make a calculated guess. Prosser."

She had gone very pale and her eyes shone like bruised velvet violet flowers after rain as she looked back at him, but there were no tears or hysterics as he might have expected.

"Well?" he demanded, his patience wearing thin. "Am I correct?"

"Yes," she said quietly.

"You know the man to be a traitor?"

"Yes," she admitted again.

"This declaration of friendship only is wearing a trifle thin, my dear. I am sure you are quite unwilling to tell me where the fellow is hiding or, incidentally, how you came to receive a message from him."

She shook her head mutely.

He sighed again and moved a fraction nearer to her. She flinched away from him and his level brows rose in annoyance.

"Do you believe I would beat the truth out of you?"

"I do not know," she said flatly, "but you would be

within your rights, I know that. Please do not ask me to betray Howell.'' She hesitated. ''Please, Martyn, I beg of you. I have my reasons and they are not what you suppose. I tell you again, there is nothing between Howell Prosser and I that could constitute a threat to our marriage.''

He sighed again then moved away from her to the window and stood staring out, his back to her.

She said softly, ''For my sake, my lord, will you let Howell Prosser go? If you do not it could harm others—others I love. I am assured the man can do no more harm to the King's cause. I swear I would not help him if I did not believe that.''

He turned, shrugging, then, abruptly, he thrust the travel permit to her across the desk which now was between them.

''Then I suggest you get this to your messenger as quickly as you can before I change my mind.''

She moved to the door and turned to speak to him again, but he had once more turned his back on her.

She swallowed back tears and left the room.

Her father looked up anxiously as she returned to the winter parlour. She handed him the permit and he gazed up into her taut, pale little face.

''Were there difficulties? You were not discovered?''

There was little point in alarming him further. Unexpectedly Lord Martyn had capitulated and given in to her desperate plea. She drew a hard breath as she thought it possible that her father might be observed leaving the house and be followed. It was a risk they all must take.

Somehow she believed that Martyn had understood her fear and would allow her messenger to pass unchallenged. Her alarm mounted as she thought that he might be well aware of the messenger's identity. If he intended to arrest her father, he surely would have done so already? She would pray to the Virgin that her family remained safe.

She said hastily, "No, all is well, but I think you should leave London very soon now. It will be safer—for all of us."

He took her into his arms in a bear-hug embrace.

"Don't think I am unaware of what you have done for us and what it has cost you. You are growing up fast, my daughter—too fast. Know that I love you very dearly. I will not endanger you again. I promise."

She forced a smile. "Go with God. Kiss my mother for me. I pray I shall soon see you both again."

He paused in the doorway. "Have you any message you wish me to give to Howell?"

Two bright spots of anger burned in her cheeks as she recalled how he had used her in that final talk they had had together on the Westminster quay.

"No," she said in a tight, hard voice. "Only that I wish him safely out of the country as soon as possible."

Sir Daniel bowed his head slightly as if he read the hidden message to her former friend in her contemptuous tone, then he left the room and she heard him speaking to a page outside with instructions to call for his horse to be saddled.

That night Martyn came to her chamber. Without waiting to be told, Alice made a discreet exit. Cressida waited apprehensively for her husband to approach the bed. She well understood that he was furiously angry with her but, as yet, he had made no move to reproach her or punish her.

He looked down at her impassively and she controlled the urge not to flinch from him again as she had done in the office.

"I have sent a messenger to your father requesting that he escort you to his own manor for the next few months until I am able to come and take you to Wroxeter."

She blinked uncertainly. "Tomorrow? That is very soon. I shall scarce have time to pack…"

"I have already given instructions for your maid and the other servants to see that that is completed very early in the morning."

She said appealingly, "I know you said you thought it best for me to be out of the capital during the coming summer, but could I not wait until you can take me to Wroxeter yourself?"

He said coldly, "I have told you what I have decided. For once you will obey me without question."

"How—how long do you think it will be before…?"

"I have no idea, but I will convey my later orders to you by courier."

His manner was so cold that he might have been dismissing some importunate mistress he wished to discard. She swallowed back salt tears. She had cost him dear too many times for him to forgive her. Was this to be the sum of their lives together, this polite endurance of a bond which had been forced upon them?

It wasn't enough for Cressida. She had tasted of the fruits of love and found them sweet. She ached to pull him down to her, compel him to love her as he once had, but knew she dared not. She could only hope and pray that in some future time he would find it in his heart to forgive this foolish child bride who had both embarrassed him and today forced him to acquiesce in an act of treason.

She wanted to weep, plead with him not to forsake her, but it would be useless, and she could not wound him further with pointless childish behaviour.

She shook back her hair and forced a smile to her stiffened lips.

"As you wish, my lord. My parents will be glad to have me spend some time with them."

He held her gaze deliberately with his own. "Your presence may suffice to prevent your father from taking part in any indiscreet actions."

Her eyes opened wide and he nodded coolly, then turned towards the door again. "I shall send Philip Kenton with you. I shall have need of Peter Fairley's services over the next months."

Her mouth went dry again. Peter Fairley was his squire. Did he expect to need the boy's services in battle?

As he raised the door-latch she resisted the urge to call him back. This might well be the last time she saw him. As if to reinforce that thought he said, chillingly, "I shall have left the house before you embark, having ensured everything for your comfort. Your father will doubtless dispatch a courier to assure me that you reached home safely and that all is well with you."

He was offering her no farewell kiss, no assurances of his devotion. This cold little exchange was to be their parting words and he had spoken of months, so he fully expected their separation to be lengthy. She waited until he had withdrawn, then buried her head in her pillows and sobbed out the agony of her grief.

The journey back to the Marches was as uneventful as their previous journey to London and Cressida's spirits were as low. She forced herself to be cheerful and excused her frequent laspses into despondency by references to the death of the Queen to whom she had been deeply attached, as her parents knew.

Not even the sight of her beloved manor could completely lift her heart, though the servants received her joyfully and she felt herself once more enclosed in the loving cocoon which throughout her childhood had always meant so much to her.

Sir Thomas Prosser came frequently to visit Sir Daniel and they seemed as much on good terms as previously, but no mention was ever made to Howell's absence and Cressida was not informed as to whether he had safely left the realm.

Despite her inner anger towards him for the way he had shamefully used her, she missed him. When she rode out towards Ludlow as before she found herself expecting to see him riding towards her. At least no word reached them that he had been arrested and they could only hope that all was well with him.

Her father dispatched a courier to London soon after their arrival home to inform Lord Wroxeter his wife was safe and well, as he had requested. He sent back formal messages thanking Sir Daniel for his care of Cressida and a brief, equally formal letter to Cressida, assuring her of his constant devotion and desire to see her soon on their Wroxeter manor. He passed no comments on events at Court and it seemed that he had deliberately determined to cut her off from any further disclosures which could possibly harm the King's cause if related to any of those barons thought to be secretly in league with Henry Tudor.

Cressida had hoped passionately that she had conceived but as the weeks passed that hope was dashed and, though her mother never referred to the subject, delicately avoiding the issue, Cressida was aware that her parents believed the marriage had remained unconsummated.

It seemed that they had obtained this information from Howell, though Cressida had regretted her hasty unhappy disclosure and had begged him to keep it to himself. In some strange way it was communicated to her that they were relieved that this was so and she refrained from informing them otherwise. Alice, she knew, could be relied upon to keep her own counsel.

News came to them through passing chapmen, Welsh minstrels and herdsmen who had driven their flocks westward towards the border towns of Hereford and Gloucester.

The King had declared John of Lincoln, his sister's son, his heir. The claim of his late brother's son, the youthful Earl of Warwick, had not even been considered. Clarence's lands and hereditary claims lay still under attainder and his boy heir was said to be simple-witted.

Cressida knew the boy was living at Sheriff Hutton along with his cousin, the Lady Elizabeth. She wondered how her friend was faring and would have given much to hear from her. Would the King consolidate his hold on the throne by announcing new wedding plans? She knew that that was politically necessary and, remembering the man she had seen overcome with anguish, understood how that would cost him dear.

Days and weeks passed slowly, or so it seemed to Cressida, who was impatient now to be joined by her husband and visit her own lands near Wroxeter as he had promised. She had always loved the coming of spring and the warm summer days on the Marches—the splendours of sun on grass, hawks hovering overhead in bright blue skies, the profusion of wild flowers—but now the procession of days seemed irksome.

She fretted against the necessity of sitting in the solar with her mother on those days when it was too wet for her to ride out, working on new altar cloths for the church and the repair of tapestries, in preparation for the draughty autumn and winter days to come.

She rode out one fine May day with young Philip Ken-

ton in attendance and returned to find considerable activity
within the stables. Grooms were busy rubbing down newly
arrived mounts and judging by their appearance the beasts
had been ridden hard. Cressida felt a sudden constriction
round her heart. It had been such a day, though in winter,
when she had come back from a ride to find that a courier
had arrived to summon her family to Court.

She had been afraid then that her father might have been
in some danger. Now she was even more alarmed. They
had received only snippets of news lately, though all their
neighbours were openly discussing an imminent invasion
by the Tudor. Had it come at last, the danger which Martyn
had known was threatening and which would cast its
deadly shadow over her father's household?

She asked no questions of the grooms, but handed over
their mounts and hurried Philip inside the manor house.
Her mother stood near the oriel window in the solar, gazing down over the herb plot, one hand pressed against her
heart. It was clear from her expression that she was disturbed. She forced a smile at sight of Cressida.

"It is such a fine day I thought you might stay out
longer."

"You wanted me away from the house?" The question
was posed brusquely and Lady Gretton glanced pointedly
at Philip, who stood uncertainly in the doorway.

Cressida said sharply, "I shall not want you for a while
now, Philip. Go and practise that new ballad you promised
to sing to us tonight after supper."

The boy bowed and withdrew.

"Is there news from my lord?"

Lady Gretton shook her head. She sighed wearily. "No,
a messenger has arrived from Rhys Ap Thomas." She sank
down on the padded window seat and stared bleakly back
at her daughter. "There are two of them, sounding out

your father's allegiance. I wish devoutly it were otherwise.''

"You are afraid for him?"

"Of course. Ap Thomas is a devious man and, in my opinion, not to be trusted. He hasn't decided on his own loyalty yet, I imagine, but could draw in his neighbours further than any of them would be wise to venture.''

Cressida gave a sharp intake of breath. "Has there—been any news of Howell?''

"Not that I have heard. He was in deep. I doubt he will risk himself just yet in England.''

"Father would not ally himself with the King's enemies?''

"No. He toyed with the idea once, I think, but not since your betrothal has he been in any doubt concerning the King's honour. But even the presence of these men here at this house could smell of treason. I wish we could openly refuse to receive them.''

"Why does not Father make his allegiance plain to them?''

Lady Gretton turned slowly to face Cressida. "I think he considers it politic to show no hostility to either side at this stage.''

Cressida was shocked. "He would not fight for the Tudor?''

"No, he would never go that far, but he is a border baron. He is considering carefully our safety should there be a change of ruler.''

"But the King could never lose, not in an outright battle for the crown. He is an experienced warrior *and*," she finished indignantly, "he is our anointed sovereign.''

Lady Gretton smiled a little wanly. "I see you have changed your tune since you met him. Less than a year ago you were all for joining his enemies.''

Cressida's reply sounded rueful. "Now I am a married woman and my husband is deep in the King's confidences. Where would he be if I were to show any counter-interest?"

"Just so, and was not this entirely in the King's mind when he pressed for this marriage?"

Cressida flushed hotly. "It was in his mind at the beginning, but I believe he saw advantage in this match for me too—when it came to it."

"Do you love Martyn, child?" It was a very direct question and Cressida drew another hard breath.

At last she said, "I—I think I do. I must. He is my husband."

Cressida's mother placed a hand gently on her daughter's arm. "It is well you are dutiful, but—but I wish he had not neglected you so blatantly for these months. It was not so between your father and I."

The two messengers rode out soon after and Sir Daniel strode into the solar, red-faced and grim of expression. Cressida guessed there had been hard words and argument between him and his visitors. He did not enlighten his wife and daughter as to what had occurred and neither Cressida nor her mother thought it wise to ask.

Sir Daniel stretched his legs out before him as he seated himself in his padded armchair.

"I hear the King has fitted out a squadron under Sir George Nevill to watch the coast and intercept any possible invaders. Lovell has been appointed to command the fleet at Southampton."

Cressida was deeply shocked. The situation must be serious indeed for the King to send his closest friend from his side at this critical time. She assumed that Martyn would still be at his sovereign's disposal and too occupied to write to her.

* * *

A pedlar called just after Whitsuntide and informed them that the King had left the capital for the north.

"It's being said, my lady," he said in his falsely bright, gossipy manner, "he will head for Nottingham to spend his time hunting and hawking, but we all know my lord the King 'as never bin one for such sports. Nottingham being the middle of the realm, like, he'll doubtless think it a fine spot to wait for news—"

He broke off as it dawned on him that he was about to speak what might be termed treason and Lady Gretton bestowed her most wintry smile on the man.

"Those ribbons will be all." She dismissed him coldly. "I imagine you'll want permission to sell to the serving girls. You may go to the kitchens."

He bowed himself out backwards, almost as if he were leaving the presence of royalty.

Cressida sat with a tangle of bright ribbons in her lap, her thoughts occupied with the fellow's news.

Martyn would doubtless be at Nottingham with the King, ready for any threatened action. She would not remain here waiting idly for news. Whether Martyn liked it or not, she would have no more of this enforced separation. Her place was at his side and she would not be gainsaid.

She stood up abruptly, spilling the bright ribbons to the polished oaken floor. They had stood out starkly against her mourning gown, which she continued to wear for the dead Queen. Now she knew that her drab gowns must soon be set aside again; court mourning would be over after these long weeks of her absence.

"I have decided," she said firmly as her mother looked up at her askance. "I shall send Philip to Wroxeter for an escort. I am going to Nottingham."

Recognising finality in her daughter's tone, Lady Gretton closed her lips on her intended protest and forced a confident expression.

"Since he has not sent for you, I take it Lord Martyn has been over-busied with state affairs. Doubtless he will be glad to have you with him." Privately she considered that unlikely to be the case, but there was no arguing with Cressida in this present mood, as she would inform her husband. Warningly, she glanced across at him as his head jerked up in sudden alarm.

He frowned, considering. "Well," he conceded after a moment's thought, "you should be safe enough with an escort from your husband's manor, but without sufficient men-at-arms to form a safe escort I cannot allow you to go. Times are too unsettled."

Cressida was determined to go whatever happened but she did not argue with him now. Instead she cast him an approving smile.

Protected by an escort of ten of her husband's men-at-arms, Cressida rode out of Gretton on a fine hot day in early July. Philip rode happily at her side and it was obvious that he was as anxious to rejoin his master as she was. The burly sergeant in command of the escort was by no means so pleased. He had been summoned to Gretton by his new Countess and, despite all his argument to the contrary and his protestations that he had no orders from the Earl to leave the manor, he had been constrained to do his new mistress's bidding.

It had been very clear to him from the beginning of the interview that this authoritative young woman was by no means the docile and biddable child bride he and the rest of the Wroxeter household had been expecting, but a very formidable lady indeed. Cressida had made it very plain that, with or without his support, she would journey to the

Midlands, and reluctantly he had given way and had agreed to provide the necessary company of armed men. Blame would undoubtedly fall upon his hapless shoulders if any harm was to come to the Countess on such a rash undertaking, but he had bowed to the force of her determination.

Now he rode sourly at the head of the escort, his eyes peeled for any possible danger lurking behind forest land and hedges bordering their road and the glint of sun on metal which would apprise him of the presence of mounted men in the vicinity.

He cursed under his breath. Anything could happen on this ill-advised venture and, whichever way events came, he would be blamed. Already he was hearing in his imagination the blistering rebuke he would receive from the Earl on his arrival in Nottingham. He had been put in charge of the defence of Wroxeter in the light of possible alarms within the volatile Border country and had been hard put to it to find a suitable man to leave in charge there.

Undoubtedly his principal duty was the defence of his Countess, but he was no happy man and constantly cast Cressida dark glances whenever he thought himself unobserved.

Cressida was far too busy with her own thoughts to give heed to the man's brooding disapproval. She was hearing again in her mind her mother's question—''Do you love Martyn, child?'' If she did not, why was she in such haste to reach his side? He would not be pleased. She bit her lip uncertainly as it occurred to her that he might well have found some other, more accommodating mistress to warm his bed.

She had been a constant thorn in his flesh since her arrival in Westminster. She had been pressed upon him, willy-nilly, by his sovereign, and the doubtful loyalties of her father made association with her family dangerous in the extreme. He had shown irritation, downright exasperation with her, but—her cheeks flushed red as she recalled the ecstasy of their love-making—he must have had some deep affection for her to give her such joy.

What did she feel for him? From the beginning he had aroused her interest. She had been piqued by his determination to treat her as a child, while the excited arousal she experienced whenever he was near told her the contrary was true. She had never felt such stirrings during her long association with Howell. She had longed for Martyn to consummate their marriage and now that he had done so she was not disappointed.

She pictured him in her mind's eye: that tall, rangy body, hard-muscled, the deceptive sleepy gaze, which gave the appearance of slow-witted joviality. She knew his mind was razor-sharp and feared his ability to strike mercilessly at those he considered his King's enemies. He would be a gallant and loyal friend and a dangerous and ruthless antagonist. In this coming struggle for the crown Richard would need him, as he would need all those loyal northern gentlemen who had been his companions since childhood.

In combat Martyn could be killed. An icy chill swept through her at the thought. She *must* reach him, beg his forgiveness for her final betrayal of his trust. Her mother's question was answered by the terrible fear she had for his safety. She loved him, desired him, ached for his nearness. All these days of separation had been a torment. Now, despite the anger she would see in his expression on her arrival, she had to be near him.

Chapter Nine

Lord Martyn handed his latest report to the King as he sat sprawled in his favourite armchair in the hunting lodge near Bestwood. Richard had left Nottingham Castle some days ago, intent on filling his restless hours in the hectic pursuit of the chase. He watched Richard now as he sat forward in the chair to catch the light the better to peruse the report.

These waiting days were trying for all of them around the King. He could see that these last months since Anne's death had aged Richard more than he could have believed possible. There were purple shadows below his eye sockets, deep lines of suffering from nostrils to mouth, and that mouth, which had always been held in a tense line of concentration and anxiety, showed signs now of rigidity, revealing a harshness of purpose which Martyn had never seen there before.

He told himself, with a sigh, that that was just as well. Richard had ever been too trusting and willing to forgive those who betrayed him. Now it was necessary for the good of the realm that he should face squarely the guilt of those who would destroy him and eliminate them without mercy.

The King looked up and sighed. "So you distrust the motives of Lord Stanley in failing to come to join our force here, insisting on remaining on his Cheshire estates? You think his excuse of poor health suspect?"

"Your Grace, one must always keep in mind that the Lady Margaret, Lord Stanley's wife, is Henry Tudor's mother. Despite his protestations of loyalty Lord Thomas would have much to gain if the Earl of Richmond were to ascend the throne. You were wise to request that Lord Strange remain at Court during his father's absence."

"As a hostage?" The King's lips twisted sardonically. "It is not a course I find to my taste, Martyn."

"But Your Grace must see the necessity."

"Yes, yes," he replied a trifle testily. "Your report informs us that the Marquis of Dorset appears to regret his offer of support to Henry Tudor and apparently attempted to leave him and return home."

"My spy is sure that that move was prompted by a letter from the Dowager Queen advising him to return to his allegiance. Unfortunately—" Lord Martyn shrugged regretfully "—he left Paris heading for Flanders to take ship for home, but was taken into protective custody at Compiègne by Humphrey Cheney and was forced to return with him to Paris."

The King's lips parted in a smile. "Poor Thom; he appears to be able to do nothing right. At least I am reassured that the Dowager Queen now seems to trust me to do what is best for her children."

Martyn nodded. "I think it behooves us to keep a very close watch upon Lord Stanley's heir, Lord Strange."

The King was about to reply when a knock came on the door and Martyn turned angrily.

"Your Grace, I gave strict instructions that we were not

to be disturbed and left Peter Fairley outside to see that my orders were obeyed implicitly.''

"It would seem that either Peter has been removed forcibly—since nothing else would cause him to desert his post—or he has something of great importance to tell us. I think we should admit whoever it is.''

Lord Martyn's squire looked anxiously at his master's grim countenance as he entered and bowed at the Earl's barked invitation.

"Your Grace, my lord, forgive me for intruding, but I thought you should know, sir—'' here he gave another alarmed glance towards his master ''—that—that my lady, the Countess, has arrived.''

Lord Martyn looked thunderstruck. "Countess? Countess of what?''

"I think Peter is endeavouring to explain that my lady your wife is here at Bestwood.'' The King was smiling hugely now.

"Cressida, here?'' Martyn was about to explode into a furious oath, but the King gently shook his head, indicating the presence of Peter.

The boy nodded mutely in answer to his master's questioning glance.

The King signalled to the squire. "Admit your lady, Peter. It would be discourteous to keep her waiting.''

"How dare she disobey me and leave Gretton without my leave?'' Martyn fumed.

"She is indeed a lady of spirit.''

"But, Your Grace, now is not the time for—''

"I know that, Martyn, and so does she. I imagine her presence here is not the result of a whim, but of a genuine concern to be near you in time of crisis.'' He turned away and Martyn was aware that his unspoken thought was that the Queen, had it been possible, would have moved heaven and earth to be by her husband's side at this time.

There was a flurry of movement by the door and Martyn turned to see Cressida curtseying low, flanked by the stolid form of Alice Croft.

The King gestured for her to come forward. "It is good to receive you at Bestwood, Lady Cressida."

Cressida avoided eye contact with Martyn as she bent to kiss the King's extended hand.

"Your Grace, I should not have dared to come to the lodge without direct invitation, but I discovered in Nottingham that my husband was here and felt I could not ask the castle castellan for lodging without his permission and I—"

He waved aside her apology. "Of course you will be welcome at the castle. I suggest you escort your lady there, Martyn, and remain there yourself for a while. You can report to me here whenever it is necessary."

Martyn began to protest, but the King was insistent. "I would like you to go at once and dictate that letter to my secretary—the business concerning Lord Strange." He rose and, placing an arm on Martyn's shoulder, moved with him to the door. "Then return here. I insist that Lady Cressida dine with us before you withdraw her from our company."

He smiled genially. "Meanwhile I shall spend one or two private moments with her. I trust you will grant me that pleasure, though I know you must now be anxious to have her to yourself."

As they reached the door he bent and said very softly, "I know you are angry, Martyn, but go easy. Take my advice, my friend; spend time with your lady. This opportunity may not come again. If I read you rightly, these moments will be very precious and who knows when or if they will ever come again?''

Martyn stared at him wordlessly. The warning communication passed between them and Martyn gave a great sigh.

''My lord…''

''I know you love her.''

''More than my life…''

''Do not waste these hours, Martyn. You and I both know there is a world of time for regrets.''

Martyn bowed his head, unwilling for his sovereign to see the tears sparkling on his lashes. He had been too close to Richard over these last months not to realise how the man was suffering the terrible pain of loss. Not even his constant occupation with the threatened invasion and perusal of the many reports from scurriers, nor the recent issuing of commissions of array, could take away the hours of loneliness when he was withdrawn from his companions.

He had, himself, felt the separation from Cressida. In the lonely hours of the night he had ached for the sight of her, but had considered it best for her welfare if she could be kept clear of this. Now she was here and he could not prevent his whole being from crying out a paeon of joy. He could not play the tyrant now and send her home, not without some time for them to enjoy each other's company for what might very well be the final time.

He said a trifle hoarsely, ''I take your meaning, Your Grace. For these next days I shall cherish her, but I must soon dispatch her to safety again.''

''You will know the time.''

The King waited while Martyn turned down an angle of the corridor and was lost to sight. His lips twisted at the sight of Peter Fairley's puzzled countenance. ''Stay at your post, lad. Never fear; I doubt that the full force of your master's fury will fall on you. More likely to descend on the sergeant-at-escort's head.''

Cressida was staring at the King wide-eyed as he returned to her side then crossed to a small travelling chest which stood on a stool near the window.

"I needed to get rid of Martyn for moments."

She started and he laughed at her concern. "I have something for you which I think you would rather he did not see."

He lifted the lid of the chest and withdrew a small book which he placed in Cressida's hands. "There is a letter inside from the Lady Elizabeth. I have been puzzling for some days over how I might get it to you without undue notice." His eyes were twinkling as she gazed down at the rubbed leather cover, then up into the King's shrewd grey gaze.

"The Book of Hours belonged to my brother. Elizabeth thought I would wish to have it. She put the message to you inside."

Cressida fumbled to extricate the message but his hand closed on hers. "I would like you to have the book. I know how you value her friendship. I have other gifts from my brother, the late King. It would please me to know you treasure it. Anne would have liked you to have it, I know."

She stooped to kiss his hands, her eyes brimming with tears, but there was no time for further words of gratitude for at that moment Martyn arrived back in the chamber and the King dismissed them, jovially ordering them to withdraw and to prepare to eat dinner in an hour's time.

The return to Nottingham Castle was made almost in silence. Cressida had hardly exchanged more than a word or two with her husband during dinner, the King having dominated the conversation, chatting pleasantly about the environs of the hunting lodge, their successes and failures in the hunts, and also enquiring politely after the health of her parents. All the time Cressida had been conscious that Martyn was sitting beside her, simmering with rage.

Partly thankful that the meal was over and with it the need for court protocol, and half-alarmed at the explosion of temper which she feared would descend upon her hapless head when they were at last alone together, Cressida dismounted her jennet in a confused mood, only glancing up briefly at their sergeant-at-arms, whose expression told her that he was as alarmed as she was at the prospect of facing his lord's wrath any moment now.

Lord Martyn ordered Cressida's baggage to be brought up to the apartments in the castle set aside for him and strode through the hall, Cressida and Alice striving hard to keep pace with him.

The Earl's chambers were surprisingly commodious. Cressida had been used to cramped quarters at Westminster, but then, few courtiers were now in attendance on the sovereign and those who were were hardened campaigners in advising the monarch as to future combat strategy.

Cressida found that, though the bedchamber was luxuriously furnished, Martyn had apparently unpacked few of his clothes or possessions—or perhaps, she mused, he had brought little with him, wishing to travel light in case of need.

Alice glanced round briefly and immediately set about unpacking for Cressida. Shortly afterwards Lord Martyn strode grimly into the chamber and dismissed the maid.

''Go and see about arrangements for your accommodation. Send one of my men to obtain a truckle-bed for you and see it set up in a room near your mistress. I'll send when I want you.''

Philip had been sent off to the great hall with Peter Fairley. The boy would soon make friends amongst the other assembled pages. Cressida would see to it that no blame would be laid at his door for her disobedient conduct.

Once alone with her husband, she decided to take the initiative. ''There is not the slightest use in raging at poor Philip or at Sergeant Chubb either. I and I alone am responsible for the decision to leave the Marches.''

She faced him squarely and he caught his breath at the splendour of her lovely young body held rigid with steely determination, spine erect, head high, chin jutting obstinately.

''I am sure of it,'' he returned mildly, ''and had no intention of punishing either.''

She was put off course by his agreeable tone and stared back at him in amazement.

''I insisted—said I would travel alone if Chubb would not provide an escort. He had to agree, but I understand he has made adequate arrangements for the defence of Wroxeter in case of need...'' Her voice trailed off as she recognised the reason for his decision to isolate her from Court in the first place.

He remained silent, seated in the window seat, staring out over the castle pleasance, which had been sadly neglected over the last year, although a climbing white rose had bloomed in spite of lack of careful pruning and its scent was heady in their chamber. He turned and looked full at her.

''Come here.''

She hesitated, then moved from the bed to come doubtfully towards him.

''I'm sorry, my lord, but I had to come. We heard news. Events were following each other so rapidly that I—I—''

"Yes?" he prompted softly.

"I—I wanted to be with you in case—in case—" She rushed on almost incoherently, "I know you cannot really want to be bothered with the need to watch over me at this time, but I swear I will not prove to be difficult and—"

"Cressida, you have always been difficult."

She swallowed hard, feeling tears threatening. How could she explain how she felt? "I am your wife," she declared defiantly, shaking back her hair. She had removed her hennin and veil, thinking that she and Alice would be alone in the chamber until he had entered unexpectedly. Her glorious golden locks streamed unrestrained down her back and her luminous eyes were lambent with unshed tears.

He had never seen her so lovely and his loins had ached for her over these long months. The light from the window limned the rounded beauty of her upthrust breasts, the thin stuff of her blue summer riding gown moulding them tight by the fashionable high waistline, for she had put off mourning for the journey.

Here was no child bride, but a mature and passionate young woman. He made a little inarticulate sound deep in his throat, stood up abruptly and pulled her fiercely into his arms.

Startled into instant acquiescence, her mouth opened sweetly under his and her body responded, pressing itself close to his, without the need for restraint. His kiss scorched her, sending waves of heat through her whole being. She had wanted this for so long. She returned his kisses passionately, accepting his absolute need for her. For moments they clung together, wordlessly, her arms stealing up around his neck while he pressed her even closer.

At last he drew away, holding her gently by the shoulders at arm's length.

"Let me look at you."

She stared back at him proudly, the ivory of her cheeks flushed with the warm glow of love.

"Sweet Virgin, how I've longed for sight of you all these months, and now here you are, a fairy queen, rather than the fairy child I was remembering."

She said softly, "I do not think I was ever the child you imagined, my lord, not even when you first mistook me for one in the tilt-yard at Westminster."

He gave a little laugh. "Perhaps you're right. You are so tiny, so exquisite, it seemed a sacrilege to touch you then."

"And you were full of guilt because you thought you'd not completed the full mourning for the Lady Elinor."

"That may be so. Who knows what guilt can do? I only know that the first time I saw you properly, in the King's presence chamber, desire gnawed at my loins."

She was content now to tantalise him a little. "You are glad to see me, then?"

"Sweet wounds of Christ, how can you ask me that? How in the name of all the Saints am I to send you back? Anywhere now you could be at risk, with armed men at large. I sent you to the Marches for your own safety. I cannot escort you myself. I—"

"Then you must keep me near you," she said confidently, "which is what I intended. Where can I feel more secure than near my husband?"

"Cressida, I must soon fight for the King."

"Will it come soon?" she asked softly, and he nodded.

"We already know Henry has borrowed considerable sums of gold from the French king. We hear he has gone to Normandy. At any moment I expect my spies to inform me he has embarked.''

Her lips parted in wonder. ''The kingdom cannot be in danger, surely? The King has all his forces at his disposal, Henry just a few disgruntled rebels.''

''More rebels than you think.'' He had released her and was about to pace the room as he often did in times of doubt. He saw her face change and put an imperative hand upon her arm.

''Your father has not foolishly involved himself in this?''

She shook her head. ''Messengers have been riding in, two from Rhys Ap Thomas, but my father has sworn he will take no part in open insurrection; rather he will put what few men he has at His Grace's disposal.''

Martyn frowned. ''He would do better to hold himself ready to defend his own land. Were it possible I would send you back forthwith to him.''

''But suppose the invasion were to come from Wales?''

Those heavy lids of his swept upwards and she saw a strange gleam in his eyes. ''You have some suspicion of this?''

''No, none at all. It is just that—Ap Thomas is in league with Sir John Savage, they say, and Jasper Tudor was Earl of Pembroke. If the Welsh see Henry as their natural leader...''

''He is no more truly Welsh than the King,'' Martyn snapped. ''I would wager Richard speaks more Welsh than the Tudor. The man is French in outlook, has spent his youth there and relies totally on French gold and support.''

She reached up and gently touched his cheek. ''You are fearful, Martyn? I think this is unlike you.''

He gave a rueful grin. ''Like His Grace, I shall be confident enough when we are on the march and know what to expect, but it has been my work to sift through these varying reports and I do not altogether like what I read.''

''You fear betrayal?''

''Aye.'' The single word was grimly uttered. ''We have had a quiet time in England after Tewkesbury, with only minor alarms and skirmishes, but men will risk much for offers of land and preferment and the Lancastrians have never been content. To add to this, the people have been disturbed by scurrilous tales of the King's perfidy, as you know well, and the doubtful fate of the Princes weighs hard against him.''

Cressida's lips tightened. ''You do not believe the King capable of…?''

''No, no. I am one of the few knowledgeable about that matter, but, for obvious reasons, Richard will not divulge the truth of this business, especially at this time, even to secure the trust of doubting subjects. He fears for the boys' safety.''

Cressida gave a little shudder. Only too clearly did she see how vulnerable the Princes would be should Henry Tudor wed their sister and claim right of sovereignty through her.

Martyn drew her close again. ''It seems I have only one course now—to protect you myself. While I am alarmed for what might come, I will not deny it will comfort me greatly to have you near me at this time. Well, wench, since you are here, I shall set you to work to refurbish my shabby banners and take charge of my domestic household.''

She shook her head regretfully. ''I fear I am no hand with the needle, as Alice will testify, and your household has always seemed perfectly disciplined, if I am any judge. I am at a loss to know what help I can be to you.''

He laughed then, uproariously. "Do you not, my lady? Then I shall very soon tutor you in the skills I require."

He laughed again as her answering flush spread from her glowing cheeks to her throat and breast.

"I shall strive to be a responsive scholar, my lord."

It was after she had retired with Alice and was waiting for Martyn to join her that Cressida remembered that she had not yet looked at the letter from the Lady Elizabeth.

It was quite short, but affectionate enough in tone to relieve Cressida's mind.

My very dear Cressida,

It was a great comfort to me to receive your message, which His Grace was magnanimous enough to forward to me. Please absolve yourself of all blame for my dismissal from Court. Unfortunately, we are all unwilling pawns of those about us. I have only regret that, unwittingly, I may have harmed the King's cause by my wish to serve him. It is necessary always to be guarded in all matters. From your affectionate and dutiful friend, Elizabeth Plantagenet.

The letter was addressed to "The Lady Cressida, Countess of Wroxeter, from the hand of the Lady Elizabeth Plantagenet, written at Sheriff Hutton on the fourteenth day of June in the year of our Lord 1485."

Hastily Cressida returned the missive to its hiding place within the Book of Hours which was the King's gift. The seal on the letter had not been broken, or so it seemed, but the tone was indeed guarded and Cressida could not be sure that it had not been read by eyes other than her own.

Had the King seen his niece's letter? She thought not, doubting that he would betray her trust in his discretion.

At all events, Cressida was unwilling for Martyn to know that she was still in contact with the Lady Elizabeth. Their friendship had always been a bone of contention between herself and her husband, and at this moment, when he gave every sign of wanting her love, she had no wish to allow this difference to come between them.

When Martyn came at last she saw that he was still troubled.

"Has there been further news, my lord?"

He shook his head. "No—or, at least, nothing of importance. One of my couriers came in an hour ago. He gives me information about the movements of one or two lords whose loyalty I doubt, but nothing to give us cause for concern."

He looked down at her and his expression cleared. Her bedgown of pink brocade had fallen open and he had a tantalising glimpse of rosy-tipped breasts as round and firm as apples just ripe to be picked. Her belly was flat and taut, yet her hips were already rounding deliciously with advancing womanhood. He discarded his clothing hurriedly and drew her hungrily towards the bed.

His lovemaking was tender, yet Cressida guessed at the desperation held in check by his determination to treat her considerately. Again, as at the first time, he wooed her body with gentle, teasing kisses until he sensed she was ready to respond. She did so with equal hunger, delighting in the ecstasy of fulfilment, and, afterwards, lying beside him content, her body glowing with the sweat of love.

Once, in the night, when she wakened suddenly, it was to find him sitting up in the bed staring down at her so intently that she wondered if the force of his desire had caused her to waken. She gave a shaky little laugh and reached up to wind her arms round his neck and pull him down to her again, revelling in the feel of his hard-muscled body against her own.

He took her passionately this time, satisfying his own need quickly, and she thought that perhaps he had not taken his pleasure with other women over these last months as she had believed. Certainly she would never question him about it. She was content to know that he wanted her now, and desired only to give him happiness.

Over the next weeks Cressida was to know nights of intense delight, tempered by the unspoken knowledge that they could end very suddenly. By day Martyn was often from her side, his duties on the King's war council keeping him fully occupied at Bestwood where the King continued, outwardly, to give the impression to his people that he was enjoying the hunt.

At the beginning of August the royal household returned to Nottingham Castle and Cressida rejoiced, for it was no longer necessary for Martyn to leave her so early each day.

During the heat-laden nights when the heady scents of lavender and rose seeped into their chamber from the opened casement—for Martyn, unlike her parents, rejoiced in the cooler air, refusing to believe that it carried contagion—she would lie in his arms replete with love, hardly daring to sleep while he rested secure beside her.

She would wake often to gaze down at him where he had pushed the sheets impatiently aside, marvelling in the ever familiar knowledge of his body, the soft brown hairs, intermingled with the lighter golden ones of his chest, the slim waist and strong, muscular thighs which would hold her fast in the act of love, even the one or two whitening scars which spoke of the battles in which he had taken wounds.

One evening she ran her fingers lightly along a deeper

grove extending from his neck to his shoulder. Here the skin was still puckered and the scar itself still purplish.

"Where did you get this?"

He guided her fingertips, feather-light, down to his waist.

"On the border. We encountered a thieving reiver band and they struck us from ambush. I fear I was ill prepared that day. One stinking borderer's sword pierced between my gorget and breastplate and our surgeon was forced to cauterise the wound."

She winced inwardly at the ugly mind picture of him being held down while a heated sword was laid flat, smoking, on his agonised flesh.

"Did you kill the man?"

He gave a grim splutter of laughter. "No; thanks to the Virgin, my lord Richard saw all and rode the fellow down, felling him with his battleaxe."

She compressed her lips. Martyn's love for his sovereign was all-encompassing and would lead him to risk himself rashly in the cause he served so loyally. She suppressed a frisson of fear and bent to press her lips to the puckered flesh.

She prayed continually that she would conceive Martyn's child. Once or twice he had looked at her quizzically, as if he feared that she might do so, and she remembered how he had spoken of his wish that her family might continue to believe that the marriage was unconsummated.

Had he such fears concerning the outcome of this coming campaign that he would wish to leave her utterly free if the worst happened? At such time, fear would freeze her very marrow until she saw the air of calm confidence on the King's face and the cheerful exuberance of his principal officers. If the King was so sure of success, why should she fear?

* * *

Very early on the morning of August the eleventh Cressida was startled upright in the bed by urgent knocking upon their chamber door. Struggling up from deep sleep, Martyn sat up blinking, leaning up on one elbow.

"What in the devil's name is it?" he snapped.

"Peter Fairley, my lord. We've urgent news from the West. Scurriers rode in during the night and—"

"Very well." Martyn was instantly awake. "I'll be down in the hall within minutes. Come to my ante-room and help me dress."

He bent and kissed Cressida's tousled hair. "I don't know if I can breakfast with you today, my love."

"You will let me know?"

"Aye, as soon as I'm sure the King is informed and everything put in hand that is needful."

She watched anxiously as he pulled the cord of his bed-gown tightly round him and moved into the small room nearby that he used as a dressing room. She could hear him talking to Peter, but could not distinguish what was said. Sighing, she rang the small silver bell which brought Alice to her side, knowing it would be useless to try to sleep any longer.

"Well?" the Earl said as he struggled into hose and shirt.

Peter bent to help tie the points. "It's come, my lord. The Tudor has landed at Milford Haven. The King has already been told and summons you to Council."

Lord Martyn grunted. "Good. Who is with him, Peter?"

"Sir Richard Ratcliffe, my lord. Lord Lovell is still in the south. Some of the northern knights—Sir Dominick Allard, Sir Guy Jarvis…"

"Jarvis? So he has ridden south, has he?" Martyn's tone was harsh. "I want you to send a messenger in haste to Master Standish. Tell him I wish him to question Lord

Strange. He is not to hesitate; he has the King's authority through me. Instruct him to get Sir James Tyrell to act with him.''

"Yes, my lord.''

Peter completed his work of dressing his master and exited as Martyn waved at him impatiently. Martyn then plunged his face into a bowl of cold water poured from the huge earthern jug by his squire and towelled himself dry. Feeling more wide awake now, he hastened below to the great hall.

The King greeted him cheerfully. "I see you've been informed, Martyn. Wales, eh? I had expected the landing to come in the south. Your lady spoke of the possibility of Wales, I believe?''

"Only because there had been some coming and going of messengers and neighbours at Gretton. She assures me her father is totally loyal, Your Grace.''

"I received a courier sent on from Sir Daniel informing me that he intended to join me with a force of some one hundred and fifty men.''

"God grant he is not prevented by Henry's advance,'' Martyn murmured.

"I shall summon Norfolk north with Surrey and Brackenbury. Comissions of array have been sent to Northumberland. I have assurances from Sir Thomas Bouchier and Sir Walter Hungerford that they intend to ride north also.''

Sir Richard Ratcliffe looked up with a grim smile from the vellum map the household gentlemen had been examining.

"His Grace thinks it best to make for Watling Street. Undoubtedly Henry Tudor will attempt to reach London, more than likely by that route, and he must be cut off.''

Martyn nodded in agreement. The King joined them after giving some instruction to his squire.

"I cannot say I'm disturbed by this news, Martyn. I've been spoiling for battle long enough. We are in the hand of God now, my friend."

"Aye, my lord."

"You look concerned. We have taken all precautions…"

"True, Your Grace. I've no lack of confidence in our ability to meet this challenge. My concern was personal. I fear for the safety of my lady. I had wished to send her home. Now that appears impossible."

The King's eyes twinkled. "She must ride out with us, Martyn. I shall go to Leicester. I am informed the castle hall roof is in some state of disrepair but, in all events, I shall not remain in the town long. Accommodation should be available for Lady Wroxeter in the castle gatehouse. See to it when we arrive."

He placed a hand on Martyn's arm. "I know how you feel, old friend, but she should be safe enough there." His grey eyes looked into the far distance as he added, "Anne would have wished to be near me at such a time."

Cressida rode beside Martyn in the army which set out for Leicester on August the sixteenth, the day following the Feast of the Assumption. She marvelled at the imposing war panoply and was not surprised by the crowds of curious townsfolk and peasants who flocked to see the King ride south.

Richard was mounted upon his favourite white charger, White Surrey, and attired in the armour which Martyn had told her he had worn at Tewkesbury, when scarce eighteen years of age. His body had thickened little since that time. Cressida had not seen her husband armoured since that first time in the tilt-yard, and then it had been in jousting armour. Peter Fairley, grave-faced, rode behind.

Through the Nottinghamshire countryside the army progressed, marching four abreast, the baggage train in the centre. The King himself with his household knights followed, Martyn and Cressida within that company, protected by the wings of mounted cavalrymen.

Cressida's heart was thumping hard against her ribcage, yet she was in no way afraid for her own safety, only for Martyn and the success of the King's righteous cause. She had received a message from her father that he would await the King in Leicester, so she would see him then. She had also received, stoically enough, Martyn's grave command that she should remain within the town when the royal army marched out.

These, then, were the last days she would spend with her husband before the battle. She wondered, fleetingly, if Howell Prosser was in the rebel army with Henry Tudor, marching relentlessly through Wales.

On the last night of the march Cressida slept cradled in her husband's arms in a curtained-off corner of the hall of some Leicestershire manor whose squire had agreed to accommodate members of the King's household. Martyn was very tender and loving with her and it was all she could do to hold back her tears. She had a terrible presentiment that all was not well.

Martyn bent to kiss away a solitary tear. "Be brave, my love. This business will take only days and soon we shall be back together in the Strand house in London."

"I have had you for such a short time, discovered my love, and now—" she gulped helplessly "—I am so afraid for you. You said yourself that there are traitors abroad. When Lord Strange tried to escape from house arrest and was recaptured he admitted that his uncle, Sir William Stanley, and Sir John Savage have declared for Henry Tudor. Can his father, Lord Thomas, be trusted?"

Martyn's voice was falsely cheerful. "I have had my doubts about the man, but Strange swears his father is still loyal and the King refuses to believe ill of him. Despite these few traitors the King has many true friends and his army well outnumbers that of the Tudor." He bent and nuzzled her ear.

"Have you no confidence in your husband's warlike skills? I'm an experienced warrior, I assure you, and too much in love with my wife to take undue risks. That is never good battle strategy in any case."

She forced a smile then for his benefit and again when they rode into Leciester town to be met by open-mouthed townsfolk and yokels who had come to see the King ride up the high street by the swine market and take up accommodation in the inn of the White Boar.

The landlord came out sweating, agitatedly wiping his greasy hands upon his apron and anxious to please his sovereign and oversee the positioning of the great bed, which the King took upon his travels, in his finest bedroom.

The town was already packed to overflowing by the supporting forces of John, Duke of Norfolk, and his son, the Earl of Surrey, Sir Robert Brackenbury, the King's Constable of the Tower and many other lords with their men-at-arms who had come to defeat the traitorous Welshman who dared to challenge Richard for the crown of England.

The King's officers were already established in the inn, ready to receive instructions and offer advice about the order of march in the morning, for the King intended no delay. Martyn excused himself and obtained permission to accompany Cressida to the castle gatehouse. The King, despite his urgent business, called her to him before she departed with Martyn.

"You will be reasonably comfortable, my Lady Cressida, until that fine husband of yours comes again to claim you. I'll send him as soon as I can. Be very sure of that.''

He looked confident but tired, and Cressida glimpsed the marks of suffering on his clever features. She bent to kiss his hand.

''God guard you, Your Grace.''

He stooped and dropped a light kiss upon her bright hair where the hood of her travelling cloak had fallen back.

''Thank you, my child. I know that you were not pleased at first by the marriage I made for you, but I shall pray for your happiness. Pray for me, Cressida, and for all of us.''

''I will, sire.''

She was determined not to give way to tears when Martyn left her in the capable hands of one of the harassed castle serving women. He had left her with two grizzled veterans who had served at Barnet and Tewkesbury and Towton before that. They were not pleased to be left behind in this decisive battle, but knew they must obey their orders and guard their lord's lady with their very lives.

Philip was with her, and Alice, and she waved to Martyn cheerfully, though her heart misgave her as he strode off to return to the council of war at the White Boar with the rest of the King's commanders.

Lord Martyn stood a little apart from the group of household knights and lords who surrounded the King on the ridge above the village of Sutton Cheney. From here he could see the countryside for miles around, green, uncultivated land, marshy in places, especially on the edges of the ridge and near the spring behind them where his squire, Peter Fairley, was even now watering Martyn's courser and his own mount.

The King had camped near the village overnight and Martyn had emerged from his tent during the evening to see the fires of the royal camp and those of the opposing army in the distance. Jack Wainwright, who had insisted on marching with the army and abandoning his kitchen, had told him that the enemy was camped near Dadlington. Jack had kin in the nearby town of Leicester and others in Shenton near here, and had some knowledge of the lie of land.

It was still early in the morning of August the twenty-second, and the heat mist was now just dissolving, so that Martyn could again glimpse the enemy men-at-arms massing for battle formation.

He glanced round doubtfully at the forces of the Earl of Northumberland drawn up close to Sutton village, a reserve force to be called on to reinforce the two main battle formations, Norfolk's in the van and the King's main force behind, as had been decided at last night's battle conference. Martyn would fight beside the King in the company of his former companions from the days of the border campaigns.

He was glad to recognise the friendly faces of Sir Richard Ratcliffe and Sir Robert Percy with the Lord Chamberlain, Lord Lovell, who was at this moment talking animatedly to Richard, who leaned close to listen. Also there was Sir Robert Brackenbury, Lord Ferrers of Chartley and other, lesser knights who had served Richard well in the past—men like Sir Dominick Allard and Sir Guy Jarvis.

William Catesby, a lawyer who had once been in service to Lord Hastings and was now deep in the King's confidence, was nervously fiddling with his mail gauntlet as he talked with the King's secretary, the bluff John Kendall. These two were not experienced knights yet both had taken up arms to be with their sovereign on this momentous day, as Wainwright had insisted he be by Martyn's side as he had been on other campaigns.

The King had heard mass in the little plain church at Sutton and Martyn had knelt on the hard floor and prayed not only for victory but also for the safety of his beloved wife, Cressida.

He fingered the small reliquary which hung by a fine chain around his neck. Cressida had placed it there after she had helped Peter with the refractory buckles on his vambrace when he had gone back to her after the war council at the White Boar in the early hours of August the twenty-first. She had risen and come to him at once when he was announced just before dawn and he had held her so tight to his body that he had feared afterwards that he had cracked her ribs.

She had kissed him hungrily and laughed at his fears for her comfort.

"What are a few bruises? Oh, my love, I thought never to see you again when you went off to the inn."

"Are you comfortable here?"

"Yes, well cared for by Alice, and young Philip is keen to serve me and rouse the slow servants, though he would have loved to go with you. The castle servants are all bewildered by events, poor souls. Martyn, how is the King?"

"Cheerful and confident, outwardly at least."

"Was Northumberland at the conference? I know you were concerned about his slowness to comply with the commission of array."

"Yes, not pleased, but there, and agreeable to what was decided. Lovell is here. The king was delighted to see him. Francis had to ride hard to reach us in time." He had bent closer, his hands urgently squeezing her shoulders as he had stared, bewitched, at the glorious hair which streamed below her shoulders to her slim waist. "Have you had news of your father?"

She had shaken her head. "No, no word. He was riding

through the border. I pray he has not been attacked by rebel outriders.''

''He may well have been delayed,'' he had comforted. ''Whatever happens, whatever you hear, remain in the safety of the castle environs until I come or send you word.''

He had seen alarm reveal itself in her widened eyes and had quickly kissed her soundly. ''Just a precaution. Trust no one with information about the battle but those you know well.''

She had nodded silently and two tears had rolled down onto her pale cheeks. ''I shall go to the chapel and pray continually. Oh, take care, my love, for I do not think I could live on without you.''

Then it was that she had given him the relinquary. ''It has an enamelled likeness of St Martin of Tours. I meant it for your birthday in October but I want its added protection for you now.'' And she had slipped it over his mailed shoulders. The chain was long and fine and he had thought it needed to be stronger for such duty, but he would not have left it off for anything in the world.

She had clung to him then, desperately, until he had gently put her aside as the dawn light grew stronger. He had turned once at the door to fill his eyes with one last sight of her, then had gone hurriedly from the room.

Trumpets sounded shrilly and destriers behind the line neighed and pawed the ground restlessly. Martyn saw men round him hastily cross themselves and did likewise. He saw the banner of the lion stream in the wind as Norfolk began the march down Ambien Hill, named, so Wainwright had said, for its single tree, to take up his position. He wondered if the message pinned to the Duke's tent flap warning him of betrayal disturbed him.

"Jockey of Norfolk be not too bold
For Dickon, thy master, he bought and sold."

Martyn approved of the King's decision to take command of the high ground. In the distance he saw a blur of green jacks as Henry's advance battle formation began also to advance under the command of the Earl of Oxford. Martyn could just distinguish the Earl's banner of the star with its streaming lines. He turned to look for the King who had now assumed his battle helmet, round which glinted the crown of England.

Martyn grunted his disapproval. Repeatedly he had argued in company with Francis Lovell that Richard should not so openly mark himself a target for the enemy. But he knew his sovereign. Richard's obstinacy was well known in the household. On occasions he could display a burst of Plantagenet temper worthy of the famed King Henry II. He fought for England, for the realm itself, and he was its anointed king. His men must see that circlet proudly marking him as the focus for their loyalty.

As yet Martyn could not see the Tudor's banner of the red dragon, but the King's personal standard of the white boar was held over his head by his standard bearer and another flaunted the royal standard of England with its leopards and fleur-de-lys. Martyn signalled for Peter to unfurl his own standard of the saltire argent over the field vert, glad this day to be identified with the family of the dead Queen Anne, the Nevilles.

"Peter, stay by me unless I give you a command to withdraw to the horse lines. Then you will obey me at once."

His squire opened his mouth to protest, then, seeing his lord's grim expression, he held his tongue and handed him his battle helm.

Oxford's men had wheeled round slightly to avoid the marshy ground round the foot of the hill and now faced Norfolk's van, which he had drawn up in the shape of a bent bow. Cannons thundered from Henry's position and the weird silence, previously only punctuated by the neighing of horses and the tramp of booted feet, was broken. A man screamed in agony as a stone ball found its mark and felled him and jeers, oaths and furious war cries came from the waiting foot soldiers.

The heavy guns appeared to have done little real damage and soon hand-to-hand fighting began in earnest. The former quiet of the countryside was now shattered by the screams and oaths, the clanging and thuds of bills and pikes, the splintering of wood as men savagely thrust and stabbed at each other. Sweat and dust from the combatants half blinded the commanders upon Ambien, preventing them from seeing much of the carnage, but Martyn had seen such sights before and hardened his heart against pity for the lives spent and bodies shattered by the brutal business taking place below him.

He heard Peter give a sudden gasp as an agonised scream sounded too near for comfort. He reached out a gauntled hand to steady the boy's shoulder.

It was a relatively short time, though it seemed hours, while they waited for further commands from the King, then suddenly a shout went up which struck them all to the depths of their courage.

"Norfolk is down. The good Duke is slain."

Martyn could see the King turn agitatedly to his close companions but could not hear what was said.

A royal pursuivant raced by him to the horse lines and Catesby walked towards him, awkwardly clumsy in unfamiliar mail.

"The King has summoned Northumberland to bring up reinforcements."

Martyn nodded tersely. It was difficult to bellow over the noise of combat and helmed as he now was. He saw men carrying the body of the stricken Duke back towards the horse lines. Norfolk was a stalwart and experienced campaigner, a good friend to the King, and this was a severe blow to the royalist cause.

Martyn was not surprised when the pursuivant returned alone from Northumberland's camp. He sensed that the man he had long suspected of petty jealousy towards Richard during their earlier joint rulership in the north had given some excuse for yet holding back his force.

Still the furious fighting continued and the stinks of gunpowder and fresh spilt blood drifted back to the commanders watching grimly upon the hilltop.

Another pursuivant rode a lathered horse up to the command post and dismounted. Martyn watched intently. The man had been sent earlier to order Lord Thomas Stanley to come to the King's support and he guessed by the rigidity of the King's head and shoulder posture that Lord Thomas had refused to obey.

Ratcliffe turned and bellowed, "My Lord Wroxeter, the King would speak with you."

Hurriedly he moved to the King's side. The royal visor was up and Martyn saw the signs of one of Richard's royal rages in the hectic spots which marked the normally pale cheeks and the hard-held line of his mouth.

"Martyn, you were right. Lord Stanley refuses to join us. I have threatened to execute my hostage, his son, Lord Strange. Send one of the squires to see to it immediately."

"Yes, Your Grace." Martyn was about to step aside when, just as quickly, he was recalled.

"No, stay, Martyn; let us await the outcome. What point

to vent my fury on Strange? He is not to blame for his father's perfidy.''

Martyn was glad of the King's change of heart. He had no stomach for executions when the terrible carnage below was exacting its full toll of dead and wounded. He knew now, as he was sure the King did, that this battle was lost. Northumberland and the Stanleys were intent on treason and though the King's force had outnumbered the rebels when they had arrived at Redmoor the combined forces of Henry's with the Stanleys', especially if Northumberland joined the fray on the rebel side, would give this victory to Henry.

Catesby was murmuring urgently that the King should fly the field and fight another day. Reason told Martyn that the man's advice was sensible and should be heeded but, wearily, he knew that no one would convince Richard of the practical good sense of it.

Already he saw squires dispatched to bring up the destriers and the King's voice carried to the household.

''Gentlemen, it seems we are bedevilled by treachery. There can be one way to end this business and one way only. A scout has informed me that, at last, Henry has joined his force. I intend to charge full into the enemy lines and confront him. I order no man to ride with me, but those who do know they ride to defend the realm and the honour of their King.''

Martyn snapped an order to Peter as the lad brought up his destrier.

''I ride with the King. Get back to the spring near the horse lines.''

''But, my lord—''

''Obey me, Peter. You have your Countess to consider. See to it that she is informed of whatever happens now and—lad—tell her of my undying love.''

Peter, wide-eyed and frightened, held Martyn's destrier steady as he mounted, then stood away from its plunging hooves. The highly trained animal had scented blood and was as eager for the fray as his master.

There was no fear in Martyn's heart, only a calm acceptance. There was still a chance. Richard was a doughty fighter and could save the day, but many of them would die on this final charge; he knew that. The household knights grouped together around their sovereign. The horses moved in a slow walk down from the summit, then, as the steepness of the ground lessened, momentum carried them into a gallop.

Martyn could see the white boar banner streaming in the wind above the King's mount and spurred his own destrier to the gallop. They were flying now into the full might of Henry's cavalry.

A giant mounted figure loomed ahead—Sir William Brandon, Henry's standard bearer. As if berserk, like his Viking ancestors, Richard cut him down with his battleaxe and the giant toppled, dragging the red dragon banner in the dust where it was trampled underfoot.

Martyn charged on, oblivious of the shouts of the men around him, determined to stay near the King, as battle-crazed now as those with him. He wielded his own broadsword vigorously from side to side, ignoring the thuds and clangs of weapon against armour, his eyes half-blinded by his visor and the flying clods of earth and grass tussocks thrown up by the destriers' hooves.

A savage blow toppled the King from his courser but he fought on valiantly on foot. Men shouted hoarsely for someone to bring the King a fresh mount and Martyn strove desperately to reach Richard's side.

He saw a sudden sun flash on red jacks and yelled a warning as Sir William Stanley's men streamed ahead of them, joining Henry's force. The King was surrounded, but still fought on doggedly.

Martyn felt a jarring crash upon his helm which paralysed his arm, still upheld to strike his opponent. For moments he remained upright in the saddle, bemused. His last thought, in the moments before the red mist hampered his vision and then the blackness engulfed him finally, was of Cressida, leaning down from the chamber window at Nottingham to smell the climbing white rose, then he lurched sideways from the saddle before the hooves of the oncoming coursers.

Chapter Ten

Cressida could hear the growing buzz of noise in the street as she returned to her apartment in the gatehouse from praying in the church of St Mary's within the castle walls. She paused for a moment in the courtyard, her hand on her heart. Was there news of the battle already? She hastened inside, her anxiety conveying itself to Alice who was close behind her.

Alice said softly, "It may be nothing, child. Crowds gather for any reason which offers some excitement. It could be some dishonest baker being carted through the streets for punishment."

Cressida nodded abstractedly. She wanted news desperately but feared to receive it when it came. She remembered Martyn's last advice to her.

"Trust no one with information about the battle but those you know well."

Philip, white-faced, was waiting for her at the door to her chamber.

"My lady, they're saying in the streets that the battle is lost to the King and Henry Tudor has been crowned on the field with the golden circlet which fell from the King's helm when he was cut down and slain."

Alice gave a little growl of warning but the boy rushed on.

"Lord Thomas Stanley had a stool brought for the Earl of Richmond to sit on and crowned him himself. The circlet was found under a thorn bush and a soldier brought it to Lord Stanley."

Cressida drew the boy within the chamber and signalled to Alice to bar the door. "They are saying the King is dead?"

"Yes, my lady." The boy blinked unhappily. "I heard one man say it was the Stanley brothers who won the day for the Tudor. They waited till the last minute and then brought their forces to cut off King Richard's men and—and the King was killed fighting on foot…"

"Then the royalist forces are in retreat?"

The boy swallowed hard and avoided her eyes. "It—it would seem so, my lady. I—I didn't wait to hear more, but came back to tell you."

Cressida sank down heavily upon the bed while Alice came to her side and put a reassuring hand on her shoulder.

"You must not give up hope. The Earl may well have escaped the field."

"My father told me of the pursuit after Tewkesbury," Cressida said woodenly. "It was more bloody than the battle itself, he said, and every man in Lancastrian livery was rounded up and—and the ringleaders executed…"

There was a terrible numbness within her which would not allow her the solace of tears. She had feared this for so long, during those last, poignantly sweet days with Martyn. Where was he now? Had he perished on the field or was he, even now, being hunted down like some animal?

She could not take it in. Martyn had kept on assuring her that the King's forces were superior to those of the Tudor, that King Richard was far more experienced a com-

mander than Henry Tudor or any of his supporters, yet
here was Philip telling her of this disastrous defeat.

The King had been despicably betrayed. In his heart
Martyn had known this was likely, yet he had kept up a
brave front before her. She turned a frightened face towards her nurse, made a little anguished sound and buried
her head in the folds of Alice's skirts.

Alice said gruffly to the boy, "Take yourself off for a
while. Do not go into the streets again but keep your ears
open for talk from the castle servants. Say nothing about
the Earl, nor are you to remind anyone, for the moment,
about the presence of your mistress here in the castle."

"But—but how are we to be served?" he stammered
fearfully.

"I will see to that personally. And, before you come in
again with more distressing tidings, speak to me first."
These last words were uttered in a threatening hiss.

The boy nodded dumbly and scrambled out of the room.

Still Cressida could not cry. At last she sat upright, one
hand still clinging to her old nurse's skirt. "What are we
to do? What will become of us? I will not be moved from
here until—" Cressida's lips trembled "—until I hear
word of Lord Martyn." She broke down finally and whim-
pered, "Oh, Alice, how could he have escaped? He would
have fought near to his King, I know it."

Alice pursed her lips. "We know nothing of the sort.
You've just said yourself your father escaped after
Tewkesbury."

"He was taken prisoner and it was only by the mercy
of the Duke of Gloucester." The last words were jerked
out brokenly as she thought of the bleakest of Philip's
tidings—that Richard, who had been Duke of Gloucester
then and spared her father, was now dead on the battlefield
himself—if the rumours were true. Wearily she faced facts.

The news *had* to be true. Why else was there so much commotion in the streets? She had heard it in the distance and dreaded knowing the outcome, even then.

Cressida refused a late dinner which an excited serving man brought to her chamber. In spite of her charge's protests Alice took the laden tray from him and placed it on a fald table within the chamber. She questioned the man as to further news of the battle. Wearily Cressida climbed to her feet from the prie-dieu where she had been praying for the repose of the dead King's soul.

The man glanced shiftily towards the Countess. "The new King is to enter the town within the next hour and—" he shifted awkwardly from one foot to the other "—some man-at-arms riding in shouted that they be bringing in the late King's—that is the usurper's—body for public view."

Alice dismissed the fellow quickly and came back to Cressida, who had turned a horrified face towards them both.

"No, no, they cannot do that," she raged. "It is not decent. It—"

Alice drew her down onto the bed. "My lady, it is customary. The new King must let the people see King Richard is truly dead. It was so with the late King Henry VI, and King Edward lay in state for his subjects to view the body."

Cressida covered her face with her hands. She had been present at the obsequies of the dead Queen, had seen how reverently things had been done, and now the King she had come to like and admire was to be the object of curiosity for every townsman or beggar in this town to come and stare at in vulgar and idle speculation.

"I must go and see." She spoke with cold determination, knowing that Alice would protest vehemently. "At least there will be two or three souls there who will mourn him in honour.''

Alice offered no objections, knowing it would be pointless to do so, but summoned the two men-at-arms whom Lord Martyn had left to guard them to accompany their mistress into the crowded streets of Leicester town. Philip refused to be parted from his mistress and, wearing a dark gown and simple cap, and a lightweight grey cloak, for the afternoon was sultry, Cressida left the castle ward. Her guards made way for her through the avidly curious and whispering townsfolk onto the high street near to its junction with the road which led westward to the little town of Market Bosworth.

The King's party rode in soon after. Cressida caught only a glimpse of the man who had been a thorn in King Richard's side for so long and who would shortly be crowned more ceremoniously in London as King Henry VII of England. He was closely hemmed in by a bodyguard of men wearing green jacks with his device of the red dragon.

Beside him and behind him rode those lords who had helped him to the crown, two of them, at least, by treachery, she thought bitterly. She saw only a tall, slim man dressed very soberly, with lank brown hair, his face shaded by a black velvet low-crowned hat. The standards of the Stanley brothers and that of the Earl of Oxford were borne triumphantly by.

Cressida could not believe she was seeing what followed. There had been ragged cheers of welcome from the crowds lining the street which the new King did not acknowledge, then the people fell strangely silent and looked back to the rear of the procession, craning their necks and whispering awkwardly.

A lone white horse was ridden by a solitary pursuivant.

Cressida's mouth went oddly dry as she recognised Richard's favourite courser, White Surrey, his head hanging low as if for very shame at the proceedings he was forced to take part in. The pursuivant, too, she knew; it was the youthful herald Blanc Sanglier, the man who had proudly carried Richard's banner of the white boar in the royal army which had set out from Nottingham.

He sat upright in the saddle, his youthful face set into a mask of seeming stone, and behind him the body of the dead King was slung ignominiously, stripped of his armour and clothing, naked, bloodstained, and wearing a halter like a common felon, the dark head lolling grotesquely downwards, as if bowing to the watching subjects.

Cressida made as if to step forward to make a public protest at this gross indignity but Alice caught her and held her forcibly back. Her own face expressed total horror and she motioned to their two veteran guards to prevent their mistress from making any further move.

Tears streamed down Cressida's cheeks and she knew she was sobbing. People near her turned to stare but she was beyond caring. No one was making any comment. One or two had the decency to turn away and one old grizzled townsman who might have been a butcher, judging from his bloodstained apron, murmured brokenly, "It ain't right. 'E was the Lord's anointed." He was hastily and nervously shushed by a fat woman near him.

Alice whispered urgently, "It cannot matter, my little darling. He feels and sees nothing. Please, you must not make a scene."

Cressida gave an anguished cry despite the grim warning when the courser approached the bridge over the River Soar and the lolling head struck one of the coping stones in passing and a concerted cry went up from the watching townsfolk. Still wary, the townsfolk continued to watch as

the white courser passed onward, bearing its horrifying
burden towards the castle and the church of St Mary,
known as the lesser, to distinguish it from St Mary's within
the castle precincts.

There Richard's body would lie for some days, exposed
to public view as Alice had predicted. The news of the
King's death would be carried from Leicester town by the
new King's messengers and by the gossip of these witnesses. Soon all England would be made aware that a new
king had won the crown.

Cressida was almost fainting and Alice was forced to
hold her upright. They were compelled to remain where
they were for some time for the crowd dispersed slowly
and uneasily, muttering amongst themselves as mounted
knights rode in at the rear and behind them, wearily, men-
at-arms on foot. Finally came the baggage train and, with
it, a pathetic group of pinioned prisoners.

At last it was possible to return to the castle and Alice
was relieved to have Cressida safely behind the locked
door of her own chamber, for she was afraid that her mistress would continue to speak out fiercely about the irrev-
erent way the body of the fallen King had been treated.

Alice was not sure if the new King Henry was even now
accommodated within the royal apartments of the castle,
but she knew that the great hall roof was still being re-
paired so he could not be installed with any degree of state.

Cressida refused to eat at supper and spent the rest of
the evening in St Mary's in prayer. Later Alice insisted on
her retiring to bed and watched until Cressida fell into an
exhausted sleep.

The next morning Cressida agreed that it would be better to remain in her chamber and Alice herself went down
to the castle kitchens for food for her mistress, herself and
Philip. The men, she knew, would forage for themselves,

and it was of those two that Cressida spoke, after breaking a frugal fast.

"They should leave here, Alice. Ask them to come to me. I shall send them home. They must not remain here wearing Lord Martyn's livery. Best that they should set off immediately for Wroxeter."

"But we do not know yet what news they should carry of their lord's fate."

Cressida's expression was set but calm. "Whatever it may be, he will be unlikely to return to his manor and his servants should be informed. These men could be arrested. You saw those wretches in the procession. These men are my responsibility now and I must think of their safety."

Alice looked at her charge keenly. Cressida was scarcely seventeen—only a year ago she had been castigating her for childish follies. Now, already, Cressida was taking on the role of sole arbiter of her husband's estates. She had grown up far too quickly for Alice's liking.

Just before Alice set off in search of dinner, Philip came to the door of the chamber, his face grave, and stammered that there were visitors for his mistress.

Cressida was talking to the two men-at-arms who were arguing, though respectfully, that their master had charged them with her protection and how could she be left alone within this now hostile castle? She lifted a hand to quell further objections to her orders, then turned and nodded to Philip to admit the newcomers.

Her heart was beating so fast that she thought it would burst free from the restraining ribs and she had to force her trembling limbs to hold still and support her.

She gave a little sob of surprise and relieved joy as Sir Daniel Gretton walked in briskly and waited for no greeting but came hurriedly to her and embraced her in a bear hug. She allowed her tears full rein then and sobbed against his shoulder.

"There, there, lass," he said gruffly, patting her shoulder in awkward sympathy. "Thank the Virgin I am here now. You can rely on me to see to your interests."

She lifted her head and stared beyond him to where Howell Prosser stood silently near the chamber door, and behind him she glimpsed a dust-stained, white-faced Peter Fairley. She gave a little choked cry and stood fully upright, putting an arm out to withdraw herself from her father's protective embrace.

"What is this traitor doing in my presence?" she said haughtily. "Isn't it enough that you betray your anointed King, but you must come and mock at me also?"

Howell bowed, his brown eyes imploring, but he did not attempt to come any nearer.

"God knows I would not hurt you by any action or words of mine, Cressida," he said quietly. "I shall not try to excuse myself. You know well my sympathies have always been with the House of Lancaster. I have served *my* King to the best of my abilities and can only rejoice that he is triumphant, but I regret that his victory causes you pain. It is ever so in war."

Cressida suddenly turned angrily to her father. "And what are you doing in this man's company? Have you too turned your coat, after King Richard honoured you so recently?"

"No, Cressida," he returned mildly. "I was on my way to join the late King's force at Leicester, but our way was blocked by the Tudor army. It was impossible to proceed. I took no part in the battle." He hesitated then added, "Perhaps it is just as well I was prevented, since I will be in a better position to protect you and guard your rights. I met up with Howell here in Leicester when I rode in with my men following King Henry's force.''

Her blue eyes were blazing and he stepped back a little from such passionate fury.

She ignored both men and held out a hand to Peter. ''What news do you bring me, Peter?'' she said at last, very softly.

He opened his mouth as if to try to speak and then turned away brokenly. Howell then advanced further into the chamber.

''I was aware how much you would wish to know of— Lord Martyn's fate after the battle. Fortunately, I encountered Wroxeter's squire with some of the other squires and pages, near the spring. As soon as it was fully light I took him to search the field.''

He cleared his throat. ''We concluded that—that Lord Martyn would be found, if still on the field, with those who died near the King at the foot of Ambien Hill. There were enemy bodies…''

He paused and swallowed as Cressida continued to look intently at him, her blue eyes now sparkling with restrained tears. He pressed on, turning slightly as if to avoid the full stare of those accusing eyes.

''We searched those. Finally we came upon the body of a tall knight—it was impossible to be sure, for most had been half stripped of their armour and armorial bearings. Already the bodies had been despoiled in the night by those ghouls who prey on the dead and prosper after battles.''

''Yes?'' The single whisper was a determined command for him to continue.

''Peter here thought—that is, he identified his master. The Earl was wearing this, though how in God's name it escaped the thieving hands of the robbers I cannot say—

possibly they left it for very shame, knowing it to be a
sacred reliquary or fearing it would be noted and recognised later.'' He shook his head.

He was holding out to her the reliquary of St Martin
which she had given to Martyn the morning he had ridden
out from Leicester with the King's force. She gave an anguished little sob and wonderingly took it from him.

"Your squire said he was wearing it when he charged
down the hill with the King's company."

Cressida's eyes met the sorrowful eyes of Peter Fairley.
She said very softly, "Is he truly dead, Peter?"

The squire could not answer. He nodded dumbly.

Cressida said woodenly, "Thank you, Master Prosser.
I—I have been very anxious to know—the worst. What—
what is to be done? My husband's body must be brought
from the field and tended. If he could be brought here…"

"No, no, Cressida, I'm sorry." Howell's voice was
harsh with embarrassment. "That won't be possible. The
King has commanded that those enemy dead are to be
buried near the field. Trust me to see to it that—that the
Earl is interred with honour."

"Unlike his sovereign," Cressida said in a brittle voice
and he winced slightly.

"You must realise, Cressida, that these things are necessary and—afterwards—I am sure that the King will arrange for—"

"I trust he will do so," Cressida said icily, "for otherwise his subjects will surely cry shame on him as a dis-
honourable victor."

Her father said weakly, "Cressida, child, I beg you to
have a care…"

She turned from him back to Howell Prosser. "Am I
not to have an opportunity to see my husband's body and
mourn him in honour?"

He drew a hard breath and looked to Sir Daniel for support. "Believe me, it is best that you do not, Cressida. He—he was badly disfigured in the charge. The following destriers must have—he must have been unhorsed early—and—"

Still she did not weep, though her mind took the full pain of the picture his words had conjured however he had sought to hide the truth from her.

"I see," she said coldly. "Thank you again, Master Prosser. And now—now, if you please, I would like to be alone for a while with Alice."

Sir Daniel drew Howell to the door, after dismissing the two men-at-arms, who were round-eyed with horror.

He spoke to Alice. "We are lodged at an inn in the town. I will come back when your mistress is less distraught." Peter trailed miserably after them.

Cressida stood staring into space until Alice came to her and gathered her close to her heart. The tears came then and she sobbed as if her heart would break. Afterwards she drew away and said briskly, "I must not give way, for there is much to be done. See to it that those men are provided with coin and send them off to Wroxeter. There is no need now for them to remain at risk here, since my father's men will escort me when it is time for me to leave. I will go to St Mary's and have masses said for Martyn's soul."

Alice nodded and went off to do her bidding. Cressida summoned Philip and set off for the church. Even now, though she had feared the worst, she could not fully take in the fact that she would never see Martyn again, never lie with him, her head pillowed on his shoulder after the delight of lovemaking, never see those sleepy lids sweep back to reveal those dark eyes smouldering with desire for her, never hear his half-humorous rebuke—"Cressida, you have always been difficult."

There was a terrible ache at the back of her throat which she knew was caused by the tears she must not shed. If she stopped to weep now she would not be able to do what must be done. There must be masses said. In spite of Howell's promise of honourable burial, she must insist that her father accompany her to the churchyard where Martyn would be laid. Later she must arrange for mourning black to be doled out to all their servants…

She was thankful that the church was deserted. As yet there was no priest in attendance. He must be summoned and given instructions for the requiem masses. She knelt alone before the altar, Philip, at her command, remaining at the rear of the nave, her lips murmuring intercessions to the Virgin and St Martin that her husband's soul would not suffer too long in purgatory.

She was sure that he must have been in a state of grace. The King, known to be pious, would have had mass said before the battle. She continued to intercede for him too. Kings had much to atone for. It was necessary that they be ruthless. Martyn had assured her that the King had done no murder, that his nephews had not suffered at his hands, but there were others who had suffered in order for King Richard to take the throne and keep the peace in England—and Martyn had been in his councils, worked with him.

She closed her eyes and prayed fervently for all those brave men, on both sides, who had fallen that day.

She knew she was still numb, that true realisation would come soon and, with it, increased suffering, but for the moment she forced herself to think only of Martyn's soul's salvation.

She was half-distressed and half-annoyed to hear booted

feet approach. She desperately needed to be alone with her grief. Deliberately she did not turn, hoping that the newcomer would see her need and leave the church quickly, but she heard a rustle of movement as the intruder knelt some paces behind her. Clutching her beads determinedly, she continued to pray.

Then it was that she heard the whisper from the shadowed gloom of the nave.

"My lady, do not despair. Lord Martyn lives."

She thought at first that she was experiencing a hallucination of her own desperate longing and shut her eyes fast. She must address herself to God and not allow false hopes to weaken her purpose.

Again came the whisper, this time even closer to her ear, as if the speaker had leaned forward eagerly to speak secretly to her.

"I have waited to find you alone, my lady. He was badly wounded." It was undoubtedly Peter Fairley's voice. She half turned but he warned her hastily, "Do not turn round, my lady; just listen to what I say. You must not acknowledge me in case someone enters.

"We searched for him last night as soon as the pursuit was well in progress and Henry's men had left the field to the despoilers of the dead." He sounded bitter. "Jack Wainwright and I, we were hardly noticed in such a company and we had both torn our Wroxeter devices from our jacks.

"We found him, more dead than alive. He wasn't conscious and Master Wainwright said that as the helm was badly dented he must have taken a blow to the head from a mace or battleaxe. His arm was broken. We feared for his life, but he was breathing, though very shallowly.

"We—stripped him of his armour, as others had been so despoiled, and found some other poor soul about his height and put some of it on him—the dented breastplate and part of the vambrace—and—and I put the reliquary round the stranger's neck. Master Wainwright, he—'' Peter gave a shuddering breath ''—he saw to it that the other man would not be recognised. He was past heeding, mistress, so it was no sin, though I—baulked at it.

''We managed to carry Lord Martyn from the field and hid him in a ditch near the marsh. I stayed with him till Master Wainwright came back with a cart and we managed to get him away.''

Again there was a hard swallow which told Cressida of the terrible horror and fear which had haunted the boy throughout all this and she clutched at her beads until the knuckles of her hand whitened with strain. Still she did not turn, obeying Peter's strictures, though her heart was pounding and her whole soul longed to cry out questions.

He gulped and continued. ''We piled straw over him, and the dung, and we got him clear of the field. There were some of Lord Stanley's men drinking near one of the baggage wagons, but they did not question us, thank the Virgin. My lord moaned, but did not come to consciousness. We thanked God for that at the time. Then I went back. Jack said that would be less suspicious.''

''Where is he now?'' Cressida asked urgently. Hope was flooding back into her numbed being—yet he was sore hurt, Peter had said—and a head wound —

''In the house of Master Wainwright's cousin, here in Leicester. We dared not summon a physician but Master Wainwright tended him. He has cared many times for sorely wounded men on other campaigns, my lady. We feared—brain damage, but once or twice Lord Martyn half came to and seemed sensible. He knew us but he kept falling off again, but Master Jack says that is just nature's way. We have hopes of full recovery, but he may not get back the full use of his sword arm. Master—''

''You must take me to him.''

''No, mistress. You must not go near him, not until the King's men have left the town—not even then until we are sure there will not be searches made for fugitives.''

She drew a hard breath. He was so tantalisingly near and yet she saw the sense of it. She must not endanger him, nor those who gave him shelter, but, sweet Virgin, even now he might die and she not at his side.

Peter explained. ''Master Wainwright says that—that because of the work my lord did for the King the Tudor would never pardon him. Already there is talk that Master Catesby must die.''

She said as calmly as she could, ''What must I do, then, Peter? Oh, Peter, take him my love…''

''He knows he has that, my lady. In his delirium he speaks your name.''

She swallowed back tears of joy and newly roused fear for his safety.

''You must continue to mourn him, my lady. Not even your father must know and certainly not Master Prosser. When it is safe I will bring you news again.''

She heard the rustle of his garments as he stood up and moved away down the length of the nave. She remained where she was until she heard the heavy door close and then fell forward, face down, upon the hard stone and whispered her heartfelt paean of praise to God, the Virgin and all the Saints that they had heard her prayers and granted her the life of the man she loved.

Cressida shifted awkwardly upon the hard bench where she waited in the ante-room to the late Queen's chamber while a page carried her request to the Lady Elizabeth

Plantagenet for an audience. It was three weeks since she had heard the heart-stopping news that her husband had escaped Redmoor field. Now she had arrived at Westminster and was fervently praying that she would be received by her friend, for only the Lady Elizabeth could offer her any hope of pardon for Lord Martyn.

Henry Tudor was already England's acknowledged King, and on his accession he had declared his intention of honouring his pledged word to the Lady Elizabeth that he would take her to wife. Elizabeth would be the new Queen and cement the union of the houses of York and Lancaster, thus making it more probable that the common folk of England would accept without protest his claim to the English throne. They had all had enough of the wars; Londoners had loved her father; they would greet this promised union with glad hearts.

Cressida could only hope that Elizabeth would still look with pleasure on their erstwhile friendship and grant her request.

She had done what Peter had told her—returned to her apartment in the castle gatehouse, outwardly the grieving widow. Her father had called several times in the days which followed to offer her clumsy attempts at sympathy. He had wanted her to return at once with him to Gretton but she had determinedly refused, knowing she could not leave Leciester until she had managed to glean further news of Martyn's recovery.

Only one person had she trusted with her wonderful secret—Alice. Her maid must know, for if there was the remotest hope of seeing Martyn Alice would insist on accompanying her.

Alice had been totally dumbfounded, but had rejoiced as her mistress had done. She was utterly trustworthy yet capable of duplicity while secrecy was so desperately

needed. She had laid out the black silk mourning gown
Cressida had worn at Court for Queen Anne's obsequies
and continued to play the supportive role expected of her
to the young widow.

Determined to play her part to the end, Cressida had
pleaded to go to the churchyard near the village of Daddlington where the bodies of the royalist dead had been
laid to rest. Howell had gently but firmly prevented her,
explaining that any outward show of sympathy for the late
King's cause could only exacerbate the King's enmity towards the families of the fallen royalist knights. Her father
had also reminded her that Lord Martyn would have
wished her to salvage what she could from the ruin of the
Wroxeter fortunes.

"It is fortunate that the Prossers have always been supporters of the new King," he declared. "Howell will use
his best efforts on your behalf to see to it that your dower
rights are protected."

Because it served her purpose, Cressida had reluctantly
acceded to their wishes. The unknown knight who was
buried as the Earl of Wroxeter had been interred quietly
but decently and Cressida had sent gold to the priest at
Daddlington to say continual masses for his soul. She had
prayed privately for this unknown man in his own right.

Howell had been proved right. Henry had shown ruth-
lessness in his determination to heap infamy upon the
memory of the dead King. A proclamation was issued accusing him of many crimes against humanity, one unspe-
cified, pertaining to shedding of infant blood, but Cressida
noted that the new King had not dared openly to accuse
King Richard of the murder of his nephews.

She wondered why that was. Was Henry himself unaware of their fate and feared that one or both of them
might one day appear to dispute his own claim—or, worse,

was he guilty of ordering the murder of the boys himself? That question she was unwilling to dwell on.

King Richard's body had finally been laid to rest in the church of the Grey Friars. Cressida had heard of the execution of William Catesby, though of what the man was guilty, other than loyally serving his sovereign, she did not know. Two other men had been hanged in Leicester town, but she knew of no other noble prisoners who had suffered so.

She was told that Norfolk's son, the Earl of Surrey, and the Earl of Northumberland, who, astonishingly, had taken no part in the battle, were to be imprisoned in the Tower. Of Lord Lovell's fate there were no tidings and she assumed that he had managed to flee the battlefield.

With the King on Ambien had died Sir Richard Ratcliffe, Sir Robert Brackenbury, Sir Robert Percy, even John Kendall, the King's secretary. She had known them all and grieved for them.

During those terrible days Cressida had grimly hung on, hoping against hope that Peter Fairley would be able to contact her again in secret. He had come to her at her apartments frequently, but there had never been any opportunity for them to speak together alone.

She had been returning from one of her usual visits to the church one day when a lanky boy, most likely one of the kitchen scullions, had come across the court then stumbled and almost fallen into their path. Alice had scolded him roundly for his carelessness but Cressida had heard to her utter astonishment, a whispered message.

"Mistress, if you would see my lord, dress in plain attire and wait for me tonight by the church lych-gate. Bring only your maid."

The boy got to his feet, apologised gruffly, and was off

before Alice could cuff him about the ears. Cressida stared after him in wonder.

After supper she informed Alice, who was equally bewildered and more than a little alarmed.

"Are you sure you can trust this messenger?"

"Alice, I must. How else will I ever know how my lord Martyn is? Can you lend me a woollen gown of yours and a simple cap?"

"Aye, of course I can, but I'll come with you, even if I have to wait outside the house. We must give it out that you are unwell—a headache has come on through overmuch weeping. Philip will stand guard outside your sleeping chamber until we return."

"What shall we tell the boy?"

Alice pursed her lips. "Tell him we are going to keep a night vigil in the church. To tell truth I think he may well suspect, but he's loyal to the core. He'll do what you command without question."

Alice was right. Philip made no objection to his mistress leaving the castle court without him, nor did he comment when he saw Cressida emerge from her chamber with Alice dressed in a skirt of brown fustian and white linen blouse. Her bright hair was thrust well under a concealing linen cap. Alice had given her a basket to carry.

Though the hour was late and most of the castle servants were engaged in serving those supporters of the new King who had remained after Henry had set out for the capital, Alice assured her that many women went out to buy cheese and bread from one or two shops which stayed open.

"The poorer folk shop when the food is less fresh and it costs less at these late hours. We will not be noticed."

They waited by the church gate, anxiously scanning the deserted street. The same lanky boy who had accosted them earlier sidled into view and beckoned. Cressida has-

tened to catch up with him as he set off. It was evident
that he did not wish to be associated with the two women
and they must simply follow and keep him in sight.

They reached the high street with its cross and then
passed the inn where Richard's officers had spent that last
night before the battle in conference. Cressida caught her
breath as she recalled the King's last kindly words to her.
The innkeeper had decided to play safe and had already
painted the white boar device on the inn sign blue.

Their guide plunged down an alley nearby. The light
was beginning to fade now and Cressida had difficulty in
picking out his outline but at last, near an old house whose
upper storey was leaning crazily towards the house opposite, she saw that the lad was waiting for her. A torch flared
on one of the nearby houses and, as he faced her, she
thought she half recognised the boy. Could it be the ill-
used scullion she had tried to rescue from dire punishment
at the hands of their cook in the Strand house?

He knocked upon the badly warped door and turned to
face them again, signalling them to enter as the door was
opened.

The familiar bulky figure of Jack Wainwright almost
filled the small room into which they were ushered. Cressida gave a relieved gasp at sight of him.

"Master Wainwright, where is Lord Martyn? He is not
worse…?"

He shook his head decisively. "We have him in a room
above stairs. We must move him soon, so I thought this
your best opportunity to see him."

Alice opted to remain with their guide in the downstairs
room. From the kitchen a woman emerged and curtsied.

"Welcome to our house, my lady Countess. I will bring
you ale and meats…"

"No, no," Cressida said agitatedly. "Do not put your-

self out. You have done more than enough in risking yourselves for my lord Earl.''

Wainwright nodded towards the plump, smiling woman
who was plainly but respectably clad. ''My cousin, Mistress Joan Wainwright. Her man, Dick, is a groom in service at the Blue Boar, as we must call it now. Come upstairs, my lady. Tread carefully; the light is dim here in
the shadows.''

Heart in her mouth and winded, for she was too eager
to see Martyn and climbed too hurriedly, Cressida was also
too breathless to question Jack Wainwright.

He moved through an upper sleeping chamber where
two pallets gave evidence of occupation by his cousin and
wife. He stooped at a low door at the rear and pushed it
open, revealing a room behind, more than likely usually
used to store apples or barrels of salted meat. The light
was dim, but Cressida could just distinguish a pallet on
which a man lay. The unshuttered window gave her light
enough to approach and kneel by her husband's side.
Wainwright stood waiting near the doorway.

Martyn was half turned from her. He was dressed like
their scullion, in brown hose and a torn fustian tunic of
some indeterminate colour. He had not been shaved and
there was dark stubble upon his chin and cheeks, though
she could detect no rank odour from his body, so he had
been cleansed and tended well. A linen bandage about his
head was marked with a seepage of blood. He was
breathing steadily and appeared to be sleeping normally.

She bent and kissed his cheek. He had not lost his normal tan, for he had spent the summer at Bestwood, often
in the chase, but there were dark bruises about his eyes
which spoke to her of suffering. She whispered his name
very softly.

''Martyn, my dear lord.''

He moved restlessly and, at length, at the touch of her hand on his, he opened his eyes and blinked at her owlishly. She was fearful that the blow he had taken to his head had rendered him witless, but at last recognition dawned and the hooded lids swept fully back. Joy lit up those dark brown eyes and he struggled weakly to turn and rise up against the straw pillow.

"Cressida, can it really be you?"

"Yes, my love. I am here. You must not try to talk too much if you are still weak."

He grinned at her mischievously. "As the proverbial kitten. They tell me I've been here for days."

"Yes, my love, you know where you are?"

He nodded. "Aye, in Leicester."

She said with a little catch to her voice, "You know—about the King?"

The dark eyes clouded and he nodded again. "Aye, God rest his soul."

She stroked his face, then traced the beloved lines of eyes, nose and chin with one questing finger. "You have much to thank Master Wainwright for. You must be guided by his advice now."

She turned to their erstwhile cook. "You say you must move him. Is there still danger?"

The burly giant frowned. "Who knows? Few have been executed so far, but my lord Earl is a special case. Many of Henry's supporters have suffered because of him."

Martyn's fingers tightened suddenly upon Cressida's hand.

"You should go home to Gretton soon now. You must not be involved in any plan to get me from here."

"Hush, hush. We shall all be very careful, I promise. Rest now." Worriedly, she saw how the least movement tired him.

"Kiss me again before you leave me." The command was almost imperative, as she remembered, and she stooped, her lashes wet with tears, to kiss him full on the mouth then on the eyes and chin.

"See her safe to the castle, Jack. Let your parents go on thinking me dead, Cressida. Do not worry about me. I'll manage to stay hidden. Jack will send you news when it's safe to do so."

Cressida was unwilling to leave him so soon, but she dared not be too long away from her chamber at the castle. She moved back to the storeroom door and turned for a last look at him, then she hastened back again and pressed into his hand the reliquary. "Keep it safe. It helped to save your life."

He coughed weakly and bent to kiss her fingers, then she hurried out with Jack Wainwright.

She conferred with him below. "How well is he really?"

"He is still weak. At first he rarely remained conscious for long, but he is much better already. He lost a great deal of blood, but his arm is mending and soon we must try to reach the coast. He is not safe within the realm."

"But I hear Henry is anxious to appear merciful and will pardon many who fought for King Richard."

Wainwright's bulbous eyes narrowed warily. "Believe me, my lady, he will not pardon my lord Earl. There is too much between them."

"Where will you take him?"

"Eventually to Burgundy, if we can make it, but the ports are watched. Travellers need licences to take ship."

Grimly she recalled the licence she had stolen for Howell. How could she obtain one for Martyn? Dared she trust Howell? But immediately she knew she could not. Only one person could possibly help her now. The Lady Elizabeth was to be the new King's bride. Martyn had shown her some hostility. Would she, for the sake of the friendship she and Cressida had shared, be willing to help him now?

Her father had made no objection to her avowed intention to travel to Westminster and had provided her with an escort of Gretton men.

"Go by all means, daughter. Your friendship with the Princess should influence King Henry in any decision he makes concerning the possible sequestration of your husband's estates. Your dower rights must be protected."

He had not added that possibly, in time, the new King would provide the widowed Cressida with a new husband.

So now she waited, hoping that the Princess would see her and remember the hours they had spent together in amity. Her fingers surreptitiously touched the modesty vest of her gown where Elizabeth's letter to her, written from Sheriff Hutton, was hidden.

The door to the Princess's chamber was opened and a page called haughtily, "The Countess of Wroxeter?"

Cressida rose hastily and he beckoned her forward.

Elizabeth was seated in a padded armchair, wearing a gown of deep purple. She rose at once, hands outstretched graciously, to greet her friend.

"Cressida, how glad I am to see you here." She glanced pointedly and imperiously towards two elderly attendants who sat stitching industriously in the window seat. "You may all leave me. Go, I say."

They moved reluctantly but the Princess stared at them coldly and at last they backed from her presence, pulling the doors to after them.

Elizabeth drew Cressida to a seat by her chair. "I'm sorry I kept you waiting. Lady Stanley has been to see me, as she does most days, and it is difficult for me to be alone, as you saw.'' She looked towards the closed door and Cressida realised that, like her late uncle, she had already discovered how a monarch was denied privacy, especially the privacy to grieve.

Elizabeth looked down at Cressida's mourning garb and sighed heavily.

"How can I say how sorry I am that you have lost Martyn on that terrible Leicestershire field?'' She turned away momentarily as if she did not wish Cressida to gauge her expression. "At least you have the right to grieve. I dare not.''

The whispered words were anguished and Cressida reached out and touched her friend gently on the arm. Elizabeth swung back to her briskly.

"You know I am to be King Henry's wife?''

"And England's Queen. Yes, my lady, and all England will rejoice on your marriage day. I wish you all happiness.''

"Do you?'' Elizabeth's question was brittle. "I shall do what is necessary, as other members of my family have done. The King honours me with this proposal and—and I must be humbly grateful.'' Then she said quickly, "I shall be a queen in name only, unlike my aunt, whose husband listened to her advice at least, even when he could not always, for the sake of the realm, accede to her wishes.''

Cressida was silent. Uncomfortably she knew that Elizabeth was trusting her with a confidence she could share with no other. Looking up fully into the Princess's blue eyes, she read the truth at last. Elizabeth had truly loved her uncle as a woman loved a man, knowing that that love was not returned, yet having no regrets, only, now, the terrible knowledge that she could never acknowledge it to a living soul.

Elizabeth said softly, "Can I help you in any way, Cressida? I can still expedite matters of a personal nature. Do you wish to return to Court when your mourning is over? I should be glad to have you with me."

Cressida shook her head very slowly, her eyes filling with tears. How lonely Elizabeth was to be in the years ahead.

"No, my lady, I..." She hesitated, not knowing, even now, if she dared to trust this woman, then plunged on determinedly. "I came to beg you—that is, to ask if you could obtain for me—a licence to travel overseas."

Elizabeth stared at her intently. "For yourself?" Cressida swallowed painfully then again shook her head. Elizabeth leaned towards her eagerly. "You need to help someone to flee the realm?"

"Yes, my lady, unless there could be hope of pardon from the King..."

Elizabeth was still staring at her, so hard that Cressida thought she could read her very soul, then at last she whispered incredulously, "For Martyn?"

Cressida inclined her head.

Elizabeth sat back in her chair and Cressida could almost see the thoughts racing through her brain, then she said very determinedly, "You could never hope for pardon, Cressida. Never allow King Henry to know your husband lives, or anyone else at this Court. No, do not tell me where he is. Even that would not be wise." One hand went to her lips as she stared across at the oriel window. "He must be got to Burgundy, to my aunt Margaret."

"But how, my lady?" Cressida murmured urgently. "I hoped—prayed that you might be able to help me. I know he was—distant in his attitude towards you, but—"

"He had his reasons, and though I was angered at the time I understood them." Elizabeth rose and moved to the window, where she stared down into the pleasance below. "I think there might be one way. Was he injured?"

"Yes, my lady. He—he received a blow to the head, otherwise I think he would have ridden on to his death with—with the King…"

"Yes." The voice was a little hoarse with unshed tears. "Is he fit to travel, sit a horse?"

"I think so, now."

"I am soon to travel to the shrine of Our Lady of Walsingham in Norfolk. I shall pray there for a child—Henry's heir. We shall not be far from the port of Lynn. If he could be disguised he could ride in my company as one of my grooms." She hesitated. "There are men in Lynn whom—whom my uncle trusted to do very special secret work for him, men with ships who sailed privily to France and on to Burgundy. Somehow Lord Martyn could be smuggled on board one of those vessels. Can you get a message to him?"

"Yes, my lady. My page is with me and some of my father's men, but they know nothing of—My father is unaware that Martyn lives."

"And should remain that way. Cressida, I shall take you with me. How natural that I should. You will need comfort from Our Lady of Walsingham as I need the great boon I pray for. It has already been arranged for me to leave in one week."

She sighed. "It will be a relief to be away from the prying eyes of Lady Margaret, Henry's mother, even from the vigilance of my own mother. I shall rest one night at St Edmund's shrine in Bury. Send to Martyn to join my train there. My captain of escort is trustworthy and will arrange for him to replace one of my servants and travel on with us. That way he will be able to approach the coast without undue notice."

* * *

Cressida was summoned to the stable of the convent where the Princess had elected to stay for the night. It had fallen out as Elizabeth had promised and easier than Cressida could ever have hoped. They had set out from Westminster escorted by twenty men-at-arms, most of whom wore the livery of the dead King Edward, Elizabeth's father, the sun in splendour badge ornamenting their jacks.

Six wore Henry's badge of the red dragon and Cressida knew they must be wary of these men, obviously set to spy upon the Princess while she was away from the King's eyes. Elizabeth appeared unperturbed by their presence, however, apparently putting her trust in her elderly captain of escort, who, she assured Cressida, was totally loyal to her.

On this, the third night of the journey, they had arrived at the shrine of St Edmund in Bury and Cressida and Alice had stayed within the little cell-like room assigned to them, Cressida's heart beating fast in anticipation and alarm.

She had dispatched young Philip to the house in Leicester. The boy had been overjoyed at her news and, despite his extreme youth, she knew she could trust him with his master's very life. He would not join her on this journey. She had sent him on to Gretton with news to her parents that she had undertaken this service to attend the Princess.

They had had no tidings. Of course, she had expected none, but now she feared that Philip had failed in his mission, or, worse, that Martyn would not be well enough to travel. Fear touched her heart at the thought that he might be recognised and arrested leaving Leciester or at any place along the route to Bury.

When Peter Fairley tapped on her door she almost threw herself into his arms at her relief on seeing him. He was dressed like a servant, his brown hair tousled as if it had not seen a comb for weeks, but his eyes were shining triumphantly.

"My lord is here in the stables. If you would see him you must come now, while the men of the escort are at their meal in the convent kitchen and the sisters are at their devotions."

She had already donned one of Alice's fustian cloaks and went with him instantly. Jack Wainwright was standing at the stable door with the boy, Wat Forrester, beside him.

"All is well, my lady. He is in there. This meeting must be brief. You understand that?"

She nodded and waited no more but hastened into the gloom. The stable smelled sweetly of straw and hay and horses—even the familiar sharp scents of horse urine and more pungent dung could not disturb her.

At first she could not see him, deep in the shadows, then he had enfolded her in his arms in the old masterful way and kissed her hard, hungrily, demandingly. She responded eagerly, her arms reaching up round his neck to pull his head down even closer to hers.

"Oh, my darling, darling Cressida." He sounded like a man who had hungered for weeks and just now had had delicious food placed before him. She murmured incoherently of her love and he strained her body to him yet tighter.

"Come," he whispered hoarsely. "Here, down on the hay. Jack will keep guard and God knows how soon it will be before we meet again."

She could not even see him clearly, but she knew every part of his dear body that was hidden from her by the unfamiliar fustian tunic and coarse woollen hose. She protested when his chin rubbed against her cheek raspingly and she realised, laughingly, that he had grown a full beard.

She surrendered to him joyfully, feeling his own shuddering delight in her nearness, his desperate longing to possess her. Death had been so close and could even now draw near again. She was here within his arms and he took full advantage of her presence. But afterwards, as she lay spent in his arms, he bent to smooth down her disordered clothing and whispered a hasty apology for his urgent roughness.

"Don't," she whispered softly. "Don't even speak of it. I have needed you quite as desperately as you have wanted me. Oh, Martyn—Martyn, I thought I had lost you—and then Peter came—and I dared not believe him. My joy was too great..."

He nuzzled his bearded cheek against her nose and then her hair.

"I could hardly believe it myself when I came to in that upstairs room in Leicester. I had to feel myself all over to be sure I was no revenant."

"Will you be safe—even now? Oh, Martyn, I could not bear it if..."

"We have come so far safely, my heart, with the care and help of these three good men. Peter has had to grow up very quickly and as for Jack—" he drew a hard breath "—he is tried gold indeed and always has been. But for his quick thinking I would certainly be languishing in one of Henry's dungeons now, awaiting—who knows?"

He bent and kissed her again as he felt her shudder with fear beside him. He gave a bark of a laugh. "As for Wat, well, his knowledge of the underworld of society stands us in good stead now. Bless the boy, he knows I saved his life and has proved a willing messenger, guide—aye, and scavenger. He says he will go with me and God knows we need his special skills.''

''The Princess says you will make for Burgundy.''

''Yes, to the Court of the Duchess Margaret at Malines if God is with us.''

''You will be very careful?''

''I swear it, my love.''

Jack Wainwright's warning whisper reached them from the doorway. ''There are sounds from the kitchen that tell us the men will be coming out soon, my lord.''

''I must go. I must not endanger you.'' She rose immediately. ''Oh, Martyn, it will be so hard not to acknowledge you when I see you in the Princess's train.''

''I know, my love. I shall hardly dare to look your way.''

He drew her close again and she felt his body go rigid with the strain of this parting, then, gently, he set her from him and she moved to the stable door. A horse whinnied and moved restlessly and she turned.

A shaft of moonlight from the open door illuminated him for her. She saw his tall, erect figure crowned with a mass of dark hair that, like Peter's, had grown over-long and was in disarray from their tumble in the hay. His eyes were shining and his bearded mouth was parted in a reluctant smile. He lifted one hand in farewell and then she stepped out into the cold, moonlit court.

Later that night the Lady Elizabeth sent for her. She had dismissed her elderly attendant and was alone with Cressida. ''He is recovered?''.

''It would seem so, my lady.'' Cressida blushed hotly and Elizabeth laughed.

''I am relieved to hear that, and now, Cressida, you should go early tomorrow back to your father at Gretton.

It will be hard for both of you to remain in my train and avoid looking with such obvious love at each other.''

Cressida's heart turned over. ''So soon? Oh, my lady, why cannot I go with him? I did not speak of it in the stable for I knew he would object, but—''

''No, Cressida; he would never manage to board that ship with you. For his sake, you must let him go alone.''

''But I must see him again, just once more—please…''

''Would you make the parting harder for him to bear? He loses everything—title, home, friends and, most of all you—but his very survival now depends on the fact that everyone continues to believe he is dead. Believe me, Cressida, I know how hard it is for you to accept that premise. I too must forgo any contact with—with someone I love—for his chance of life.''

Cressida stared at her hard but Elizabeth shook her head decisively. ''You must let Martyn go. If he is taken, he will endanger more than his own life.''

''But will I ever see him again—and won't he look for me at least to say goodbye? He will think I have deserted him for my own comfort, knowing he has nothing to offer me in exile but a life of hardship.''

Elizabeth did not answer. Her eyes glittered oddly and Cressida was not sure if that was due to unshed tears or steely determination. Cressida sighed, curtsied, and made to withdraw.

Elizabeth said softly, ''I will send my new groom on some errand. He will not see you ride out early. Trust me. My friends will see him safe, at risk to their own lives.''

Next morning, when Cressida rode out early with Alice and two of the men from Elizabeth's own trusted escort, she looked back once towards the stable, busy now with grooms and ostlers preparing mounts for the Princess's departure for Walsingham. There was no sign of Martyn. She rode forward towards the convent gate feeling as if her heart would break and die within her living breast.

Martyn of Wroxeter looked up at his friend, Lord Lovell, with a wistful smile.

"I wish I were going with you, Frank," he said.

Lovell drained his wine goblet and rose to his feet. "You will be considerably more useful to the cause here in Malines," he replied. "Your collation of information gathered from all sources will be invaluable. The Duchess Margaret needs you and there is the boy to think of."

Martyn shook his head. "I know it, but I hate to skulk here in safety while you risk your life in England to sound out the northern lords for rebellion. Henry will have spies everywhere."

Lovell smiled grimly. "The Staffords are still free and I too have my companions who are ready to lay down their lives to bring Henry Tudor down."

He took his leave after the two grasped hands. Halfway down the stair he said, "Do you wish me to have someone contact the Lady Cressida?"

Again Martyn shook his head regretfully. "No, I will do nothing that could endanger her. Keep well away, my lord."

He returned to his seat near the window and looked down over the street below. His lodging was not large but it was comfortable and conveniently placed for his work at the palace of the Duchess Margaret of Burgundy.

He had come here with scarcely more than the clothes he stood up in, but Richard's sister, Margaret, had welcomed him warmly as she had other survivors of that débâcle on Ambien. As Lovell had said, he had soon slipped into the work he had done for King Richard, acting as the Duchess's spymaster and collecting all information which came to Malines which could help in the cause of dealing Henry Tudor a blow mighty enough to topple him from the English throne he had usurped.

Martyn had never needed luxurious accommodation; he had rooms on this second floor which served for his use and that of his squire, Peter Fairley. Below in the kitchen Jack Wainwright ruled benignly over the serving and kitchen wenches. Wat Forrester slept with Wainwright in the attic rooms at the top of the house and, for the most part, went his own way about the town, though he too had his uses. He met English and Burgundian merchants in taverns and brought back a wealth of information.

Martyn gazed about the room thoughtfully. The furniture and hangings were somewhat spartan, but he had been far less comfortable many times in his life on campaign. No, it was not concern for his bodily ease which brought the hint of brooding sadness to his dark brown eyes or the wistful downward turn of his lips.

It would soon be the Holy Season of Christmas. Last year at this time he had not met the fairy child whom he had made his beloved bride. She had been the King's pawn, wed to weld her father's allegiance to King Richard, and though the ploy had been successful it had all come to naught in the end with the fall of the King at Redmoor.

Martyn had not thought then that he could come to love that exquisitely beautiful child with all the passion and devotion of his heart. He missed her desperately, knew she was secure upon her father's manor at Gretton, but longed with all his being to have her with him now.

He had little to offer. His title meant nothing here and he had no fine town house nor rich estates on the Welsh border. Despite all their intended efforts to dislodge Henry from the royal seat, Martyn could not dispel the thought from his mind that he would never have those things again.

No, Cressida was best in England. Her parents considered her a virgin still. It might yet be possible for her to obtain a dispensation and wed again, some man Henry favoured. He ground his teeth in bitter desperation at the thought.

A knock came at his door and he called for Peter Fairley to enter.

He did not look up at once and wondered why the boy remained in the doorway and did not state his errand. Then he turned.

She stood, framed against the lintel, the formidable form of Alice Croft beside her, and behind them, shuffling uncomfortably in the confined space of the landing, young Philip Kenton and the stolid frame of his former captain of escort at Wroxeter, the redoubtable Sergeant Chubb.

At first he thought he must be hallucinating, then she gave a little inarticulate cry and moved towards him. Alice shooed away the others and withdrew herself, leaving them alone.

She was real; he could feel her close to his heart. He pressed passionate kisses upon the top of her head, then pushed back her hood, tilted up her chin and kissed her again on her mouth, cheeks damp with happy tears, eyes, chin again. At last he drew away to arm's length, holding her hands still, and took in his full sight of her.

He said, hoarse with emotion, "I—I cannot believe you are real. If I continue to look, will you disappear from view like the fairy you are?"

She laughed merrily. "I am very solid indeed, my lord, more so than usual for—for I bring you an heir." She was blushing rosily in shy embarrassment.

Again he stared at her, then abruptly enclosed her in his arms again. This time he could not hold back a sob of amazed joy.

"I had meant to be more decorous than that and tell you more gently," she confessed, "but—oh, Martyn, I have waited so long to see you that it could not wait."

She stared back at him now wonderingly. He was again the elegant courtier she had known at Westminster. His beard was gone, his cheeks smooth-shaven, and his dark hair was combed back from his face in sleek waves and fell to his shoulders. She drew a hard breath and laughed again in sheer delight at reaching him at last.

He drew her to the chair and, sitting her down, knelt before her.

"I think either the Virgin has answered my prayers or you yourself, with your magic, heard me call to you across the sea. Oh, my darling. How is it possible you are here?"

"The Princess convinced me that I must not leave with you. It would endanger you, she said, and I must return to Gretton and pretend you were indeed killed, so I did." It was so simply said, with no mention of the immense difficulty of accomplishing that, that he had to laugh aloud.

"It had its problems," she confided, "especially when I discovered that I—was to bear your child. I told Alice, of course." Her expression sobered. "I could not even tell my mother.

"And then Howell came to Gretton." Her clear blue eyes looked deep into his. "Howell loves me. He believed I was a widow and—and he proposed to me—after my period of mourning was over, of course."

"And you said?"

"I told him that could never be and—and he guessed, because he loves me, I think. He said we could still get a dispensation if it was believed I had been no true wife—and—and that he would say the child was his."

Martyn gave a little hiss of protest.

"I had to tell him then how dearly I loved you—that

even if you were dead I could never give my heart to another man.'' She was silent for a moment, then said, ''He is a very honourable man, Howell, even though he supported the Tudor. His allegiance was given there, as yours was to Richard. At last he said he would help me to come to you if I truly wished it. Oh, Martyn, how much I wanted that.''

He sat back, regarding her with a little crooked smile. ''And so you came. You never let little difficulties prevent you from doing what you wished, did you, my wife?''

''Never.'' She reached down and kissed him. ''Alice had to come, of course, and Philip. I could not ask my father, so—Sergeant Chubb insisted that he could not let his Countess embark upon the high seas without her sergeant-at-escort. Besides, he wants to be with you.''

He stood up and held out his hand to her to rise, then took from her her cloak and looked hungrily at her beauty again. As yet there was no sign of impending motherhood. She was, as ever, tiny, resolute, holding herself with the grace of a queen, and her blue eyes shone with love for him. Suddenly her expression clouded. ''You will not send me away?''

His voice was almost choked with tears as he said, ''Never, never, my darling.''

She looked round anxiously. ''You are happy here? The Princess indicated that you would work for the Duchess Margaret.'' She hesitated. ''She also said you would endanger more lives than your own if caught. Did she—did she mean one of her brothers, Martyn?''

He nodded slowly. ''Richard of York has been here in Burgundy for almost two years. It will be my duty to serve him.''

''And the other Prince?''

He shook his head regretfully. ''I do not know. Edward

was sent north to Barnard Castle with Sir Guy Jarvis. Guy came south to fight at Redmoor. I cannot say what has happened to the boy since then. I hear Jarvis and Allard both survived and have paid heavy fines and returned to their manors.'' He did not add that he believed both would be active in Lovell's proposed rising against Henry.

Cressida said quietly, ''Elizabeth saved your life. Martyn, I believe she truly loved Richard.''

''I know. In that lay the danger.''

She sighed again. ''How lonely and unhappy she will be in the coming years. She is to marry Henry in January. We shall all grieve for the death of the King. I have a Book of Hours he gave me and will treasure it for ever.''

''We must pray he has his wish and he and his beloved Anne are reunited. He would have wished to die like that, fighting gallantly for the realm.'' He was gently stroking the palm of her hand. ''You do not mention the problems of your journey.''

''Howell found us a ship sailing from Milford Haven— ironical, wasn't it?'' She dimpled. ''It was very uncomfortable. We were all sick, then the journey was hard. Alice said I must travel slowly because of the child.''

''And now you are here and there will be eons of time to hear all about the long days we have been separated, but for now we must think of our happiness together. My darling Cressida, I have little to offer you but a life lived in the Duchess's favour, for which I am grateful. I brought little coin and no treasure from England.''

''But I did,'' she said happily. ''Alice and I sewed jewels into our clothing and they will keep us remarkably comfortable for a while, at least.''

He threw back his head and laughed aloud. ''Truly you are a redoubtable Countess of Wroxeter and will always be the love of my life.''

She offered herself for his embrace and he drew her into his arms. Christmas would come here at Malines and he would rejoice with his lovely bride by his side.

*   *   *   *   *

Elaine Knighton grew up in California, riding her horse through the grassy, windswept hills and dreaming of romantic, heroic adventures. Now she lives in the misty and mystical Pacific Northwest and writes about romantic, heroic adventures instead of only dreaming about them. Elaine has roots in Poland, England and Scotland, a mixture in which there may be some hope of finding a balance between passion and reason, but she thinks she'll always be a dreamer at heart.

To my wise and beautiful daughters,
Asmara and Angela

The Alchemist's Daughter

by

Elaine Knighton

Prologue

The Holy Land
Somewhere between Jerusalem and Acre
Spring of 1197

"Lucien! De Brus has fallen. We must stop."

"Aye, Allan, I expected it to be so." Lucien de Gris-wold's heart sank as he turned in the saddle and looked back over the straggling line of weary men and horses. De Brus, who had gone with them on pilgrimage to Jerusalem only to please his lady-wife, had taken a deep sword thrust to his thigh. The attacking tribesmen, in search of plunder, did not respect the uneasy truce between west and east, no more than did many Crusaders.

The dry wind kicked up a spiral of dust and heat shimmered over the sand and rocks. This desert, this place…the Holy Land…was not a land of milk and honey, but of blood and pain and thirst. Only the Saracens, with great determination, faith and skill, were at home here.

Allan had dismounted and helped the ailing De Brus to

the shade of an overhang. Lucien left his horse in the care of a servant and knelt beside De Brus. The knight's wound was poisoning his blood. His red, sweaty skin, his leg so swollen that his foot was mottled, testified to that fact.

"He needs more medicine than the camp leech can provide, even could we get him there before he dies," Allan whispered.

De Brus opened his eyes. "Don't bother trying to spare my feelings now, Allan. I know full well I am a waste of further food and water. Just leave me here in the shade."

"Be quiet, Brus," Lucien said. He drew Allan aside. "There was a *caravanserai* going east. They may know of a physician in a town nearby. It is worth a try."

"A Saracen physician?" Allan's brows knit.

"Aye. They have the skill Brus's leg requires. I have seen what they can do. I fear otherwise he will indeed die while our leech deliberates and Brus argues with him. He won't be able to argue with a Turk."

"Very well. But be swift, for we dare not tarry here overlong. If you must go, at least take someone with you. Do not go alone."

Lucien shook his head. "To the Arabs we Franj are dangerous wild animals. A pack of us will only make them defensive. One of us may get a better result than many. And if I should fail, there will be fewer of our party at risk. No one in Acre even knows we are here, so we have no hope of them setting out to look for us."

"But Kalle FitzMalheury is due to return this way. No doubt he would come to our aid."

A surge of distaste filled Lucien at the mention of the knight whose reputation for brutality overshadowed his brilliance as a commander. "I hope we are gone long before then, for I have no wish to encounter Kalle Fitz-Malheury—especially if I need him."

"Aye." Allan rubbed his dagger hilt. "I know what you mean. He is a restless lion amongst men."

"All the more reason for me to make haste." After downing a mouthful of warm water, Lucien set out in pursuit of the *caravanserai* whose dust was still visible in the distance. It was a small procession, no more than a dozen heavily laden camels, but well supplied with guards, a mixture of Turks and mercenary Franks.

With a final burst of effort from his horse, Lucien caught up with the vanguard. He brought his mount around, just close enough for them to hear his shout. Some of the guards had already turned, arrows nocked and ready to fly.

"May peace be upon you, all honor to the Prophet!" Lucien began in Arabic.

But the guards' bows stayed taut, the arrows level; the red tassels on their horses' bridles fluttered in the wind.

Lucien took a deep breath. "I seek a *ṭābib*. Know you where I might find a man skilled in medicine?"

"Why should we help a murdering Franj?"

To Lucien's surprise, one among them replied, "Because it is the Law of God, both Christian and Muslim, to show mercy to those who ask it of us, if that is within our power to bestow."

The man rode toward Lucien, his white robes pristine despite the dust and heat. "I am Palban, known in these parts as al-Balub, a physician come from Cordoba. What is the problem?"

As he drew near, Lucien saw that whether a Saracen or

no, this Spaniard was fair of complexion and not one of the Turks by birth. He quickly explained Brus's predicament and added, "I swear to protect you and see you safely back to your escort. I can but offer you a promise of compensation, as at the moment I have nothing of value beyond my honor and gratitude."

Palban smiled. "I see you have manners befitting a prince, if not the wealth of one. And I consider the former of more worth than the latter. It would be a refreshing change to minister to a wounded knight be he French or English or German, instead of an overfed emir. Let me collect my things." He galloped back to the caravan and returned with a bundle strapped to his saddle. "They will await me here, for a few hours only, while they rest the horses."

Lucien's heart leaped with hope and he led the *ṭābib* toward De Brus. As they rode he plied the physician with questions, of medicine, of philosophy and of alchemy, an area in which he had a deep interest. Compared to this country, where such exalted knowledge was openly sought and arcane pursuits were more valued than feared, England was an abyss of ignorance.

"I seek a teacher in these arts," he confessed to Palban at last. It was a vast understatement. He longed for knowledge of beauty unseen, of words unspoken, of music unstruck. Beyond that, he owed his lady-mother a heavy debt of the heart, and realizing the fruits of alchemy had become his last hope of easing her pain…and his own nagging guilt. But as this campaign in the Holy Land had unfolded in a sea of blood and anguish, he had begun to despair of ever realizing such a nebulous dream.

"Ah." Palban smiled again. "There is an old saying, 'When

the student is ready, the master appears.' Have no worry, Sir Lucien, you will find a teacher when the time is ripe."

Lucien smiled grimly to himself. He had been ready for a long time, with no such manifestation.

As if Palban had read his mind, he said, "But in Acre, you should visit a man named Deogal. I have not seen him in years, but I think he may be of value to you."

"My thanks, *effendi,* learned one. I hope one day I will be allowed the honor of repaying this boon of your service."

"You can repay me by being of noble service to others, my young friend, that is how I was taught."

Lucien marveled that in this desert he had been guided to such a jewel among men. Then, as they drew near Brus, he swallowed against the lump that formed in his dry throat. He could not bear another pointless death and prayed that he had not brought Palban too late. "He is just over there. The sun has moved, but I think there is still enough shade."

Lucien waited while Palban remained at Brus's side until the sun neared the horizon, a crimson blaze deepening into the dusky blue of evening. At last he rose and came to Lucien, his white robes no longer pristine. "I think he can be moved to Acre now. And once there, if his wound is tended properly, he will live. But there is no time to waste. I have spoken to your comrade, Allan. He knows what measures to take in the meantime. Now I must return to my own journey."

Lucien looked to De Brus, who dozed peacefully, his lines of pain gone. "Many thanks, *effendi.* You have eased more hearts this day than you can know. I'll summon a proper escort and see you back to your party."

After a quick meal that put the final seal upon their

friendship, they set out with a half dozen men. As they left their resting place behind, a rumble of hooves met Lucien's senses. It was part hearing, part feeling and part knowing—danger approached, and would be upon them in but a few moments.

Allan looked to Lucien. "What shall we do? There is no cover."

Lucien shook his head. "We cannot outrun them, our horses are too weary. We must simply keep moving as we are and meet them when they find us. Keep Palban in our midst."

The sound of pounding hooves grew louder and the last few rays of the sun caught the helms and lance heads of a group of warriors as they neared.

"They are ours!" Allan stood in his stirrups and waved, his relief apparent. "It is FitzMalheury!"

"Then do not invite him to join us!" urged Lucien. But it was too late. Kalle FitzMalheury, who had been expelled even from the ranks of the Templars because of his extremism, came upon them in a whirl of dust and clanging metal.

He brought his horse up short and it reared. "What are you doing, Lucien de Griswold, wandering in the desert? Should you not be in the safe company of your men?"

Lucien resented having to explain himself to anyone, but decided not to argue. "De Brus needed help. I found someone to provide it and now am returning his savior to his own people."

Kalle glared at Palban. "Savior? Whom do you serve? The lords of Constantinople, or of Cairo, or of Jerusalem?"

The physician sat his horse stiffly. "I am of Cordoba, my lord. I am here on an errand, upon the request of al-'Ādil the Just, may he live forever. But I serve no one but God."

"Which God?" Kalle pressed, his pale eyes gleaming. His gauntleted fingers twitched upon his sword hilt.

Palban raised his chin. "There is but a single God. It is you Christians who are the polytheists, worshiping a trinity."

"A cursed tongue have you, dog of an infidel." Kalle swung his head to face Lucien. "You have done Brus no favor, Lucien de Griswold, by turning his leg into a pagan offering!"

"FitzMalheury, have a care as to your words," Lucien said softly, and began to ease his horse between Kalle's and Palban's.

"FitzMalheury?" Palban's face paled as if he had heard of Kalle's reputation.

Kalle sneered. "And you, Lucien, watch your empty head, lest I send it rolling along the ground as a lesson to all friends of Salah al-Din's brother."

"Allan," Lucien, his heart pounding, kept his gaze upon Kalle. "Take Palban on to his destination. I would stay here with Kalle and have it out with him to my satisfaction."

"Had you the least respect for your betters, you'd not even think of raising your hand against me. But be advised—I've seen to it that nothing remains of the *caravanserai*. And I will send this Saracen to join his friends, to be purged by the hellfire that surely awaits him."

Kalle spurred his horse forward, his sword unleashed.

"Nay!" Lucien sought to block his advance, but the heavy destrier's shoulder knocked his own tired mount off balance. Palban tried to rein his horse around to flee, but Kalle was almost upon him. In desperation, Lucien kicked his stirrups free and leaped from his saddle to land behind Kalle, on the destrier's rump. Anything to slow him down.

But Kalle's speed was beyond stopping. Palban screamed as the knight's blade flashed. A burst of red showered through the air. Then, with a snarl, FitzMalheury rammed the pommel of his sword backward and hit Lucien between the eyes.

And Lucien thought, as the blackness swooped in, *Kalle has robbed Palban of his life—and me of my honor....*

Chapter One

Acre
Capital of the Kingdom of Jerusalem
Early summer, 1197

The crunch of booted feet on packed earth and the rattle of swords echoed in the narrow, steep-walled lane. Shifting her precious bundle of glassware, Isidora hurried through the arched stone gateway into the courtyard of her father's house.

She pushed aside her linen veil and looked back. Drying fabrics streamed and billowed like pennants from windows high above, creating a serpentine play of light and shadow on the street. Below, bareheaded in the sun, as if it were not the middle of the afternoon when sensible folk came in out of the heat and dust, a group of brawny young men strode nearer.

Tall, broad-chested warriors. Franks? English? She was not certain. But they moved with bold assurance, taking up more space with their extravagant movements and loud voices than was either seemly or wise in this city of many cultures.

When the great Salah al-Din had ruled, isolated westerners like she and her father had usually been left in peace. Then the city had been retaken by Richard Coeur de Leon and King Philippe.

Little enough blood had been shed when Acre shifted hands that time, but many a Crusader did not bother to determine who was Christian and who was Muslim before striking out.

Isidora's stomach fluttered at the sight of the men with their fair heads and long swords. She swallowed her rising fear and took another peek. She had to admit they were glorious—like young, unruly chargers.

But joking amongst themselves and occupying half the lane, they acted as though they personally ruled the place.

Whatever their purpose, she should bar the gate before they drew any closer.

"Marylas, quick, help me." Isidora put the glassware down.

The serving girl was a Circassian, her face and arms heavily veiled because her flawless white skin could not tolerate the desert sun. But she was strong and willing, and helped Isidora push the heavy wooden gate. It swung a short way, met a stubborn resistance and stopped short.

Isidora's body stilled at a creak of leather and the faintest whiff of sandalwood. She looked around the edge of the thick planking. Her gaze moved from a gauntleted hand, up a muscular, linen-clad arm, and to the vivid blue eyes of the man who remained firmly in the way.

"Oh," she breathed. If the lovely Marylas resembled a

woman made of silver, this was as comely a man as could be imagined, made of red-gold. A straight nose, set in a lean, sculpted, sun-burned face, with high cheekbones and a wide jaw. Hair that flowed past his shoulders like liquid copper.

His eyebrow quirked. A charming, perfect eyebrow.

"Ma demoiselle?"

And a voice to match the rest. Resonant yet soft. Rich with nuance.

She blinked and was ready to kick herself. *What am I thinking? One bewitching stranger cannot sway me from what I know to be the truth. Fair men are perfectly capable of destroying one's life and happiness, just as are ugly ones.*

"Pardon me, do you speak French or English?" he asked, still not releasing the gate.

"Or Latin? Or Greek? Lucien knows them all," came another voice from beyond him, accompanied by male laughter.

"You are Franj?" Isidora ventured in French. His eyes were as blue as the sea beyond the walls of the city. *Beteuse! What does it matter who he is or how handsome? Tell him to go away!*

"Nay. But we need—guiding—to the, em, bathhouse. Can you help?"

His companions groaned. "Lucien—you and your hot water obsession! Why not ask where the nearest ale house is?"

Her father's voice rang out into the courtyard. "Isidora! What's keeping you?"

She glanced over her shoulder. "Nothing, my lord! Just some travelers looking for the *hammam*. It is up that way," she added, and pointed in the direction they should go.

"God speed you!" she urged the young men, but they did not depart.

Then her father, Sir Deogal, emerged, tall and spare and out of sorts. His eyes glinted dangerously from beneath his heavy gray brows. He moved in the stiff but determined way of old warriors, his faded blue robe dragging along the stones of the courtyard.

Isidora threw him a concerned look. He would still pick a fight, even though outnumbered and unarmed. Strong he might be, but men like these could cut him to pieces if they chose.

"Father, please do not trouble yourself. They are just leaving." She turned and met the handsome intruder's gaze squarely. "Are you not?"

Clutching the slender neck of a glass alembic in one hand, Deogal threw the gate wide with the other to reveal the group of four young men.

"Take yourselves off from here. Go find someone who has time to squander dealing with the worthless likes of you!"

Just this once, curb your temper, Father! Isidora's heart pounded and she balled her hands into fists as the knights exchanged dark looks and fingered their swords. All but the one at the gate, whose eyes smiled even when his mouth did not.

The stranger gave a dismissive wave. "My friends, waste not your strength upon a demented old man. Go on, I will catch up with you later." When they hesitated, he fixed them with his gaze and said but one word. "Go."

"Don't get *too* clean, Lucien, or we won't take you back." They resumed their joking and moved down the lane, away from the *hammam* and toward the closest wine merchant.

Deogal shook his flask at Lucien and its contents danced in silver waves. "How dare you speak of me thus, you sorry whelp of a—"

The young knight raised his gauntleted hand. "Sir, I could not but help notice that is quicksilver in the vessel you hold there. I have an appreciation for such things, but my friends do not, so forgive me for having discouraged them in the way that I deemed best for the situation…may I speak with you?"

"You may not. I have work to do and no time for curiosity seekers. Isidora, get inside."

As Deogal retreated, slamming the workshop door behind him, Isidora was struck by the disappointment reflected on—what had they called him?—Lucien's face.

It was similar to her own, what she felt every time her father barred her from entering his *sanctum sanctorum*. From the part of his life that mattered most to him.

This fellow did not belong here. Her father needed help, aye, but she would provide it, not some stranger off the street. As much as she resented the Work, it was indeed important, and given time, Deogal would surely let her in. She was of his flesh, his only child. Sooner or later he *had* to….

But for now, the least she could do was show the knight that manners did exist in this household. And that she was not afraid of him.

"Lord, would you like some wine?"

The knight, who she assumed belonged to Henry of Champagne, the King of Jerusalem—known to the native residents of Acre, his capital, as *al-Kond Herri*—took a long breath. He crossed his arms and seemed to consider her proposal, looking at her carefully all the while. Then he nodded, once.

She had half expected him to stalk away. Half hoped that he would. But here he remained, so Isidora ushered him into the small garden where her father received his rare but usually important visitors.

All was in order. A small fountain burbled, red-flowering vines wound around the carved sandstone columns and birds chirped, flitting in and out of the shadows.

"Please sit, sir." Isidora indicated a polished marble bench. Off to one side, Marylas stood staring, her hand clamped over her mouth. Isidora gave the girl a reassuring look and she hurried toward the kitchen.

Marylas was easily frightened by the presence of armed men. Before coming to this household, she had suffered indignities that Isidora did not want her to be reminded of by anyone. Even this Lucien.

He settled his elegant limbs, removed his gloves and dabbled long, strong fingers in the fountain's pool as he looked about. When Marylas returned with the refreshments, and hesitated before him, Isidora saw that Lucien recognized the maid with courtesy instead of treating her as an object of contempt.

He inclined his head to her and murmured something that actually made her eyes smile. No doubt he was hoping to lay the foundation for a future assault. He would meet with a sharp, unpleasant surprise, should he try. Marylas never went without her dagger.

Isidora poured a measure of water into a mazer, then topped it with the wine and handed it to him.

"My thanks." Lucien raised the bowl but did not drink. "Will you not join me?"

"Nay. Forgive my rudeness, I have but little time to spare."

In truth, every moment she was with him unnerved her more. She found herself staring like a foolish girl might. He was so foreign. Gleaming. Beautiful. He glowed, like a painting of a heavenly herald.

Her mind wandered, as if along the golden curves of the lettered illuminations she labored over each day. For one ridiculous, embarrassing moment she imagined him to be sent by God, to distract her from the frustration of working for her father. Working for him, but kept apart from his work. *The Work.* It was all that mattered to him.

A familiar constriction squeezed her heart at the thought. She adored her father, but the Work had become her enemy, for it always stood between them. At times she hated it, as much as one could hate anything so ethereal and elusive.

Isidora looked away, for fear the young man would see her loneliness and pity her for it.

But he did not seem to notice anything amiss at all. He took a swallow of the wine and wiped his mouth with the back of his hand. "I am Lucien de Griswold. What is your name?"

"Isidora," she managed.

"Ah. *Gift of Isis.* A fitting name…for an alchemist's daughter."

She made a small sound. At his knowledge she was truly surprised and not a little alarmed. "You know of the Work my father does?"

"Of course. It is why I am here."

Oh, dear. Isidora decided to have a drink of wine after all. She had to get rid of him. For his own sake, as well as that of her father. Deogal wanted no more outsiders, and few were likely to tolerate his deteriorating, increasingly erratic temper.

But "Gift of Isis"? Curse of Isis was more like it. Even her name was not meant for her, but only as a reflection of her father's complete preoccupation with alchemy. And now here before her was a stranger, come out of nowhere. One who, it seemed, was only interested in the Work. Just like her father.

She filled a mazer without first adding water and, sitting upon the bench opposite Lucien, gulped the wine down.

To her chagrin, Lucien's mouth curved into a wry smile. "You do not approve of me?"

Already the wine had a certain fortifying effect on Isidora. "It is not my place to approve or disapprove. I assist my father and do his bidding. Beyond that and my attempts to protect him from ill-informed churchmen or greedy fortune seekers, I have no part in it."

Lucien leaned forward and rolled the wooden bowl between his palms. He met her gaze. "I am neither a cleric nor do I seek my fortune. I would be his student, his apprentice, if he would allow it."

Nay, not another one! Kalle FitzMalheury had been fair of face and words, but he had hurt her father—and been the downfall of her mother.... Isidora would not let anyone hurt Deogal again. "What *do* you want, then, my lord Lucien?"

He looked away and the wine in his bowl shuddered. With his eyes still averted, at last he spoke. "I want the truth. I need to find the Elixir."

"I see. Then all you wish is to attain perfect enlightenment and to live forever. Nay, I would not call that seeking your fortune." Isidora had not intended for her words to sound cutting, but from the way Lucien's brows drew together, it seemed he had taken them just that way.

"I need it for someone. Before it is too late."

The sincerity and quiet regret in his voice touched Isidora despite her mistrust. Perhaps there was more to him than good looks and assorted weapons. But it was not likely to be much.

She could not help him. He was from another world and did not belong here. "There is nothing I might say to my father to make him change his mind." Not that she wished to try, in any event.

Lucien's resultant sad smile made her bite her lip. How did people as tempting as him come into being, after all?

"Nay, *Demoiselle* Isidora. If I cannot convince him of my merit, then it is not meant to be."

There came a shuffle of leather-soled slippers. "What's this—you are still here, boy?" Sir Deogal loomed at the edge of the courtyard. "Why?"

Lucien immediately rose to his feet, as did Isidora. Lucien was much taller than she. Broad-shouldered and well-made, he stood mere inches away. He smelled of smoke, horses and that elusive air of sandalwood.

In all her life she had never been this close to a man not related to her. And this man, she knew, from some secret place within her, was potent. Like mead or the red inks she used—a little would go a long, long way....

"I invited him in, Father. It is hot outside. It was a matter of simple courtesy."

Lucien bowed. "I would have returned, in any case, and waited until you gave me audience, sir."

Deogal raised his chin. "What do you want from me, then?"

"The chance to learn from a master alchemist, my lord."

"Do you, now?" Deogal came closer and waved a hand at Isidora. Her nerves on edge, she tried not to spill as she poured him some wine, after a liberal dose of water in the bowl.

He sat beside her on the bench as if she needed protection, and looked Lucien up and down. "I have had students before. They invariably proved themselves either fools or corrupt, and had to be thrown out on their heads."

Isidora closed her eyes against the flood of painful memories those words evoked. Not so many years past, Kalle, her father's last partner in the Work, had brought Deogal's wrath crashing down upon himself by his betrayal. Her father had beaten Kalle nearly to death. Then he had shoved her mother out onto the street…and lived to regret it the rest of his days. Isidora bit her lip.

She well remembered the look of rage, aye, and loss on Kalle's bloodied face. She shivered despite the warm day. He was an enemy worthy of the fear he inspired. And her father, strong as he once had been, was no match for the cunning and evil Kalle was now rumored to be capable of.

Isidora eyed Lucien appraisingly. She had to consider that he might make himself useful as a champion to Deogal, and protect him from harm in ways Isidora could not. He seemed honest…but Kalle also had sounded sincere at first.

Lucien had remained standing. "I do not believe I am particularly corrupt or all that foolish. But I cannot promise that one day you would not be tempted to throw me out, on my head or otherwise."

Deogal grunted a laugh. "We shall see, then, just how

badly you want to be my student. But do not bother Isidora, do you understand? She is too trusting by far, to have spoken to you and allowed you entrance. Sometimes I regret raising her as the Franj do and giving her such freedom, instead of keeping her hidden away."

Isidora refrained from groaning out loud. What freedom? The freedom to go to the marketplace and purchase supplies for his Work? And why must Father delude himself into supposing that a wealthy stranger might take interest in her?

After all, she was dark, and too outspoken. Often as not, folk mistook her for one of the servants. However, she knew who she was—the proud daughter of a noble house, and it mattered not what anyone else thought.

Lucien crossed his arms, as if closing a door around himself. A bastion not easily swayed. "I have no intention of bothering your daughter, sir."

Then, the rogue disproved his words with but one look. His lips parted slightly and his eyes glittered with the light reflected from the fountain's waters. His gaze swept Isidora's skin in a hot wave and made her cheeks catch fire, as if she stood naked in the public square. How dare he show such insolence!

Isidora had to force herself not to jump up and run off to hide in the house—just to avoid losing control and slapping him. But she would not give Lucien the power to affect her so, or give her father cause to either worry or question her actions.

Chapter Two

Lucien came every day after that. He spoke but little as he sat and waited for her father to emerge and accept him as a student of the Work. At first his friends accompanied him to the gate. But as time passed and he still made no progress, one by one they fell away, until he remained alone.

Leaving his sword in Marylas's charge, he would bow to Deogal but say nothing. His request did not need to be made out loud, for it seemed he was asking with his whole being.

Day by day his face lost some of its air of ruddy confidence. But he had a presence that seemed to take up more space than he did physically. He wore sumptuous clothes and his surcoat of raw, red silk and fine leather boots added to his princely air.

Despite Lucien's silence, or perhaps because of it, Isidora wanted to know everything about him. Where his home was and what kind of life he led there. But she could not bring herself to ask him directly.

He was quiet, but seemed bigger than life—as though his skin couldn't quite contain him. He made her nervous, and he might mistake her inquisitiveness about the rest of the world for a personal interest in him.

Each day she offered him unleavened bread, dates and butter, figs and honey and wine, which he occasionally accepted. But of course that was only a matter of courtesy on her part, not concern.

Lucien was polite, without ever paying her enough attention that she might engage him in true conversation. His mind was always upon his goal. He would not endanger it by "bothering" her, she was certain. But she was also just as certain that eventually he would tire of waiting and leave them in peace.

But one day Deogal emerged from the workshop, his blue robe sooty and smelling of sulphur. "Tell me again why you want to partake of this Work, boy."

Lucien jumped to his feet. "Because I must, sir. It holds the greatest fascination for me. I sense…I know—that there are worlds of knowledge waiting to be discovered through the arts of alchemy, through the patience and persistence of those who dare venture past the mundane and into the arcane. I cannot believe that my life's achievements are only meant to be what my father envisioned—nothing but breeding and a series of acquisitions by force of arms."

Deogal looked down his aristocratic nose at Lucien. "You are dissatisfied with your lot? With your enviable position of privilege, rank, honor and wealth?"

Lucien gazed at Deogal and spread his strong, lean hands. "I am not ungrateful, Master Deogal. I simply cannot bear to accept that I might miss something else, something so huge and divine and all-enveloping that I cannot see it without the guidance of a man like you. Beyond that, I cannot put it into words."

Deogal raised one shaggy gray brow. "And what makes you think I have the means to guide you? Why should I be anything other than a bad-tempered old fool puttering with substances better left alone?"

"I have heard talk…but beyond that, I felt it, from the moment I stepped over your threshold. This is the place I belong. And you are the one to teach me."

Isidora had to hide her amazement. This cool, aloof young man had such eloquence, such passion? Only for the Work, she reminded herself.

Deogal let a smile spread across his face like the slow rising of the sun. "Then so be it, Lucien de Griswold. You will take the oath revealed to Isis and swear by Tartarus and Anubis and Cerebus and Charon and the Fates and Furies. You will do as I instruct you, and you will go to your grave with the secrets I reveal—"

A numbing cold spread through Isidora, freezing her lungs, her heart… To see her father smile like that—to hear him offer his trust, his sacred knowledge, to this stranger who had only waited a fortnight for what she had waited her whole life—it was beyond bearing.

After all that had happened, how could he trust someone who might turn out to be another Kalle—perhaps even worse than Kalle? Then the numbness gave way to a fury she did not know she possessed. To a shameful jealousy, unworthy of her.

It took her off guard, like a blow from behind. Kalle's apprenticeship had never produced such a reaction. He had never won her father's love.

Isidora's body shook, she could barely breathe, and she was possessed by a sudden, dreadful hope that Lucien would collapse in fits from the glare she bestowed upon him, before leaving this house for good.

Did he not deserve it, for reducing her to such a wretched, despicable state? But he never saw her daggered look. His eyes were shining with joy and his full attention remained on her father, waiting for him to finish.

Deogal frowned at Isidora. "You, child, should not be here listening! Go to the scriptorium and find something to copy!"

"Father…" she whispered before her throat tightened beyond words. She refused to look any longer at Lucien. The hateful usurper! Her face burned as if she had scrubbed it with nettles. Yet again she was banished from all that was important to her.

But she loved her father, no matter what, and would serve and protect him as long as he needed her. Whether he wanted her to or not.

"Excuse me." She stood and forced herself to walk slowly, with decorum. But once out of sight, she grabbed her skirts and ran through the house, up the stone stairs and into her haven. In the tiny scriptorium, a sense of calm gradually enveloped her. Here was *her* Work.

Isidora blinked, sniffed, swallowed, and as her heart slowed its wild beating, she regained the control that had long stood her so well. She looked at the scrolls and piles of parchment on the shelves, the bowls and bottles of colored inks that she mixed herself, from oxgall and ground lapis and all sorts of ingredients, both rare and common.

She had produced ornate manuscripts and painted portraits that had been purchased by princes and bishops and satraps. She wrote letters for those who could not do so themselves. It was how she best helped her father, for ingots of silver and vials of mercury did not come cheaply. Nor did the gold leaf or vellum she used in her finest scribing.

Isidora slipped onto the wooden seat behind the slanted table and reached down to open the small cupboard behind it. She felt for the folio inside and brought it out into the light of day. Carefully she opened the heavy leaves.

A painting of an exquisite face smiled at her from the calfskin surface. Luminous brown eyes, skin like the petals of a dusky rose, jet hair peeking from beneath a silken veil.

Here was her treasure…an image she had created, of Ayshka Binte Amir. Of her mother, as she had once looked. Before Kalle FitzMalheury had begun her death… Before her father had completed it…. Isidora swallowed the tears that threatened.

Unlike the fabled Elixir, her art was real. People could see it and feel it. It had meaning and value. Creating it was a solitary occupation, by its very nature, but such was her lot in life. Like Marylas, who had lost everything, to hope for more, for a loving father, much less for a loving husband, or children, was to ask too much.

She had seen the suffering of the truly unfortunate. What she had should be enough. Aye, she should be grateful for the bounty she possessed. Her sight, her limbs, her very life. Enough to eat and a place to sleep…even alone. It was best that way.

Why think twice about a man like Lucien? So what if Deogal wanted him to stay? So what if he brought Deogal some companionship in his labors—was that not a good thing?

Nay, not if it is at my expense!

But it was wrong to think thus.

She had her path and Lucien had his. They would be parallel for but a short time. The inevitable divergence would come, no doubt when *al-Kond Herri* called the knight back into service, and she would be rid of his enviable presence.

Isidora rested her cheek on the cool surface of the table and gazed out the window. Just beyond the walls of the city, the sea glistened as the afternoon waned. The sail of a returning fishing boat slid by, gilded and backlit by the sun.

Isidora gave thanks for the beautiful sight and made up her mind to banish all selfish thoughts. Her father was getting old; he needed help with the Work. God had sent him Lucien, and whether she liked it or not, she had to accept it. Just as most women had to accept so many things.

She thought of her once-beautiful mother, Ayshka, ravaged by disease and now dead. The unwelcome tears stung her eyes at last. She knew passion was possible, that true love existed. Even after banishing Ayshka, Deogal had loved her with an unseemly desperation, and that was what had fueled his love of the Work. That was what still fueled his guilt.

The Work had been his lady-wife's last hope for a cure, short of a miracle or the touch of a saintly king…. The Work could provide the Elixir, and the Elixir could cure all ills. Even the worst—that which had afflicted her mother.

A dread disease that carried with it a terrible stigma of implied dishonor, which tainted the whole family. Indeed, it might be the real reason no man had ever asked for Isidora's hand.

For her mother, shamed by one man and turned out of her home by another, had been visited by God's cruelest wrath of all...leprosy.

Chapter Three

Acre
The palace of Henry, al-Kond Herri, King of Jerusalem
High summer, 1197

"My lord Henry…can you be serious? To ally your-self—a bastion of Christianity—with Sinān, the heathen Grand Master of the Assassins? It is unthinkable!" Kalle's fist thumped the table.

The company of Henry's knights and noble advisors stirred, murmuring their disapproval of this outburst. Lucien remained silent, as he had throughout the meeting, but narrowed his eyes as FitzMalheury took a visible grip on his temper. "Surely it is not necessary for you, appointed as regent here by Richard himself, to make a pact with such a one?" Kalle asked.

Henry leaned back in his great chair and stared at Kalle. "You of all men should know the value of an alliance with them. They are deadly, but capable of reason, for they pay the Templars to leave them alone—and you should have seen what took place during our conversation at *al-Kahf.* Sinān demonstrated his power—he ordered two of his men to leap from atop the fortress. They did so without an instant's hesitation and fell to their deaths upon the rocks below. I had to beg him not to repeat the spectacle…but I will ask you, Kalle—would you have shown *me* such unswerving loyalty?"

Henry tilted his head and did not wait for a reply. "Sinān offered me another sample of his skills…he thought surely there must be someone I would like them to murder." Henry leaned toward FitzMalheury and smiled good-naturedly. "I declined, but of course, dear Kalle, you came to mind as a first candidate, being commander of the garrison as well as my closest rival."

At this the company roared with laughter, but Lucien saw that Kalle's mirth did not reach his eyes. The knight cleared his throat. "You flatter me with such a designation, my lord. But how you came by this opinion is quite beyond my understanding."

He then gave Lucien a direct look. One that pierced him with its enmity and stirred his own desire for revenge. "There are other candidates for elimination. Indeed, there is a man present who spends so little time amongst his own kind, one wonders whose side he is on," Kalle said softly, still looking at Lucien.

Lucien replied, his voice as velvet as Kalle's, "And there is another present who gives his personal ambitions priority over the interests of his lord."

"Enough," Henry said firmly. "Sinān is someone I want to be close enough to that I may keep an eye on him. I need not adopt the ways of the Assassins, only learn what I may about them, to ensure the safety of others."

Kalle stood and bowed. "As you will, my lord. I am yours to command, as ever."

At Henry's nod of dismissal, the group began to break up. Lucien was halfway to the door when Kalle stopped him.

"Never challenge my honor like that again, Lucien, or I will make you sorry you were ever born."

Lucien squared his shoulders and looked down at Kalle. "Just be advised, my lord, I am loyal to Henry, and he knows it. And just because you have made an enemy of Deogal does not mean he is anyone else's enemy."

Kalle's smile struck a perilous chord in Lucien. The man was like a rabid dog. And should be dealt with as such.

Kalle continued, "I shall have to pay the old man and his daughter a visit one of these days, hmm? See what progress he has made with the Work? Or perhaps you'd like to tell me yourself and spare him the pain?"

Lucien bristled. "Stay away from them. I will cut you to pieces if I catch you."

Kalle laughed. "Of course. If you catch me. A very small likelihood. But nay…the thought of playing inquisitor with you appeals to me much more. After all, Deogal would not last more than a day or two as my…guest. And what Isidora is likely to know is hardly worth the sweat of finding it out…whereas you, Lucien, could prove entertaining, indeed. So have a care, the next shadow you see might not be your own, eh?"

Isidora wondered at the change in Lucien when he returned from the court of *al-Kond Herri*…his somber moods, his rude questioning of her servants about who they saw and to whom they spoke from outside, his pacing and restless nights....

His evident distraction even caught her father's notice. "What is wrong with him?" Deogal frowned as he dipped a piece of bread into his bowl of sauce.

Isidora shrugged. "Perhaps he is ready to move on, at last. Perhaps he longs for home."

"He cannot! Not at this stage of the Work. We are just purifying the red essence of— Never mind. Just tell him I want to see him after vespers." Deogal pushed his half-eaten food aside and stalked back to his quarters.

Isidora stared at the carved marble bowl her father had abandoned and worry yet again twisted within her. He ate less and less, looked more and more haggard. She felt so helpless. How could she stop his decline? He paid her no attention, found her concern an annoyance.

"Isidora?"

That smooth voice, from behind. Lucien. She closed her eyes and did not move. She could not quite face him with her fears still so evident. "Aye? There is food left, should you want it."

"Has all been quiet? Nothing amiss?"

"Nothing."

"Why do you keep your back to me? What is wrong?"

At last she turned around. His beautiful face was limned by the golden glow of the oil lamps, accentuating the hollows of his cheeks. He, too, was in a decline. "Why don't you tell me? You are the one who knows what is going on, Lucien. You have known for months and are making all of us miserable as a result."

Lucien put his hand to his brow and pinched the bridge of his nose. His fingers quivered, and her alarm grew. "What is it? What has happened?"

He met her gaze. "Tonight you will hear a clamor, for the city will be in mourning, as soon as word spreads. Henry is dead."

A sense of cold struck her, as if she had jumped into the winter sea. "What? How can this be?"

"He fell to his death…from a window in his palace. Kalle FitzMalheury has taken charge, only until a succession is sorted out, or so he says. I have little hope that this was an accident, Isidora. You and your father are in danger with Kalle now free to run wild."

"He is no threat to us. We have friends more powerful than he, and well does he know it."

"You do not know what he has become, Isidora. He is growing inside of himself, like an abscess of pride and corrupt power."

"Then lance him," she replied, shocked at her own bluntness.

Then Lucien shocked her even more when he caught her shoulders in a firm, warm grip. Her surprise kept her in place, as well as the dizzying effect of his nearness.

"Do not speak so," he said. "I expect better of you. I would like…" His voice trailed away and the muscles in his jaw clenched as he searched her eyes.

Her belly tightened in an unfamiliar way. She felt an invisible pull, as if from his body to hers, and the tension grew until it was all she could do not to either break from his grasp and run or throw herself into his arms. "What would you like?" Isidora prompted, and yet held herself still and stiff, and closed her eyes against his gaze.

His voice emerged in a low growl. "I'd like to be finished here. Done with this place. I need to go home."

Isidora's cheeks burned as though he had slapped her. Why did she take his remarks personally? She did not care. Indeed had she not been looking forward to the day this troublesome knight left at last? But she had more than herself to consider. "You cannot go. M-my father needs you still."

"Look at me, Isidora." When she was focused on his flame-lit, blue eyes, he continued. "We are close to the Elixir. Very close. But the slightest mishap could make us have to start all over again. I am but trying to protect him, and the Work…and you. Should anything befall him, or me, all will be lost. Indeed, I cannot think why he has not included you, to ensure preservation of our progress, but I am sworn to secrecy and must respect his wishes."

As she allowed the truth to rise within her, Isidora began to tremble. "You know, Lucien, he chooses to believe my mother yet lives…that he can still restore her to health with the Elixir. That desire is all that keeps him going. If one day he wakes up and remembers that she is dead, he, too, will die."

Then the unthinkable happened. Lucien drew her close, wrapped his arms about her and held her to his chest, as if she were precious to him. "I won't leave, unless you command me to go."

Here was the moment of his obedience…she could tell him, right now, to be gone from her home, her life, her heart. But instead she replied, "You have our thanks, sir.

My father is too proud to say it, but I say it on his behalf." That was all there was to it. All there would ever be. Her father and his needs.

Lucien eased away from her and bowed, his bright hair gleaming. "I will go once more and find out the state of things in the city." Shouldering his sword, he disappeared out the door into the darkness. He did not return that night or the next.

Weeks passed, then months…her inquiries met with no results. It was as though he had been swallowed up in the ensuing maelstrom of grief and confusion that whirled through the streets after Henry's death became known. Perhaps Lucien had decided to go home, after all.

But Isidora knew that was not the case. And she had a good idea of where to go to next for answers.

Chapter Four

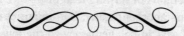

Lucien de Griswold, knight of the realm—sovereign lord of the village of East Ainsley, he reminded himself—and now prisoner of Kalle FitzMalheury, lay on his back in a dungeon of Acre. A Christian knight, in a Christian dungeon, in a city that lay months from home.

He squinted as a shaft of light penetrated through the wind hole, far above. Its feeble rays made his eyes ache. He had been here for what felt like forever, and time had lost all meaning. His capture had been the result of a fleeting slip of his attention…and a solid blow to his head.

What mattered now was the constant gnawing of his stomach, the thirst that made swallowing difficult, and the deep ache of his battered body.

It had been days since anyone had thrown him anything. Indeed, it had been days since he had seen or heard another human being. He wondered if Kalle had forgotten him.

Or perhaps some wild shift of fortune had caused the city to return to Muslim hands and the Saracens did not know of this small, isolated hole in the bowels of the keep?

The place was like a rabbit warren of ancient tunnels and chambers, and he doubted if any one man had ever explored all its secrets.

But he would rather suffer repeat questioning than be abandoned. FitzMalheury had not been able to beat any information out of him. He was but a student of the Work, not an adept. He was not privy to magic keys or unfailing methods of turning lead into gold. Now, silver into gold was another matter, but unlike Kalle, Lucien believed all that to be secondary to the true Work, not its goal.

Lucien forced himself to move, to raise his throbbing head and sit up. But the resultant swaying of the world forced him to seek the wall for support. And, in addition to his hunger and weakness and pain, he was so filthy he could barely stand himself.

They had doused him with latrine water to wake him up when he passed out. Apart from the murder of Palban, that indignity alone made him hate Kalle enough to kill him.

But he had to smile. Aye, even now, had he a bowl of water, he would save a bit of it to wash with. So he could not be all that close to death. When he cared no longer, then he would worry.

"Lucien?"

Footsteps on the stone floor. A feminine voice. A familiar accent, part French and part Arabic.

"Isidora?" He strained to see. There came a rustle of fabric. She peered over the lip of the pit. A thick strand of glossy black hair had escaped her veil and hung in contrast to the paleness of her face.

Her eyes widened. Warm, brown eyes that needed no

kohl to enhance their luster. "Oh, Sir Lucien! What have they done to you?"

It *was* Isidora. At this moment, the most welcome, beautiful sight in all creation. She lowered a basket to him and he amended his thought. Nay, *this* was the most welcome, beautiful sight in all creation....

He tore into the treasure and put the first flask to his mouth. Pomegranate juice...the potent liquid ran down his parched throat in a stream of pure bliss. A lemon, apples, figs, dates... Lucien paused in his ravishment of the fruit and frowned. "What are you doing here? How did you find me? You should not have come!"

"Do not eat it all at once, you'll make yourself ill, sir. And you will need your strength if I am to get you out of here."

"Out? How?"

"Never mind. Just catch hold of the rope and climb up. I have tied it to a ring set in the wall."

His mouth crammed full, Lucien could not immediately respond.

"You've had enough for now, you must move quickly!"

He eased himself to his feet. "Take the basket up first."

"I can get you more food, just come!"

"Nay, take it. I'll not have it go to waste."

"You are as maddening as ever, my lord!" she complained, but retrieved the basket on its tether.

Lucien caught hold of the rope and hoped his body would not fail him. But it was all he could do just to hang there, much less haul himself up hand over hand.

"You're not a side of mutton. Walk up the wall, Sir Lucien."

Her tone was light, but he heard the undercurrent of urgency in her voice. It was like a breeze that cleared the fog from his mind. She had risked her life to come for him. He had to get out, as much for her sake as his own.

He renewed his grip and put his bare feet to the cold, gritty stones of the wall. With agony chasing each increment of ascent, he climbed. As he topped the edge, his hands began to slip. "I can't hold on…"

Isidora caught the clothing at the scruff of his neck and pulled until she fell backward and Lucien landed on top of her, his face resting cozily on her bosom. For a moment neither of them moved.

Oh, God. What a time and place for such a happenstance. She had revived him with her basket of fruit. Only too well. She smelled clean. Like freedom. Like a woman. For one delirious, beastly instant he nearly moved against her. But even if he stank, he wasn't an animal. Not yet.

"Lucien!" She shook him as best she could. "Get up!"

He opened one eye. Of course, he had almost forgotten. She had made it clear that she wanted no part of him. He eased himself off of her and immediately wished he could lie down again.

"Oh, Isidora. I'm going to be sick."

"Not now. We have to go."

Taking command of himself, Lucien agreed. "All right." He grimaced and sat clutching his stomach.

"Here, put this on." She unfolded a garment from the bag she carried and helped him pull it over his head.

"Oh, my God." His hands smoothed the red cross sewn over the breast of the white surcoat. "Templar's garb? Where did you get this?"

"It is my father's." She hurriedly scrubbed at his face with the cloth from the basket.

"But—"

"There is no time, sir! Just do as I bid you!"

He stumbled and lurched down the corridor, sucking on the lemon as he went.

"Sir Lucien, you will have to straighten up and walk properly. If anyone sees us, keep going, as if your business is done. If they question you, just freeze them with an arrogant gaze—you are quite good at that. I will follow behind you, as a servant might. Now go left, then take the first right turning and then right again, and I will show you the passage."

The merest breath of air announced a side opening. With that hint of freshness, for the first time, Lucien began to believe this scheme might actually work. He forced himself straighter, composing his face into what had once been a habitually haughty expression, as Isidora had so kindly pointed out. But no more.

"How know you this way, Isidora?"

"Shh! I am privy to a few things worth knowing."

Lucien's mind churned. The Templars had more secrets than the Pope had ducats. So a hidden passage was not surprising. But her father, Deogal the Learned, his teacher of the arts of alchemy—was a Templar? An ex-Templar, no doubt. All that mattered now, Lucien thought, was that he had a chance to see the full light of day once again.

"Where are we going?"

"Your place is arranged on a ship to Cyprus, then to England, once you are out of here."

He paused in astonishment and turned around to face her. The expense should have been far beyond her means. "How?"

She gave him a shove. "Never mind! Just go! Get as far away from FitzMalheury as you can."

"What about you? I think I have proven myself worthless to him, but you—"

"I am staying here with Father."

A lump formed in Lucien's throat. "I will send you compensation, Isidora, as soon as I may. But I do not want to leave—"

"You must. Your family is powerful. They can help you. Father is not well. There is nothing left for you here."

Lucien came to a halt and caught her hand. It was compact but strong, her skin soft except where her pens and brushes had calloused her fingers. "How so?"

She pleaded with her dark eyes. "Lucien, what does it matter? I can help you, now, in this moment only. You can do nothing to help him, ever. So go while you can. It is what he wants. It is what he commands."

Nothing? Ever? A command to go? With the bitter finality of those words, all Lucien's other troubles faded. His studies under his beloved master were at an end, just when he might be close to the knowledge he sought…to the cure he sought…for the agony he had caused his mother…for the agony inflicted upon her long-lost daughter, his own beloved twin, Estelle. He had failed to protect her, just as he had failed to protect Palban—though at least Brus had gone home with both legs intact.

There *had* to be a way to find the Elixir, even if it meant struggling on his own the rest of his life. Or so he still hoped. Slowly he let go of Isidora's slim fingers and returned to trudging up the corridor.

Chapter Five

Wales
Saint Crispin's Day
October, 1202

"By the Rood, you don't much resemble an excommunicated outlaw to me." Lucien raised an eyebrow at his friend, Raymond de Beauchamp, who sat by the central fire with a contented, plump baby in his lap.

"Nor do you look much like an overeducated horse's arse to me, Lucien, though we both know it to be God's honest truth," Raymond said agreeably, and planted a kiss on the baby's head.

Raymond's squire, Wace du Hautepont, sat cross-legged on the floor beside him, mending arrow fletches. At his master's remark, the young man looked up from his task and grinned at Lucien. The lad had filled out and looked like a grown man, nearly ready to become a knight. Lucien grinned back at him.

"Well, I must admit, fatherhood has sweetened your temper, Raymond. Has it not, Ceridwen?"

Raymond's lady paused in her refilling of Lucien's bowl of mead and glanced fondly at her husband. "Indeed it has not. But who says his temper ever needed sweetening?"

At Raymond's resultant growl of laughter, Lucien looked heavenward in mock supplication. "The pair of you make me positively ill. Such a rogue does not deserve your devotion, Ceridwen, nor your defense. As I have said before, Raymond, you are a lucky man."

"Aye, I know it full well, Lucien. Here, hold Owain while I show this wench my gratitude." Raymond stuffed the child into Lucien's arms and caught Ceridwen, neatly turning so that his body shielded her from view.

Lucien, quite unused to infants, peered into the baby's round blue eyes. The child's soft weight was unexpectedly satisfying. Black curls—obviously Ceridwen's contribution, since Raymond was blond—peeked out from the tiny linen coif he wore, and his cheeks were round and red.

The wee thing chortled, grabbed fistfuls of Lucien's hair and yanked. "Oy! What have you taught him to do?"

"Eh?" Raymond released a breathless, blushing Ceridwen, who came to Lucien's rescue.

"He ever escapes his swaddling." She swept up Owain with expert confidence and recontained him in his wrapping.

Raymond sat in his chair once again and placed Lucien's mazer back into his hands. "So, Lucien, when are you going to follow in my footsteps?"

"Steal Ceridwen away from you, you mean?"

"Nay," Raymond said gently. "When will you give up this dry path of…of metallurgic sorcery you have chosen and attend to the stuff of life? Alchemy is for old men, Lucien, who have nothing else to do—or lose. You have lands to defend, crops to grow, and it is high time you took a wife."

Lucien sighed. His bitter disappointment in his ongoing alchemical failures since returning from the Holy Land ran deep. It had been nearly five years. Knowledge of the Divine—of the Essence that could cure all ills—carried a high, painful price. He could be close, without even knowing it.

And a wife would only get in the way of his paying the debt he owed his mother… "Wives require time and attention," he said at last.

"Marriage is not the penance you make it sound, Lucien," Ceridwen said. "Even Raymond no longer believes that." Her hip met Raymond's shoulder as she stood beside him and he slid a powerful, possessive arm around her thighs.

That in itself was a small miracle, to see Raymond, so recently the terror of the marches, now basking in the glow of his lady's affection. Though no less a warrior, he was a better man for it.

"But even supposing you are right, where am I to find a woman to put up with me as you do him?"

Ceridwen gave an unladylike snort. "Lucien, I can hardly believe my ears. Do you not notice those who follow you—nay, *devour* you with their eyes—at every feast or fair or market you attend? You have but to give any of them the slightest favor. Heaven knows their fathers will be delighted to hear from you. You are a prize, Lucien. A lord both handsome and wealthy, and unlike some around here, possessed of exquisite manners."

"There you have it! From one who has *me* to compare

you against, at that—true praise, indeed!" Raymond received a nudge of his wife's knee in his ribs and grinned.

Their encouragement only sounded like a lot of effort, fraught with risk. Then an inspiration came to Lucien. If he would pursue the Divine, he could also seek its help. "I shall pray and ask God for a sign. I will let the choice be up to Him."

"Let us hope the sign is not like it was for me, finding my bride impaled on the end of my sword…" Raymond looked up at Ceridwen, who gazed back at him with sultry eyes and ran the fingers of her free hand through his thick hair in a slow, sensuous movement.

Wace's cheeks reddened and he pointedly remained absorbed in his work.

Ceridwen smiled. "Never mind, my lord, it was for the best. I would not trade my scar for anything. But look, I have caused Wace to blush, and you have bored Owain to sleep, bless him. I shall retire. Good night, Wace, Sir Lucien. Worry not, all will be well."

"I am not worried," Lucien lied without remorse as he rose and bowed to Ceridwen. "So, you feel secure here, Raymond, at this keep? Do you need any men?"

"Ceridwen's brother and I make a good team, as it happens. We have enough men. And I do not think it wise for you to fight alongside us. You are established too far into England, you might bring down the anger of King John upon your head."

"I will fight for whom I please, Raymond, make no mistake."

"Aye, I know. Just be careful, eh? Come get some rest, now. You have a long journey to East Ainsley tomorrow." Raymond cuffed him good-naturedly. "But mind you, I shall be sending Squire Wace to visit whilst the year is yet new, and take measure of your progress toward a wedded state."

"I look forward to it, Beauchamp."

Lucien sighed and lay down by the fire, cocooned in blankets of both wool and the pleasant haze of mead. He hoped, as he did every night to little avail, that his dreams did not take him back to Acre, to the nightmare of the dungeon and the inexplicable, nagging sense of something left undone whenever he thought of Isidora....

Acre

With tears streaming down her face, Isidora knelt at her father's bedside, holding his blue-veined, wasted hand. There was so much she needed to tell him, so much she needed to hear from him, and so little time.

Since Lucien's departure, Deogal's illness had worsened day by day, for months and years until she despaired of him ever getting well. He had the flux, could hold nothing down; he often did not recognize her and sometimes he raved.

But now, at the end, by the grace of God, he looked at her and spoke her name.

"Isidora...the Work..."

Even at the moment of his death, he spoke of the Work but not how he felt about her?

"My daughter, you must take the scrolls to Britain, to Lucien. My notes. And the small bundle, there, on the shelf behind the antimony...it is imperative. Promise me you will do this."

She squeezed his trembling hand but said nothing. Even

had she a way to find Lucien, she could not face his mild, brotherly regard again, nor deliver into his hands a fresh obsession that would undoubtedly drive him to death and madness as it had her father.

Deogal returned her grasp and pulled himself up to face her, his eyes burning with feeling. "You *must,* Isidora. Please…I beseech you. It is the Key, at long last…of all my students, he alone will understand its significance and bring the Work to a magnificent conclusion…"

"Why have you never shared your knowledge with me, Father? I—I might have been closer to you that way."

"Nay, it is not for lasses such as yourself. Besides, your mother, God rest her soul, made me promise not to involve you. In order to protect you. But now, I have no choice. I beg this of you, before it is too late."

Her mother made him promise? *To protect her?* Such isolation had not felt like protection! And now he would burden her with these dark arts, when all she wanted was to burn the texts in the athanor!

He loves me, even though he hurts me. Yet again Isidora felt the heat of shame for her ingratitude.

Deogal lay back, as if the effort of his entreaty was too much. "You are the only one I can trust, Isidora. This must be from Acre, taken as far from FitzMalheury as it can be."

Despite the tearing of her own heart, Isidora could not bear the anguish in his eyes. She could not nay-say him, whatever the consequences. She took a deep breath.

"Of course, Father. I will see it done." She pulled out the small, gilt Maltese cross she wore and kissed it. "I swear upon the Holy Cross and upon the grave of my adored mother, Ayshka Binte Amir, and upon the love I hold for you, my dear father, that I will complete the task you have set me, or die in the attempt."

He smiled. "Good girl…" He sighed. His eyes closed and his fingers relaxed completely. Irrevocably.

"Father?" Disbelief, fear, grief, rage and desolation all competed for dominance within her. She fought to breathe, fought not to weep all over again.

He was gone! Leaving her nothing of himself but an errand. Not a word of love, only his habitual, "Good girl." Just as one said, "Good dog."

Isidora wailed and embraced his body in death as he had never allowed her to do in life. The overburdened moment froze for an instant. The scent of mint rose from a bowl of water she had used to bathe him as a warm, dry breeze wafted through the small window. But it did not stir Deogal's sweat-dampened hair. Nothing could touch him now.

He was safe, beyond suffering.

Kalle FitzMalheury hurled his goblet against the sandstone wall of the castle's refectory and rounded on the bearer of bad news. "What do you mean, Deogal is dead?"

The knight, a member of Salah al-Din's own extended family, nodded gravely. "A few days ago, *effendi*. He was buried this morning."

"Then where is the book, the material? The *stone?*"

The knight shrugged. "There was nothing but broken glass and crockery to be found. It looked as though a whirlwind had passed through the place."

Kalle approached the man and sneered, his pale hair

hanging in greasy wisps about his face. "And the girl? The half-breed?"

The knight did not retreat by even a fraction of an inch. He met Kalle's chilly gaze. "She is gone, as well, *effendi.*"

"Her father had the protection of the Templars, but I doubt that she does. So find her, Faris al-Rashid. Bring her back and I will see to the rest."

Faris bowed to Kalle, even as his fingers longed to grasp the hilt of his dagger. *La*—nay. Jesus Christ frowned upon cold-blooded murder even as did the Prophet. And, Faris had the feeling, even though newly baptized, that by his forbearance he himself would prove a better Christian than Kalle FitzMalheury.

He would seek out Isidora Binte Deogal, for he had his own reasons to find her.

Her head down, Isidora crept warily along the docks, avoiding the gaze of passersby. Sailors, merchants, thieves and beggars. Strangers, and dirty, dangerous ones at that.

Her heart thumped erratically in her chest. She had managed to smash what crucibles remained before she'd slipped out of her father's house—just ahead of the man who had come searching—for what?

She did not know if he was a robber or an assassin— but Lucien had been taken once, by Kalle FitzMalheury, so it was not so unlikely to think they might be after her.

Especially if they thought her father had passed on his secrets to her. Which, apparently, was exactly what he had done.

Not for the first time, she cursed the Work. She needed a way to get on a vessel bound for England, or even France.

In truth, she had little idea of how to go about it. Lucien's voyage had been made possible with the aid of her father's mysterious and invisible Templar allies.

But she had no idea how to contact them for help for herself. Her father's wretched *Work* had eaten up what remained of their resources. All but a few pieces of silver and the items she had been charged to deliver to Lucien.

Seabirds screeched and the scents of tar and the briny low tide filled her nostrils, along with rotting fish entrails. Despite that, she was hungry and soon it would be dark. What could she do?

If she managed to get aboard some galley in secret, and was caught, the ship's master might sell her into slavery to obtain his payment for her passage. Nay, she needed a better way. Perhaps one of them could use a cook or a washerwoman— A hand on her shoulder made her shriek, even as a gull cried out.

"Be not afraid—I mean thee no harm."

She whirled about and looked into the deep brown eyes of a man—one clad in a contradictory mixture of eastern and western garb. A Franj surcoat over doubled links of the finest Persian mail. A modest turban crowned his head, but he was clean-shaven. His sword was not curved, but his dagger was, the hilt crusted with jewels, as well.

She found her voice at last. "Who are you?"

"I am here to help you. I am known as Faris al-Rashid. Kalle FitzMalheury sent me— Nay, wait!" His hand restrained her instant attempt at flight. "But my mother…my mother was Ayshka Binte Amir."

Isidora chose to ignore the last part of his statement and concentrate on the first, for he still held her arm. "Please explain yourself, sir, for Kalle FitzMalheury is no friend of mine."

Faris glanced about and drew her into a doorway, out of sight. "It was the only way I could get close to you, without arousing his suspicion."

"Why do you want to get close to me?"

He caught her shoulders. "Because, Isidora, you are my sister—half sister—but my blood kin all the same. You and I are all that are left. The wars have taken everyone else close to us."

His flimsy story was hard to believe. But she saw the reflection of her mother in his eyes, in the elegant sweep of his brows. "Take off your turban and let me see you properly."

He unwrapped it to reveal wavy black locks and a central, down-pointing hairline at his forehead, just like hers. "Why now, and not before?" she whispered.

"She was widowed when my father was killed and I was sent to be fostered in one of the royal palaces. I did not know she had remarried, nor of your existence, and in my ignorance of the Franj, would not have wanted to know. In battle, I sang the praises of Allah as I cut the infidels to pieces, right along with everyone else.

"But afterward…afterward, something happened. I had a vision, Isidora. And I received instruction from an angel that my path was no longer with the army of Salah al-Din, may his great name be honored forever. For though his brother is wise and just, my heart was no longer in the *jihad*. Before she returned to God, I went to see *umma*."

"You did?" Isidora's eyes glazed with tears. She had seen her mother only once after she was taken to the house of lepers. Deogal had kept her close, isolated from others. He had been determined that Isidora not fall prey to the same disease. It had taken her much time and secret effort to find Ayshka. But her mother had forbidden her ever to return, and Isidora had not seen her again before she died.

"They say it is a judgment of God, to be afflicted thus, but she was in no pain, I swear to you. She asked me to find you and to give you this…" Faris produced a small, exquisitely carved wooden box, inlaid with ivory.

Isidora took it and carefully opened the lid. Inside, beneath a layer of red velvet, lay a beautiful but oddly crafted ring of silver. It was smooth on one edge and had rippling indentations on the other. She had never seen it before. But from her mother, it was a treasure indeed.

Faris spoke again. "She said you would know what to do with it, when the time is right. And she also said to tell you that Deogal loves—loved—you as a bird loves the air, for you were all that he had left of her, like the scent of jasmine, lingering…"

Isidora swallowed hard. Her father loved her only as a reminder of her mother? But what was wrong with her, that she could not rejoice for what blessings she had, instead of pining for what she had not?

"I—I have a brother. I am not alone. Oh…" Isidora covered her face and began to weep, as she had not done since the day her father died. Only the day before yesterday.

"Shh…" Faris held her and muffled her sobs against his sturdy chest. "We need to leave this place."

But Isidora was not done. She wiped her eyes. "How is it you can be associated with Kalle? He is a mad dog when it comes to Muslims—"

"I converted, Isidora."

She stared at him. "Not for me, please do not say it was for me."

"Nay, because of the angel's visitation, I was sincere. I am still sincere. And I sincerely hate Kalle, may the one God forgive me."

"Aye, I, too, am guilty of that. But I need to get to England, Faris, to find a student of my father's. Can you help me? W-will you come?" It was too much to ask, too much to hope for.

He grinned, a flash of white in the deepening shadows. "If I am to journey, I'll need a squire, and you look a promising lad, eh?"

At this, Isidora's heart began to feel a good deal lighter.

Chapter Six

Three months later
Ainsley Hall, England...

Lucien slouched in his great chair, absently watching his servants clear away the remains of the night's dinner. Venison—heavy—and ripe as old cheese. Such leftovers would probably choke the paupers who received them.

He missed the foodstuffs of the east. Fruit and rice and pulses. Fare that did not immediately put one to sleep. But, he was indeed grateful for what he had. None of his people were starving this winter. The hall was festooned with greenery and folk were in a state of pitched excitement, for tomorrow began the Christmas revels.

For weeks the celebrations would continue, the Feast of Fools being the highlight for those whose chief pleasures were drunkenness, dung-tossing and bawdy displays of dubious wit. The festivities would no doubt leave him exhausted, when he had much to ponder in the privacy of his solar. And such privacy was a rarity. Indeed, even now, Lucien felt a presence at his back.

"My lord."

Mauger, his not-to-be-denied seneschal. An impeccable man sent years ago by Lucien's late father, to keep an eye on him. One who had appointed himself advisor, bodyguard and chief nag.

Aye, who needed a wife with one such as he at hand?

"Sir Mauger. How may I be of service to you?"

The impressively large seneschal came 'round to face him and bowed. "Really, my lord Lucien, don't mock me thus."

Lucien smiled thinly. "How can I do otherwise? Even your plea for the betterment of my manners comes forth as an order. Dare I hope you will be chosen King of Misconduct for the Epiphany Feast?"

Mauger shook his head, making his dark curls bounce, and raised his eyes heavenward, his palms together. "I must pray for patience, Lord Lucien, for as much as I love thee, I'd see you improved as your father, God rest him, wished."

"One might think if I have not improved sufficiently yet, I never will."

Mauger put his fists on his hips. "What you must improve is your attention to the ladies who attend the revels, my lord. Your duty is clear, as is mine to remind you of it. You must produce an heir. Your uncle Conrad and ladymother are as set upon it as was your father."

Lucien shifted in his seat and avoided the seneschal's flinty gaze. As much as Lucien loved his parents and still respected his uncle, their plans for him had not taken into account his own desires. "Plenty of time for that."

"There is not. Children take years to grow, and often

don't survive. You must start now, Lucien, and your lord father charged both me and Lord Conrad to see that it comes to pass."

"Oh, and what do you intend to do? Chain me to some hapless female and instruct me step by step?"

Mauger stared at Lucien, his eyes frankly challenging. "If you refuse to cooperate, then I'll secure for you a suitable bride. Upon your uncle's and lady-mother's approval, of course."

"Not mine?"

"If you force me to such action, your approval is forfeit."

Lucien rubbed his unshaven chin with the back of his hand. "From your tone, Mauger, one might think you nursed a grievance against me."

"You nearly got yourself killed in Acre—and not in any noble, Christian cause! If you'd allowed me to go with you, no such misery would have taken place. And furthermore, had you returned in a timely manner, the marriage your father had already arranged would've taken place long ago and we'd not be having this discussion."

Lucien allowed himself a small sigh. "Ah, so it is that old complaint—I left you behind! Nay, Mauger. I needed you here, and a marvelous job you made of it. Nary a revolt, nor a shilling lost, nor a lamb or cow unaccounted for."

Mauger's ruddy face darkened even further. "Your description of my worthy efforts sounds like an accusation, my lord."

"Your worthy efforts make me nearly superfluous, Sir Mauger. I am apparently only required as a means to sire offspring."

"Indeed, look at it any way you like. You've been home

quite long enough to settle down. But there's yet another matter of great concern, my lord."

Lucien waved a hand toward a carved, leather-seated chair to his left. "Please, take a seat, Mauger. Had I known this would go on so long, I would have offered it immediately."

The seneschal sat heavily in the chair that Lucien's lady would have occupied, had he a lady. Mauger leaned forward and spoke in a lowered tone. "My lord Lucien, this unsuitable preoccupation of yours, this dalliance with sorcery—"

"Alchemy is not sorcery, Mauger. Only the ignorant believe thus."

Mauger clenched his fists. "I am not ignorant, and it *is* sorcery, make no mistake. Any art that aims to bend the course of nature to one's own will is magic. 'Tis blatant heresy, as well, Lucien, and you risk bringing ruin—aye, even damnation—upon yourself and your family by its pursuit!"

Lucien ground his teeth and narrowed his eyes. "I will not be threatened."

"I'm doing no such thing! I am but warning you of how most clerics view such conduct."

"I am fully aware of the Church and what it cares about, Mauger. As long as I am free of excessive wealth, and make no enemies of priests, bishops, abbots or cardinals, I have nothing to fear from them."

"What of the king's spies, then, Lucien? What of any visitor, with connections you know nothing about? 'Tis one thing for foreigners in outlandish places to dabble in alchemy, but quite another for a young man of good repute to do so right here in the English countryside."

Lucien gripped the arms of his chair, then rose. The seneschal did likewise and they met eye-to-eye. "Are you quite through, Mauger?"

"Nay, my lord. I am, though loath to do so, going to put a certain pressure upon you, in your own best interests. If you don't give up this obsessive study—and apply yourself to finding a bride—I shall inform your uncle and mother of the situation. Then we'll see."

Lucien's heart constricted, as if in the grip of an iron fist. It would be the death of his mother, should she learn of what he did in the wee hours, even though it was for her ultimate benefit… "What I would like to see, Mauger, is the two of us engaged in single combat, that I might be rid of your cursed interference once and for all!"

Mauger looked truly shocked. "You wound me, my lord, indeed you do. So little gratitude. *Someone* has to look after you, as you refuse to look after yourself!"

Lucien took a deep breath and crossed his arms. He knew that Mauger would no more give up this battle than a dog would a bone, for Mauger would carry out Lucien's father's wishes to the letter or die in the attempt.

"Nothing will keep me from my studies, Mauger, and you might as well face that right now. If and when I so choose, *I* will find myself a bride, not you or anyone else— so you had best leave off this well-intentioned persecution."

"Aye. But—"

"Nay. I am no longer the stripling you could browbeat into submission. You will say nothing to my uncle—or my mother—about alchemy or any other pursuit of mine that is none of their business. Or yours. If you value my respect— and if you wish to remain here as seneschal—you will agree."

Mauger gave him a long, appraising look, as if measuring the strength of his resolve. "I see. I can only assume that you, being the son of your father, will do the right thing. But—if, and when—you must choose the correct woman, Lucien. Not one you can easily set aside while you mix your—"

"Enough! Do not presume too much, Mauger. I am yet lord of this manor, so by God do not push me. Are we agreed?"

"Agreed." Mauger spit on his palm and offered his hand to Lucien, who tried to hide his distaste for the ritual as he followed suit. Mauger's face creased into a grin. "Lucien the Fastidious, that should be your name."

"And yours should be Mauger the Meddler."

"You'd best be off then, to the tonsor for a shave, my lord, and—"

"Aye, so I will do. No more advice, Mauger. Let me do this my way."

"Of course, my lord." Mauger smiled, bowed as low as his girth allowed him, and Lucien knew his troubles were just beginning.

Chapter Seven

It was more than a fortnight past Christmas, and on the ice-rimed road to East Ainsley, Isidora's horse attempted to snatch a mouthful of dried grass from a huge bundle carried by an overburdened man. She pulled back the reins with cold-stiffened fingers, but the horse was more determined than she.

"Oy!" the serf shouted.

"Your pardon. Though, as I am squire to the great lord Sir Faris, here, you should be honored to have a chance to feed my beast." Isidora attempted to wink at her brother. Somehow, pretending she was a squire made her bolder than she would have been otherwise under the circumstances.

The man grunted. "I'll feed yer beast, all right. It can be the main course for tonight's feasting!"

Isidora exchanged looks with Faris, who understood more English than he could speak. But from the blue tinge of his lips, Isidora doubted he would be speaking in any language if they did not soon find shelter.

"We seek Ainsley, the hall of Lucien de Griswold. Is it

nearby?" She could scarcely believe, after weeks of travel both under sail and overland by horse, that they might be in sight of their goal.

"Aye, 'tis so, that's where I am to deliver this load, by the lakeside, for the wounded to lie upon."

Isidora's breath caught. "Wounded? What do you mean? Is there a battle?"

"Yer no from these parts, are ye then, laddie? Well, follow me, you and yer great lord there might like to join in and get warmed up."

Faris indicated the man with his chin and addressed Isidora in French. "What is that impudent fellow talking about?"

"I do not know, Faris. But I would rather follow him than wander these foul roads any longer."

"'Ere's the shortcut."

The serf led them from the road to a lane and thence to a path that wound through thick woods. A freezing gray mist crept between the gnarled tree trunks. Everything looked the same, in any direction.

Close and still, the forest gave Isidora the feeling it was creeping up on her. So different from the long views the desert afforded…but she could not think about that now. She concentrated on guiding her horse over roots and stones, every now and again looking back at Faris.

Often as not, she saw he rode with his eyes closed, his teeth gritted together. So far, England had not suited him in the least. He needed food, and a fire. "How much farther?" she asked their guide.

"Not much," he grunted.

She could hear the faint drumming of tabors. And the

occasional swell of voices, as of a crowd shouting. After a while, a meadow opened up before them, teeming with people.

All sorts, it seemed, from high-born ladies bundled in furs to the lowliest of pig-herders. They clustered around various fires and there were ale-tuns at regular intervals.

At one end was a frozen pond—a sight at which she no longer marveled. At the other was a slope of rising land, striped fields and pastures. Past a wooden wall, presumably sheltering the village of East Ainsley, the view culminated in a rocky outcropping with a small but well-situated castle.

So this was Lucien's home. But where was he? Isidora did not know whether she dreaded seeing him or not. Her stomach churned and her heart pounded so hard that she felt quite ill.

A trumpet blast pierced the frigid air. "Hear ye, hear ye! The mêlée is about to commence! The valiant but outnumbered forces of Sir Lucien, to be faced with the Blessed Host of the Lord of Misrule! There is to be no fair fighting, no shows of bravery and every man for himself!"

At a great shout, to Isidora's astonishment, two hordes of jubilant men poured onto opposite sides of the ice-covered pond, bearing all the accoutrements of battle as well as of farming. The smaller group seemed to be better dressed and equipped, but throughout were swords, spears, flails, staffs, clubs, forks and even digging tools.

Some rode stick horses, others had bones strapped to their feet, which seemed to allow them to glide over the ice faster than those who merely slid around in boots or shoes.

Isidora was completely baffled. Had they all gone mad?

"Knights, to the fray!" With a roar, the smaller force surged toward the center of the pond. Their opponents fell back at first, then rallied and soon the battle was fully under way. Isidora picketed the horses and coaxed Faris to warm himself at one of the fires while they watched the spectacle.

A red-cheeked young woman smiled at them. She was dressed like a troubadour, her head capped by a jaunty hat with a turned-up brim. "You're not joining in the fight?"

Isidora bowed. "*Demoiselle,* we are strangers here, and are unfamiliar with this custom."

"Oh, it is the tradition! The Feast of Fools is the one day of the year when serfs and servants are the equals of the master and his men. They battle out on the ice, and Lord Lucien is as apt to be beaten as any other. There is no fear of reprisal, and all are allowed to participate."

"That sounds—" Isidora had been about to say "barbaric," but amended it. "Entertaining."

"Aye, indeed it is. My lute teacher is out there, giving as good as she gets, I'll warrant."

Faris asked, "Which is Lord Lucien?"

The girl raised up on her toes and peered at the mêlée. "Aye, there he is—on his knees, doubled up, with his arms over his head. Taking quite a thumping— Oh dear!"

Isidora's jaw dropped at the sight of several rough-looking men belaboring their lord with wooden rods. These English had to be mad! Then a massive fighter came to Lucien's rescue and tried to drive off the attackers with a flaming torch. But yet again, the mob surged toward them.

Panic surged through Isidora. She had witnessed bloody, lethal fights in the crowded streets of Acre on the heels of *al-Kond Herri*'s death. This looked no different. Lucien was about to be killed and she could not stand by and watch. She ran toward the pond.

"*La!* Isid—boy! Stop!"

Isidora heard Faris shout after her, but paid no heed. She bounded across the icy surface, only realizing her mistake when she found she could *not* stop, nor indeed even stay upright.

Her feet went skyward and the impact knocked the air from her lungs. She sprawled onto her back, spinning and sliding until she rammed something larger and heavier than she was. Then she knew she had made yet another mistake, for she had no weapon.

The recipient of her skidding blow was about to deliver one of his own—a fist aimed at her face. Lucien's eyes blazed like blue flames and she squeaked in terror.

"The devil—*Isidora?*" he breathed, frowning, and then lowered his arm. "Good God!"

"Hold!" Faris shouted.

There came a thunder of hooves. Her brother was coming to protect her. "Nay, Faris! Stay back!"

Lucien looked up and his face paled. The horse landed on the ice and an ominous groan sounded.

"Everyone off the pond! Now! The ice is breaking!" Lucien scooped Isidora into his arms and made his way with amazing speed to the safety of the shore.

But he dumped her there only to go back out onto the ice, his skill with the bone-clad boots making him swift.

Faris had jumped clear and was attempting to help his floundering horse out of the hole he was in. Some men were racing back to land, others were still so caught up in the mêlée they had not heard the warning.

Lucien grabbed the burning torch from the huge man who wielded it and shouted until he had their attention. "*Oyez!* Listen to me—the ice has cracked and is broken in places. Make your way back as lightly as you can. Spread out, and do not run or cause any more vibration than you have to. If you must, slide on your bellies to spread your weight, do you understand?"

Isidora watched, her heart in her mouth. The men, common and noble alike, slowly regained the shore, leaving red patches on the ice where the fighting had been fiercest. When all were safely in front of them, Lucien and the big man followed.

Faris's horse lunged, found its footing and scrambled out of the water. Then, with a shriek beyond anything Isidora had heard before, a gash ripped the ice open like a strike of lightning. The black water swallowed Faris up as if he had never existed. Only an echo of his cry remained.

The Persian mail! With so much metal weighing him down, he might as well have held a boulder in his arms and jumped in. She felt helpless, as if a tide were sucking the last remnants of her life away. This nightmare could not be true....

Lucien raced to within a few feet of the ice's edge, then lay on his stomach. Wet and half frozen himself, he scooted to the brink and held the torch over the water. The stranger might have a chance to surface, if he knew which way was up. If his eyes could yet see...

All were silent. The only sound was the irregular creaking of the pond's crust. Then came a small splash and Lucien grasped an ice-cold hand in his. A dark head emerged, and the stranger gasped for breath.

"Mauger, hold on to me! Get someone to pull us out with rope!"

His men quickly formed a human chain and tied something to Lucien's belt. It took all his strength to hang on to the drowning man's hand. Then his wrist. Then both wrists, and he came slithering out, as if newborn from the waters.

"Come, you can make it," urged Lucien.

"Mâshallâh!" croaked the fellow through chattering teeth, and Lucien nearly let go of him in surprise. *An Arab?* A handsome devil, no less, and obviously high-born. But what was he doing here?

"My mail, *effendi*. S-see to it, I b-beg of you."

Lucien blinked in confusion. Then the Arab pulled down an edge of his surcoat to reveal the shiny links.

"Of course, I will not let it rust. But let us get away from here first."

"Shuk-r'n."

"I only do as God allows, my friend."

A gust of freezing wind skittered across the pond and the Arab began to shake from head to toe. Lurching and slipping, Lucien guided him until they regained the shore at last.

Lucien wrapped a cloak around the man and helped him back onto his steaming, shivering horse. He tried to untie the rope from his belt, only it was not a rope, but a long length of cloth, and his stiff fingers could not undo the wet knot.

Climbing up behind the man, Lucien took the reins and halted the horse before Isidora. "This Turk belongs to you?"

She nodded, her face white even with the snow as a background. "He is not a Turk. But, aye, that is his turban. I gave it to your men, for there was no rope."

"Larke!" Lucien called out, his gaze sweeping the crowd.

The troubadour girl came running. "Are you all right, Lucien? Is the man all right? And the horse?"

"Aye, aye, have no worry." He indicated Isidora with a nod. "This is my friend. Take her to the hall and get Mauger to go with you. Isidora, my sister, Larke, will attend you. Kindly do as she says."

Isidora stared. "You have a sister? And in all the time with us you never told me? What is the matter with you, Sir Lucien?"

"Never mind, we'll talk later. This man needs to get warm, and my cuddling him atop his horse is not going to do much good." Lucien then turned to address his people. "This was but a minor mishap. All the revels will continue as usual, and I congratulate the fools who routed us!"

A cheer rose and Lucien breathed a sigh of relief. At least this farce was over for the year. But Isidora? In England? With a Saracen escort? He needed some hot mulled wine before he could take on such a puzzle.

Isidora sat before the fire in Lucien's solar, sipping warm wine from a wooden bowl that still rattled against her teeth, she was yet so cold. As was Faris, no doubt.

He dozed in Lucien's bed, dark against the white linens. No wonder Faris was exhausted. He must have found the strength of many men, to have risen in the water despite the mail coat he'd worn.

She felt a stab of fear for him, that he might be singled out and targeted by someone for the color of his skin. But so far, though many had stared, no one had said a word against the guest of their lord. He was yet safe, his sword but an arm's length away.

And, his mail now hung from a rod, Lucien having made certain it was dried and oiled. Faris would be glad.

But to her, the situation was utterly overwhelming. The journey, the dangers, the weather, the English themselves, and now this place, Lucien's home. It offered slender comfort, by eastern standards. Though clean enough, it was rudely furnished and only vaguely warm despite the roaring fires. Still, in any event, she did not belong here. Did not want to be here.

But perhaps he was merely a land baron now, and no longer possessed by alchemy. Perhaps she need not give him the things she had come so far to give him. Things she did not understand and that were certain to be dangerous.

"Isidora."

Lucien's voice, smooth and rich and heady. He was here with her, as if summoned by her thoughts of him, just as spirits—and devils—were summoned. Despite his coming up behind her, she did not jump in startlement.

Instead she was suffused by a flood of warmth. Nay, this was all wrong! She must stay strong and keep her heart her own....

"Isidora?"

The weight of his hand upon her shoulder. She closed her eyes. She would not speak, would not move, was glad she was already sitting. Maybe he would go away.

"Isidora, I do not know why you are here, or why you are garbed as a man, or who this person in my bed is to you, but…"

The intensity in Lucien's resonant voice made her open

her eyes. Now he was on his knees before her. His eyes shone in brilliant blue contrast to his blood and dirt-darkened skin—indeed, his face appeared little better than it had the last time she had seen him, but was still so handsome that he was almost painful to look upon. She shifted her gaze to the bed where Faris lay heaped with furs.

Lucien plucked the bowl of wine from her fingers and engulfed her cold hands in his even colder ones. "You shield yourself in silence, Isidora. It is not necessary."

"Is it not? Silence reveals much, if one is patient."

"But you must have news…an explanation?"

"I am on a grim errand, Lord Lucien. I will explain it when I am ready. Not before."

He gazed at her, searching her eyes. "Isidora, you have come a long way, and I…I am not sorry you are here."

Before she knew what was happening, he had pulled her into his hard embrace. Her cheek pressed against his wet surcoat, his heart pounded beneath it. She could scarcely breathe, he was squeezing her so tightly.

"I thought I would never see you again," he whispered. "I was afraid that Kalle might have— I should never have left."

"Nay, Lucien—I wanted you to go. You know that."

Despite Isidora's words, he did not push her away. And for reasons unknown to her, she did not try to escape.

Then the solar door creaked open.

"My lord?"

A young woman's voice. One sounding confused, perhaps even dismayed.

"Goodness, Lucien!" That, Isidora knew, was Larke's amiable, if surprised, response.

"Unhand Isidora, you Saxon!" A man's growl—that

of Faris. The hiss of metal being unsheathed. That of Faris's sword.

Lucien cleared his throat and eased Isidora from him. He looked at her as if he had just awoken from a deep sleep and could not believe where he found himself.

"*Effendi,* by God, that is my sister, not some camp follower!"

"My lord Lucien, who is this woman?" the unknown young lady asked, her voice quavering.

Isidora remained silent. Only her eyes questioned him.

Lucien cleared his throat and stood. "Lady Rosamunde, allow me to present Isidora, daughter of Sir Deogal, a brave knight of Acre." He gestured at Faris. "This is Faris, ah—"

"My half brother," Isidora supplied.

Faris nodded. "Faris al-Rashid, great-nephew to Salah al-Din the Magnificent, may his name be bathed in eternal glory. I am a Christian knight, even as you are, Lord Lucien. But I hold my sister's honor more dear than do you, it seems."

Isidora saw that it took Lucien a moment to take in this information. But he recovered quickly, only to deal her a blow for which she had no defense.

"Isidora, this is Rosamunde d'Artois. Daughter of the Count Hardouin. My betrothed, as of this New Year's Day just past."

Chapter Eight

Mauger marched into the solar and took in the scene at a glance. "Milady Larke, kindly take fair Rosamunde back to her quarters to await Lucien's apology." Once they had gone, he rounded on Lucien and shouted, "What in the name of all that is holy has been going on here?"

Lucien sat on his bed, to whence Faris had retreated, and sighed. "Should you not be supervising the Mass of the *Festum Assinorium,* Mauger? There will be much more to disapprove of there in the chapel than here."

"Aye," growled Mauger. "But a bunch of drunken peasants dancing naked in church with a donkey is not as serious as the Lord of East Ainsley kissing strange Saracen lads before the very eyes of his intended!"

"Even on Feast of Fools day, when all must be forgiven?" Lucien offered. "Besides, I was not kissing a lad. I was not kissing anyone at all."

Mauger's green eyes bulged and he glared at Isidora.

Lucien winced as she rose to his defense.

"I am not a boy, my lord Mauger. I can prove it, if you like. Nor am I a Saracen. But for that you must take my word."

Lucien shook his head. How could anyone mistake Isidora for a boy, no matter what garb she wore? "For God's sake, Mauger, leave her alone. It is not her fault."

Isidora drew herself tall and raised her chin. "Indeed it is my fault, Sir Lucien, for I have placed myself within your reach. You did not kiss me, but you might have done so without censure, because I owe you my gratitude for saving the life of Faris."

Lucien put his hand to his brow, then looked at her through his fingers. "I had God's help. But, I thank you for your courteous speech, Isidora."

Isidora bowed her head and her dark tresses fell in waves about her face. Through a gap in the curtain of her hair, Lucien saw that a tiny smile graced Isidora's lips.

Full, pink lips that he had not just been kissing.

He hurriedly looked at the fire. A conquest by an invader from Acre? He thought not. It had merely been a slip of control. She had surprised him, when he had not held a woman in God only knew how long.

Lucien indicated the door. "Sir Mauger, please go see to Rosamunde's comfort. She requires your subtlety and decorum."

Mauger's face reddened. "What of this knight in your bed?"

Lucien shrugged. "Oh, I daresay he will keep his hands off me. Will you not, Faris al-Rashid?"

Faris grunted incoherently. Lucien suspected—and hoped, especially since the man had drunk a great deal of mulled wine—that he did not fully understand the exchange.

With obvious reluctance, Mauger withdrew.

"So, Isidora. I…" Lucien tried to keep his voice light, as if he cared not one way or another that she was here. But her presence brought forth waves of memories—of hot nights, of the scents of jasmine and roses—and burning charcoal—and sulphur.

Of the excitement of discovery in Deogal's workshop, of secret knowledge and solemn dedication and joyful, mutual understanding, all lost to him now. One did not often meet such a skilled and highly principled master of the Work as Deogal.

Lucien wanted to catch Isidora in his arms again and hold her, to try to regain some of what he missed so much. But instead he turned to her and asked, "Why have you come, Isidora?"

"To see you, Sir Lucien."

"A long way, just to see me. Tell me the truth."

She looked up at him, her brown eyes soft and serious. "I cannot. I am not ready to tell you. You must give me time."

"Very well."

She played with the lacings of her tunic. "Are you truly going to marry that girl?"

"Isidora…"

"Are you?"

His composure slipped and clawed for a purchase. He forced himself to answer. "I have promised."

"Then that makes my task all the more difficult, for now I must consider her well-being in addition to yours."

"What are you talking about?"

Isidora tipped her head to one side. "Are you still an alchemist, my lord?"

Lucien blinked. What else was he, if not that? "Aye. Not a very good one, perhaps, but I am yet trying."

She gazed steadily at him. "I see."

"You are driving me mad, Isidora. Speak your mind!"

Isidora strolled around the brazier, jabbing at the coals with a poker. "Have you told her yet? Does she know of your unnatural delight in lead and quicksilver and acids?"

"Well, nay, I have not mentioned it. But why do you call it—"

Isidora interrupted him, waving the iron stick in emphasis. "You must tell her, Lucien. Otherwise it is just as if you wed her without mentioning that you already had a lover you were unwilling to give up."

He stared at her as if she had grown an extra head. "Not so! I will not be allowing her near the Work, in any event."

Isidora's smile was anything but humorous. "She will find it sooner or later, my lord, and right or wrong, she will draw her own conclusions."

His belly muscles tightened. "I cannot give it up."

"Then you should give *her* up."

Lucien jumped up and began to pace. "You do not understand."

Isidora threw down the poker with a clang and crossed her arms. "Then explain it to me, so that you might in due course explain it to her."

He stopped before her, wanting to shake her for such impertinence. "What gives you the right to come here, without warning, and tell me what to do?"

The liquid look she gave him then, of pain, and yearning, and love forsaken, was enough to make his own heart begin to ache. He took her hands in his once again and drew her to a wolfskin-draped bench before the brazier.

She sat stiffly and gazed at the red glow of the coals. "I have no right. Forgive me, my lord."

Lucien straddled the bench and leaned toward her, his elbows on his knees. "Tell me what has happened, Isidora."

She still did not look at him and, one by one, great tears began to slide down her cheeks. "Father is dead, Lucien. He went mad and he died."

Lucien's heart convulsed, as though it had been crushed by the careless blow of a hammer. "Oh, Isidora. I am so sorry. It must have been difficult for you."

She grabbed up the poker again and stirred the coals into a seething mass of heat and sparks. "Difficult? Oh, aye! To watch him being eaten alive by the Work. To know it would only be a matter of time before Kalle FitzMalheury tried again to gain his secrets. But Kalle was too late, may fleas infest his nether parts! And it was too late for me, too. Father died thinking of *you,* Lucien. Of you and the Work and my mother. That is all he ever thought of."

Lucien sat back, chastened. He remembered. Isidora peeking into the workshop and being driven away. Isidora serving him and her father food and drink as they spoke, watching and listening, but never included. Clever, inquisitive Isidora, always kept apart from what was truly important to her father, and to him.

She gently set the poker down. Her slender shoulders began to shake and she turned her face from him.

"Come, Isidora, it is all right." Lucien shifted closer, wanting to do something to comfort her, but not sure what she might accept. Then his body took over where his usually reliable mind stumbled. He drew her into his arms, so she was between his knees, and hugged her. "Shh, don't cry."

She wept all the harder and her body trembled.

When he rubbed her back with his palm, she turned to him. She pressed her wet face to his chest and neck, wrapped her arms around him and hung on as if he were her only refuge.

He swallowed against the closing of his own throat. "I miss him, too, Isidora."

"I know," she whispered.

Lucien found her shining, black hair beneath his hand and carefully squashed the urge to stroke it. To tip her head back and kiss her... He cleared his throat. "You had best go to bed now. The women's quarters—"

"Please, Lucien. Do not send me away."

Her whispered entreaty cut him to the quick. "You cannot stay here with me. It is improper."

"But I am afraid, Lucien. For the first time in my life, I am afraid, and I feel so alone. Next to you, I feel that much closer to how things were when Father was still alive."

He was helpless to deny her. She had come so far with nothing but false hopes, and had nothing to return to. "You are a brave lass, make no mistake. And you are not alone."

Isidora pulled herself upright, away from his warmth, and looked into his eyes. "You say that because you feel sorry for me. But you are still going to send me away. Aren't you."

"Not tonight. After all, it is still the Feast of Fools."

Her heart beat faster. "Must I be coy and deceive you about how I feel, like an English maid might?"

"I wish you would, Isidora. It would make it less painful for me. But you are still cold from the pond. If I shove your brother over a bit, you can get into the bed between us. I will remain awake, on the outside of the covers."

A tiny spark of heat ignited within her. "And if Sir Mauger comes in?"

A corner of Lucien's shapely mouth quirked. "I will tell him there is no room for him to join us."

Isidora smiled. "No wonder he is so vexed with you. But are you not supposed to go give an apology to Lady Rosamunde?"

"Aye."

Lucien's coppery hair gleamed in the firelight as he gazed at her. She wondered what Rosamunde would discover in him, and do with him, and if he would be happy married to her…indeed, what would it be like for any woman to be wed to Lucien de Griswold?

His eyes narrowed. "Isidora, you are thinking thoughts you should not be thinking."

She sniffed. "If you know what they are, then neither should you be thinking them."

Isidora felt the tension rise in his body, and slowly, Lucien eased farther from her and stood.

"This is all wrong, Isidora. You never should have come here. You must go home as soon as the weather allows."

With his warm strength now out of reach, she hugged herself instead. "I cannot leave until I do what my father bade me do."

"And what is that?"

"I cannot tell you."

"Why not?"

Now Isidora got to her feet and looked him squarely in the eye. "Because I must first determine if you are truly worthy."

His jaw muscles tightened. "Of what? Who appointed *you* my judge?"

"My father—your master—did! He asked me to bring you a gift. But I will not give it to you until I am convinced you are ready for it."

"What makes you think I want any such gift?"

"Oh, I know you do, Sir Lucien. You want it as much as you want your next breath of air."

He grew still and she could see a pulse pounding in his neck. "Do not tease me, Isidora, or I swear I will make you sorry for doing it. Tell me the nature of this gift."

The brazier's glow seemed to increase, perhaps because they were both breathing so hard. "It has to do with the *Tabula Smaragdina*…"

Lucien's eyes grew wide. "The Emerald Tablet?"

Isidora nodded. "…'It is the power stronger than any other power, because it can overcome—'"

"'—every subtle thing and penetrate every solid thing,'" Lucien finished for her, then put his hand over her mouth as if she had continued the utterance herself. "You must never, ever speak of such things to anyone. Anyone but me. Do you understand, Isidora?"

His hand remained over her mouth so she could not reply.

"What do you know of this? Were you paying heed, all that time, to the bits and pieces available to you? A little knowledge is like a little fire, Isidora. It can do good or it can get out of control and destroy everything in its path. Oh, had I known!"

He released her and began to pace again.

"What would you have done, cut out my tongue?"

"Don't be stupid."

"I know enough to see that the Work consumes men, like flesh is consumed by a wasting disease. I know enough to see that nothing I can say to you will stop you from this folly."

Lucien stopped and rounded on her. "Tell me what your father sent me."

"Nay." At her refusal, his eyes blazed so fiercely that she took a step back. "Not until you have proven yourself to me. I trusted Kalle once, did you know? And he betrayed me, and my father and mother—all of us."

Lucien took a deep breath. "What do you want me to do?"

"When I know, I shall inform you. I must allow the Divine to guide me in this."

"Right. In the meantime, allow *me* to guide you." He scooped her up, strode to his bed and set her down upon it none too gently. True to his word, he pushed Faris to one side to make room for her. "I will be back once I have spoken to Rosamunde. When I return, I want to see that you are asleep."

His arrogant regard for her well-being both annoyed and warmed her. "As you will, my lord Lucien."

Lucien swept out of the room as if he were an outraged king, not just an angry man. An impossibly handsome, excessively intelligent and altogether overwrought man.

Isidora lay still, with the furs draped over her exactly as Lucien had placed them. Then she turned and curled up on her side. Why had she come? *Because I promised Deogal.* But Deogal was the one who had faith in Lucien, not she. And here she was, in his care, at his mercy.

Chapter Nine

Lucien approached the women's solar with dread seeping higher and higher in his gut. He hated scenes, and he had already had too many women weep over him, whether pining for his attentions or nursing his wounds.

Rosamunde had appeared on Christmas Day, accompanying a group of his guests. She had stood in the hall, surrounded by greenery, haloed by candlelight, fresh and glowing and oh, so willing to obey her mother and father, who had apparently sent her, their youngest, to catch the eye of the wealthy Lord Lucien.

When she smiled, everyone else in the vicinity faded by comparison. Lucien was not smitten. Nay. But he knew a good thing when he saw it. A pretty lass, biddable and easy to handle, one who would not ask too many questions, and one who, once she was got with child, would be too busy with her own concerns to bother about his. Aye, she was the perfect solution.

And he was a heartless, mercenary horse's ass to even think of marrying an innocent maiden when he felt nothing for her, no matter what Mauger had to say about it. But it would not be the first time he had broken a woman's heart. He steeled himself and knocked on the door. "It is I, Lucien, *mesdames.*"

A servant opened it, to reveal several women, including unwed female guests and a few who were married but chose to spend the night with lady-friends instead of their husbands.

A wide bed with its curtains parted provided seating for some, others rested on chests or four-legged stools. Gowns of varied hues and fabrics were draped over a wooden bar suspended from the ceiling beams.

Lucien experienced an uneasy instant of feeling that he had just gained entrance to a harem—one not his own. No doubt he had spent too long in the east. He bowed to the ladies, received a soft chorus of well-wishes, and a small pack of lap-dogs scrambled to him, wiggling their bodies and trying to lick his fingers.

He could not accommodate them all, so he bade the dogs be patient, and they settled back down. Rosamunde sat stiffly by the fire, her face white and her hands clasped in her lap. To Lucien's surprise, Mauger also sat nearby, stroking his dark beard, fidgeting, and his face shone with sweat. He looked extraordinarily uncomfortable.

"You took your time, Lucien," he growled.

"Aye, I had good reason. You may go, now, to your well-earned rest."

"Nay," Rosamunde said. "I wish for him to stay. He does not frighten me the way you do."

Lucien could hardly believe what he was hearing. He glanced at their rapt audience then back to the young lady.

"Em, mayhap we should have this conversation in a place more private, Lady Rosamunde?"

"Nay. What I have to say might as well have witnesses."

Now Lucien was thoroughly taken aback. "I frighten you that much? But I have not so much as—"

"Not in that way." Her eyes grew round and bright with tears. "It seems to me you are here, Lord Lucien, and yet you are not. Always, I see your mind is churning with thoughts—about what, I cannot fathom, but I know that they are not about me, nor are they anything you will ever share with me. You are not a man one can get close to. I do not want a husband who will make me feel that I am alone even when we are together."

Lucien swallowed. So, he had been in error about her. She was pretty *and* perceptive. "I see. I beg your pardon, Lady Rosamunde, for my inattention."

She rose from her cushioned chair. "That is not necessary, my lord, for after tonight's display of passion, I see no reason for me to stay, even if my parents punish me for returning. I will not marry a man who lusts after boys."

The resultant gasps and titters made Lucien want to crawl into a hole. "But—"

"And especially not a man who shows absolutely no remorse or shame about it, Feast of Fools notwithstanding."

"I can assure you, Lady Rosamunde—"

A spot of color appeared on each of her cheeks. "I need no assurances, sir! If you had embraced *me* in such a blatant and…and…lewd—manner, I should not be half so offended! But as it stands…"

Her lower lip began to tremble and Lucien braced himself for a flood. But yet again, the girl surprised him. She bit the tremulous lip and took visible control of herself.

Mauger opened his mouth to speak, but Lucien scowled and threw him a quelling look before going to one knee before the beautiful Rosamunde. "My lady, even if you will not accept me, please accept my heartfelt apology for what you witnessed this night. I can explain, but I fear you will like the real truth no better than what you have mistaken for the truth."

She looked down at her hands and must have heard his sincerity for she spoke in a small voice. "I know it was not a boy. I only said that because the thought of you wanting to hold another woman was so unbearable to me. I know what life is like for a woman whose man strays. My mother…"

Lucien stood and took her hand in his. "What does your heart bid you do, then? For I cannot, in good conscience, wed you merely to please your family. Or mine. I want you to be happy."

She took a deep breath. "Then release me from this betrothal. I can see only heartbreak in it, Sir Lucien. For you think too much and are far too attractive. I should marry someone older, plainer, someone who would feel absolutely blessed by my acceptance. Then I might shower him with bliss and feel his devotion for me alone."

Rosamunde glanced at Mauger, who shifted yet again, as though he had just landed in a pile of gorse. Lucien raised his brows. Mauger coughed and squirmed some more. "Indeed. Mayhap Sir Mauger has proven his charm to you?"

"He certainly understands women better than you do, my lord."

An inexplicable wave of relief swept Lucien. He was

free again… "I release you, Lady Rosamunde, and I wish you much joy."

Mauger got up and shrugged himself into order. "You and I shall have a talk, sir, on the morrow."

Lucien bent over Rosamunde's hand, which he still held, and kissed the backs of her white fingers. "I hope, my lady, that you do forgive me. But I fear you are wise to refuse me. I am indeed selfish and preoccupied."

"Oh, Lucien!" She choked on a sob, then said with admirable calm, "Good night, my lord. God keep you well."

"And you, my lady." He bowed to her and the assemblage, then retreated as quickly as politeness allowed.

Mauger took a bit longer.

Chapter Ten

"Did you listen, Faris, or are you truly asleep?" Isidora asked, looking at the back of his dark head on the feather-stuffed pillow. Even with all her clothes on, she was yet chilled.

"I listened," he admitted, and turned to face her. "And I will tell you, Isidora, this knight, this self-proclaimed *alchemist*, will break your heart in the end. I advise you to come away with me, and let us return to Acre. This was a fool's errand."

Isidora sat up and drew the bed furs about her shoulders. "My father was no fool! If he sent me here, it was for good reason. And I will not fail him. You go home if you like, but I am staying."

"I will not leave you here with Sir Lucien. From what I have seen thus far, his morals are worse than those of a Franj, which perhaps he cannot help, for he is a Franj and a Saxon combined." Faris punctuated his statement with a sneeze.

"So you would have preferred that he did not risk his life to save yours this day?"

Faris punched down his pillow. "It is a measure of his

own foolishness that he did. For he should realize that I will not stand by and allow him any further liberties the like of what I witnessed earlier. And that after he had pledged himself to another!"

"You know nothing of what you speak, Faris. Had I thought you would make yourself so disagreeable, I would never have allowed you to accompany me here!"

Faris gave a long-suffering look toward heaven. "As if you could have stopped me! And had I the least bit of sense, I would not have allowed you to leave Acre in the first place. I have many friends, strong, well-favored knights, any one of whom might have made you a better husband than this fellow."

"Who, pray tell, has ever suggested that Lucien be my husband? Thus far, only you, my lord brother, and I would thank you to keep such remarks to yourself in future!" With that, Isidora turned her back on him and scooted beneath the furs.

With a creak of old wood and iron hinges, the door swung open to admit Lucien. Lord of this place. Lord of many female hearts, no doubt. But not hers. She squeezed her eyes shut so that he might not see anything beyond her exhaustion.

Only when she felt his weight settling next to her did she open them. Here Lucien lay, right beside her, but he might as well have been across the room, he felt so distant.

But she could see that a strong pulse beat in the hollow of his throat. His cheek was ruddy and smooth but for the stubble of his beard. His red tunic, of soft, thick wool, had intricate embroidery along the neck and seams. Griffins and wolves intertwined in fantastic combinations of lapis and gold thread.

Who could afford such expensive clothing? He could,

apparently. He blinked, a slow sweep of thick, dark lashes, and then turned his blue eyes upon her.

"You are supposed to be asleep."

"One cannot order another to sleep, my lord. One must be taken upon the angel's bosom in its own good time."

"What does that mean?"

"It is what my mother used to tell me. That to sleep was to be carried through the night on the bosom of an angel. It made me less afraid of the dark."

"I never knew you feared the dark."

"There is much you do not know about me, my lord."

"So, your coming after me into Kalle's dungeon took great courage."

"Nay. I needed no courage for that. Something else carried me that day."

Lucien swallowed and his voice grew husky. "I have never properly thanked you for helping me."

"The fact you are alive is thanks enough."

"Isidora, such talk makes me ill at ease. I feel as though you want from me something I do not even possess, much less can give."

She propped her head up on her hand. "Sir Lucien, you are ever searching outside, but there is a wealth of treasure within you as yet undiscovered. Have you not learned that in any of your studies?"

He looked into her eyes, a piercing, poignant look that spoke of a terrible yearning. "Nay, you are wrong. I am still empty. I have yet to find the—the touchstone that would fill me, and save my....save what is dear to me."

Isidora felt her heart catch. "Is that what the Work means to you, then?"

"I see you know me little better than I know you, after all." His tone was flat with disappointment.

She almost reached over to touch him, to reassure him, but it was too soon. For her, as well as for him. "Given time, we might each learn a great deal, my lord."

"Ahem." Faris was awake. Indeed, so awake that he sat up in the bed. "I wish you two would be silent. I prefer not to listen to such a private conversation, especially one I cannot properly understand."

Lucien gave Isidora a wry smile. "Your brother is indeed mannerly, is he not?"

"Aye," she agreed. "And had I a longer acquaintance with him—beyond these recent few months at least—I would feel more at ease telling him to stop trying to protect me!"

"I think Faris is to you what Mauger is to me. Mayhap the two of them should not be allowed to communicate. God knows what well-meaning horrors they would come up with for us were they to get together."

Faris bristled. "You, sir, are as close to single combat with me as you'll ever be and still live to talk about it."

Lucien was off the bed and on his feet faster than Isidora would have thought possible. Cold fury poured from him and in a panic, she threw herself back against Faris.

"Hold, both of you! Faris al-Rashid, I humbly ask that you offer an apology for this affront to our host. And Lucien de Griswold, please overlook my brother's ill-considered words."

Faris, looking only mildly repentant, said, "May God forgive me for such rudeness."

Lucien relaxed a fraction. "I do not know about God, but I am willing to let it pass. We have no quarrel, Faris al-Rashid. I have no designs upon your sister. She is beyond reproach."

"Your behavior is not!"

Isidora lay back down. "I am going to sleep. Surely you two can find something more important to fight about in the morning?"

But Faris was not finished. "You cannot change the subject so easily, Isidora Binte Deogal! I want assurances from you that you will behave as befits a daughter of the house of Salah al-Din, may his name be emblazoned upon the heavenly firmament for all eternity!"

Isidora threw a helpless look to Lucien, who seemed to have understood Faris's outburst of Arabic perfectly. He awaited her response with his arms crossed upon his chest and one eyebrow cocked.

She took a deep breath. "Very well. Sir Lucien, I forgive you for your intrusion upon my person. And I am sorry for the way I felt about it, as well as for the way it seems to have made *you* feel."

Lucien shook his head slowly and half turned from her. "I will find somewhere else to take my rest. This situation is most unseemly. I cannot remember a time when I was more mortified, unless it be a short while ago, while explaining this same infamous *behavior* to Lady Rosamunde." He bowed to Isidora and Faris. "I will send a guard to sit before your door, with instructions to allow no one entrance, not even me."

With that he swept out of the solar, leaving a faint scent of sandalwood in his wake. Isidora turned a furious eye upon Faris. "I hope you are satisfied, brother!"

"I am, at that. The Saxo-Franj has been humbled at last."

Isidora grabbed the majority of the covers and jerked

them over to her side, then changed her mind and tossed some back. "I do not want you snuggling against me for warmth in your sleep."

"No need, sister, for your anger throws off enough heat for me to keep my distance and still stay warm."

She ground her teeth and no angel came anywhere near for her to settle upon its bosom.

Lucien stalked his keep like a restless wolf. Women! If ever had there been a king of fools on this feast day, it was he.

Rather than risk disturbing his guests who slept in the main hall, he threw his mantle about his shoulders and went out a side door into the still, frozen night. The moonlight showed him that the narrow stone stairs were slick with ice, but he made his way down without mishap until the reassuring crunch of the bailey grounds met his feet.

Across the yard were the mews. Aye, horses were the best company he could keep just now.

He stepped into the dark warmth of the stable and soft nickers greeted him. He could just see a groom dozing in a pile of fodder. Careful not to wake the lad, Lucien took several handfuls of dried grass for each of his beasts, as well as the horses of his guests. The resultant contented munching soothed his heart. At least these creatures were well satisfied with him.

But his uncle would not be. Indeed, he never had been. At least, despite providing him with the best of everything, the stern Lord Conrad had never told him so.

Lucien sat down on an old, folded horse blanket and prepared to put himself into the contemplative state Deogal had taught him.

Unum in multa diversa moda—one in many manifestations. The Great Work. The distillation, reduction and ultimate fixation of the many into the Perfect One.

Nigredo, albedo, citrinitas, rubedo…black, white, yellow, red, stages of separation of every particle of dross from the impeccable substance that constituted the essence of purity—the Elixir. Omniscience and eternal life…a cure for all evils.

What made him think he, Lucien of the Grey Forest, had the character, much less the right, to pursue such divine knowledge, such power? Deogal must have been mistaken in accepting him as an apprentice. Such things were not meant for such as him, men who used their brawn as much as their brain…were they?

But was that not the point? Were not ordinary men capable of ultimately achieving unity with God, just as base metal might be transmuted into pure gold? Mauger was right about at least one thing—the very idea was Gnostic— and utter heresy.

Lucien sighed and put his head into his hands. All he could do was to keep on struggling. Alone. As ever. Aye, on the morrow he would rid himself of all these guests.

Including the estimable Faris al-Rashid *and* his sister.

Chapter Eleven

Isidora kicked at the bed furs. She envied Faris his sound sleep. By the sliver of light on the floor, the moon had moved halfway across the night sky and she still lay wide awake, staring at the brazier's glow, listening to the occasional pop of the coals.

How many times at home in Acre had she observed her father at his athanor, the clay furnace in which he heated the metals to their various states? It had seemed an endless, pointless task. Dry and dusty and inexplicable.

What was he doing? And why? It broke her heart to see him so absorbed. At times she was certain if she had dropped dead before him, he would have merely stepped over her body to reach his tongs and alembic or whatever crucible he needed.

Isidora hugged her pillow tighter. If only her father were still alive, she would gladly suffer his unwitting neglect. Glancing at Faris, bundled with his back to her, she wished the brazier in Lucien's solar threw off more heat. It would be a long time before she got used to the English cold.

Indeed, she hoped she would have the opportunity to get used to it.

"Milady? I am Larke, here to see you."

The soft voice reached Isidora from the other side of the door. Rather than risk waking Faris, she slipped out of bed to greet the young woman. Her bare feet alternately met wolfskins and wooden planking as she hurried across the chamber.

The girl was wearing a voluminous, white nightdress, and with her wild, red-blond hair cascading about her shoulders, she resembled some kind of escaped denizen of the heavenly firmament.

"What brings me the honor of your presence, Lady Larke?"

"Oh, but I am not a lady, just ask Lucien!" The girl grinned and caught Isidora's hand in one of hers. "Are you comfortable? I thought I'd see for myself, as I cannot rely on my brother to know enough to provide adequate blankets and so on."

"Well, I—" Isidora glanced over her shoulder: Faris yet slept on "—he is certainly comfortable enough. In fact, Lucien piled us with furs. But I am still a bit cold."

Larke raised the candle she held and peered into the solar. "Ah. Your Faris was the most handsome man at the mêlée, I trow! But come with me, my quarters will be more to your liking, perhaps."

Isidora felt a small thrill. To think that Larke had troubled herself to seek her out—what a joy, to have a friend in this place! "That sounds lovely."

Then she started as she realized a man stood in the shadows, but a few feet away, with a pike in his hands.

"Larke…who is that?"

"Oh, that is but Jager of Cumbria, whom Lucien sent to guard your door. I gave him a penny to let me by, but he will let you out for nothing—won't you, Jager? Come on." She gave the guard a smile as she towed Isidora past him.

Wood had long given way to rough stone beneath Isidora's feet and she wished she had donned her shoes. Larke led her around the perimeter of the central hall's upper expanse to a door set into the corner.

Larke ushered her into a small chamber, nearly filled with a bed and brazier, and much warmer than Lucien's solar.

"Now climb in and get under the covers," Larke ordered. "Just elbow your way in if those vixens won't move over," she added.

Isidora saw the bed already had at least two other occupants. The "vixens" giggled and made room. She sank into the feather bed with gratitude, and Larke followed.

"Now," her hostess began, "we can talk properly. Isidora, these are Brannwenn and Eyslk, cousins to the Lady Ceridwen, who is wife to Lucien's ally, Raymond de Beauchamp."

"Aye, the very same," chorused the girls.

"They are fostering here, and my task is to keep them out of trouble until they are wed. No small challenge, that! But the important question, Isidora, is what think you of our Rosamunde?"

"Oh, well, she is very beautiful, of course."

Larke snorted. "Of course! But is she good enough for our Mauger? *That* is the question!"

At this, Isidora could only open her mouth in surprise.

* * *

Lucien woke to something warm and heavy in his lap. Nothing that purred or licked his face, but it had its arms and legs wrapped around him in blatant invitation.

He opened his eyes. He had slept in the mews. And now this girl—delightful creature that she was—had climbed atop him. "Daphne? What are you doing?"

She yawned and snuggled closer. "Nothing, more's the pity."

"Get off of me and find someone else to do nothing with, then."

A lass from the village, Daphne was a luscious temptation, though one he had never succumbed to despite her best efforts. But why not? She was comely, reasonably clean, and more than willing…as willing as his own body apparently was. But that was beside the point, and she had made no move to obey him. "Get off. Now."

Something in his low tone must have gotten through to her, for she sat back, her pale, tousled hair haloed by the dawn. "My lord?" She quickly disentangled herself and got to her feet, her eyes wide.

Lucien followed and gazed down at her. "Who did you think I was?"

"I—I, forgive me, lord. I did not mean to make so bold with ye."

"Of course you did. But you should take more care in the dark, Daphne. You leave yourself far too vulnerable. You might have woken to find someone much more unpleasant than I between your legs. I could have been anyone."

She twisted her hands together. "Nay, you are like no other, Lord Lucien. Everyone says so…"

"Says what?"

"T-that you'll bring bounty to those who can get near enough to touch ye."

That nonsense again! "Do not listen to idle gossip, Daphne. And do not let me catch you in the mews in future, for any reason. Horses are no more toys than are men."

"Aye, lord." She curtsied and ran out, her breath clouding the cold air.

Bounty? Someone had had too much to drink and nothing better to do than to make up such a story. It had started upon his return from the east. Folk had begun the irritating habit of laying hands upon him with the flimsiest of excuses. Especially women. All ranks and ages.

With the horses clamoring for someone to break their fast, he woke the stable lad and headed out into the bailey.

Mauger approached, his long strides looking far too energetic for the early hour. "Ah, there you are! I saw that wench fly out the gates and I wondered."

"Wondered what?"

Mauger stood with his arms crossed over his chest. "If she fled your inevitable rejection, of course."

Lucien walked right past Mauger toward the hall of the keep, where his guests still slept, as he wished he were doing. "Aye, Mauger. I must keep myself pure for the Suitable Bride. But, as a matter of fact, the winsome Daphne only wanted to make use of me as a talisman, by touching as much of me as she could, all at once. That is my sole appeal, apparently. So I sent her packing."

"Hmm." Mauger caught up and fell into step beside him. "I wonder what started such a ridiculous notion?"

Lucien shrugged. "The summer drought ended when I

returned. We had a winter of few losses. The lambs and calves were born healthy and the cows' milk stayed sweet. And there have been no raids upon us."

"So they give you credit for all that?"

"And so they should! I sold my soul to my near name-sake, Lucifer, on their behalf."

At Mauger's look of dismay, Lucien had to laugh. "My good sir, please, you must know by now when I am jesting."

Mauger shook his head. "With all that goes on behind closed doors here, I know less than I ought, I'm certain."

"Do you wish to observe my operations, then? Do you want to become my assistant?" Lucien challenged him.

"Nay! I have no desire to be tainted with the vapors of such deviltry. It is bad enough we must send the Lady Rosamunde back to her family."

Lucien halted. "I thought she expressed an interest in you, Mauger. What of that? Surely such beautiful prospects do not often cross one's path?"

"She knows nothing of me. I was but a ready ear for her troubles. She likes to think I might grovel at her feet in gratitude for her attentions."

"And would you not?"

Mauger hesitated a fraction too long before his denial. "Nay…"

Lucien grinned. "Of course not. She will flee your 'inevitable rejection' as Daphne did mine."

"And what of this Saracen and his outrageous woman?"

"Isidora is his sister, Mauger. And Faris is not a Saracen, but a Christian, even as we are. But, I would see them return to the east as soon as possible."

"Why did she come all this way? It had to be important."

"I—"

At that moment Isidora emerged from the hall, looking pale but lovely in a blue-and-silver over-gown that Larke had been given but never worn. The sun struck gold on some small ornament around her neck—the Maltese cross she wore, Lucien recalled.

Behind her, Larke and Rosamunde emerged, as well, and Lucien's sense of being outnumbered went far beyond their three to his one. He bowed to them and nudged Mauger, who was staring stupidly at Rosamunde, to do the same.

"I bid you good morning, ladies. Glad am I to see you have made such cordial acquaintance." Indeed Lucien was not glad at all. Such an alliance could prove his undoing, in ways he no doubt could not as yet imagine. "Are you preparing to journey home, Rosamunde?"

"She is staying, Lucien," Larke announced. "Isidora and I believe you and your household may benefit from our continued presence."

"How?" Lucien blurted.

"If one stays, then so must both, Sir Lucien," Isidora said, as if he were a witless dolt. "A young lady alone in residence at your hall is a scandal. Two young ladies, and it is merely a happy gathering."

"But why should either of you—"

"My lord!" Larke surprised him with her sharp tone. "Isidora has reason for being here, the awkwardness of it caused only by your stubborn refusal to cooperate. She has explained everything to me. And I have decided that helping her is the least I can do, for by doing so I will also help you."

"Cooperate? What have I refused to do? I need no help. Pray enlighten me."

Larke stood upon his steps like a queen on high, declaring a proclamation. "Rosamunde tells me Mauger had much to say whilst they were closeted awaiting you last night. And Isidora, who could sleep no more than could I, came to me, as well. Rosamunde has decided, as your former betrothed, that since she has thrown you over, you should wed Isidora instead."

Lucien remained speechless for a moment, then turned to Mauger, who was still staring. "What did you tell her? Nay. You will not command me in this, nor in any other thing! None of you!"

Fists clenched at his sides, Lucien climbed the stairs to where the women were. Rosamunde backed off a step, making him ashamed of being so obvious in his anger. But better that they see it rather than feel it. He pinned Isidora with his gaze. "What say you to this grand scheme of Lady Larke's and Rosamunde's?"

Though her color was now high, Isidora remained steady. "She flatters me with such an impossible suggestion, my lord. Well do I know you have no intention, much less desire, of keeping me underfoot any longer than you must. I am unwelcome here, and I beg your pardon for arriving unannounced with my brother."

"I never said you are not welcome, Isidora."

"You did not have to say it, it is obvious."

"Oh, then it was not you I embraced, after all?"

She blushed and looked at her feet. "Let us speak of it no more. Please, show me where you do the Work, my lord," she asked.

"Why should I?"

"It will help me decide about the gift I yet hold in trust for you."

An unreasoning panic rose within Lucien. "I will not show you, for it is none of your concern. It is a private place and a private endeavor."

Rosamunde put her hands on her hips. "And had I continued with the betrothal, you would not have told me of this endeavor at all, no doubt?"

Lucien began to feel like a cornered beast. "No doubt whatsoever."

At last Mauger found his voice. "Em, ladies, let us amuse ourselves in some way other than baiting Lucien, here, shall we?"

"Aye, why do you not take them out on a ride over the fells, Mauger? Go hawking. Play hoodman-blind." Lucien waved a hand vaguely. "Or something."

"Many thanks, but no," said Rosamunde, as if he had been serious. "I would not like to leave your other guests behind."

"What will your lord father say, Lady Rosamunde, when he learns of this turn of events?" Mauger asked.

She smiled, revealing a mischievous charm Lucien had not seen before. "He will probably come here to give Lord Lucien a thrashing in person. Then he will agree to whomever I have my heart set on."

Lucien fumed. "Oh, that is something to look forward to, indeed! Who do you have as an alternate, then?"

"Why, Sir Mauger, of course. I thought I had made that clear already."

"Just to be certain, lady," Lucien said weakly. He exchanged looks with Mauger. It was one thing to avert the whim of a maiden, but quite another to avoid the will of her powerful father. Just as his own father's will could not be denied, even from the grave.

Perhaps he could help Mauger escape Rosamunde's trap, in exchange for being left unfettered himself a while longer. "What say you, Mauger?"

Mauger opened and closed his mouth, then bowed over her hand and uttered the fateful words, "Lady Rosamunde's will is my command."

Lucien pulled the seneschal aside. "What are you doing?"

Mauger turned a hard gaze upon Lucien. "I know how your mind works, my lord. If I can marry, then so can you. Our agreement remains intact and I need not summon your uncle."

So, Mauger thought to sacrifice himself, his independence, to bring Lucien to heel? Nay. "You want her, in truth, Mauger, admit it! You are lusting after a highborn maiden, as you ever have urged me to do."

Mauger stole a glance at Rosamunde. "There is more to her than meets the eye."

"Such as her father and brothers and uncles, I trow!" Of a sudden, Lucien remembered he had spent the night in a horse barn. He looked down at himself. Straw, dirt and wisps of dried grass adorned his mantle and leggings. He was hungry and cold.

"I need to gain the sanctity of my solar, Mauger. I will have no more talk of marriage this day, to anyone or about anyone, but I promise you I will think upon it. Let us first see to my other guests."

Mauger nodded his assent and Lucien was relieved he did not have to shake another spit-besmeared hand.

Isidora watched as Lucien returned from his private consultation with Mauger. He did not look any happier, but nor did he look angry. He paused before her and she gazed up at him.

A nimbus of light from the morning sun crowned his head. Except for a black eye from his beating on the pond, he looked little different than he had the first time she had seen him on the street in Acre. Just as handsome, just as lordly. Why did she care, when all he showed her was indifference?

Aye, he had held her close. But now he returned her gaze with a look of puzzlement. Not affection, nor concern.

Merely an expression befitting a man who has discovered something wholly unexpected at his door and knows not what to do with it.

"Isidora…"

His voice, so smooth, saying her name…

"We needs must have a talk."

Her heart sank. "As you will, my lord."

"After nones, then, once I have seen everyone off."

"Where?"

He hesitated. Swallowed. Then took a deep breath. "Meet me in the chapel. From there I will take you to my *laboratorium*."

Before she could show her appreciation for the enormity of his offer, he had stalked away ahead of her up to the hall.

Chapter Twelve

The midday meal was long over and most of the guests from the revels had departed. Head to head with Faris, Mauger was attempting to win a game of chess. Lady Rosamunde cast him glances as she worked her embroidery by the wintry light of a small window.

Isidora did not know exactly when nones was, but thought it better to be early than late. She declined Larke's offer of a maid or servant to accompany her on her supposed quest for fresh air and made her way out of the hall.

Even with a woolen mantle drawn about her face, the chill air bit into Isidora's nostrils and seeped through to her skin. What a place. She missed the warm breezes of the east, the graciousness and easy affection of the people. Small wonder these English were so hard, having to live under such conditions.

By the time she reached the chapel she was shaking with the cold. A vine, its leaves tinged with red, climbed its walls, creeping toward what light and warmth it could find. Isidora admired its tenacity.

She touched the door's great round, iron handle, wondering if she should go in or wait outside. A crunch of footsteps came closer. She turned to see Lucien, walking about as if it were not a frozen, uninhabitable place he lived in. Beside him lumbered a large, shaggy hound of some sort.

"Your hand will stick to that if you don't wear gloves in this weather."

"I have none," she admitted.

Lucien stopped before her and took one of her chapped hands into his leather-clad ones and examined it. "Larke will give you some. But for now, wear mine."

Before she could either accept or object, he had doffed his gloves and slid them onto her hands. The leather was fine, they were lined with soft wool, and so large on her she could scarcely keep them from falling off.

But they were wonderfully warm. From the heat of his body. To her own dismay, she shivered again at the very thought. "M-my thanks, sir."

Lucien frowned and swept his mantle from his shoulders to hers. She closed her eyes for an instant. Now she was wrapped in not only his heat, but his scent. Elusive, smoky sandalwood…

He jostled her with his elbow. "Are you going to sleep? Come. It is not here."

He walked away, as if Isidora's following him was inevitable. Only the dog had the courtesy to pause and look back at her. She trotted to catch up.

"What is this dog you have? It seems an unlikely companion for one such as you, my lord. I would have thought an elegant gaze-hound to be more of your liking."

Lucien grunted his amusement and scratched the beast

behind its ears. "You have some odd ideas about me, Isidora. But this wolfhound was given me by my friend Raymond de Beauchamp. One does not refuse such a princely gift. Not from Raymond, at any rate. He adores its sire and considers my having the pup as strong a bond between us as if I had wed his sister, had Raymond a sister."

"Pup?"

"Oh, aye, he will be twice this size before he is done."

"Heavens. What have you named him?"

"Raymond named him Gawaine. Though I have not noticed his strength increasing before noontide."

"Ah. Well, let us hope he has some of Sir Gawaine's other characteristics, then."

Lucien brought her to a wall covered in the same leafy vines as was the chapel, into which was set a low, arched door. He unlocked it with a stout key and shot the bolt free. Its heavy hinges creaked and the nails studding the wood were set in the shape of a triangle. After the briefest hesitation, he motioned her through.

"Watch your head."

"I thank you, Sir Lucien." Isidora ducked as she entered and, with a fresh shiver, looked about. The chamber was built into the thickness of the wall itself, lit by windows high up, so one could not see in or out, except the sky. The walls were white, plastered stone, which reflected even more light.

But drawn upon them, by a skilled hand, were all manner of signs and symbols. Suns, moons, stars, runes, dragons and animals and humans…nothing like her father's stained and smoke-smudged workshop.

Where his had been a jumble of whole and broken

crockery and glass vessels, bowls and jars of unlabeled substances, discarded failures and hopeful but incomplete experiments, Lucien's *laboratorium* was a place of order and clarity.

Crucibles were arranged by size, tongs and tools hung neatly on racks. He had an immaculate balance, with brass weights, and each of his containers had a label—though not decipherable to the uninitiated.

Dominating the space at one end was the athanor, the smelting furnace, where each metal endured a trial of purification by fire. But it was unlit, and if possible, the chamber was even colder than outdoors.

The whole of it filled her with both dread and longing. She missed her father so much. And with all her heart, she did not want Lucien to travel that same desperate, impossible path to nowhere.

There was one thing written on the wall that she could read. *Ora, lege, relege, labora, et invenis.* Pray, read, re-read, work, and you shall find. She turned to face Lucien, who stood in the only shadowed part of the room. Watching her every move. "I did not know you could draw, Lucien. These figures are quite marvelous."

"Is this enough for you, Isidora? I would rather we leave now." His voice was low, emotionless, yet she knew it had cost him much to bring her to his secret place.

"Sir Lucien, from what I have seen here, your approach to this is a bit skewed."

"How so?" He stepped toward her, a challenge in the set of his broad shoulders, in the elegant tilt of his head, in his velvet voice.

She blinked. "Oh…no doubt I am mistaken."

"Finish what you were going to say."

Somehow he now had her backed up against one of the tables built along the wall. "Perhaps, my lord, you are too...too aggressively methodical. Alchemy requires method, aye, but it also requires intuition, subtlety and inspiration."

"This you learned from Deogal?"

Isidora started to nod, then shook her head. "I learned it from the texts."

Lucien put his hands upon her shoulders. "And those are...?"

"The ones I took from Kalle FitzMalheury's dungeon."

"What? You did not!"

"I did! His guards had found a pile of scrolls in an alcove, they were burning them to stay warm at night. I had bribed them to let me pass and I saw symbols of the Work on one of the scrolls they had not yet touched, and others had marks like what one sees in Egypt. I picked up a couple of them and hid them in my skirt. I made a joke about putting good use to worthless old letters, and continued on my errand—to free you—without giving them back."

Lucien's fingers tightened on her upper arms. "Fitz-Malheury would have skinned you alive, had he known. But they probably are indeed worthless, and you should not have taken such a risk!"

"Well, I did have cause to regret it, because a few days later I saw those same foolish guards hanging from the curtain wall. At first I assumed it was because they had allowed your escape. Then later, once I had had a closer look at the scrolls, I thought perhaps it was because Kalle had found out they had been burning a long-lost library full of ancient secrets."

Isidora wondered at Lucien's hold on her, even though she was certain he was barely aware he had her in his grasp. For once again, she saw that look in his eyes. The faraway look so familiar to her she would recognize it in her dreams. The look of an alchemist who has only molten metal on his mind.

By God, she wanted to slap it right off his face.

Instead she pushed herself away from the table edge and impulsively threw her arms around his middle. At this assault, Gawaine, who had been sitting patiently all the while, stood up and barked, the sound echoing in the cold *laboratorium*. Isidora buried her face against Lucien's chest. Warm. Fragrant with his unique scent. "Do not ask me to show them to you, please."

He had not put his arms around her, but nor had he pulled away. "You must, Isidora."

"It is too dangerous. They are incomplete. You yourself told me what danger a little knowledge presents."

Now he did step back from her, the better to look her in the eye, no doubt. But he still loomed over her, holding her hands, and his voice was quiet and stern.

"A little knowledge to one who has none to begin with is dangerous, aye. But to one who already has much, it could lead to the final piece of a vast puzzle that has been painstakingly assembled for years on end. Knowing your father's struggles, knowing mine, how can you even consider withholding this from me?"

Isidora did not know what to say at first. To be so near Lucien, in such a short time, after such a long while, and after so much bitterness was like drinking too much wine at once. She felt his warm hands move around her waist, to settle at her back, and the words came at last. He deserved the truth from her, if nothing else.

"Because, Lucien, I do not want you to take what you believe to be that final piece and have it lead you astray to madness and death, as it did my father. So, do you see now? I killed him! It was my fault, it was my bringing him the scrolls that pushed him over the edge into the abyss."

"Oh, Isidora, do not think such things of yourself."

"It is the truth."

"Your father was a brilliant man, devoted to the Work. It would take much more than some moldy old scrolls to bring ruin upon him. Put your mind at ease."

She withdrew from him. "Let me see your hands, Lord Lucien."

"Why?"

"Just give them to me!"

He held them out and she took them into hers. They were strong, shapely hands, with long fingers and broad palms. They also had black stains of various degrees of intensity, along with rusty red ones, nicks and abrasions and a few blistered burn marks.

"Look at the abuse these have suffered, all for the cooking of mercury and antimony!"

"Anything worth having bears a price."

Isidora looked into his eyes, still holding on to his hands. "You would not want to pay the price, if you knew just how dearly bought is the Elixir. There are worse consequences, much worse than sore hands."

To her surprise, Lucien's fingers squeezed hers in a gentle caress, and he spoke in a voice to match. "Do you not understand the nature of the Elixir, Isidora?"

A vision of her father came to Isidora, as he staggered and fell in his madness, unable to eat or sleep, his body withering, his mind a wasteland… Her eyes brimmed, her throat closed, and she could not answer.

"Let me tell you…just as it can turn base metal to gold, it can cure all ills. *All* ills, Isidora. Body, mind and soul. Do you realize what that means?"

She shook her head. She did not want to know.

"It means that even if all the afflictions you spoke of were visited upon me during the course of the Work, a single minute speck of the Elixir, mixed in a barrel of water or wine and a sip swallowed, would effect a cure. That is how powerful it is."

"B-but, Lucien, all it takes is the smallest misstep in its preparation, perhaps months in the making, requiring certain seasons to aid specific processes—aye, I know these things—and there would be no Elixir. Just a worthless puddle of disgusting elements. And that is all your efforts will ever come to, do you not see? If my father, the great Master Deogal, could not do it after years of effort, how can you ever hope to succeed?"

Lucien straightened and released her hands. "You came so far, by land and by sea, to tell me that? I do not believe you, Isidora Binte Deogal, and I do not think you truly believe it yourself. Elsewise you would not be here."

"Nay, Sir Lucien. I am here because my father charged me to come with his dying breath. But I do not know what is worse—breaking my vow to him or giving you what I fear will lead to certain death."

Lucien put a hand to his brow. "Do as you will, then. I will carry on, no matter what. With or without the gift you brought. Come, let us take our leave of this place, as it obviously brings you no joy."

With a heavy heart, Isidora went back out into the fresh air and waited while Lucien relocked the door. The frost on the tree limbs sparkled, birds chattered and she even heard an occasional drip, as if some hidden warmth was melting the ice from the eaves of the workshop.

Gawaine stationed himself in front of her and gave her a toothy grin, his tail thumping the ground. She knelt down, stroked his head gingerly, and he rewarded her with a generous lick to her mouth.

"Ugh!" She hurriedly stood and wiped her lips with the back of her still-gloved hand. It hardly tasted better.

Lucien faced her with a grin even more charmingly idiotic than his dog's. "Better his kiss than mine, eh?"

"I would not go that far, my lord. But then again, I have no idea what your kiss is like."

The smile vanished from Lucien's face and was replaced by a raw, hungry, dangerous look. He would not allow such a challenge to go unmet.

He stayed his ground.

And for once, she stayed hers.

He clenched and unclenched his jaw. "What would you have me do, Isidora? I scarcely know whether to flee before you or to throw you on your back and—"

She stared at him. "Pardon me? Is there not some course in the middle you might consider, my lord?"

Lucien's eyes darkened. She heard a growl—either from him or his dog—and in the next moment he caught her in a hard, breathless embrace. His mouth moved over her neck, burning along the curve of her jaw, across her cheek and at last to her lips.

Lucien. His blood, heating hers. It was bliss. As close to pure happiness as Isidora had come in her life. Her heart pounded, expanded and soared with delight. She abandoned herself to his kiss. It might never happen again. Indeed she could not allow it.

But his arms bound her so tightly, with her feet barely touching the ground, she could not have escaped even had she wanted to. Though she had first met him as a knight, she had had no idea that the Lucien she had come to know—the scholar, the alchemist, the landlord, could also be the impassioned man who held her now.

Then, just as suddenly as the kiss had started, it stopped. Lucien, breathing hard, eased her down and away from him. It felt as though she had been torn from a comfort she could not live without. Her eyes welled with tears against the loss.

He looked at her, aghast. "I should not have done that. I am sorry, I—"

The hurt grew to an unbearable pain. "Nay, you misunderstand. I am glad of it, Lucien, truly."

"Nay, that is not right."

"Why not?" She could contain herself no longer. "Are you so heartless, my lord, or merely blind?"

He stared, now astonished. "Obviously, I must be both, if you are asking."

"For one with such a keen intellect, you are woefully lacking in powers of simple observation, my lord."

"Oh, indeed. Tell me what I have missed, then, Isidora.

The fact that you hound me with your gaze whenever we are together? That your cheeks flush whenever I so much as flicker an eyelid in your direction? That you hang on my every word, and can doubtless quote back to me every pearl I have spoken since I first walked through your door in Acre? That you adore me from the safety of your self-imposed inferiority?"

Isidora gasped. She knew that a truly highborn woman would have slapped him for saying such things, or at least tried. But it was not in her. And, the only reason she had to slap him was that everything she had goaded him into saying was true. Yet her pride could not allow him the last word.

"Oh, you are worse than any *advocatus,* my lord. I pity the woman you finally marry."

"Indeed?" His soft tone told her he doubted the truth of her second statement, not her first.

She shivered, all alone inside his mantle. "I mean, she had best keep her wits about her."

Lucien crossed his arms and nodded his agreement. "She will need them, and more besides. And the same goes for the poor besotted fool who takes *you* to the marriage bed."

To her own pathetic surprise, Isidora found herself encouraged by this. "So, you do not consider my being wed one day a possibility beyond the scope of mind or magic?"

"Not entirely." He gave her the smallest of smiles and, once more, for that moment, all was right with her world. Then, with his next words, he put it all to ruin again.

"I should tell you, Isidora. I think I should give up on Mauger's idea that I must be wed. He has threatened to expose my activities to my uncle, but I am coming to the point where I would rather have Lord Conrad put me under siege than make me marry against my will. Or, as you have pointed out to me, inflict my heresies upon some unsuspecting woman."

Isidora bit her lip as a terrible, wonderful idea formed in her mind. "Your uncle, Lord Conrad, is on his way?"

Lucien shrugged. "Maybe not now, but he could easily be, once the roads dry a bit."

"Then consider this, Sir Lucien. What if you were to present me to him as your choice of bride? All we would need do is convince him until he leaves. Then I could be called away by my family, decide to become a nun, or even conveniently die, and you would be free. Especially if I died, you would be in mourning for some time, would you not?"

"Oh of course! What an idea, Isidora. The very thought is absurd. We would fool no one. And he would still want me to produce an heir."

She lifted her chin. "That would all depend upon how convincing we were."

"But what of Mauger, and my people? They would surely see through such a farce. It would hardly be fair to you, either, Isidora. The risk to your reputation would be awful."

"How badly do you want to continue the Work? You are lord here, no one would dare question you. As for my reputation—is it of any concern at all? I have no family beyond Faris. I am an orphan. No one cares if I become a harem girl or even a whore."

"I care. And, I would hope, you care. I will not use you in such a way, Isidora. I must simply face my uncle's anger as it comes."

"Why will you not let me help you?"

"I do not need your help, Isidora. I know you mean well. But it is not proper."

She dug her nails into her palms. "To hell with what is proper!"

Lucien's face paled. "This has gone far enough. You must return to Acre before you are entirely ruined."

"You are mistaken. I am already ruined, Lord Lucien!" *I see no one but you. Nothing but your face in my dreams.* "I have nothing to return to. Only a shell, for Kalle's men have destroyed my father's home in search of the Elixir. I will end my days scribing merchant's contracts in the marketplace."

He turned partly away from her, as if he could not bear to face her pain. "I know your fear, Isidora. My yearning for forbidden knowledge has separated me from much I might have been blessed to be a part of. But there are some things I cannot explain, cannot put into words. It is like trying to describe the taste of honey to one who has never had it. Or love… Do you see?"

"How can I? If you know this, then you are simply mad to continue. Perhaps you have truly earned your loneliness."

"I never said I was lonely!"

"Oh? Then why is it you kiss me and hold me as if you were a drowning man?"

"That is different. You…you beguile me. I cannot help myself. Yet another reason you should be away from here." He rubbed his arms. "Let us go back to the keep. It is too cold yet for such fresh-air dalliances."

"You should take back your mantle. Here." She started to unpin it.

"Keep it, I pray you. I know how long it took for me to

get used to the cold again, once I had returned from the east, so you must be suffering the same."

Aye. My suffering has not changed at all. I am still alone as ever despite people all around.

Chapter Thirteen

"But, my lord…to go so far, when the prize is not certain…?" Earm's big hands shook as he poured wine into the silver goblet upon the table in Kalle FitzMalheury's refectory.

Seated in his great chair of carved, imported oak, Kalle curled his lip in a way calculated to make his would-be advisor, Earm, cringe even more than was his wont.

"England, far? To one who has pirated the coasts and trampled the peasants of half the known world? It is my opinion, Earm, that your hesitation to return to your homeland is due to the fact that I've explained you'll be hanged if anyone recognizes you, not because it is 'far.'"

"If you say so, my lord, then you will of course understand if I do not accompany you—"

"That is all the more reason for you to accompany me! I will wring from you every last drop of the servitude you owe me, Earm, but I will also protect you, and in the end, make you a wealthy man. Trust me."

With that, Kalle curved his sneer into a grin and Earm's face turned a gratifying shade of pale gray.

"B-but, how do you know the girl took anything of value with her when she fled?"

"Because, my dear fellow, nothing of value was found when my men searched the *laboratorium!* Deogal had reached a critical point in the Work. I felt it in my bones— that is why I left him alone for so long. When he died— and damn his timing—who else did he have to confide in but that impertinent girl of his? His old Templar comrades? Hardly. But she slipped away, despite Faris being sent to hold her.

"And now he, too, is gone. So, Earm, I have two things to accomplish in England. One is to recover the Key to the Work, and the other is to punish Faris for his treachery. No one escapes having once betrayed me. You'd do well to re-member that yourself."

"Aye, milord."

Kalle took a closer look at Earm. The man was sweating! A mass of quivering, terrified flesh that had once been a bold soldier of the cross. Perhaps he'd been too harsh of late. Aye, he needed Earm to at least be able to sit within a lance length of him and not shake like a maiden on her wedding night.

"Go and relax in the baths, Earm. It will do you good. I'll have Shunnar send Lina herself to attend you."

Bewildered gratitude spread across Earm's face. He sagged with apparent relief.

"Go! Before I change my mind."

Earm rose and straightened his broad shoulders before bowing to Kalle FitzMalheury.

Earm sank up to his neck in hot, silken water. Rose pet-als floated upon its surface and curls of steam wafted their perfume to him. Lina, a lovely Berber woman whose sorry fate, like his own, was to be part of Kalle's household, rubbed Earm's tight shoulders with practiced hands.

She paused for a moment. "You are unhappy tonight, my lord?"

"Every night, Lina."

"What misfortune dogs your steps, then? It seems you have the favor of the master, to be here like this."

"That is like having the favor of the devil. I am damned, with or without his patronage."

"Why do you say that?"

Earm turned his head, so he could see her face as he replied. "Do you know, Lina, 'Earm' is not my true name? It is a name *he* gave me, as a jest. It means 'wretched.' And he was right."

"What then, is your birth name, *effendi?*"

Earm shook his head. "I was struck down in battle. I do not remember my name. I know nothing about myself, save the unpleasantries which Lord FitzMalheury tells me."

She slid her hand over his shoulder and gave his chest a slow, light caress. A tremor ran through him, much different from those he had experienced earlier in the evening. Her voice matched the touch of her fingers.

"You should speak no more of these sad things. I will give you another name, one that will make your heart shine anew. It will be our secret."

Earm found himself smiling. "Truly?"

She put her cheek next to his, and whispered, "Nadir. *Beloved.* That is what you shall be, from this moment forward."

"Why show me such kindness, Lina?"

In one graceful movement she was in the water, facing
him, her bare legs straddling his and her chemise afloat and
billowing. He could scarcely breathe for the swift effect she
had produced. Lina caught him around the neck.

"Because, Nadir, I see in you a champion, and I have
great need of a champion. I wish to leave my lord Kalle,
and I can help you do the same."

"Aye," he murmured, already becoming lost in the
waves of her loose, dark hair. He cupped one of her lush,
round breasts and kissed it through the wet fabric. She
arched her back and wrapped her legs around his middle.

From a dark doorway Kalle watched Lina work her
magic on the hapless Earm. As a tester of men, the girl was
priceless. To know the weaknesses of those he used was
always wise.

And to know that he himself could resist her potent
charms—indeed, resist those of any woman at all—gave him
a well-deserved sense of superiority. The benefits of a pure
bloodline, brutal training and high rank would ever outweigh
those of love. Only the weak fell prey to fleshly pleasures.

And yet…something stirred in him at the sight of their
impassioned embrace. Not lust…nay, it was far worse than
that. A despicable sense of yearning…it occurred to Kalle
that he had not felt a kindly intended human touch in more
years than he could recall.

Ayshka… Even now, he wondered if she had kept his
gift…. He closed his eyes against the sudden pain.

There was no profit now in wanting something so vulgar
and common as love. He ground his teeth and turned away.
Let them have their moment together. It would not last.

Nay. The only thing of permanent value was the Elixir—and the gold it would bring. Brother Deogal had been close, very close. His daughter was not as stupid as she pretended.

And Lucien, the one who had taken *his* place—the one he had not been able to break—now, mayhap there was one capable of finishing what the old man had started.

He would find them both. And take from them what was rightfully his—for might, of course, made right.

Chapter Fourteen

Hoofbeats thundered over the drawbridge and Lucien's stomach tightened into a knot. In the cobbled bailey, he straightened from his examination of a slight puffiness in his palfrey's foreleg. Aye. No one made such a noisy arrival as his lord father's brother, Conrad.

"Mauger!" Lucien bellowed. "Get you down here and tell me you did not send for Lord Conrad."

The seneschal ran down the stairs to the courtyard, quick on his feet despite his size. He halted before Lucien and crossed his arms over his massive chest. "I did not send for Lord Conrad."

Lucien stroked his horse's shoulder and nodded to a groom to lead the beast back to the mews. He met Mauger's hard gaze, then glanced at the heavy beams of the gate, opening even as they spoke. His heart sank.

"Oh, God. What do I tell him? I swear, Mauger, you must decide this day whether you serve him or me. You cannot do both." For an instant, Lucien caught a flash of sympathy in the seneschal's usually frowning countenance.

Mauger uncrossed his arms. "Never will I lie to your uncle. But nor will I ever reveal to him anything that I do not honestly believe is important to your ultimate welfare."

"In other words, you will play the same game you ever have. Keep me on the edge of torment while trying to satisfy him."

"Lucien, that is not—"

Mauger was cut off by the clatter of hooves into the bailey. As one, he and Lucien turned and bowed to Lord Conrad as he trotted to them, his retinue following, all clad in the red and white of his household.

"Lucien!"

His uncle jumped down and caught him in a hard embrace. Lucien froze, not certain how to respond to this unexpected overture.

"My lord, I hope the journey was not difficult."

Conrad shook his head and actually smiled through his close-cropped, gray-streaked beard. "A bit, but no matter. Your mother is coming, too, a few days behind me."

At this, Lucien could scarcely gather his wits to speak a coherent sentence. "What brings such favor from you, my lord? I did not expect a visit until full spring was upon us. I fear I am not yet prepared to honor you properly."

"Come, my boy, you need not be so formal!"

Lucien narrowed his eyes at Mauger. Since when had his relationship with his uncle ever been anything *but* formal? Though the thought was terrible to contemplate, there remained the possibility that Mauger had lied right to his face. What might have brought his uncle here, with a smile on his lips?

Mauger slowly paled under Lucien's gaze, but Lord

Conrad did not seem to notice. "The pigeon arrived in good time, Mauger. Bearing good news, for a change! So, Lucien, I would meet your Rosamunde right away."

Mauger studied the buckle on Lord Conrad's reins. *Later, sir,* Lucien promised with his eyes. "Uncle, please have some dinner first, it is getting on toward evening."

"Surely she will be dining with us?"

Lucien could not let this go on. "My lord, there has been a misunderstanding. Rosamunde—"

"Rosamunde is no longer amenable to the proposal," Mauger blurted. "But there is an alternate choice."

Lucien had to make a conscious effort not to grab Mauger and shake him. The announcement of such a turnaround should not be received by Conrad on an empty belly. What had come over Mauger? Was he *trying* to make things worse?

Then, at that moment, they became so, without Mauger's help. For, no doubt having heard the noise of the new arrivals, Isidora, Larke and Rosamunde all emerged into the bailey and approached them.

Before Conrad could respond beyond the deep frown he had assumed, Mauger said, "Here she is now. Ah, Lady Isidora! How good of you and your companions to brave the cold."

Lucien bit his lip. Isidora and Larke looked at each other, then Isidora smiled and curtsied before Sir Conrad.

"Good evening, my lord."

Conrad threw a sharp glance to Lucien and cleared his throat. "What a charming accent! It sounds almost Byzantine. But of course that is absurd."

"Ah, well, my lord, my brother is of late from those lands, and we are so close, his ways rub off on me."

She raised her brows at Lucien. What did he want her to do? He and Mauger were up to some game, that much was clear. But Mauger stared at his own feet, his face pale and his brow furrowed.

Lucien gave her a forced smile. "Allow me to introduce you to my uncle, Lord Conrad, lady."

Conrad interrupted with a wave of his gloved and be-ringed hand. "Surely if this be your choice, it is her father I would meet."

At this Lucien's jaw looked hard enough to split a rock. His nostrils flared and his mouth set in thin line. Isidora was afraid if she mentioned her father was dead, she would merely increase his ire.

Finally, Larke spoke. "I hope, my lords, that you might wait until our lady-mother arrives before conducting any marriage negotiations."

"Aye, let's do," growled Lucien. "For I have made no 'choice,' as you well know, Uncle."

Conrad glowered. "Indeed, there will be no choosing beyond what I and your mother agree upon. Such a matter of import cannot be left up to you alone."

At this something very like a sneer curled Lucien's lip, then vanished. He met his uncle's gaze.

"It is too cold to stand out here talking." Lucien led the way back inside, not seeming to care whether anyone followed or not. But the return to the relative warmth of the hall was a relief.

"We will settle this when your mother gets here." Conrad threw his sword and dagger down onto the table with a clatter.

Isidora felt the situation spiraling out of control. Now

that this man of immense power and influence had arrived, no one's will but his mattered. Not even Lucien's.

Within two days Lucien's hall was overflowing with nobles. His uncle's retainers, friends and hangers-on, all hoping for a moment of Lord Conrad's attention. In addition, a bold and well-favored young man, Wace, who hailed from Raymond de Beauchamp's household, arrived on the heels of the rest.

In the midst of such chaos, Isidora wondered what Lucien's mother would be like. She herself had long been without one. Leaving her respectable widowhood to marry Deogal had cost her own mother her life and her honor.

Apart from Ayshka's family's rejection was the subsequent shame of leprosy. The Franj believed that leper women had loose morals, were lustful and full of vice. And that God had made his judgment upon them painfully obvious.

Isidora wondered…how could Faris have found the woman who was their mother and not taken Isidora to her? Was it only because of the terrible disease—or was there reason beyond that? She should ask him.

She found him in the solar, looking at various books and scrolls Lucien had there—more than she had ever imagined existed outside a monastery. "You are recovered, Faris?"

He casually set aside the manuscript he had unrolled. "I am, thank God for his mercy."

Isidora approached him and put her hand over his. They had spent many long hours in the saddle, aboard ships and afoot. Too many for there to be any lies between them.

"Faris, tell me, could you not have brought me to see our mother, one last time?"

He looked at her, then out the narrow window that allowed light into the small space. "She forbade it, Isidora. I could not disobey her. And, in truth, I was more concerned with my own questions…I asked her who my father was."

"Oh, Faris. That is hard, indeed."

"She would not tell me, other than that he was of the house of Salah al-Din. She said the risks were too great." The corners of his mouth lifted. "But, her gift to me was knowledge of you."

Isidora's heart rose like a feather on the wind. "A gift?"

"Aye." His smile faded as he met her gaze. "I was in the service of Kalle FitzMalheury, Isidora."

"So you said before." But she wished it were not true.

"He sent me to search your father's workshop—the *laboratorium*. All I found was rubble and an empty house. So I came after you. But I swear to you, Isidora, that never would I have robbed you, nor harmed you, no matter what Lord Kalle had ordered."

"Harmed me? Why would he order you to do that?"

Faris cast his gaze about, as if in search of something that might ease his shame. "He did not. But he expected me to find you and…question you. I would never have done so in the manner he questioned Lucien."

"Of course not, Faris."

"By the holy shoes and beard of Allah—nay. But Fitz-Malheury surely knows by now that I have betrayed him. He will come after me. I should not remain here any longer, for it is only a matter of time, and I would not draw him to you."

Isidora's hand tightened over Faris's. "But, if he wants

to punish you and to 'question' me, then what difference does it make if we are together? And, no doubt, he wishes to reacquaint himself with Lucien, as well. Should we not try to make a united stand?"

"Against whom?"

Isidora dropped Faris's hand and whirled about to face Lucien. She had not intended her actions to resemble those of a guilty person, but she was aware that so they must appear.

"My lord Lucien, you startled me."

"My apologies, lady. Sir Faris, do you feel stronger now that you have had rest and food?"

Faris bowed. "I do, and many thanks. Isidora and I were speaking of Kalle FitzMalheury and his inevitable pursuit of me."

The sight of Lucien's grave, beautiful face made Isidora lose the thread of her thoughts. Indeed she scarcely heard his next words.

"I have a thing or two to discuss with Kalle, myself. I will welcome him to my hall, should he come so far."

The undercurrent of menace in Lucien's tone took Isidora by surprise. "Please, stay clear of arguments with him. He is ruthless and deadly. A sorcerer."

Lucien smiled without humor. "He caught me when I was off guard. I will not be so easy to catch again. Indeed he may find himself in an uncomfortable situation one day."

Faris said, "Do not make him more of a foe than he is already. Let him think you have learned your lesson. Be wary. Be prepared."

"Aye, have no worry on that account. I bid you excuse us, Faris, I would have a word with your sister."

Once they were alone, a hard hand gripped her arm. "Isidora." Lucien's voice was low but serious. "Do not create any more lies about you and I being wed or betrothed. I command you in this, as I cannot command Larke or Rosamunde."

"Why not?"

"Because such lies do not make it—"

"Nay, why command *me?*"

"You are not under anyone's protection but mine whilst you are in this country. Faris has no power or influence here."

"Except for what he enjoys by the mere fact of his being a man."

"Aye, as do I."

"But he is my brother."

"Do you obey him, any more than Larke obeys me?"

"Nay, but I have only known of him these few months."

"That does not matter, he still should have authority over you—if you truly believed him to be your brother."

Isidora's breath caught. "If I did not, would I have been in the same bed with him?"

Lucien smiled wickedly. "You were with me."

Isidora sniffed. "You have never posed any threat to my virtue, I think."

"You should be glad of that, Isidora."

But was she? Well, if she did not know for certain, then he had no business knowing, either. "Aye, so I should," she replied firmly.

"Which is precisely why I am telling you not to play any games of pretense with my uncle. He has no sense of humor when it comes to matters like my marriage."

"You are fortunate to be of so wealthy a family you need

not wait for an inheritance or marry an heiress to have your own household."

"Aye, so I am. But that does not mean that they keep any less a grip on their purse strings."

"What do you want, then, Lucien? To be free of the prospect of a woman and children of your own?"

Lucien raked a hand back through his hair. "My mother expects me to marry, she is counting on it, for I am her only son."

"But will you?"

"Aye. I will. But on my own terms."

Isidora could not help but smile. "It will interest me to meet your lady-mother when she arrives."

Lucien scowled and did not reply.

Chapter Fifteen

His lady-mother did arrive soon thereafter, borne in a curtained litter like some eastern queen. In the women's solar, with her ladies out of earshot, Lucien took his mother's cool, slender hand. She looked up at him, her eyes liquid with feeling. With love. But she said nothing at all. He would have felt less guilty had she ever even once ranted or raved or shouted or ordered him beaten.

But no such thing had ever happened. Sometimes he wanted to shake her, to jar free the anger he was certain still lurked beneath her long-suffering surface calm.

As if in compensation, his father had rarely revealed anything but a stern acceptance of Lucien's expected successes, whether at learning to play the lute or to smash an enemy's skull with a mace. And Lucien's uncle was of much the same mind as his brother, Lucien's father, had been.

In that, and in the way he gazed at Amelie, betimes... No, that could not be so. Could it?

Lucien looked at his mother's head, now modestly bent as she worked some kind of stitchery in her lap. The linen of her coif was white, pure and clean and soft. Just as she herself was. If only he could get past that purity and reach her, without destroying her...

"*Mere...*"

She did not look up, but her hands grew still.

"*Mere,* I am sorry, you know that, do you not? I will be sorry for the rest of my life." Lucien got on his knees beside her. "I would do anything for you, anything at all. Just ask me."

Then she turned and met his gaze with hers, blue and fever-bright. "Marry the girl, then. Marry Isidora of the dark eyes. That is what I wish of you."

Lucien blinked and tried to calm the sudden roar in his head. "May I ask why?"

"Why? B-because someone must be happy! If not me, then her. You must please her. You must!" Amelie burst into tears.

Lucien was horrified. But he did what instinct told him and caught her close to his chest, wrapping his arms about her until her sobs dwindled.

Her women gathered around and Lucien gave her up to their care. Once again, she was childlike, allowing them to guide her to bed, saying nothing, not even a farewell as Lucien headed to the door.

Bewildered and discouraged and dismayed, he excused himself and ran down the stairs. Women! Who could possibly bear them, much less understand them?

As he rounded a corner he nearly collided with Mauger, and blurted, "I am stifling here with so many folk about, all wanting something from me. I am going for a ride."

"I'll accompany you."

Lucien aborted a dismissive gesture. "I am telling you as a courtesy, not as an invitation, Mauger."

"And I am telling you I'm coming along, not asking permission. There are still too many unsavory leftovers from the revels hanging about the woods."

Lucien decided to ignore Mauger, since the man did not listen to him, much less obey him. He strode out into the bailey, but Mauger was the one who ordered up the horses.

With relief, Lucien mounted his big gray courser and took up the reins. He guided the beast out the gates and across the narrow, ice-slick drawbridge.

The afternoon sun had crept in a low arc across the pale, watery sky. Now it hung just behind the beeches and oaks, silhouetting their bare limbs. The great wood lay silent and waiting, in a dark blanket beyond the stubble of the fields.

"Don't go in there!" cautioned Mauger.

"If that is the only way to escape you, perhaps I will," Lucien replied. Though he shared some of his friend Raymond's dislike of the woods, it was more of a vague uneasiness than outright fear.

But he kept his horse to the muddy path and patted its warm, rough-coated neck. "I do not want to be continually butting heads with you, Mauger. I have more of a problem now than I did but a few days ago. You have helped create it, and I expect you to help solve it."

Mauger pursed his lips. "All you need do is obey your uncle's wishes."

"Has he informed you as to what they are?"

"My lord Lucien, you speak as though he and I are in collusion against you. We only want what is in your best interests, and those of the family."

"Aye, of course." Lucien cocked his head and listened. The small noises of the surrounding fields and coppiced hedges had dwindled. He halted his horse, the better to hear, but nothing seemed amiss.

"Mauger, let us turn back. I feel uneasy."

"As you wish. The horses do seem a bit twitchy."

Lucien reined his horse around, then paused and leaned an elbow on the pommel of his saddle. "Do you truly want her, Mauger? Do you want Rosamunde?"

The seneschal's strong jaw tightened and released. "If her father agrees."

"Nay, Mauger, listen to yourself. I am not asking if you want to marry her. I am asking, do you want *her?*"

Mauger's mouth pursed into a rueful smile. "I might ask the same of you in regard to Isidora. But, aye, Lucien. I want Rosamunde. No doubt I'll live to regret it, but I do."

Lucien nodded and allowed his horse to move forward. "I will help you then. For I would see you well content, Mauger. The happier you are, the less shall you pester me."

Mauger grinned. "You may be right. But you have my thanks, for lending your support to my cause."

"Oh, don't think it is out of the goodness of my heart, Mauger. Well do I know, you are a man of prowess, and I want to avoid making an enemy of you."

"Lucien, you are not even aware of the depths of your own heart, so speak not to me of its goodness or lack thereof. It shall be tested, and then you'll know."

Lucien took a deep breath. The goodness of his heart. It had already been tested. And failed.

* * *

Having met Lucien's mother, Isidora saw from whence he got his purity of skin and coloring. Much younger than Isidora expected, Amelie was like a delicate flower, her head bowed modestly and the fragrance of roses about her. Lucien and his uncle both fell over themselves to please her, though she seemed to ask for little.

Isidora sat in the hall by the fire, opposite Lady Amelie, who stared into the flames but said nothing. Isidora's heart ached for the woman, who seemed so frail and all alone. What was wrong with her? And why did Lucien not speak of it?

There was a rustle of the heavy curtain that blocked the draft from the anteroom and Lucien entered with Mauger behind him.

Lady Amelie came to life, turning to face her son, yet still she did not smile. He came in, smelling of fresh, cold air. He bowed first to her, then to Isidora, took a seat beside his mother and he, too, said nothing.

Then, without warning, as she sat between them, Amelie caught Isidora's and Lucien's hands and put them together. Isidora stared first at Amelie, then at Lucien, whose face was now as red as she had ever seen it. But, to her immense gratitude, he did not jerk his hand from hers.

Instead he swallowed and, with a flicker of a look toward his mother, leaned toward Isidora.

"Em, my lady, this—" he gave her fingers a squeeze "—is how it is to be between us, from now on. Lady Amelie has expressed her desire that I have you. And I am agreed."

Isidora nearly choked. Lucien had agreed to his mother's desire that he *have* her? As *what?* "Pardon me, my lord, but I do not understand. Just what does *this* signify?" She returned his subtle squeeze.

Amelie broke her silence. "He will have you. You will have him. Be glad of it."

We will be wed? Isidora's heart felt like the froth on a mazer of ale. Light and heady. Full of intoxicating promise.

Then, daring to be bold, she looked into Lucien's eyes.

And felt as though she had been slapped. They were not joyous or loving. Just a steely blue. Determined. And they held no promises at all.

The cold, terrible truth crashed into Isidora like a warrior into a shield wall. He was not doing this because he loved *her*. Of course not. He was doing it because he loved his mother. And because he felt guilty about something.

"Isidora." Lucien held on to her hand as she tried to pull away. "Not now. Please."

He was right. Why should she be upset? Husbands and wives were not meant to love each other with passion.

Moderation was in order. Propriety. Conserving one's strength for the trials ahead. Good wives gave their love to God and obedience to their husbands.

Look what happened to those who loved with abandon. Look what had happened to her own mother!

Isidora bit her lip. To hell with good wives! She would never be one. But she could not bear the thought of being a bad one, either. Bad for wanting more from Lucien than distracted glances and his duty to provide her with children…she wanted him, heart and soul.

For poor, wounded Amelie's sake, Isidora gave him a false smile in return. Aye, soon enough Lucien would have to face his bride and just how she felt.

Chapter Sixteen

Lord Conrad cleared his throat as he approached them. "Let me escort Lady Amelie to her quarters."

He held out his hand for her to take, and for the first time Lucien saw something he had never before noticed. His mother looked at Conrad. With glowing eyes and trembling lips, blushing cheeks and quickened breaths.

The way a woman in love looks at a man.

Lucien stared at her, then at his uncle, who immediately frowned. But not quite fast enough to hide a flash of longing. *My God!* How long has this been going on?

They are in love! Lucien backed away, both from the thought and from his mother.

The two of them slowly mounted the stairs. Nay, this was crazy. And so was he, to agree to wed Isidora, the alchemist's daughter, just to please his mother! But was that not what every son and daughter was expected to do?

To obey their parents and accept whatever choice they made for them in regard to marriage? It was. Who was he to question it?

Never mind that most matches took months, if not years, of negotiation and planning. That they were arranged when the principals were children, not fully grown and fully capable of making their own choice, were they allowed. But a man was always a son to his mother. And Isidora had no one but her brother—*Faris!*

Lucien's heart jolted. Important relatives who were left out of the consent process—the bride herself notwithstanding—might be so insulted that they did violence to whomever they felt had slighted them. Especially a proud warrior like Faris, with a most traditional bent of mind.

Lucien turned to Isidora. "We must tell your brother on the instant."

She eyed him, her face already turning toward the door. "Oh, aye, it is a fine thing, to tell him after the fact. He will appreciate your consideration. As do I."

Lucien caught her arm as she was about to flounce away from him. "You and I will discuss this later. Accompany me or not, but I will speak to him now." It was imperative.

"Faris!" Lucien called as he made his way upstairs.

The wooden steps shuddered as Mauger ran after him. "Lucien, let me come, too. We will explain your lapse together."

"I would not have him think we are mounting an offense against him."

"Nay, we are showing him the respect he deserves, by the both of us addressing him."

Isidora followed them and Lucien did not try to stop her. They found Faris making ready as if to go out. He wore his Persian mail, a heavy surcoat and woolen mantle. His dark hair was combed back; hollows shadowed his cheeks.

"Sir Faris. You look as though you are missing your homeland," Lucien offered cautiously.

Faris jerked on a gauntlet. "So I do. I like it here, surprising as that may seem, but I fear I may have stayed too long already. While at first I had my doubts, I see now that Isidora is safe here, among friends."

"That is what we wish to discuss with you, Faris. My, em, family wants me to take Isidora to wife. I would ask for your blessing."

Faris stared. "What does Isidora have to say on the matter?"

"I—"

Lucien cut her off. "She is well content."

Faris pulled his other gauntlet on and flexed his fingers. "As I have said before, your courting customs are unseemly by our standards. I believe you have taken liberties with Isidora and that her honor has been jeopardized. In fact, had you not made your announcement just now, I would have insisted upon it before taking my leave."

"But—" Isidora began again.

Faris held up his hand. "Nay, Isidora. You must listen to me. You have nothing to return to in Acre. You are much better off here, with these English and Welsh. They are more amiable than the other Franj, I think."

"But you cannot go now," Mauger said. "The roads are not yet decent. At least wait until after these two are wed, which cannot be long, because it must take place before Lent begins."

"Please stay, Faris," Isidora pleaded.

He looked at her, into her eyes, and she saw pain and

regret in his. She held out her hand to him, but he turned from her and addressed Lucien once more.

"*Effendi*—Sir Lucien—it is best that I leave. I cannot explain further. My journey has been long, but it must end with my return to Acre. You have my thanks for seeing to my health, and for taking charge of Isidora Binte Deogal. I wish you many long years of happiness and many fine sons to make you proud. Fare well."

Isidora clenched her hands into fists to stop them from shaking. Bit by bit, her world was crumbling....

"I will escort you to the borders of my land, then, Faris," said Lucien.

"That is not necessary. I can take care of myself. This land is a garden paradise compared to some places I've been."

"Then take my gray courser as your own, he will see you past many dangers, with more grace than any other horse I have."

Faris smiled. "I am honored by your gift, sir." With an elegant gesture of finality, Faris strode past Mauger and Lucien, headed for the stairs. Then, just as he was about to pass out of sight, he halted and turned. With a crook of his finger, he bade Isidora come to him.

She had to stop herself from running, from begging him to take her home. Away from these merciless English...

"Isidora, forgive me," he whispered. "Do not lose the box I gave you from your mother, eh? Keep it as a remembrance of me, will you?"

She nodded, any words she might have uttered were locked behind the tightness in her throat. Despite her efforts to prevent them, tears began to stream down her face. With Faris's departure, she lost not only him, but all connection to everything that had once been so familiar…warm sandstone, sunny blue skies, the flowers and birds and refined subtleties of manners and chivalry she had always taken for granted. Now she understood how rare they were.

Faris raised his hand and, with the back of his gloved forefinger, wiped her cheeks. "No tears, *habibti.*"

She swallowed hard. "Faris, grant me one boon, if you will."

"Name it."

"Find Marylas, the Circassian woman who served in my father's house, and make certain that she is safe and happily situated."

"I will. Have no worry for her."

"My thanks. Go with God, Faris al-Rashid." Isidora watched him descend the stairs to the main hall, Mauger at his heels. Somehow she feared she would never see Faris again. She felt more alone than she had ever felt at home, even with her father paying her no heed.

Then, just as she was about to turn and run, warm hands settled upon her shoulders. Lucien's hands. She held herself still, not wanting to give in to the immediate sense of safety his touch brought, however fleeting. Nay, it was not fair at all. She would not be pitied by him, or used.

There was always a nunnery as a choice…

"Isidora, it has been a trying day. You should go to bed. My mother is already settled in the women's quarters."

His breath was warm against her ear, for he had bent his head—so that he could keep his voice low, she assumed.

"Lucien, I will go to bed when and where I choose. I have lived long enough to be fully capable of such a decision."

"Have you? I wonder, even at your age, that you do not need some guidance in that regard, or at least some inspiration?" He turned her around. "Do you *want* some…inspiration?"

At the sight of him, so close, the feel of him, living, breathing, a pulse beating in his neck, his eyes gleaming in the firelight, his male scent proving his nearness…for once, his attention focused upon her alone…Isidora had all the inspiration she could handle.

She felt positively dizzy. She wanted to fall into his arms. Kiss him. And beat him with her fists, so thick-headed was he. Had he no idea of the torture he put her through? What was the matter with him? She could not ask.

"Lucien, this should wait."

"What should wait?" He slid his hands from her shoulders to the small of her back, drawing her even closer. His eyes had darkened and his lips parted in a small, beguiling smile.

Apparently helpless to do otherwise, Isidora's arms wound around his waist. She took one last glorious look at him, then shut her eyes and tilted back her head. "*This,* Lucien, God help me. Yet again."

"He will not," Lucien whispered in a low growl. "He cannot. Not now."

"Blasphemer. Then He should help *you.*"

"Aye, by making you stay quiet for a moment…"

His hand roamed lower.

"Oh!" Isidora could tell he was truly smiling now. Indeed, he nearly purred. She wriggled at the warm expanse of palm against her backside. That small movement brought her body to his, his mouth to hers, in a hard, hot and all-consuming kiss. A mingling of breath and essences, of scent and skin, an illusion of unity that gave her such pleasure she could not describe it.

It was not until he withdrew that she opened her eyes, was able to breathe, and realized her thigh had climbed his during the encounter. She felt blood rush to her cheeks and quickly put her foot back on the floor. "My God, Lucien!"

"Eh, He *was* quite helpful, after all…"

"Stop this!" She pulled her arms back to her sides.

"You mean the same 'this' we were just doing?"

"Aye, the very same."

"Why? Did you not enjoy it?"

She would not lie, but she would indeed sidestep. "You toy with me. If you intend to marry me, then you should have a care for my honor."

A look of stunned bewilderment crossed Lucien's fine features. "Of course I care for your honor. How could you imagine otherwise?"

"You are not indifferent to me, true, but you allow lust to be your guide, my lord. That is what must wait. I should not even be having to say such things to you."

Lucien's hands fell from her waist and the loss of their comfort brought an ache to her heart.

Of a sudden his color rose. "Indeed, you should not. But, lest you fall victim to my…lust…again, mayhap you should keep to your quarters, or do not roam about unescorted."

"I will not be made prisoner here, just because you cannot control yourself."

His jaw tightened. "Oh, Isidora, if I am such a threat, then so shall you be kept safe from me by the same God that brought you here!" He turned on his heel and stalked away.

Now what had she done?

Chapter Seventeen

What have I done? Lucien crossed the cobbled bailey in the night, kicking bits of stone as if they were himself as he went. He had tried to seduce a woman to whom he was betrothed but did not want to marry? Where was the reason in that? Had he lost his mind?

Never had he intended to hurt Isidora. There was simply something about her that made him want to seize her and—and what? Kiss her? Bed her? Aye, both. But it was not her fault. And she deserved more—and better—than that.

By the dim flicker of the oil lamp he held, Lucien made his way to the *laboratorium*. It had been days upon days since he had last seen to the Work. It was all that was truly right and real in his world.

Dropping his mantle onto a hook in the wall, he lit the candles in their sconces and the lamps upon the workbench. He looked about. Dust coated the glassware and crucibles. One should have an assistant to keep such annoying impurities at bay, he thought.

With a sigh, Lucien took a bit of rag and began to rub

the bubbled, green-glass surfaces clean. The pure drudgery of the task was soothing in a way. He picked up a flask, still laden with the liquid, silvered remains of a failed effort.

Nay, he would not give up! He could not…not if Amelie's happiness meant anything to him, and as far as he could see, she had none. That was what he must remedy, his debt to her—atone for the death of his sister, a tragedy that had broken his mother's mind.

His fingers tightened around the flask and it shattered in his hand. Pain burst into his consciousness. A heavy, curved piece of glass had impaled his palm at an angle, and shards were scattered all over, mingled with spilled mercury. Lucien pulled the glass out, cutting his other hand's fingers in the process.

He pressed the rag to the wound, then looked at the mess of discarded quicksilver. The heavy liquid ran over the stone table's top, its racing metallic edges crimson in the firelight. It seemed to have a life of its own, pooling here and continuing there…at last it came to a stop.

Lucien stood, his eyes wide, his bleeding left hand forgotten. The liquid had formed a shape. Like the graceful, gray body of the horse he had given Faris. There was even a suggestion of a rider upon its back. A splotch of red disturbed the image. Then another.

Shaken, Lucien clenched his dripping fist and wrapped the rag tighter. Something was wrong. He should never have allowed Faris to leave as darkness approached, much less unescorted. Knight or no, one man was not always enough. He grabbed his mantle, extinguished the lamps, slammed, bolted and locked the door before running back to the mews.

Gripped by a sense of urgency he could not explain, Lucien did not wait for a groom. His wounded hand left him clumsy, but he managed to saddle Mauger's palfrey, a fine Andalusian, for apart from giving Faris his gray, he had sent his other courser to cover a mare at an adjoining estate.

Lucien was nearly out the gate before remembering he had not brought his sword. He halted the long-maned, restive horse outside the portion of the keep that provided the barracks and armory for his men.

"Oy, are any of you lads awake in there? Or is Daphne visiting?" he shouted.

A blond head, perpetually touseled, to Lucien's observation, preceded the emergence of a tall, strikingly fair but solidly built man.

"Milord?" he rumbled.

"Jager, you're here. Good—" It struck Lucien that Sir Jager looked even more pale than usual. And stiff.

Then another body emerged through the low doorway from the dark confines of the men-at-arms's quarters.

"Oh, hullo, Lucien!" Larke smiled cheerily as she straightened to stand beside Jager, only reaching the man's shoulder. She was garbed in her usual inappropriate attire—a long hunting tunic, torn leggings and a voluminous, muddy woolen mantle.

Jager did not twitch a muscle. Indeed, he seemed frozen to the spot. Lucien breathed in deeply and released the air slowly, until the blood stopped pounding in his neck. He could not fault Jager for succumbing to his sister's persuasive and persistent ways. "Larke, go back to the hall."

She frowned. "Whatever for? Sir Jager is just about to show me where the orb of Venus is to appear tonight. I was going to bring Isidora along later, so she can see it, too. And Rosamunde."

Lucien took another deep breath. There was no point in shouting. "Jager is needed. Venus will still be there tomorrow night. Or ask Mauger where it is."

Larke brightened. "Oh, indeed, a splendid thought, Lucien. Jager, I thank you for your time." She swept the man a bow, as if he outranked her and she were another man.

If she wanted to behave thus, then she could make herself useful, as well. "Larke!"

She turned on her heel. "Aye, Lucien?"

"Bring me Isenbana."

A flicker of darkness passed across her face and her smile vanished. "Aye, Lucien, at once."

Jager's eyes moved to follow her departure, then he closed them briefly. "Lord, I meant no—"

It was becoming more and more difficult to rein Larke in. She needed a husband. Soon. Lucien raised his hand. "I know, Jager. Never mind. Just find another two men, I need an escort."

By the time Jager had readied himself and his men, Larke, too, had returned, bringing Lucien's heavy sword to him. Isenbana. *Ironslayer.* An ancient thing, but well had it served him. He strapped it about his middle.

But, confound her, Isidora had followed Larke from the hall! No doubt to see why Gawaine was barking so loudly, tugging against his chain.

"Let's go." Lucien urged the courser forward, ready to simply ignore the young women rather than argue with them about their being left behind. Besides, he did not want to tell Isidora that he feared for Faris's safety.

With Jager mounted, his men, afoot and bearing torches, fell into step beside Lucien's horse. At the gate, as the porter opened it, Lucien risked a look back. There stood Larke and Isidora, their breaths clouding the air, looking forlorn and abandoned.

If only Larke had the sense of a pea-hen, things might be all right. But she was far too clever for her own good.

Isidora watched as Lucien and his men ventured into the evening mist. She put her hand on Larke's arm. "I don't like this. Did he say where they are going? Or why?"

The girl shook her head. "Nay. But we can find out, if we dare."

"Dare what?"

A mischievous grin lit Larke's features. "Well, you have your mare and I have mine. We could follow them."

Isidora looked about, at the red glow of the sun's last rays as they tinged the bellies of the clouds. At the black rooks lining up along the battlements of Lucien's fortifications. The forest swayed and creaked in the wind. It was far too cold and late for any such adventure.

But she had not come all this way to simply stand by while Lucien rode off into the night for no apparent reason. She could follow him, as Larke suggested, for she still had her clothing from posing as Faris's squire.

Faris! The pain of his departure was but hours old and not hers alone. She had seen a bond form between Faris and Lucien. Isidora turned to Larke. "What if Lucien has decided to pursue my brother, to bring him back? Or to find him, that he might accompany him past his borders, after all?"

"It is just the sort of thing Lucien would do, after the fact," Larke declared.

"They do not have much of a start on us. If I could see Faris even one more time, it would be worth your brother's ire."

"And I, too, would like to see *your* brother one more time."

"Why? What do you mean?"

"I told you, he was the most handsome man at the mêlée on the pond. Except for Lucien, of course. Nothing like what I had imagined a Saracen to be—no pointed teeth, or scales, none of that. One does not get to see such sights as Faris often. So dark, yet so brilliant—"

"He is not a 'sight,' Larke, nor a Saracen any longer, but a man. A good man, whom I love and might not ever see again myself."

Larke bit her lip. "I know."

Isidora frowned. "What is it?"

"Nothing. He is not married, is he? Or if he is, does he yet have his full contingent of wives?"

"Larke! Of all the foolish notions! He is not married. But if he were, it would be to a Byzantine princess or one from the family of an eastern Frankish king. He has no ties to England, no reason to ally himself here."

"I never thought you capable of such…such elitism, Isidora. I thought you were my friend."

"Oh, Larke, so I am. I but want to protect you from heartbreak. Did he show you any interest whilst he was here?"

"Nay. I do not think he even noticed my existence."

"So for that, you would place your heart at risk?"

"I never got to say goodbye! I made him a good-luck charm."

Larke sounded so earnest that Isidora was moved to co-operate. What a pair of fools they made! "Very well, Larke, but we must tell someone we are going."

After her initial smile, Larke's brow creased. "Not Mauger. He would be most vexed. But...we could tell Rosamunde."

Isidora tucked her chin to her chest. She wanted as little to do with Rosamunde as possible, for both their sakes. The whole situation was a stew of dishonor.

"Come!" Larke strode into the stable, barked orders to the grooms and walked with Isidora back to the hall.

"But, Larke, if Lucien thought it prudent to take three men along with him, what about us? I have my bow, but..."

"Oh, what bother! Our darling Lucien is always over-prepared, for anything he does. We can bring Gawaine along, he'll protect us! You're not afraid of the dark, are you?"

Isidora met Larke's clear, fearless gaze. "Aye, I am. The dark holds the unseen. And the unseen are not to be taken lightly. This I know..."

It was how her mother had been saved and cursed...starving and stumbling in the dark, until she received help from those who were not supposed to be out amongst the ordinary living. Nay. Ignorant folk believed that lepers were no longer fully human. But some of the afflicted had more compassion than many a sound-limbed man.

"Well, Izzie, dear, I trow there's nothing like a warm horse between one's legs at night to chase the devil away, eh?"

Isidora put her hand over her mouth and stared at Larke. Then they both burst out laughing.

"What's all this?" Mauger's deep voice put a quick end

to their mirth. He moved toward them, just as a bear might amble toward an object of interest. Faster than one might expect and just as impossible to stop.

"Em, mere speculation, sir," Larke offered with a winning smile that obviously had no effect upon Mauger, who crossed his arms. "You should be in bed soon, Lady Larke. Night is nearly upon us."

Larke put her hands on her hips. "I beg your pardon, Sir Mauger, but I am no longer an eight-year-old. Kindly address me as befits my station. And yours."

Mauger cleared his throat and pursed his lips. "As I said, my most esteemed Lady Larke, you should be in bed soon."

She stood up on tiptoe and peered over his shoulder. "What of Lady Rosamunde? Should you not be seeing her to bed, as well?"

The resultant crimson of Mauger's face was not pleasant to behold. He uncrossed his arms, bent to Larke's level and lowered his voice to a hiss. "If she is behind me, and heard, Lady Larke, I swear upon my grandfather's beard, your hind parts will have cause to regret the indiscretions of your fore parts!"

Isidora thought Lucien's sister an outrageous minx, but her next move topped all those heretofore witnessed. Larke caught Mauger's broad face between her palms and planted a noisy kiss on his lips.

"Nay, Rosamunde is not behind you," she announced. "Elsewise I would not have done that. I *am* fond of you, despite your grumpiness, Mauger."

He straightened and backed away. "By God, young woman, you have much to answer for!"

Larke smiled sweetly. "I'll just tell Rosamunde you will be up shortly to see her."

Isidora could have sworn she heard Mauger growl.

Chapter Eighteen

A short while later Larke and Isidora slipped through the hall and out to the mews where their mounts awaited them. Gawaine had to be admonished, so that he did not entangle himself amongst the horses' legs.

Larke carried a horn-paned lamp, which was not enough to see by but better than nothing. Isidora was so intent upon climbing atop her horse, she nearly fell off at the sound of yet another authoritative male voice behind her.

"Where are you two going at this hour?"

She righted herself in the saddle and looked down at the speaker. Wace, the squire from Wales, though he himself was not Welsh. Good-looking and arrogant, Wace had hair of dark auburn and a clear-eyed gaze that missed little.

Before she could reply, Larke did. "What business is it of yours, Wace du Hautepont? Your master did not send you here to nursemaid us, did he?"

Wace grinned. "Had Lord Raymond known how badly you needed it, he might have, Lady Larke. He has tamed much wilder women than you!"

Larke raised her chin. "Do not speak to me of taming, sir, if you wish to be my friend. You *do* want that, do you not?"

"Em, well, aye, I suppose."

"Declare thy intentions convincingly or be gone!" Larke commanded with a flourish.

Isidora could see Wace's resolve harden before her eyes. But his response was not a capitulation, as she expected.

He crossed his brawny arms and stood with his weight on one leg. "Why do you behave like a child, Lady Larke—now before me, and especially, before your brother? You know better."

Larke placed one hand upon the other on the pommel of her saddle. "But *he* expects me to act witless! Perhaps he knows I am not, but he is more comfortable having his expectations met. He has much on his mind, Wace. I love him and I want him to be happy."

Wace snorted. "Has it occurred to you that he might be happier if he did not have to always worry about what you next might do? If he could count upon you to behave properly, as a modest maiden should?"

Larke gave Wace a withering glare. "Mayhap that is what would make *you* happy, Wace? Do I shame you?"

"You shame yourself, when you behave like an imbecile!"

At this Larke urged her horse around, so that Wace was forced to step out of the way. "You, sir, have much to learn about how to address a lady."

"And you have much to learn about acting like one."

An icy void of silence spread between them, then Larke proved his point by declaring, "Oh, go dunk your head in the tanning vat!"

To his credit, Wace did not fall prey to her taunt. "Not

before you've told me what you are up to. Dragging Lady
Isidora out into the freezing night."

Larke looked to Isidora, who replied, "We are on a
quest, Squire Wace. To guard Lucien's back."

"What do you mean? Where has he gone?"

Larke snugged Gawaine's leash tighter. "We do not
know. But he needs us."

"Then so do you need me. I am coming with you."

Larke rubbed her chin, as if considering his statement.
"Very well. But I am in charge. And on no account must
you tell Mauger or anyone else."

Wace grinned again. "Of course not. Where would the
fun be in that?"

Larke beamed from ear to ear as Wace collected his horse.

When they approached the gates, the porter challenged
them. "What's this, milady? Yer goin' out?"

Larke winked at Wace and whispered to Isidora, "I am
a much better liar than you, so let me do the talking." Then
she replied to the porter, "Aye, 'tis but a game, nothing to
worry about. Squire Wace is going to show us how to night
track certain wee beasts. We will be back soon."

The man cranked the portcullis up with shrieks of protest from the iron chains.

"You need some fat in there, porter!" Larke called as
they trotted through. Once outside and across the drawbridge, the dusk-befallen fields and woods spread before
them in a misty array of muted greens and browns. The air
smelled of wet leaves and woodsmoke, and cattle grazed
upon the common, with a herdsman beginning to gather
them up for home.

The lane skirted the forest for some way, then once past

the pond, dove into the cover of the trees. A shiver of dread coursed through Isidora. These woods—so dense, so close, even in daylight. And at night…

Gawaine howled and Isidora started. Her horse jigged, and Larke's lamp swayed and bobbed like a cork on the sea. The shadows danced to the motion of the swinging light, as if the trees were beings fully aware of their passing.

They progressed farther into the forest, then the path forked. The mud was hoof-marked in both directions. Larke turned to Isidora and Wace, her eyes wide. "Em, how do we know which way they went? The right turning goes back to the main road, the one you came on, no doubt. The left goes to another village, down the valley."

"It is your wood. I am merely here to protect you, not lead you," Wace said coolly.

"Stay right," Isidora said, not knowing why she said it.

But Larke reined her horse to the left, as if she had not heard. "I think they went this way. Lucien has no sense of direction."

Farther and farther they went, the trees moaning as the breeze quickened, until Isidora was shivering with the cold and the darkness had become nearly impenetrable. "What is that ahead? That flickering?"

Larke halted her horse and peered forward, but Gawaine leaped against his lead and jerked it from her hands. He bounded toward the golden light ahead, barking as he went.

"It must be Lucien he's sniffed!"

"Nay, Larke, we should not go any closer!"

But Larke urged her horse on and Isidora had to follow. She half expected to see a fairy ring—she had heard such things were common in England. The place was so strange and eerie, anything might manifest. But the sight that met her eyes when her horse stepped into the clearing was beyond anything she had imagined.

A striped pavilion had been erected in a meadow and a fire burned off to one side, with a cook pot suspended from an iron tripod. A wagon had a pair of carthorses tethered to it, and picketed beyond them were a fine bay palfrey and a chestnut rouncy.

Blue and yellow pennants hung from a cluster of lances propped together in a circle. The device on them looked familiar… *I must be mistaken.* Isidora's stomach curled at the possibility she was not—

"This looks welcoming, eh? Hello!" called Larke.

A short, stocky man walked out of the darkness, bearing an armload of wood, and stopped at the sight of the riders. Another, tall and dark, came out of the tent, a frown upon his face.

"These are strangers and we are not a welcome surprise, Larke," Isidora whispered. "Let us turn around and go."

"But they may have seen Lucien. At least let me inquire. Your pardon, sir, but—"

Larke went quiet as yet another man, far more imposing than the first, emerged from the pavilion and straightened to stand before the fire to warm his hands. He, too, was tall, but fair-haired and grim, with strong, sculpted features and startling gray eyes that barely spared the women a glance.

"Bon soir, Isidora," he said softly.

She swallowed back a sick, rising fear. She had not been mistaken. "Good evening, Lord FitzMalheury."

"Earm, kindly provide the young man and these *demoiselles* with some hippocras."

"Our thanks, but no," Isidora said. At the moment, even the thought of drinking sweetened wine, warmed and spiced, made her ill. "We must be going. Perhaps some other time."

Kalle glowered at them. "You would refuse my hospitality? Have you already forgotten how civilized people behave since you came to this godforsaken country?"

Wace's hand rested on his sword hilt and Larke looked at Isidora. "You know him?"

Isidora nodded. "Please, Larke and Squire Wace. I will handle this." A flash of anger speared her and sweat trickled down her sides, even though she was cold. "My lord, I have forgotten nothing of your hospitality toward Sir Lucien."

Larke's brow creased. "Lucien knows him, too?"

"Shh!" hissed Isidora.

Kalle laughed, a deep, rich sound. "What a pretty pair of doves you make. All a-flutter. What think you, Earm?"

The dark man inclined his head. "I think whatever you command me to think, is that not so, my lord Kalle?"

Kalle's gaze narrowed into icicles of light. "It would seem everyone is forgetting their manners tonight."

Larke stirred and sat up straight in her saddle. "Oh, indeed not, sir. I bid you come to our hall and make yourselves comfortable."

Wace and Isidora looked at the girl in dismay.

"They will be outnumbered there," Larke whispered.

"A fair enough invitation," Kalle said. "Earm, tell Cooke to dump that mess out of the pot and pack up."

With a careful glance at Kalle, the short man set his wood down and bowed, as if begging to be spared.

Kalle ignored him while he pulled on his gloves. "I will

ride along with these *petits oiseaux,* Earm. No doubt you can find the way yourself."

Earm brought Kalle his palfrey. "Aye, God speed, milord."

Isidora clutched her bow, little use that it was in such close quarters. She had only ever shot at targets, not at a living being. And Kalle…he was so hard, and no doubt surrounded by protective spells of some sort, the arrows would probably bounce off him.

Kalle mounted his horse, which shook its head and pawed the ground. He brought it alongside Isidora and leaned on the pommel with one elbow, the picture of relaxed detachment despite the beast's restlessness.

The knight smiled, ever so subtly. "So, Daughter of Deogal. Shall we call a truce, until we can meet on trodden ground, as it were? I do not want you fleeing into the wilds on account of me."

Isidora stiffened and her grip on her bow grew even tighter. "You mock me, sir, with such a suggestion, and flatter yourself. I am not my mother, may God forever bless her innocent soul."

At this Kalle's smile and easy manner vanished. A seething cloud of rage and pain seemed to surround him. "In that you are indeed correct," he snarled, his teeth flashing white against the tan of his face.

Larke cleared her throat. "Em, Isidora, good sir—let us be on our way before we freeze. You can best sort out any differences at the hall."

Isidora had to force herself not to do just what Kalle had said—flee into the wild at a gallop, to put as much distance as possible between them. His presence brought back an unbearable burden of wretched memories.

Of her father, his fists bloody, the night he nearly killed Kalle. Of her mother, weeping, forced out onto the streets because of Kalle. Of herself, screaming, being restrained by servants to keep her from running after her mother.

But in truth those memories remained a part of her, whether Kalle was present or a thousand miles away. He was a danger, aye, to Lucien for one set of reasons and to herself for another. And Lucien? What was he to her?

Something, for certain, elsewise she would not have come chasing after him into the forest at night.

Kalle spoke again, this time addressing Larke. "So, I take it you are not Isidora's servant, though you've dressed the part." He scrutinized her profile and she nudged her horse, putting Wace between herself and Kalle.

Isidora understood her apparent desire to hide, but had to remind her, "Larke, you have the lantern."

The girl held out the light to Isidora. "Take it, please. I would not have him look at me thus."

Wace leaned over and caught hold of the lantern's bronze handle and the flame flickered precariously in the growing darkness.

Kalle chuckled. "Ha, no matter, I have it now. You are the young sister of Lucien, but no longer a child. Aye, I learned a great deal about our Lucien whilst he was in Acre. He had another sister, as well, did he not? His twin? And he let her die cruelly at the hands of vicious outlaws."

Isidora stared, first at Kalle, then at Larke. What was he talking about?

Larke looked over her shoulder. "You, sir, are cruel, to bring up such a thing. I pray you do not speak of it in my presence again. Nor in Lucien's, if you value your life."

Kalle's eyes crinkled at the corners. "I see he has not mentioned it to our Isidora. But all in good time. Then shall you have the full measure of your precious Lucien."

A stick cracked. Out of nowhere, a horse and rider loomed ahead, barely visible in the gloom, but Isidora knew the set of those broad shoulders and, as they approached, the familiar gleam of coppery hair.

Gawaine whined and broke free of his leash yet again, to roil toward Lucien as Jager and the other two men brought up the rear, carrying torches.

Isidora felt a pang that was a mixture of alarm and relief. "Perhaps you may have his full measure *now,* FitzMalheury."

Again, Kalle's teeth showed white as he grinned. A cunning, predator's grin.

"Sir Kalle." Lucien held up his empty right hand. "Somehow it does not surprise me to find you here. But leave these women out of any business that only belongs between you and me."

Kalle shook his head, like a lion shaking his mane. "Have no fear for them, Lucien. I am but escorting them home from their ill-advised outing. But why you allow such delicates to roam at night is beyond me, especially with all the wild animals in the woods. I came across quite a ferocious specimen earlier, in fact. He got away even after I wounded him, but I expect he's finished by now."

Isidora felt rather than saw Lucien stiffen in response. The atmosphere went even colder than it already was. Still, it was strange, how the shared experience of captive and captor created such intimacy between the men. Strained to its limits, no doubt, but intimacy nonetheless.

Lucien frowned at Larke and Isidora, and scowled at

Wace. "Fascinating. But these three shall hear from me upon that score. Later."

At this ominous remark, Isidora exchanged a glance with Larke, who, for once, said nothing, and Wace's look of utter calm did not ring true.

Lucien continued. "Jager, Wace, light the way for the ladies. FitzMalheury, ride alongside me, if you will. I know you have not come all this way to kill me, you could have done that long ago."

Kalle laughed in his mirthless way. "You have more use to me alive than dead, Lucien. I do apologize for having forgotten about you in my dungeon, but of course, that is the purpose of an *oubliette*. You were indeed fortunate that our Isidora decided to pay me a visit sooner rather than later."

Isidora's heart lurched. If Kalle said another word…

"Oh, aye, *our* Isidora is quite the resourceful one," Lucien agreed, as if he knew all about it. But the very quietness of his tone made Isidora more uneasy. She would have to talk to him. Not that it was any of his concern. She had saved his life, was that not the important thing?

"Em," Larke squeaked. "Lucien, can we hurry? I'm hungry!"

Lucien did not reply. Not to her, nor to any more of Kalle's baiting, for the rest of the ride home.

Chapter Nineteen

As they entered the gates of his keep, a black stew of hatred boiled within Lucien, begging for release. Begging to be visited upon Kalle FitzMalheury's arrogant head. He dismounted, gritted his teeth and kept his hand well away from his sword hilt.

It was he himself who had failed Faris, and if he was hurt or dead, Lucien could not place the blame on anyone else. Jager and the others knew to keep an eye on Kalle, for the moment. Lucien looked at Isidora, still atop her horse, her face pale even in the red-gold glow of the torchlight. He went to her.

The loss of Faris would be a terrible blow. But by God, she needed a leash more than did Gawaine! Or his own fiendish sister! Riding astride, through the woods, in the dark— And Wace! That boy had much to answer for.

"Get down, Isidora. It's icy. I will catch you."

Rather too meekly, he thought, she kept her gaze downcast and swung her right leg over the high cantle and the horse's rump, and deftly kicked her other foot free of the stirrup as she went. Halfway to the ground he caught her about the waist and turned her around, more roughly than he had intended, and his wounded hand began to hurt again.

"What were you thinking? I expect such idiocy from Larke, but not from you. Have you any idea the sort of wicked folk who inhabit those woods?"

"I do now," she replied. "But you forget, Lucien, I traveled all the way from Acre, and have ridden through many such woods."

"Aye, with Faris at your side to protect you. A battle-hardened knight."

Her eyes widened and glittered with sudden tears. "Faris…he told me he worked for Kalle."

Lucien's grip on her waist tightened and he glanced over the horse's back. Lord Conrad had come out of the hall and was speaking to FitzMalheury. "Is that why Kalle is here? To meet with Faris?"

Isidora shook her head. "I do not think so. I think Faris loathed Kalle."

"As do many others. I had a bad feeling, Isidora. I went to look for Faris and provide him escort. But we did not find him. I am sorry."

Isidora looked up at him and her face was such a picture of pain and regret that he wanted to make it all go away. To kiss her and kiss her some more, and then—

"The animal! The wild animal!" Isidora cried, and tore herself free from Lucien's grasp. Dagger in hand, she ran across the bailey toward Kalle, who caught her easily even as he disarmed her.

Lucien followed and felt a fresh stain of anger spread through his heart at the sight of Kalle's hands upon Isidora.

"Let go of her!" he snarled.

Kalle locked gazes with Lucien and smiled, but did not release Isidora. He casually began to toss her dagger into the air, catching it by the handle each time.

Conrad stared at the spectacle. "What is this? Has this woman lost her wits, Lucien, that she should attack Sir Kalle? Confine her, by God, or I will do so!"

Lucien fought down his inclination to challenge Kalle to a fight. "Let her go, FitzMalheury." Lucien pulled Isidora away from Kalle. "She merely has had a touch of moon madness, my lord."

"Nay, I am not mad! He has mur—"

Lucien clapped his hand over her mouth. "Not now, Isidora. Come with me." He looked for his sister, who was still holding her horse's reins, staring at him and Isidora. "Larke! Get yourself up to my solar. Wace, I will speak to you later."

Larke jumped, then hurried to obey, Wace at her back.

Once upstairs, behind closed doors, the servants dismissed and a goblet of wine quaffed, Lucien wished—not for the first time—that Larke had been married off at a very young age to some unsuspecting knight of sturdy constitution. As it was, she would see him to an early grave.

She and Isidora huddled together, sitting side by side on a chest.

"What came over you, Isidora?" he asked, weary of ever being the inquisitor and disciplinarian.

She gave him a soulful look. "I merely acted upon the impulse you yourself have been stifling, Lucien, is that not so?"

He would not lie to her. "Aye."

Isidora took a shaky breath. "I believe Kalle came here to kill Faris. And I think that is what he meant when he spoke of wounding an animal in the forest. He looks at Arabs in that way. Even those who have converted to Christianity, I trow." *Except for my mother...* She twisted her hands together.

"You may be right. I hope not." Lucien did not want to admit to her that he himself had rushed into the forest on the strength of what seemed to be a sign.

Larke, who now showed no sign of contrition, peered at Isidora. "Here, you've bloodied Isidora's lip, Lucien! How could you?"

Momentarily shocked, Lucien knew not what to say. "I did not mean to."

Isidora touched her mouth. "Nay, I am not hurt. I think it is you who are hurt, Lucien. What is that soggy thing wrapped around your hand?" She got up to see, with Larke following.

Lucien backed away. "It is nothing. Just a cut."

Isidora looked at him, her brown eyes serious. "It is more than that. Else you would not try to hide it."

Lucien pointed to the door. "Larke, leave us now. Go to our mother and reassure her."

Larke, who obviously wanted to stay and hear more, reluctantly withdrew.

With the heavy, timbered door closed after her, Lucien continued. "I broke a glass vessel from the *laboratorium*— Larke does not know all that I do there. My blood spilt and formed a shape along with the quicksilver, and I had the foolish thought that it meant something I could remedy. I was wrong."

"Oh, Lucien. Every man who comes near me seems to end up either dead or in harm's way, sooner or later."

Lucien smiled a little. "Nay…that is simply the way of the world, not you. You are not *that* powerful a force to be reckoned with." *Or was she?*

"Do you believe Kalle has killed Faris?" she asked.

"There is little I believe without seeing it for myself." Now, seeing the hope in her eyes, he was ready to lie to her, after all. "Nay, I do not believe it."

She gazed at the floor, her dark hair coming over her shoulder in a thick, shining braid, and he knew she struggled not to show what she felt. Just as he did. Right now.

With his fists and teeth and gut clenched hard, the only way he could think of to keep himself from envisioning her…Isidora, of the east, naked, fragrant and willing…in his bed, an invitation in her eyes, his name upon her lips…her body, supple and warm, beneath his—

"Lucien, I must tell you something, about me and Kalle."

His fantasy shattered. "I don't want to hear it. Not now. I must go down to see what is taking place. Kalle and my uncle seem to be on friendly terms. For all I know, Conrad may be selling Larke to him at this very moment."

What could be worse than that? The thought of Isidora in Kalle's embrace? Was that what she wanted to tell him? Nay. He would not let her, even if it were true. She could save that for her confessor.

"I will go down with you," she said.

"Nay."

"Please, Lucien. I have a right to be privy to this. And I should apologize to your uncle, if not to Kalle. Do not treat me like you do your sister."

She pleaded with her eyes and something inside Lucien cracked. He had thought himself angry, frustrated and longing for solitude. But with Isidora here before him, he only wanted to touch her. "Not like my sister? What do you want, then? This?"

He drew the back of one finger along her cheek. She shut her eyes and her lips parted slightly.

"Or this?" His hand slid around to stroke her neck, then moved down and around to bring her up against him. She still said nothing, but her lips trembled.

"Enough of that," Lucien said in a voice he himself barely recognized, so hoarse was it. He looked upon the fresh, pure skin of her face, at her eyes, now open and searching his. Brown and gold and beautiful. He took her mouth, in a savage, sweet kiss, drawing from her a moan— of pleasure, he hoped.

"Do you want me, Isidora? Say you do." He did not wait for an answer—could not wait—and kissed her cheeks, her brow, her throat. Her arms wound about him and her whole body began to quiver.

"Lucien, I—you m-must stop."

"Why? Are we not to be wed?" He held her closer and spoke into her hair.

"No one has asked me. I have been told, that is all."

An icy pang struck Lucien's heart. Why had he assumed she must love him? "I see."

"I doubt that very much, Lucien. You see only what you want to see, what you shape and create to your own design. You are used to having your way, to being obeyed. And I, I am used to being obedient. But I do not want that any longer, Lucien. I want to be free."

Slowly he pulled away from her so he might see her expression better. "Free? But you are!"

"Nay, not when I must come when you call, sit when you tell me to, sleep when and where I am told, my movements restricted, my choice of clothing, of food, of husband, dictated by someone else. All my life. Either by my father, his relatives, or Kalle, or Faris, or you, or Mauger, or your uncle, or even your mother."

"But…but that is the way of things. For the good of everyone, yourself especially."

"Oh, Lucien. Do not be so thick. I will not be your shadow, forced to watch you as you pursue the Work, to aid you in its pursuit when it will only consume you and leave me more alone than I was to begin with."

"But what about…" He kissed her again, tenderly at first, then relentlessly, until she opened to him and he could taste her desire.

With a small cry she pushed him away. He stared at her, like the dumb animal he was at the moment.

She shook her head and her braid began to come loose. "Nay. This shall not be the way of it. Not until I say so."

"Oh, God." Lucien sat heavily on the edge of his bed and wanted to roll into it and go to sleep. But he still had to go downstairs. "Give me a few moments and I will leave."

"Why do you need any time? It would be best if—"

"Isidora, I do not want to be seen—in this state."

"What state?" She looked him up and down, turned pink, and stammered, "O-oh. I am sorry."

"I am not. Nor should you be, though priests will tell you otherwise. It is the one thing you can do to me that I cannot control. So, if you want power over me, you have it already."

"Doesn't every woman have that power?"

Lucien found this amusing. "Of course not. Not over me, at least. Not when I am conscious, anyway," he added truthfully, remembering Daphne in the barn.

A small furrow formed between Isidora's brows. "I do not understand."

Lucien caught her hand in his. "Whether I care or not makes a difference, Isidora. Does it not do the same for you?"

She pulled her hand back. "I—I do not know. You see, my mother, it seems, had this same effect upon Kalle."

"What?"

Isidora hurried on. "Though I do not believe she cared for him. And if he felt something for her, that does not mean it was her fault, does it? But if he has grown bitter over the years, and hurt you and Faris because of it, I could not bear that."

"Isidora, what Kalle feels or felt about your mother has naught to do with what I feel about you or you feel about me."

"But it does! It is all tied together. Lust or love—there seems to be little difference—caused my mother to be cursed, my father to be damned, and Kalle, who, believe it or not, was once much like you, to become wicked and cruel. I cannot be a part of any such disaster again."

"There is a difference between lust and love."

"Is there? Can you prove it to me? Like the knights of old, who for the sake of love, freely allowed their lives to hang upon their lady's merest pleasure? With no hope of reward, beyond her smile or a fleeting kiss?"

"That was not love, but lunacy. What could you expect from Provençals, anyway?"

"Kalle is a Frank."

"Even worse. Not only French, but an uneducated boor, no doubt."

"He was once not only a Templar, but a priest, Lucien."

"Good Lord." Lucien wiped his face with his palm and took a deep breath. "You know more about him than do I."

"When he lived with us, I was but a child. But I heard a great deal. More than I should have. More than I wanted."

Lucien put one hand to his thigh and stood. "I am going down now. I do not think it wise for you to accompany me. Let me find out what Kalle wants. I will convey your regrets, and you can make amends properly later, though in truth I don't see why you should. I will take you to my mother and sister on the way."

"You are angry with me."

"Nay, Isidora. I am angry with myself, for being such a blind, prideful fool."

Isidora gave the slightest of shrugs.

"Oh, so you agree! And, no doubt have the same opinion of every other man of your acquaintance."

"Some are worse than others," she admitted, and a tiny smile dimpled one cheek.

"Come, let me take you out of here before I do something I'll regret."

Grateful she did not argue, Lucien left Isidora with Larke and his mother in the women's solar before heading down to face his enemy.

Chapter Twenty

Earm put his shoulder to the back of the wagon and shoved—with all his might and all his rage. He had put up with a great deal, in the service of Kalle FitzMalheury, but doing the work of a beast of burden, up to his ankles in mud, in the middle of the night, was beyond the call of any such duty.

"Cooke! This is futile. We will leave the damned cart and continue with the horses."

"But, sir, Lord Kalle will have my head, should I fail to meet his request, or lose the implements we've brought so far—"

Earm caught the cook by the front of his tunic. "*I* will have it, by God, long before Kalle, if you do not help me unharness these beasts! You can carry your pots and pans on your back if you like, but do not look to me!"

"Nay, do not speak so, sir!"

"Then do as I say or I will leave you to find your own way." Scum of the earth, were kitcheners and the like, thought Earm. He felt unclean even having touched the fellow's greasy clothing. But Kalle had such a fear of being poisoned, he ever dragged his own cook about with him.

But the people he had ridden off with—the woman called Isidora had seemed familiar, as had the knight called Lucien. The others, the girl and lad, were complete strangers to him. Earm ground his fist against his head as a searing pain shot through his temples. Not for the first time, he wished Kalle had simply left him to die on the plain of Hittīn.

If, of course, that was indeed where Kalle had found him, because he himself could remember nothing. Nothing but waking up in a clean bed in Kalle's household, finding his wounds bound and Lina feeding him sweetened, watered lemon juice.

What he had never understood was Kalle's dual capacity for both kindness and cruelty. It was as though a demon sat on one shoulder and an angel sat on the other. Ach, but this was not the sodding cook's fault. "Come on, then. I will tell Kalle that I made you leave the cart behind, eh?"

"You have my thanks, sir." The cook staggered forward, a copper vessel balanced on his head.

Earm rode the rouncy and led the two carthorses. Cooke had never put a leg over a horse in his life, and if he preferred slogging through the ice-cold mud to trying it now, that was his affair.

"So, Cooke, what was Kalle hunting while I was mending harness? Did he tell you? Or did you sneak it into the pot he had you dump?"

Cooke puffed in order to keep up. "Nay, nay. I have no idea. I never saw a thing. Never heard a thing."

"What good fortune for you." Earm chewed his lip and

tried to warm his hands, one at a time, between his thighs and the saddle, as if that might make his brain work a bit faster. What had Kalle gone after, to be that smug about it? But he himself was so cold and tired, it was all he could do just to concentrate on which way to go. Whatever had happened, it was bound to be something unpleasant.

Faris al-Rashid! the voice in his head called, louder and louder. His mother's voice…at last. Faris opened his eyes and admitted that he was yet alive.

But it was still dark. Still freezing, and he was soaking wet. Kalle's powerful arm had sent an arrow that ripped through his mail shirt and pierced his side, as no arrow had done before.

He had known it would only be a matter of time before Kalle found him. That it had happened on this night, on this lane, in this dank forest and in this foreign country, were merely details of inevitability. But the fleet gray courser had saved him, outrunning Kalle's heavier horse.

He must have passed out and fallen off. He did not know how long he had lain here or where he was. Now Lucien's horse nuzzled him, with warm, hairy lips and steamy, grass-sweet breath. That was a comfort, to not be alone. Faris felt for the arrow and found it was broken off, several inches from where the fletch end had been.

He ran his hand along the horse's jaw and up until he caught a fistful of mane. The animal obliged him by raising its head and thereby helping him get to his feet. He sagged against the warmth of the big body, then, fighting the weakness that made him want to lie down again, hauled himself back into the saddle.

He knotted the reins loosely, then dropped them, giving the courser its head, and whispered, "Take me where thou wilt, oh swift one, anywhere but back to my enemy, for I have no strength left to guide you."

Indeed, Faris was reduced to the extreme of having to hold on to the pommel, as a tiny child just learning to ride might do. It bothered him, even though there was no one to see. But the horse stepped along confidently, as though it were used to such useless burdens.

It carried him through the woods, until they began to thin, and Faris saw a blur of golden light ahead. Saw light and heard men singing. A beautiful chorus of voices, in a perfect blend of pitch and cadence.

The grey took him closer. And closer. The voices grew clearer, and louder, even as Faris's eyes grew impossible to keep open. He heard the clop of iron-shod hooves on stone. The sound changed, then echoed, and the courser came to a halt. The singing stopped. He swayed.

"What is that horse doing in here?"

"Look! A Moor! God save us!"

"He is hurt. Get Brother Percy, he knows about wounds."

"Nay! Not Percy—you know what the Saracens did to him—"

"Shh! Here he comes, be quiet."

Faris opened his eyes as strong hands pulled him down. Candles. Gilt. A crucifix. His heart caught in an instant of fear. He was in a church. These were monks. Christian monks.

Then he remembered. He, too, was a Christian. Surely these men of God would recognize that. But perhaps he should help them.

"Jesus, Mary and Joseph," he choked out in a haze of pain. "Hallowed be thy name. Forgive my horse, he knows not what he has done by this trespass."

Someone chuckled. "It is all right, brother. Be not concerned, I understand. We are Cistercians, not grim, dirty Dominicans."

The soft words, in Norman-French-accented Arabic, were spoken by one of the monks as they carried Faris through the cloisters and laid him on a bed.

"Brother Percy, you need not attend him. We can make ourselves understood well enough. And—"

The soft-voiced monk replied, "I will attend him. Just bring me the usual things—hot water, clean cloths and the salves and unguents."

Faris looked at Brother Percy. A grown man, well made but slim, fair, yet smooth of cheek, and his voice…somehow familiar. His fingers, long and slender.

Faris swallowed. He had been around eunuchs all his life. At home they might be slaves, or hold posts of great honor and responsibility. But never had he expected to meet one face to face in an English church.

Chapter Twenty-One

Isidora tried to look demure, sitting with Larke in the presence of Lady Amelie and her companions. But it was difficult, still clad in muddy men's clothing, with Rosamunde and the other women here, and Larke looking guilty one moment and trying not to laugh the next.

Isidora nudged the girl in the ribs and whispered, "What am I to say? Does your lady-mother truly expect Lucien to marry me just because she said so?"

Larke squeezed Isidora's hand. "Lucien will do anything to please our mother."

"No matter how distasteful?"

"I did not mean it like that! He feels responsible for what happened."

"And what did happen? What Kalle mentioned? Was that true?"

Larke glanced at Amelie, whose attention was now on her sewing. "In truth, I don't know all the details, for no one speaks of it. But Lucien had a twin. Our sister, Estelle…she was as lovely as he is handsome. Many years ago, they were out riding together—of course they weren't children anymore, but they still shouldn't have gone alone—and were set upon by thieves.

"They took Estelle and…and used her ill, and she died at their hands. I was very small, but I still remember seeing Lucien return with her in his arms. He was covered in blood. I never knew if it was his, or hers, or the thieves'. But it was horrible. He has never been the same since, nor has our mother."

Isidora looked at Amelie and saw her pale, sad face in a new light. "But that is terrible. Does she blame Lucien?"

"I don't know. But she does nothing to let him think she does not. It makes me so angry, betimes. She still has us, after all. She lost one child, does she want to lose another, by driving him away with her grief?"

Larke's voice broke as she finished speaking and Isidora returned the squeeze of her hand. How ironic—Larke lived in Lucien's shadow, with their mother, just as Isidora had lived in his shadow with her own father. He was well-named—Lucien, person of light. Without trying, he seemed to attract the most attention, wherever he went.

Isidora had yet another question. "But, Larke, why has your mother chosen me? Why not insist upon Rosamunde? She is one of you, after all."

"So? It seems obvious, does it not, that you and he are meant for one another?"

"You are being absurd."

"Your lips look like someone's been kissing you rather a lot." Larke looked upward, as if pondering deeply. "I wonder who that could possibly have been?"

Isidora could not reply for the heat burning in her cheeks.

"Nay, if I can see it, anyone can, even my mother. Her acceptance of you is the one thing that convinces me she may have forgiven Lucien, that she wants him to be happy."

"But what about your uncle?"

Larke scoffed, "Oh, no matter! He will let mother have her way in any and every thing. It has always been so, ever since *Pere*—died…" She turned to stare at Isidora. "I only just realized…"

"What?"

Larke looked away. "Nothing. I am speaking of things that I should not. I wish Lucien would hurry up. It is so boring in here."

Amelie glanced up from her needlework, but said nothing.

"*Mere,* we would like to go and bathe and change our clothes, may we be excused?" Larke asked hopefully.

Amelie gave the tiniest of nods and Larke grabbed Isidora's arm. They made their escape, and as one, headed not for warm water and clean garb, but down to the hall where the men still sat around the fire. Talking, Isidora saw to her relief, and not fighting.

Around a corner by the stairway, they stood just out of sight, but not out of hearing. Lucien had given his chair to his uncle, while Lucien, Kalle and Mauger sat in lesser seats and Wace made do with the floor.

All of them had mazers in hand, but their weapons were by the anteroom entrance.

Lucien nodded to Kalle. "So, pleasantries aside, what brings you to these parts, FitzMalheury? Surely you are not here for your health?"

This brought a general round of laughter, even from

Kalle himself. "Nay, Lucien. Perhaps to see to the health of others, but not my own. Already one of my goals has been met and you hold the *key* to the other. I have an interest in your...*work*, you see."

Lucien's throat went dry and he caught Mauger's swift and unnecessary "I told you there'd be trouble!" look.

Conrad drained his cup and held it out for Wace to refill. "What work is this? Horse breeding or keeping our lands out of the king's hands?"

Lucien began, "It has to do with—"

Kalle interrupted. "Aligning worldly interests with those of God, Sir Conrad. As should be the goal of all work."

Then he smiled at Lucien, a smile of such subtle conspiracy that Lucien knew not what to think. Kalle was the last person on earth with whom he ever expected—or wanted—to be allied in pursuit of the Work.

Wace came to Lucien's shoulder with the wine ewer and murmured softly as he poured, "Forgive my intrusion, but did you know, Sir Lucien, that Lord FitzMalheury was friend to my lord Raymond's late brother, Alonso? That they were together on King Richard's Crusade, along with Sir Percy?"

Lucien's jaw tightened for a long moment, then he replied, without looking at Wace, "Nay, but it surprises me not at all. I thank you for telling me."

Kalle and Alonso. Perfect for one another. Each a master of his own form of cruelty. And to think that Raymond's younger brother, Percy, also on the crusade, had been at their mercy. He had returned, starving, mute and nearly broken beyond recovery, years after the others had long been home. Alonso had abandoned him to the Saracens.

But wicked as Kalle might be, Lucien did not think him capable of the kinds of evil Alonso had found it a joy to make habitual. Nay, his ill temper was more the sort caused by a pain of long duration, that makes the sufferer lash out unexpectedly, like an animal that has been pushed too far.

Then he caught a movement out of the corner of his eye. Near the stair. "Pardon me." He rose, bowed to the company and made straight for Larke's and Isidora's hiding place. Catching them each by the scruff of her neck, he marched them back up the stairs.

God, he was sick of females and their antics! Why could they not simply behave as women were supposed to behave? As Rosamunde behaved? Never a peep out of her, after that first disastrous evening. Indeed he did not think twice about her.

He released Larke into her chamber and considered where to take Isidora, still his captive. He dragged her off to his solar; there he could speak to her alone. With the door closed behind them, he stood between it and her. She faced him defiantly, eyes flashing, her dark hair in wild disarray about her face and shoulders. He wanted to cup her face between his hands and kiss that perfect mouth, steal her breath away, show her what he could not tell her…

"What in God's name am I to do with you, Isidora? You imperil not only yourself but now my sister? Think you Kalle is a foe easily turned aside from his goals? Think you that I can handle him with your constant interference and getting in the way?"

She stood with her feet spread and her fists clenched, but her words did not match her fighting stance. "Aye, I do think so. I think you can do anything, Lucien. It is one of

the most frightening things about you. Your own blessed-
ness, that you seem not to be aware of, but instead com-
plain about inadequacies that in anyone else would be
considered virtues. You are exhausting, my lord, to yourself and all who care for you. After a while, one despairs
of being forever left behind you."

"Nay, that cannot happen. I do not know of what you
speak, except that anyone who engages in the Work must
strive to meet standards that exceed the ordinary. And so I
must. You yourself said that unless I prove myself worthy,
you will not give me the key you hold for me from your
father. What is it you would have me do? Tell me, and I
will do it."

At that moment with his earnest face and eloquent hands
and strong, beautiful neck that moved when he swallowed,
a neck that met powerful shoulders and a muscular chest and
waist that went on to meet tight hips and thick thighs and—

At that moment Isidora wanted to tell him to simply take
her into his arms and allow her to lose herself in his
strength, in his scent, in the sound of his voice, in the feel
of his skin next to hers.

Instead she bit her knuckles, felt her face turn red and
wished she had fled her father's house before he had had the
chance to burden her with any such gift for Lucien. A gift
that would both bind him to her and forever take him away.

She squeezed her eyes shut against the sight of him.
Having him was too much to hope for, and that very having would be too much for her heart to bear. She did not
want him. "Lucien," she whispered, helpless to stop his
name from forming on her lips.

"I am here, Isidora. Gift of Isis…"

She gasped as she found herself wrapped in his arms. Kissed soundly. Uplifted and carried to his bed. He drew back the furs.

"Get out of these clothes, Isidora. Let me see you. Let me touch you…" His voice was low and husky. He began to kiss her mouth and throat and mouth again, all the while working her dirty garb off of her, stripping her as efficiently as any maid did her mistress or any squire his lord.

Part of Isidora wanted to say no and part of her wanted to beg him to ignore any plea she might make for him to stop. Then she realized what a falsehood her protests would be, a mere show of modesty when in truth her body cried out to meet his.

Isidora held her breath as Lucien paused to survey what he had readied for plunder. She lay before him, wearing nothing but gooseflesh. *Am I pleasing to him?*

"You are a goddess, indeed." He pulled his tunic off over his head, threw it and his boots aside, cast off his leggings and braes. There was nothing left between them but a few shreds of self-restraint and the fact that they were not yet formally wed.

Then Lucien tugged the bed furs over them both. He was hot, melting against her. Irresistible. But she had to try. He deserved that much, to save his soul.

"Lucien, wait—oh—what are you doing?"

"Kissing you. Are you frightened?"

"Nay, I know you are kissing me, Lucien, it is just that—"

He lifted his head from her breast. "What?"

She could not bring herself to tell him the truth. "This is all so fast."

"I'll go slower."

He resumed his caressing of her body. She had never been touched before. Certainly not like this, and certainly not in all these places. "Nay, I mean…I mean, oh, I forgot what I was going to say…"

He shifted, so that he was on top of her, hard between her thighs, blood pulsing visibly in his neck. His eyes shone in the firelight and long, coppery hair spilled over his shoulders.

"Isidora, do you want me to stop?"

Just as breathless as Lucien, she could barely find the words to reply. "Y-you ask me about stopping, when you have not yet asked me about starting, Lucien? What am I to say…when you and your desire eclipse all else?"

He grinned. "Say, 'Nay, please, please, Lucien, do not stop.'"

Then he bent his head and kissed her mouth again, her breasts again, until she writhed beneath him, incoherent once more. Where had such wantonness in her come from? It had not merely rubbed off from Lucien, though he was generously doing his best to share his passion with her.

"Isidora," he murmured against her neck, the length of his body pressing hers. "Saying nothing is not the same as saying you want me. But I will not ask you a third time."

Why must he insist she take responsibility for her part in this? Other men did not give women such choices…. But then, Lucien was not like other men. His muscular warmth, his arms around her, great, delicious Saxon that he was…these alone were quite enough satisfaction, weren't they?

Nay, they were not. He was quivering with the effort of

holding himself back, as was she, with waiting for him. She could ease his torment and her own…and it would bind him to her, would it not?

A certain desperation possessed her. "I want you, Lucien. Now. Take me now."

He looked into her eyes, smoothed the hair from her brow and slowly, with exquisite care, kissed her lips. Then he pushed himself back, so she was between his arms, like pillars bunched with muscle, and his weight was on his hands, indenting the feather bed on either side of her.

He drew a long breath and his chest gleamed with the motion. "Nay…there is something not right, Isidora," he said softly, sadly. "Something you are not telling me, I can feel it. If this is to be, I want nothing to come between us."

Isidora might have borne Lucien's anger, his condemnation, but she could not bear his disappointment. With a small, animal sound, she twisted over and away, so she lay with her back to him, and hid her face under one arm before the tears that threatened could escape.

He stroked her shoulder with a broad palm. "Forgive me, Isidora. I have asked too much of you."

He did not understand. Perhaps *that* was what was too much to ask of him. She turned around. Sat up to face him and wiped her eyes with her wrist. Then she slid her arms over his solid shoulders and around his neck, pressing her face to his smooth hair as it fell forward across his cheek.

Isidora inhaled his scent and savored the moment. For all she knew, he might never allow her to be this close to him again.

"Lucien, I cannot give you the scrolls, or the Key from

my father, in exchange for your love." Nor could she tell him the truth. That by breaking her promise to her father—breaking one of God's commandments—she was breaking her own heart, as well.

He spoke, his chest vibrating against hers. "Isidora, is that what you think me capable of? That I would try to sell myself to you?"

"Oh, that is not what I meant!"

He pulled away from her and straightened. Suddenly Lucien was huge, blocking out the firelight. "Then what *did* you mean?"

"I cannot say. Please, don't make me!"

At that moment the door opened and Mauger stepped into the solar. "What's taking you so long, my lord? We are all awaiting— Oh! I beg your pardon. Ahem." He turned away, then looked again before directing his attention toward the floor.

"Glad as I am to know you are pursuing your duty, should this bedding not wait, Lucien, until you have the proper witnesses? And no other business to attend first?"

Isidora scooted back under the covers in an agony of shame.

Lucien looked over his shoulder at the seneschal. "I thought this *was* the business you and Conrad wished me to attend first, Mauger. Kindly get out and tell them I'll be down as soon as I may."

Mauger bowed as he exited. "Your pardon, *demoiselle*."

Isidora brought her head back out. "You did not bar the door, Lucien? At least I suppose that proves you did not plan all this—business—in advance."

"It proves only that I am master here. I need not bar my

door, because only Mauger would forget himself so far as to enter without knocking."

"So you did plan it in advance?"

"Nay. How can one plan anything around a creature as unpredictable as a woman?" In one graceful movement he launched himself from the bed to gather his scattered clothing from the floor.

Isidora drank up the sight of his haunches, his well-muscled calves and his—

"Do *I* stare at *you?*" He tugged his tunic down and hopped on one foot to pull up a legging.

"Aye, so you have done."

"Well, then, get used to it," he growled.

"Excuse me?"

"Whether you like me, love me or hate me, it makes no difference to the fact that we will be married before Lent. That is what my elders want. It is a prospect I find tolerable, therefore it is what I will do. In addition, it is what your brother expects, I believe it is what your father would have wished, and now that I have…have dishonored you even further, it is something you yourself should hope for, as you have no other choice but to starve."

Isidora opened her mouth, then shut it again. No other choice? Did he not know she was an artist? "I can support myself, with my scribing and illuminations. I do not need you to feed me *or* to marry me!"

"But you need me, just the same." Now dressed, he returned to the bed, sat beside her and stroked her cheek with his thumb. "To protect you."

She pushed his hand away. "But who is to protect me from you?"

"Who indeed? Kalle, perhaps?"

She swallowed and wished she had the advantage of her clothes, as well. "Nay. It was not like that."

"*It?*" Lucien's voice was too soft to be safe.

Isidora raised her chin. "Aye, our bargain. The price I paid Kalle to spare your life in Acre, Lucien."

He lowered his gaze for a moment, then brought it back to rest upon her. "I feel such shame. Whatever you paid was too much, Isidora. You should have left me there to rot, if the price was so high."

"Nay, Lucien. I know what you must be thinking. Indeed, had he asked for my virginity, I would have given it sooner than what he actually wanted. Something quite different. Something worth far more to me."

"What, then?"

Isidora twisted the sheet in her fingers. "A portrait I had painted, of my mother. The only thing I had of her. It was…so painful to give it up. But I do not regret it, Lucien."

"Oh, Isidora." He lifted her hands and kissed their backs. "I will get it back for you. I swear this, upon my father's honor and the Holy Cross."

"Nay! What are you saying? You cannot. You must not try. Kalle will kill you. It is only an image. A symbol. Not her."

"But we cling to such things, do we not? Sometimes they are our only comfort when all is dark. Like the lock of my sister's hair that I keep. It reminds me of her and of what I must do. It is why I pursue the Elixir."

"Estelle?"

He nodded. "Larke told you?"

"Aye, but she herself knows little beyond what she saw.

So do not concern yourself that I know any secrets you wish to keep."

"When I have paid what I owe Estelle and our mother, then I will tell you about it. For if you are with me, you, too, will have to live with the consequences of my actions until then."

"As you will have to live with the consequences of mine."

"You mean, your withholding of what may be the Key?"

"That, and other things besides."

He rewrapped the linen bandage on his hand, which had soaked through with blotches of crimsom. "Eventually, you will give me what I want. All of it."

"You cannot force me."

"But I can persuade you. Besides, it cannot be hidden far. Don't tell me you have dropped it down the well."

"You will not find it, not without my help."

He just smiled at her. "We shall see, Isidora. Your father was not the only teacher I ever had in Outremer."

"Either let me see to your wound or go away," she said.

His lazy grin broadened. "You are dismissing me from my own bed, my own solar?"

"What does it sound like to you?"

"Very much like a wife."

"Then listen again. Go away."

Chapter Twenty-Two

When Lucien regained the all-male sanctity of the hall, the others were just draining their mazers and preparing to disperse. It was late, and it had been hours since they had met in the woods. Lucien's head and hand both ached. Among other things.

He approached Kalle. "FitzMalheury?"

The knight turned and gave him a look that might have soured milk. "What?"

"When your man and servant arrive, Mauger will see to their comfort. You and I can finish our business on the morrow. And if I find you have killed Faris al-Rashid, you had best prepare to pay his honor price."

"Very well. *A demaine.*" Kalle stalked off toward the door, a path clearing for him as he went.

Mauger sidled up to Lucien's elbow. "How went your—you know what?" he asked quietly, without a hint of lasciviousness.

Lucien crossed his arms. "It went nowhere." Indeed *it*

was most disgruntled by the whole unsatisfactory affair. "I decided she was not ready, and she told me to get out."

Mauger's broad face looked stunned. "Oh, my God, Lucien. You did not tell her that, did you? Surely you made some other excuse, to take the fault upon yourself?"

"There was no fault. What do you mean?"

"Have you nothing between your ears but quicksilver? By *you* making the decision to stop…wherever it was you stopped, and saying it was because of *her* that you stopped—can you not see how that might seem to a proud young woman?

"She would expect, and rightfully so, that her beauty would inflame you to such passion that nothing could stop you except Isidora herself. You have taken that power from her and shamed her. 'Tis a wonder she did not throw something at you instead of just asking you to leave."

Lucien rubbed his brow wearily. "You know, Mauger, Rosamunde said you had a better way with women than me, now I think I begin to understand."

Mauger frowned. "Rosamunde should mind her own business. What's that mess there? Let me see your hand."

Knowing it would make his life easier in the end, Lucien allowed Mauger to unwrap his wound and fuss over it.

"Not good, not good at all. Look at this, my lord, what your careless neglect has produced."

Lucien looked. A still-oozing wound gaped on his palm, the angry redness of its edges puffing toward his fingers and wrist. Bits of glass and silver material still glinted within it. "So?"

"So! You never washed out whatever no doubt noxious things are therein? You never had Jager or me check it. You are irresponsible, Lucien. You need to be able to fight with this hand. Soon it will be so swollen you'll not be able to hold your own mead bowl."

"Then do what must be done, Mauger."

"I will, and the more it hurts, the less I will feel sorry for you!"

The next day, by the stream where the women did their washing, Daphne draped a linen sheet over her shoulders and ran in circles, so it billowed like white wings behind her.

Bent over the shallows, her mother looked up and shouted, "What are ye doing? Are ye daft, lass? That is Lord Lucien's! Bring it back!"

Elated, Daphne laughed and merely raised the sheet in her fists, so it flew even higher as she ran. "Look at it, Mama! All will be well! There will be an heir, these lands will remain Lord Lucien's, and all of us can stay here forever!"

"Stop yer noise and bring that here before ye dirty it more than it—" As Daphne approached, the woman's eyes rounded and she covered her mouth as a slow grin grew. "I see! He's done it! He's had her! Look there!"

The goodwives gathered to examine the evidence. A red stain, in the middle of the linen. "We should not wash this. We must show it to the Lady Amelie, and Lord Conrad, if they will allow us audience. A wedding must go forward, now, as it should have years since!"

"I'll do it!" Daphne cried.

"You will not! You'll get yer bottom smacked, more like. Nay, we must give it to someone they will listen to. Someone we can trust."

"Lady Larke?"

"Nay, bless that child." Daphne's mother tapped her wrinkled, pursed lips. "I will speak to our Jager, for he eats in hall, and he can give it to them."

"I like Jager very much, I can take it to him," Daphne offered once again.

"Nay, ye sweet wee slut, he'll be as likely to tumble ye as anything. Somethin' this important to folk, we should all go. Ye did well, lassie, to show it to us."

Daphne smiled. "I told you our lord Lucien was good luck." She pressed the cloth to her bosom. "I just wanted some of it for myself, so I'll have lots of babies. Did I ever mention the time when he fell asleep in the horse barn? He was soo-oo big when I woke him!"

The women laughed and waved Daphne away. She skipped up the lane toward the castle. Maybe Jager was back from his patrolling and she could whisper the good news to him ahead of time.

At table in the hall, Isidora sat beside Lucien as the company finished supper. It was Friday, so the main fare had been cod, as it was every fast day and would be for all the long weeks of Lent. Saxon-Norman food…sometimes she would rather starve. She took a sip of ale to try to make the taste fade.

How it produced men like Lucien was beyond her understanding. Or perhaps such men were to be expected. One is what one eats, and Lucien, after all, had about as much sensitivity and insight as did a cod. He had proven that beyond a doubt. After humiliating her beyond bearing, how he expected her to hold her head up and pretend nothing had happened was also beyond her understanding.

She welcomed the distraction as Sir Jager got up, bearing some sort of bundle, and bowed deeply before Lady Amelie. The lady turned uncertainly toward Conrad. Isidora followed suit, looking at Lucien, who in turn shrugged and raised his eyebrows just as Conrad was doing.

Jager cleared his throat. "My lady, the villagers have brought something of importance to my attention. They petition you, most humbly, that you act upon their discovery, with all due haste, and bring your son to his duty…and the altar."

Amidst the growing murmurs of the assembly, Lucien jumped to his feet. "What is this about, Jager? And why have you not spoken of it to me first, if it concerns me?"

Jager turned to Lucien. "This concerns not only you, my lord, but the welfare of the entire castle and the lands around it. And a good thing, too, that it has come to light, as such things will, by the grace of God."

He shook out the bundle. At first Isidora did not recognize it. Then she saw and was certain her face was as red as the stain on the fabric. *Discovery,* indeed. Only, the villagers were wrong. Jager was wrong. How…? She thought back.

The only blood shed that night must have been from Lucien's hand, when he'd leaned over her. The memory of him, strong, beautiful, ready for her—but ultimately finding her lacking—rushed through her senses in a hot, painful wave.

She would happily wring both his and Jager's necks, if afterward she could run and hide, so mortified was she. Beside her, apparently oblivious to her distress, Lucien caught her shoulder and squeezed it for a moment.

Amelie and Conrad remained as if frozen to their seats,

their faces unreadable. Then, with barely a glance toward Isidora, they both looked at Lucien and smiled.

"Of course we shall regard this as being under the honorable assumption that Lucien has merely made formal his intent to marry," Conrad said. "The wedding can take place at once, with just the family present. Then may the celebrations be arranged, once our friends have been invited. The question remains, of course, as to precisely whom he has chosen, though Lady Amelie looks favorably upon Isidora, here."

Lucien stood as if struck dumb, breathing rapidly, through his mouth. Just like a cod, Isidora thought. One out of water. Well, she would not help him in his plight.

She, too, stood and inclined her head to those gathered. Amelie and her ladies, Conrad and his men, Mauger, the Welsh cousins of Lady Ceridwen, Rosamunde, Larke, Wace and any number of others of varied rank. Though God may have revealed the sheet, she had Him to thank that Kalle refused to take his meals with them, preferring his private cook and pavilion to Lucien's hospitality.

"I beg your pardon, my lords and ladies," she said. "But I must assure you that the blood you see on that cloth is not of *my* body."

The sudden intake of multiple breaths was the shocked reaction that should have taken place when they first saw the stain, Isidora thought. But these folk were completely obsessed with the furthering of their line, no matter how it came about or, apparently, with whom.

"Then what virgin has Lucien been swiving, if not you?" Conrad roared.

"I have not been—swiving—any virgin, my lord!" Lucien protested.

Conrad's face began to darken toward an unhealthy purple.

"Oyez!" called a clear voice. All heads turned as Rosamunde got to her feet, pale and solemn. "My lord, I claim that blood as mine," she said, and fixed her gaze not upon Lucien, but Mauger.

Another cod! Isidora noted, as everyone watched Mauger begin his own gasping imitation of a fish. A clever move upon the quiet Rosamunde's part. She could make that claim, without telling a lie, for she had not said the blood came from her person, only that she claimed possession of it.

Which indeed, having once been betrothed to Lucien, she had every right to do, had she known it was his.

Then Isidora's eyes filled with tears as the innocent Mauger looked helplessly at Rosamunde, went down on one knee—and proved himself a true knight and faithful lover.

"I crave your forgiveness, my lady."

"As well you should!" exclaimed Conrad. "I see we have much to do, and perhaps little time in which to do it. Given the apparent fecund air of these premises, I insist upon vows being taken forthwith, before Lady Rosamunde's father descends upon us with his men-at-arms. And that goes for you, as well, Lucien. Enough has been said. It is time to act."

Mauger was still kissing the hand that Rosamunde had triumphantly offered him. Larke stood by, looking almost as furious as did Lucien, who joined her in glaring at Rosamunde.

"How dare you twist this situation to your own advantage?" he demanded, but softly.

Rosamunde tossed back her flaxen mane. "Would you have preferred that I made you keep our original bargain?"

She smiled at his stricken look. "I thought not. This way, I get what I want and Mauger gets what he wants."

Aye, the poor man! Isidora narrowed her eyes at the maiden, but was glad for Lucien's sake. She would not wish Rosamunde upon anyone.

Mauger lumbered back to his feet, and leaving Rosamunde to her wait-women, grabbed his mazer and headed for the nearest pitcher-bearing maid.

Isidora saw that Lucien was cradling his arm as his mother came up to him. Amelie drew his face down and kissed his cheeks, right and left. "You will make me happy, Lucien, I know it," she said, barely audible, then she left the hall in the company of her ladies.

Isidora's heart ached as Lucien followed his mother with a pained gaze. It struck her how alike Amelie and Rosamunde were…both of them as manipulative as they were beautiful. Perhaps it was more than coincidence that Lucien had chosen Rosamunde out of all who sought his favor.

A welcome distraction, Gawaine whined at his master's side. Lucien patted the dog's head, then turned to Isidora. "Help me," he said, his voice thick.

"All right, Lucien. I can see your uncle will not leave until this thing is done. Your desire is to please him and your mother, who will never be happy until she sees you wed."

Lucien blinked slowly. "Nay, Isidora. I mean help me with this hand."

She looked at him in alarm. He was sweating, which she had attributed to the spicy food and the emotion of the moment, but now she saw that he was in pain. "We'll see to it in your solar. Larke, come with us."

After having a basin of hot water brought up and shutting the door, Isidora unwrapped the caked bandage. The wound was ugly, festering, and Lucien's hand was alarmingly swollen, with a red streak climbing his forearm.

"This is more than cleansing herbs can remedy, Lucien. How did Mauger deal with it?"

Lucien closed his eyes. "He dug out the bits of glass and quicksilver that were in it."

"What did he use?"

"His eating dagger."

Isidora closed her eyes, too, and prayed that she did not beat Mauger over the head when next she saw him. These English knew nothing of the kind of physicking with which the Arabs had great skill. She examined the wound again. "He did not wash the knife first, I take it?"

"He wiped it on his tunic. It looked clean enough."

Isidora looked Lucien in the eye. "My lord, I must bring FitzMalheury in to see this."

"Nay. Why? I'll not have him touch me."

"And you yourself will be touching things only half as much, if this hand has to be cut off!"

"Nay. I'd rather die."

"Do not be absurd, Lucien. It has not come to that—yet. But if you insist upon being stupid, it may. I do not even know if I can coax Kalle to come up and help. But you will be fortunate if he does, Lucien. Believe me, I know he is cruel and dangerous, but he also has great knowledge.

"If the hand must be taken, that is better than dying. Whatever you think you may prefer at this moment, I assure you, even should you lose it, you will feel quite different about the loss in a few months' time."

Lucien covered his face with his good hand for a moment, then shoved his fingers back through his hair. "All right. Bring him if you can. If you cannot, then fetch Jager. He has some experience with limb-lopping. It will serve him right, for bringing in that sheet."

White-faced, Larke watched and listened, without saying a word. Then she turned on her heel and marched toward the door.

Lucien called after her, "Larke?"

Isidora was struck by the grim determination in the girl's face.

"Brother, I will return. Make no decisions about your hand until I do." She whirled out of the solar.

"Oh, God, what is she up to now? Isidora, have someone go after her, will you?"

When Isidora made no move, he started to get up himself, but she shoved him back to his bed. "Lucien, she is ten and seven. Nearly a grown woman. You must let her find her own way. She has a great deal of sense. More than you, at times. Do not worry so much."

Isidora did call for Mauger, but it was to have the seneschal come up and prevent Lucien from leaving the solar. She ordered a warm rosemary poultice and some hypericum ointment. Then she descended the stairs herself, put on her mantle and, with a heavy heart, went in search of Kalle FitzMalheury.

"Faris al-Rashid…"

Faris opened his eyes. The monk they called Percy stepped closer, then sat on the edge of the infirmary bed. The room's fire snapped comfortingly, the linens covering Faris were pristine, and the singing of the monks put him at peace. He felt weaker than he had ever been in his life.

Percy held a cup to Faris's mouth. "Of the host of Salah al-Din, I remember your name as being one of renown, despite your youth at the time."

Faris swallowed the bitter liquid, grateful that the worst was over. Thanks to the deft hands of this monk, the arrow was gone from his body and he yet lived. "No doubt such praises were an exaggeration."

"Do you not now have a Christian name, to which you were baptized?"

"That detail must have been overlooked, *effendi*. But what were you doing in the east? You do not seem the kind of man who would join a Crusade."

Percy smiled ruefully. "If you knew the sort of family I am from, you'd understand. They lust for blood, one and all, whether knights or clergy. I went with Richard Coeur de Leon, and regretted it in the end." He grew quiet for an instant, then continued. "But more to the point, how is it you are here? In England, I mean, for I know horse sense brought you to this particular place. And he is being well taken care of, by the way."

"That I am glad to hear. I came on an errand, to escort a kinswoman to see Lucien de Griswold."

"Indeed! He is a good friend of my brother Raymond. Not a brother here, mind you, but my actual brother. In fact, I am expecting him any day now."

"He lusts for blood, you say?"

Percy smiled again. "Oh, he does, at that. But he is much more selective nowadays about whose blood he sheds than he once was. And, he never went on Crusade with us. He'll have nothing against you, mark me."

"I believe his squire Wace is already at Lucien's hall."

Percy raised his brows. "Is he? They've started early this year, then."

Faris waited politely for Percy to explain his statement, but the monk did not. "You've been very kind, my lord. I thank you."

Percy rose and inclined his head. "God grant that you be well soon. Rest now. *Adieu.*"

Faris relaxed against the pillow as the monk departed. Having found such a place of dignity and kindness as this, he felt reassured to be leaving Isidora in England. Perhaps it was not completely barbaric, after all.

Chapter Twenty-Three

Isidora hesitated at the castle gate. Beyond Lucien's walls, Kalle flew blue-and-yellow striped banners from his lances. His grand horses casually nibbled at the bedraggled dead grass of the practice grounds. It looked as though he was settling in, playing at a siege encampment, she thought.

But a tiny one. Apart from the dark man and the cook she'd met in the wood, he had no more than a half dozen warriors with him as his personal cohort. He was the only one with a pavilion, however. The others had to make due with what shelter they could find.

She picked up her skirts, walked across the field and approached Kalle's guard outside his tent. "I would speak to your master."

The guard, who smelled as though he had spent a hard night drinking, narrowed his reddened eyes. "Who are you?"

Before she could reply, Kalle's deep voice rumbled from within the pavilion. "Let her in."

The guard lifted the heavy cloth door and Isidora

stepped through into the sumptuous private world of Kalle FitzMalheury. Instead of rush matting, thick carpets intricately woven in reds, blues and gold were layered on the floor. A brazier glowed and he had candles lit all around.

He had even brought a bed and mattress, complete with a stuffed coverlet and tasseled pillows. Isidora knew, however, that Kalle was as tough a man as she had ever met. This opulence did not reflect his inner being. It was merely for show and, perhaps, to put potential enemies off guard.

She had witnessed how her father had beaten him without mercy. At first, Kalle could have easily stopped the older man or even killed him. But he had allowed the awful battering to go on, and on. She had always wondered why, and thanked God that Deogal had stopped short of murder.

Kalle's forbearance on that long-ago night was the only reason she was willing to have any dealings with him at all.

She squared her shoulders. "My lord. Apart from our meeting in the forest, it has been quite some time."

Kalle did not smile as he gazed at her; his eyes shone cold and steady. He held out the goblet he just been drinking from and only spoke after she had declined it. "*Oui,* so it has. What do you want, Isidora Binte Deogal?"

Despite the warmth in the tent, Isidora hugged her mantle closer. She might as well take full measure of the man while she had the chance. "Why did you not fight back when my father came after you?"

Kalle set his drink down upon a small, carved wooden table. "I did not want to kill him in front of his wife and child."

"You could have run away, but you did not."

He sat on the edge of his bed and crossed his arms. "Your father was once a Templar, you know that, of course."

"Aye."

"Such a distinction does not fall away with either age or changing fortunes. I was the stronger, but I had to remain, and yield, for as long as it took Deogal to feel honor was satisfied."

"But my mother...she never...she was innocent!"

"*Oui*. But I was not." Kalle paused, his eyes glittering. "I decided that if he wore himself out on me, there would be less anger to vent upon her. But...he still managed to kill her in the end. And for that, I hope he is burning in hell right now and for all of eternity."

Isidora covered her face with her hands. "Do not say such things!"

"It is the truth, Isidora. Is that not what you came to me for, the truth?"

She looked at him at last. "Aye. Did you kill Faris?"

Kalle did not flinch from her gaze. "I have little doubt that I gave him a mortal wound. He vanished into the mist."

Isidora bit her lip to keep herself from weeping. "Why?"

"He disobeyed me, he betrayed me. I cannot tolerate that, from anyone. But why do you care? Did he seduce you? Capture your heart?"

"He is a good man, Sir Kalle. One with purpose and morals and honor. Do you not know that Ayshka was his mother, too?"

Kalle went pale. "Nay...I did not. You mean, he is your brother?"

"Half brother."

Kalle examined his tented fingers for a moment and his face regained its mask of hardness. "Now you think I owe you compensation?"

"Nay. But you owe me a favor, at least. Look at a wound Lucien has—"

"*Non.* Lucien can die and rot in hell along with Deogal, for all I care."

Isidora balled her hands into fists. "You have taken from me everyone I ever loved! Now you take him, too?"

Kalle smiled, a chilling prospect. "You love him, do you?"

"Nay—"

"Do not deny it. You've already saved him once. Now you want to do so again? Is he truly worth it?"

Isidora stopped the protest that came to her lips. "Worth what?"

Kalle stood, towering over her in the small space. "I do not believe you came here empty-handed, Isidora. Tell me what you have to offer."

Kalle had such skill to make people talk, he must have been privy to many secrets when he was a priest. Despite that, a great knot of refusal threatened to bind her tongue. But she must do what had to be done. "I have some items, from my father's workshop."

Kalle's demeanor subtly changed. He could not hide it from her.

His jaw knotted. His pale eyes darkened and gleamed at the same time. She knew that look—of men who lusted after impossible things. Of alchemists.

"Where are they?"

Isidora drew back from Kalle. "Hidden."

"Does Lucien know of them?"

"Aye. But he has not seen them."

Kalle paused, then took a step toward her, his head slightly tilted. "Does he not see *you?*"

"I know not what you mean…"

"You have the look of your mother." Kalle frowned and brought himself up short. "Bring me these…items, and I will decide if it is worth my time to help your Lucien."

Isidora raised her chin. "Nay. The exchange will be as simultaneous as is practical. But Lucien must be improving, first. You will accept my word of honor upon the matter and you will give me yours."

Kalle's white grin spread slowly. "Spoken like the Templar's daughter you are. Very well."

He retrieved his sword from where it lay on his bed, put its tip into the exquisite rug on the floor, and knelt with his big hands on the hilt. "I, Kalle FitzMalheury, Knight of the Cross, do swear by life and limb, by heart and hand, and by my soul's salvation, to attend Lucien de Griswold in his time of need." He genuflected, kissed the rounded pommel of the sword and got back to his feet. "Satisfied?"

"I had better be, my lord Kalle, or your soul will be in peril. We shall expect you." Hoping he could not see her trembling, Isidora turned and departed, brushing past the dark man who was waiting outside.

Earm, still tired from his muddy ordeal, watched her go, graceful and proud. Kalle's voice startled him. "Keep an eye on her, Earm. She needs looking after. Indeed, before this is through, she may even be coming home to Acre with us."

Home? Earm sighed. He had none, not that he could remember, at least. But, in Acre was also the rare and beautiful Lina. If he won her heart, he would need call nowhere else home.

Chapter Twenty-Four

Larke cantered through the forest, with Wace hard on her heels. She could not lose him, even if her horse had been the faster—which it was not—because of the poor footing, low branches and failing light. But she could stay just ahead, because her mount was nimble and she herself was a skilled horsewoman.

"Larke! Befuddle and confound you! Stop!"

Over the wind rushing past her ears, Wace sounded quite angry, Larke thought. In that case it would be a mistake to stop. Best to push on. There was a clearing ahead, she could see the pale, early evening sky above the trees.

Then, quite unexpectedly, he thundered past her on his big, elegant courser, spun it on its haunches and forced her palfrey to a splay-legged stop that nearly put her over its head.

Wace grabbed Larke by the back of her jerkin and saved her from falling. But he did not let go and when her mount shied away from his, Larke dangled for an instant before Wace heaved her facedown before him on his horse.

"Leave go!" she gasped, her head filling with blood, and her behind awkwardly sticking up.

"This presents a most tempting opportunity to teach you a lesson, Lady Larke," Wace said. "But it is not my place. Not yet."

"*What* did you just say?" she demanded, outraged.

"You heard me."

"Put me down and prepare to defend yourself!"

"As you wish." Wace leaned down, easing her to her feet with one arm, and she was amazed at how strong he was. She smoothed her clothes back into order and put her hands on her hips. "Well? Are you going to get down?"

"You said to defend myself. I think I am safer up here than down there. I know you certainly are safer with me up here, too."

"From you, you mean?"

Wace shrugged, grinned, and said nothing.

"Look what you've done. My horse has run off!"

"Oh, dear. I guess you'll have to walk home then, will you not?"

"Wace du Hautepont, when next I see Lady Ceridwen, I shall tell her of your behavior this day."

This threat made him take pause, as she knew it would, more than anything she might tell Sir Raymond.

He shook his head. "Larke, what you are doing out here again? If you must go on these nocturnal expeditions, you simply cannot go alone. How many times must I tell you?"

"Nay, Wace, first, you tell me what you are up to here at my brother's keep. No good, I warrant, and not just to torment me. Why is your lord not with you?"

Wace studied her. "Why should I tell you?"

Larke met his gaze and saw that affection glimmered behind his arrogance. "Because, I will ride on your horse's rump and embrace you from behind if you do."

Wace smirked, as if her offer meant nothing to him. "Well, knowing you, you'll find out sooner or later anyway, since you cannot seem to keep your nose out of anyone's business. My lord Raymond and I are running horses to the Cymraeg."

It took a moment for Larke to fully realize what Wace had just said. Her jaw dropped. "You are smuggling horses into Wales? Why?"

"Get up here behind me first. We'd best be moving on to wherever you were headed before your horse gets home and everyone comes looking for you." He extended his arm for her to jump up and ride behind him. She settled on his mount's warm haunches and slid her arms around his solid middle.

Wace was wearing a felted haqueton, the under-padding for mail, though he had none on, with a leather outer layer strengthened by metal studs. His double-wrapped belt bore his sword and dagger. A tiny shiver ran through her. Despite the bulk of his attire, Larke could tell that the squire was fit, indeed.

He exuded an air of confidence that only came from actual experience in battle and she knew Sir Raymond trusted Wace with his life. Under the circumstances, she could do no less. "I am sorry, Wace, for causing you worry."

"I am beginning to think that is your sole purpose in life."

"I am only trying to get to the Cistercian abbey, to see if Sir Percy—I mean, Brother Percy—can help with Lucien's wound."

"Ah. I should have thought of that myself. Very well."

"You were saying? About the horses?"

"Aye. The crown is rather strict about horse-breeding, as you must know. A lot depends upon the quality of a knight's mount. The lords of the Cymraeg appreciate fine horseflesh, and they are willing to pay handsomely for it. So, Raymond and Lucien—"

Larke was shocked. "*My* brother?"

"Aye, of course. We can't do it without havens along the way. Lucien, and others, loan their stallions out to stud with certain sympathetic owners of broodmares. When the likely colts and fillies are yearlings, we take them in small groups across the border. Just to keep the bloodlines fresh."

"But is that not treason?"

"Not when one has been betrayed on the scale that Raymond and Percy have been."

"Percy is involved, too?"

"The Cistercians cannot support themselves only by singing, can they?"

"I want to help!" Larke exclaimed.

"Absolutely not!" Wace reached back and thumped his gloved hand onto her thigh, as if in emphasis. Then he hurriedly withdrew it, as if he had only just realized where it had landed. "We'd better hurry, if we are to get back before midnight. Your brother may have me drawn and quartered as it is."

"I think not. I think he would be relieved to know anyone at all besides him was willing to put up with me."

Wace laughed, his voice rich and low. "Oh, so you think I do this willingly?"

"Of course. Indeed, I think you harbor a certain fondness for me, Wace."

"What makes you think that?"

"Because…" She found an edge and slid her hand inside the warmth of his haqueton and around to his chest.

"What are you doing!"

"Your heart beats faster when I touch you, Wace. That is how I know you like me."

"What rot. I am ticklish, that's all."

"I don't believe so. But there is one way to find out."

"What way?"

Larke smiled. "It will have to wait. You might topple from your horse, otherwise."

"You'd do well to see that you yourself stay on. And if you cannot behave, I will put you on a lead and make you run beside me."

Larke's smile just widened. The more vexed he got, the better she felt. "I shall just hold on to you a bit tighter, then, so I do not fall off." She hugged Wace from behind and there was not a thing he could do about it.

At last Mauger had dozed off, and Lucien made his escape from bed. He fumbled with the lock on the door to the *laboratorium*. It was ice-rimed. His wounded hand felt like a hot brick and was about as useful.

There was a soft crunch of footsteps. "Lucien?"

He jumped. "What are you doing out here?" He turned to see Isidora walking toward him. The moon was just rising and it shed a silver light upon her. She had pulled her mantle up over her head and it framed her lovely face in soft, crimson folds.

"I might ask the same of you. Give me that key." She held out her hand.

Still no gloves! He hesitated.

"I won't keep it, Lucien. Let me help you."

He held out the great iron key.

She took it and wrestled with the lock until it gave way. Then she handed it back to him. "What do you plan to do?"

Lucien pushed the heavy door inward. "I come here to think. It is more of a church to me than the chapel. I am so far behind in the Work…there is a phase of the moon coming up, that is necessary for— I've done nothing, for weeks and weeks. It is a great lack in my heart. And I am starting to feel it is an endeavor beyond hope." He picked up the oil lamp he had set down before the door, set fire to a twig, and started lighting the candles in the chamber.

"Let me do that."

Lucien allowed Isidora to take over the task. He picked up a handful of kindling from a basket in the corner, laid it in the stone-lined aperture of the athanor with some wood, and dribbled oil over it. The flames burst into life with a satisfying whoosh, glowing from the niche in the wall.

His skin was wet with sweat and he felt cold and hot by turns. He dragged his chair over to the fire and collapsed into it. "You should go back to the hall, Isidora."

She moved to stand before him. "Kalle will come. He promised. If you do not want to receive him in here, you, too, should return."

"I need to think. Alone." As if he could think about anything with the throbbing he was enduring.

"About what you'll do with only one hand?"

"Nay. About my purpose, in this world."

"Ah."

"You sound angry, Isidora."

She sighed. "So I am. Why are you so stubborn?"

He looked up at her. "Oh, and I suppose you are not?"

"There is a difference between stubbornness and stupidity. Unfortunately, some people display both qualities at once. You should be in bed. You should be conserving your strength, to better serve your people in future."

"I do not trust Kalle. He may cure my hand, and yet introduce some agent that will lie within me, slowly working poison, until I am rendered useless."

"Nay, I do not believe he would. He would not betray the daughter of Ayshka."

"He already *has* betrayed her! The moment he compromised your mother, he betrayed you both, as well as Deogal, and Faris. And we have yet to see how he has truly rewarded Faris."

Isidora's eyes shone bright with tears. "We have no choice! Kalle has the skill, the herbcraft. Things that do not even grow on this side of the world, he has! Knowledge of medicine that was thought lost when the ancient library of Alexandria burned, he has!"

Lucien had to smile. "Isidora, it is not some rare disease that ails me. It is but a simple wound gone bad. It happens all the time."

"And folk die of such wounds, all the time!"

"Oh, so now we've gone from me losing my hand to losing my life."

"I could not bear it," Isidora whispered, sinking to her knees.

Lucien wiped his damp face with his sleeve. "And I cannot bear seeing you this way."

"Then accept Kalle's help. You said to bring him. Do not put the effort I made to waste."

A chill struck Lucien's heart. "I should not have asked you to do such a thing, for any reason. What has he demanded of you this time?"

"N-nothing. He is doing it as a knightly gesture."

"Oh, do not insult me with such a story! Kalle FitzMalheury does nothing merely for the sake of chivalry. He left such ideals behind him long ago. But, Isidora, if you will not tell me the truth, I will not press you into a lie."

She said nothing, but stared at the fire.

"Isidora?"

At last she turned to look at him.

"I will let him look at it. I promised you as much. But if I feel any falseness from him, I shall withdraw my consent."

She smiled, then, a tender, vulnerable smile, and Lucien held out his good hand to her, to help her rise. Then he heaved himself to his feet and looked down at her. He pushed a strand of her hair back beneath the mantle's edge. "Why do you bother about me, when I have only neglected you?"

"You follow alchemy, a path of slim hope. You should know why."

"I cannot offer you spiritual bliss, physical perfection or endless wealth, though."

"I want none of those things."

Lucien did not want to ask the next obvious question. He did not want to know her desire, which, even if she told him, he doubted his ability to fulfill. He had begun to feel queasy, light-headed, indeed, quite ready to tip over, like a tree being felled.

"I think, Isidora, that perhaps you are right. I should be in bed." He did not want to fall on top of her, as he had in Acre, when she had helped him out of the pit. Or the way he had been just the other night. Poised to enter…oh, God, if any more blood drained from his head, he would have to be carried from this place.

"Come, Lucien. Let me help you outside. Then give me the key and I'll put out the candles and lock the door after us."

Isidora put her shoulder beneath Lucien's arm and steadied him until she had him propped against the exterior wall. She ran back into the *laboratorium* and took a swift look around as she extinguished the candles. As she moved toward the athanor, she spotted what she was looking for.

A space, beneath one of the stone-topped worktables. The slab rested on a ledge built into the wall. There was a gap, between the slab and the wall, about a hand span wide. She took the small bundle from where she had tucked it under her belt and stuffed it in the crevice.

It was not obvious, but still in plain sight from the correct angle. An earthenware urn rested on the floor. She tugged on it and rocked it sideways, so that it blocked the view of the hiding place.

Then, with all the fires dead but the athanor's, she ran back out, heaved the door shut and clicked the iron lock into place like a manacle. Lucien was standing with his eyes closed, looking like a ghost.

Isidora wondered if she had the strength to get him back to the hall. "Done. Shall I fetch Mauger?"

"Nay. Just walk beside me. Act as though nothing is wrong, all right? If anyone shows concern, scoff at them."

It was one of the longest walks of her life. To be beside Lucien, knowing he was slipping farther from her with each passing moment. The stairs would be the worst of it. If he lost consciousness there, there was nothing she could do to stop him from breaking his head on the stone steps.

As they entered the hall, Mauger came to meet them, looking like a storm cloud. "Where—"

"Say nothing, sir," Isidora whispered. "Just get him to the solar. Laugh, as if you are jesting with him. Then we will wait for Kalle."

Mauger nodded and for once did not argue.

Chapter Twenty-Five

"How does it feel, Lucien?" Isidora asked. Sitting next to Lucien in his bed, pinning the covers with her weight was the only way she could keep him from getting up, short of sitting *on* him.

Lucien glanced at his hand, elevated on a pillow. "As if it were in labor, about to give birth to something twice its size. It could not feel any worse, I think, unless you poured boiling oil over it."

Mauger poked his head around the bed curtain. "Fitz-Malheury is here."

Lucien grunted in response, his expression surly.

"Bon soir, mes amis." Kalle's bulk filled the doorway. He had brought the dark-haired man and his cook, as well. "You have not been introduced to Earm, your fellow countryman, Lucien. I picked him up off of a battlefield in the Holy Land. He remembers nothing of who he is. So I brought him with me to England, in case he sees something that looks familiar."

Kalle slid a sideways look at Earm, who nodded, but

seemed worried. "He is going to hold you down, Lucien, while I work. Isidora, you should leave. Lucien will not want you being privy to his screams."

She bit her lip. "Nay. I will stay."

Lucien raised himself on one elbow. "Earm, if Sir Kalle is your lord, I would not have you disobey him, but be warned—do not handle me. If you, Kalle, require me to be still, then I will be still."

"Whatever you say, Lucien," Kalle replied in a bored tone as he unrolled a velvet cloth that held instruments of various sorts. Knives, scissors, pincers—

The cook had set a pot of something to heat on the brazier coals. Kalle pulled a stool up to the bedside and motioned to Earm. "Bring more light. Lucien, I am going to touch you now. If you fight me in any way, I will have you tied down, do you understand?"

Lucien looked as furious as Isidora had ever seen him. His eyes were mere slits, his jaw clenched. "Be certain you want to cure this hand, Kalle, because if you accept my challenge, I will use it against you in single combat."

"Of course. As you wish, Lucien. May I proceed now?"

"Shite," said Lucien.

"I take that as permission." Kalle pressed Lucien's neck, counting his pulse. He put the back of his hand against his forehead. He examined the fingertips of the affected hand. "Can you bend your fingers and thumb?"

Lucien bent them, but the swelling did not allow much movement.

"Good. The tendons are intact, then. But your blood needs cleansing, to balance the humors. Cooke has a potion for you to drink. You must take it as often as you can stand, at least four times a day, for a sennight. It is a pity the moon is waxing, but that cannot be helped."

Kalle shifted his seat so that his back was to Isidora. Lucien's hand lay on a towel on a board over Kalle's knees. "Now, hold still."

Isidora did not know what would be worse: to look at what Kalle was doing or to have to watch Lucien suffer. But when she turned to him, he gave her a reassuring grin. "It will be all right, Isidora."

Then whatever Kalle did next made Lucien go quiet. He stared up at the beams of the ceiling for a long time, without blinking. He breathed slowly, in regular, deep breaths.

Kalle cursed in Arabic and flung something down that clanked onto the floor. Cooke hovered, offering various bowls and pots. "Earm, more light!" Kalle demanded. "Isidora, pull my damned hair back out of my eyes, will you?"

She did not want to touch Kalle, for any reason. But from behind him, she smoothed his blond hair away from his face and braided it for a few turns, to keep it collected. His cheek was rough with the stubble of two or three day's worth of beard.

It was strange. Doing him that small, intimate service, for Lucien's ultimate benefit, made Kalle seem more human.

Kalle was intent upon Lucien's hand, as if he truly cared. But then she remembered. She had agreed to betray her father's trust to save Lucien. And to that same end, deny Lucien his heart's desire.

She slipped from her seat and came around to see Lucien's hand. To see what her betrayal had bought. To her surprise, though there was a lot of blood, the edges of blackened flesh were gone. A small, jagged piece of green glass rested on the linen next to the instruments.

Kalle was drawing the wound closed with a needle and silk thread, around a slender, rolled up piece of fine linen that stuck out from Lucien's palm.

"What is that, Sir Kalle?"

"A wick. A drain. To keep an abscess from forming again. You can pull it after two days. You can cut the stitches after a fortnight. Make him keep this clean and dry. If he does not follow my instructions, do not bother asking me to return. He can chop his hand off himself."

Kalle wrapped Lucien's hand in fresh linen and positioned it back on the pillow, above the level of Lucien's heart. "See that he drinks the potion."

"You need not speak as if I were not here, Kalle," Lucien said.

"You took that rather well, though it was minor."

"Deogal taught me how to endure things. It is how I survived your treatment in Acre, Kalle. You may live to regret that you did not slay me when you had the chance. But, I do thank you for using your skill on my behalf this night."

Kalle shrugged. "I try my best, whatever it is I do. But I would not have taken the trouble, if I did not consider you an opponent worth saving, Lucien. Even if only so I may slay you later."

Lucien offered Kalle his right hand. "Until we meet again."

Kalle clasped hands with him. Then turning to Isidora, he gave her a look, as if to remind her of her promise, then he bowed. She nodded to him and he departed, taking Earm and Cooke with him.

She shut the door with relief. Even Mauger was not in the chamber. But for Gawaine, resting by the fire, she was alone with Lucien. And her guilt.

"Come lie beside me," Lucien suggested.

"That is not proper, you said so yourself."

"Well, I am delirious just now, so you have an excuse."

"What if I do not want to lie beside you?"

"Then lie on top of me. Would that be more to your liking?"

"You certainly *are* delirious."

"You won't know until you try."

"Go to sleep, Lucien. Have you finished the medicine?"

He grimaced. "Bah. It tastes like stale pig piss."

"And of course you are intimately familiar with that."

"Don't ask."

She took the cup away from him and sipped a bit of the liquid. It was black, pungent, bitter. Isidora wiped her mouth and shuddered. "It tastes worse, I'd say. Now, finish it. If you do not, I will ask Mauger to make you."

"I am not a child, Isidora." Lucien took another swallow. "I don't know why I am trusting Kalle not to poison me. *He* certainly does not trust anyone else."

Isidora perched on the edge of the bed. "He respects you. As a fellow alchemist."

Lucien gave her a long, sideward look, then closed his eyes. It struck her that she had not seen him eat in days. His flushed skin was still beaded with sweat. He seemed utterly exhausted.

She got a cloth, dipped it in a bowl of the fresh water that had been provided for Kalle's ministrations, and wiped Lucien's hot face, his neck and upper chest. He had blue shadows around his eyes and hollows in his cheeks. She thought perhaps he was dozing at last, but he spoke.

"It is a pity all this bother should be over such a small wound, especially one not even honorably taken, in battle. I might as well have been washing crockery or something equally demeaning. Indeed I was, wasn't I…but I never managed to break any of your father's alembics."

"That is because he would have thrashed you for it."

"Nay. Knights do not lay hands upon fellow knights. Blades, aye…but only peasants use their fists on one another."

With an inner tremor, Isidora pondered this. Her enraged father had bloodied his fists on Kalle, but the younger knight had not fought back. Now, with Kalle's explanation, it made a kind of dreadful sense.

Deogal should have challenged Kalle to an honorable single combat instead of simply knocking him down. Kalle had tried to lessen the shame of it—perhaps for both of them—by not retaliating in kind. And, he had said he wanted to draw Deogal's wrath upon himself. To spare her mother.

But she had not been spared, after all.

Men. When would she ever come to understand their simple minds? As if to prove her point, Lucien sat up and caught her about the waist. Apparently he was not as exhausted as she had thought.

He smiled. "You look good enough to eat."

"I can bring you food."

"Bring me water. And bolt the door, please."

"All right, but I think we are safe from Kalle for the moment, if not Mauger." She poured water into a goblet and he drank deeply.

"Now you have some." He held out the goblet.

"Why me?"

"Because, Isidora, I am going to kiss you, and you have the same pig piss still in your mouth that I just washed out of mine."

"I will gladly drink the water, but you are not going to kiss me." She took a few swallows.

"Better?"

"Aye. Now I should—" She stopped as Lucien's right hand found its way into the side lacing of her gown. So that is why they call it a "devil's hole," she thought.

"Just for a while, Isidora, I want you next to me. Then I'll drink the rest of that potion and you can be about your business."

Isidora looked at Lucien and a profound tenderness welled up in her heart. "But what business have I to tend, other than you?"

"Only you know the answer to that, sweeting." Then with his arm around her waist, he pulled her close and kissed her mouth, her neck, her cheeks and ears and brow, then back to her mouth again. By the time he returned there, she was ready to accept him.

It was as though some inner floodgate had been released. As though she had been primed for years, and it took only this one last kiss to trigger all of her pent-up desire. She ached to have him inside her. "Oh, God. Lucien, what have you done?"

He smiled. "What I have wanted to do for some time now. Don't fight it, Isidora, please, let it happen, let us have this time together, just for us—not for my family or any other purpose..." He tried to bring his other arm around her.

"Nay, Lucien, keep your hand there. I will come to you, you do not have to come to me. Oh, God, this is such sin!" she moaned even as she tugged her laces free and pulled her gown and chemise over her head.

"Aye, is it not? Delicious, golden, beautiful skin." He cupped her breast and took a mouthful of it.

"That—oh!—is not what I said. *Sin* is what—I—ohhh…mayhap it is not sin after all?"

"Of course not…I would never allow you to sin. I am your husband, for all intents and purposes."

"This is for us, remember? Not for church or parents or the village—" Isidora climbed beneath the sheet and found him there, warm and willing, and by all the signs, more than ready. She ran her palm lightly over the muscled ridges of his abdomen.

"All right, I am your lover, then."

"You are not at all ticklish, Lucien."

"I know. You can touch me anywhere you like."

Lucien pulled her astride him. He was solid, firm. All male. She felt vulnerable with her thighs spread, and yet to be on top gave her a certain sense of control. "You've not been with an Eastern-bred woman before, have you?"

He tipped his chin back, exposing his throat to her. "Do not tell me that the Circassian wench let slip any tales of my prowess!"

For an instant he had her fooled. But the laughter in his eyes gave him away. She decided to play him one better.

"Marylas told me, all right. How she had you on your knees, night after night, begging for mercy, pleading with her to spare you, to allow you to rest, to unlock your chain and let you crawl back to your own bed. Oh, aye, I know all about it!"

Lucien raised an eyebrow. "But did she not mention the parade of her friends she had in tow? One after the other, all weeping and fighting to be first—though of course it made no difference, they were all equally pleased in the end."

Isidora rolled her eyes. "Well, the only one you must please now, is me. Can you do that, Lord Lucien?" She squeezed his ribs between her knees.

His gaze darkened and grew serious. "I can but try, *demoiselle*... Indeed, I can feel that you...you are already halfway there..."

She felt her cheeks flush, that he should be so aware of the private wants of her body. Then, without warning, with both hands he caught her—as if the wounded one were pain-free—and lifted her and lowered her, and met her with himself, until they were as one.

"Oh, my God." The pleasure of him filling her was intense. Deep. Satisfying.

Lucien's eyes were halfway closed. "You keep calling upon God, Isidora. But we need no miracle, for *you* are the miracle. We need no salvation, for you have saved me twice over—and we need no absolution, for you are absolutely the only heaven I crave..."

She smiled, and moved.

Lucien shut his eyes. "Oh, God, mayhap you were right to call upon Him."

She moved again.

His eyes opened wide and focused upon hers. "Methinks I should take charge of this, sweeting, before you

Elaine Knighton 231

get any more of God's help." In a twinkling, he had rolled her onto her back, without leaving her.

Then, he moved.

Now it was Isidora's turn to open her eyes wide, then shut them tight as fresh sensations rippled through her. Lucien smiled. Kissed her. And moved again.

And again…until she was caught hard in his rhythm, in his breath, in the pounding of his heart against hers. She was spinning, rushing in a torrent of liquid fire, headed for an unstoppable conflagration. For something she knew would be much, much more explosive than she had ever imagined possible.

"Look at me…" Lucien growled.

Isidora opened her eyes. His were dark, gleaming, passion-filled. They were her whole world. He drove into her. Her world burst into rapture. He lifted her and came again.

She cried out. Arched forward and bit his neck.

Lucien caught her hair and pulled her head back, then covered her mouth with his as his life essence pulsed into her. He held still, for many long minutes, and she was glad of that. Lucien stroked her hair, kissed her tenderly and lay back beside her.

Isidora snuggled up against his body, still in wonderment at what had just taken place between them. It had happened so fast. She had not resisted. It had felt…so good. The coals in the brazier had burned down to a comforting red glow that made the damp skin on his chest glisten.

"Lucien."

"Aye?"

"Nothing. I but wanted to say your name."

"Not God's?"

"I'm afraid not."

"Don't be afraid. I am here with you."

"I'm glad."

"And so you should be, for this was just the first course."
He grinned at her.

"Very glad," she admitted.

"Me too."

"Truly?"

"Aye. I would never lie to you, Isidora. About anything."

A chill crept into her heart. Lucien was a pure-hearted
soul. And she, by withholding the truth from him, did not
deserve him.

Chapter Twenty-Six

The Cistercians refectory was a place of quiet beauty, Larke thought. Arching stone buttresses, stained-glass windows and carved, smooth oak tables and benches. She spooned the warm, savory soup into her mouth with relish, dipped some bread into it and stuffed it after.

Raymond de Beauchamp sat across and up from her, talking with his younger brother, Percy. He had arrived not long after she and Wace. She had heard a great deal about Sir Raymond's exploits, and had met him several times, but had not actually ever said an intelligent word to him, being too young for such a feat, until now.

He was every bit as handsome as a living legend should be. Thick, shiny, dark-blond hair, a perfect, straight nose and those blue eyes—a pity he was already married and madly in love with his Welsh wife, who, according to Lucien, had once been betrothed to Percy. How that had all come to pass, she did not know.

Someone—Wace, of course—gave her a rude nudge in

the ribs. "You should stop staring and mind your sop, there, milady."

"What?" she said, her mouth still full. Then she felt the rivulet cooling on her chin and hurriedly wiped it. To her horror, this exchange had drawn the attention of Sir Raymond. She gulped down the sodden lump of bread.

"Wace, go find another bottle of the Rhenish I brought, will you?" Raymond said mildly.

Wace bowed and went on his errand immediately.

Raymond leaned toward Larke conspiratorially. "If he gives you any trouble, Lady Larke, I can show you some moves to keep him at bay."

Larke smiled. "It seems that someone has trained Wace rather well, my lord, for I find that a few choice words usually do the trick."

A pair of creases formed between Raymond's brows. "Ah, so he *has* been giving you trouble."

"Nay—truly, my lord, he is a perfect example of chivalry, em, that is, when he is not correcting me."

"I see. Shall I have a word with him?"

"Oh, nay, please, my lord—that is not necessary." Larke did not want to imagine what it would be like for Wace to stand before Sir Raymond and be subject to any "word" he might have with him.

"What brought you here, in such a hurry, so late, milady? Percy says Lucien is injured?"

"Aye, it is but a cut gone bad. I fear I have worried overmuch. I thought Brother Percy might help."

"Sometimes we must do as we are moved to do, no matter what," Raymond replied with a small smile. "And if it is a mistake, we learn from it. I much prefer boldness to dithering."

"Aye," Larke said, relieved to find in Sir Raymond a kindred spirit.

Percy turned to her. "I meant to ask you, Lady Larke, do you know of a man, one who brought his relative from the Holy Land to see Lucien?"

Larke's heart caught unexpectedly and her eyes stung. "Why, indeed, that would be Faris al-Rashid, brother to Isidora, the lady Lucien is about to wed."

"What! You don't say!" Raymond grinned and looked quite pleased with himself.

Larke continued. "It is true, my lord. H-have you seen Faris, Brother Percy? We feared he might have been killed in the woods."

"He is here, Lady Larke, and you may visit him, if he is awake. He has an arrow wound and is improving, but I hesitate to leave him just yet."

Relief flooded Larke at this news and the tears that had threatened began to fall.

She was glad when Percy seemed to misunderstand her reaction—indeed, she herself did not understand it—and asked, "Has Lucien been taken so very bad?"

"Lady Isidora was worried enough, she was going to fetch Sir Kalle Fitz-I-know-not-who to help. But it is Sir Kalle we suspect tried to kill Faris."

"How can that be?" Percy threw a questioning look to Raymond, then back to Larke. "FitzMalheury?"

Larke was taken aback by the intensity of Brother Percy's gaze. What if she said the wrong thing and started some kind of war, right here in England? "Aye. He is encamped on our practice grounds."

"Why?" demanded Raymond.

"I do not know," Larke admitted.

Percy rubbed his chin. "Well. Kalle is a fine physician. If he agrees to help, Lucien is better off with him than me. But if—"

Raymond leaned toward his brother. "Parsifal," he murmured. "Leave it. Wace and I will go. Physician or no, Lucien cannot be left alone with such a wolf at his door."

Percy frowned. "Raymond, you ever seem to forget that I am a...a man now. I can make my own way in this world."

Raymond caught him by the shoulder. "Indeed, you are a man. But of God, not of this world. And you know what *I* am."

"Aye. You are a hero."

Raymond shook his head. "Nay, brother. I am a killer. A fate you have been spared. Be glad of it."

Percy and Raymond exchanged a look then, of such depth that Larke felt both privileged and shaken to behold it. It was as though she had a glimpse into a secret world, one few women were allowed to witness.

No doubt these men did not count her as a woman, because of her youth. But, in case they had forgotten her presence, she thought it best to speak up. "We should leave right away," Larke said.

"You will stay here, where it is safe." Raymond stood, ready to move on, as if his word was law. Which, whether she liked it or not, it was.

Larke, too, rose. "My lord, nothing will keep me from my brother's side."

Wace appeared in the doorway, a brown, earthenware

bottle in his hands. "Sir, I fear she means what she says. It is why I am myself here and not there with Lucien. The necessity of following her, I mean."

Raymond assessed Larke from beneath dark brows. "If you ride with us, you will obey me and you will obey Wace, do you understand?"

"Aye, my lord. My thanks."

"Then get ready."

As Raymond and Wace left the refectory, Larke tugged Brother Percy's sleeve. "May I see Faris? Then I can report to Isidora."

Percy's face creased into a charming smile. "Let us check on him."

Larke followed the monk out and around the perimeter of the cloister to a chamber not far from the chapel itself. In the infirmary were a few beds, all empty but for one, Faris being the only patient. She walked across the stone floor, her footsteps echoing in the high-ceilinged room.

It appeared as though he had not stirred since being placed there. The linens were perfectly folded and smooth over his chest, his arms lay at his sides, his long, black hair fanned across the white pillow. He looked much paler than he had the last time she'd seen him. Indeed he looked barely alive. Beside the bed, a young cleric was praying, but at the approach of the visitors, he rose and bowed.

"Many thanks, brother," Percy said, dismissing him. "Do you want to be alone with Faris, Lady Larke?"

Suddenly she found that prospect overwhelming. "Nay, please stay." Percy stood near the foot of the bed and Larke sat on the edge. "Sir Faris? Are you awake?"

At first he did not open his eyes. Then when he did, they

were that same, deep, melting brown that she remembered. He favored her with a small smile. "Greetings, Lady Larke, fair flower of Ainsley. Forgive me, that I do not rise to honor you as you deserve."

Larke felt a blush creep over her cheeks. "Please, do not tire yourself by such elegant speech. I am so very glad to see you mending. And Isidora will be beside herself with joy to hear of it."

A pained look crossed his face. "Lady Larke, not for me, but for the sake of these holy men, you must not tell Isidora that I live. If Kalle should learn his arrow failed…" Faris paused to catch his breath. "He will come here to finish what he started, and all these innocent men will be in peril. Isidora is not very good at falsehoods."

"I know," Larke said.

"So let her grieve. I ask God, and you, to forgive me for hurting her this way."

"But, Sir Faris, when she realized Kalle had made this attempt on your life, she tried to stab him with her dagger. I do not believe that allowing her to think Kalle succeeded will produce any milder result."

Faris closed his eyes again for a moment and coughed a little. "Isidora could not possibly kill Kalle. And he would not harm her, for reasons I prefer not to explain. It is more important that he believe me dead. And if it is only you who need playact, so much the better."

Larke started to ask about Wace, then she realized that he had been out of earshot when Percy had told of Faris being yet alive. He, too, needed to be kept in the dark, and Sir Raymond would need to agree to the secret.

"If this is your wish, my lord, then so shall it be. Brother

Percy, will you speak to Sir Raymond for me? I dare not approach him on such a subject."

"Brother Percy," Faris began, "I cannot ask you to lie. But I ask that you pray we be forgiven."

Percy looked down upon them solemnly. "I understand your position. And indeed, I will not lie. But I will ask our Abbot to give you and Lady Larke absolution in this. And I will tell Raymond what he must do. It will be a good thing, Larke, if you are not entirely alone in such a deceit."

"And, it may turn out not to be a lie," Faris added with a tired smile. "We do not know God's ultimate will in this. I am not yet so far removed from heaven's gate as to give up the thought of entering it. In that prospect I can find some joy, as may you on my behalf, though this is not the same as dying in battle."

Larke swallowed hard, unable to accept such a possibility. "Yet, once you are healed, surely we can tell Isidora the truth? Surely by then Kalle will have gone home to Acre?"

"Let us hope it will be thus." Faris coughed again. His chest sounded thick. He groaned and coughed some more.

Larke looked to Percy. "What is wrong?"

The monk shook his head gravely. "I will see to him. You should go now, get ready to leave." His lips were set in a firm, grim line.

"I thank you, Brother Percy." Larke took one last look at Faris as he struggled to breathe, then fled the infirmary. As she ran, she remembered with a pang that the good-luck charm she had made for Faris was still around her own neck.

Chapter Twenty-Seven

At last Lucien slept. *Riding on the bosom of an angel.* Like one dead. Isidora was certain she had tasted opium in Kalle's potion, but that would ease Lucien's pain as well as help him rest. As long as there was not too much of it.

Now it was time for her to keep her part of the bargain. She descended the stairs, expecting to have to go out and find Kalle, but he and Earm were still in the hall. Mauger stood by, fidgeting nervously in the absence of Conrad, who had gone to find a priest to perform the wedding sacraments.

Isidora still had the key to Lucien's *sanctum sanctorum.* "My lord FitzMalheury, a word?"

Kalle rose, overshadowing Mauger, who looked not a little dismayed. Isidora tried to give him a sign to stay away, but he came ahead anyway.

"This is private, Sir Mauger, forgive me," she said.

He narrowed his eyes. "If it has to do with Lucien in the least way, then it is my business, as well."

Kalle stood by, with his arms crossed. "I hope this does not take long, Isidora."

She raised one hand. "Please, a moment more." She drew Mauger aside. "Listen to me, Mauger. You want Lucien to cease his pursuit of alchemy, do you not?"

Mauger glanced at Kalle, then nodded.

"Well, I am doing my best this night to see that it comes to an end. I cannot explain quickly. But you must trust that I am doing this out of—out of love for your lord. And he must not know that Kalle was a part of it. Please."

Mauger nodded again. "But you will not go anywhere alone with FitzMalheury. I will go with you."

Isidora looked into Mauger's eyes. "Trust me. You must say nothing. Promise me this."

"I promise."

"All right." She turned to Kalle. "I thank you for your patience. Sir Mauger will accompany us on our walk outside."

Kalle smiled in his feral way. "I am confident that Mauger will not cause me a moment's hesitation in any decision I may make."

They proceeded outside into the frigid air, with Earm carrying a torch. Isidora's heart felt as cold and heavy as the stones beneath her feet. What she was about to do felt as large and irrevocable as tipping a boulder over a cliff— one that would crush her ideals and dreams as it tumbled, as well as Lucien's. One that could never be put back into place once it was set into motion.

"This way." She led them to the courtyard by the chapel and stopped. "I will be back in a moment."

Earm followed her with the light. She took the heavy key from inside her tunic, hung on a cord around her neck. Once the door to the *laboratorium* was unlocked, she turned to Earm. "There is still light, from a fire we had earlier. Stay here."

He nodded, peering wide-eyed into the chamber. Indeed, if Isidora had not seen it in daylight, she, too, would have been frightened. With the shimmering light of the athanor's dying fire, Lucien's fantastic drawings upon the wall seemed to dance and writhe as if the creatures had come to life. The translucent alembics along the shelves took on an eerie glow, the bubbles in the thick green glass winking like so many eyes.

She made her way to the niche and sighed with relief to see the bundle was still here, though she had no reason to think it would not be. But it would be best to check it once more. Untying the silk cord that bound it, she unrolled the protective leather.

The scrolls, three of them, wound around wooden dowels, each one with the head of some strange beast intricately carved in red stones set at either end.

She felt a warm presence at her back, looked up and had to stifle a scream. A monstrous shadow loomed before her on the wall, casting Lucien's figures into darkness. A heavy hand came down upon her shoulder.

"Cerebus," Kalle said softly, and his hand slid down her arm's length to ease one of the scrolls from her fingers. "The Key…" he breathed.

Isidora began to tremble and her teeth chattered with fright.

Kalle continued in his smooth voice, as if giving a lecture. "Each scroll bears one of the three heads of Cerebus, the dog who guards Hades. And opposite them are another three—the Fates. And this…" He reached around her with his other arm, so she was trapped between him and the table's marble edge. He was a solid wall of menace and she had never felt so helpless in her life.

Kalle unwrapped the final treasure. She felt a tremor go through him as the object slid into his hand. "I cannot believe you would give this to me, and not to your darling Lucien. Perhaps you do not understand its true significance."

She looked down at what he held. She had felt it before, through its wrapping, but had not actually looked at it. Indeed she had been afraid to. But it was a simple sphere, perfectly smooth, that would fit in the palm of her hand. It was of a mirror-bright, red-gold color. *Like Lucien's hair in the sun,* she could not help thinking.

"I am glad you are with me to savor this moment," Kalle whispered, and she could feel the pounding of his heart at her back. "Though I wanted it to be Ayshka."

"Lord Kalle, she would not have savored any such moment, and neither do I. I bear no love for alchemy, nor did she. It is what killed my father. It is what would kill Lucien, if I gave him these things. It is what will kill you, too. I know now what caused it—father's mind and body were poisoned by the concoctions of dreadful airs and powders from boiling acids and molten metals."

To her surprise, Kalle agreed, as if it mattered not. "*Oui.* That is why alchemists feel they are racing against time. Your father was also running a race—indeed, that was the whole point of his pursuit of alchemy—after he threw Ayshka out. To find the touchstone that would have cured her. And to think I was sitting on the solution the whole time. In ignorance. Until you happened upon it. Indeed, Isidora, you have some kind of magic about you. The Fates pulled your hand to the scrolls. And now they are returned to me, as God intended."

She had found the key to her mother's cure? But too late? She had kept these texts hidden away…from her father. From Lucien. And now she was giving them to an enemy? To get rid of him, she told herself. Kalle had to be wrong. There was no Elixir, no touchstone. It was all a delusion.

That was the only conclusion she could bear. She stared at Kalle's powerful hands, still holding the scrolls. He wore an irregular-looking ring on his left heart-finger. It seemed an incongruous ornament for a man of such malice. "Where is Mauger?" Isidora asked, suddenly afraid for him.

"Out. Cold. He should have known better than to try me one on one."

Isidora swallowed and said a silent prayer for Mauger. "You have what you want. Let me go. Leave us in peace."

Kalle deftly rewrapped the bundle and stepped back from her with it in his hand.

She spun around to face him, pressing her hands on the table edge to support herself so that she did not beat her fists against his chest. "I had intended to apologize to you properly, Kalle, for striking at you with my blade, but now I wish I had bitten you with it, right to the heart."

Kalle laughed. "Why? For telling you the truth? The truth, Isidora—there is nothing left for you here. Only heartbreak. You must come back with me, to Acre, to your home. I know you miss it."

"And Faris? I am supposed to simply forget you murdered my brother?"

"Hmm, I do wonder if he is dead. I think my aim was skewed when my horse jigged. Elsewise I would have brought his head back as proof. As for him being your brother, well…who knows?"

Kalle was mad. And cruel. And right about Lucien. A horrible, unbearable combination. "Go away, I beg of you. Please, just go away!" Isidora heard her voice rising toward a scream and bit her lip hard to keep the sound inside.

Kalle stared at her, as if she had just slapped his face. An act, no doubt, no one else had ever dared commit. He seemed to fold in on himself—not shrinking, but as though he had grown more dense, more opaque. Darker.

"As you wish," he snarled. "But you will have no peace now. Not once Lucien finds out you have betrayed him. An alchemist's nightmare…like a dream one has of drowning in blackness, of swimming with one's last breath and bit of strength toward the surface, toward light and purity and bliss, only it is too far, and the swimmer is too slow, and he awakens, gasping for air, knowing he has failed yet again, only this time it is forever, because this was his very last chance. That is all he will ever see in you, Isidora, from this day forward."

There. She looked up at him, white-faced, as though her heart had been poleaxed. Kalle felt a pang of remorse. If that had not been a death blow, he did not know what was.

"Should you change your mind, Isidora, you can find me on the other side of the river, but only until two days hence, at the nooning. After that, I will have gone."

Kalle turned and strode out of the *laboratorium*.

But he had to force himself not to run. The little bitch. *Just go away!* The words still echoed in his mind, after all these years. Ayshka's last words to him. Even from the dark pit of her life as a leper, she had refused him. Preferred shame and starvation and filth and death to any help he had to offer. Preferred them to him, to the love he bore her.

In that instant he had wanted to strangle Ayshka. To crush her slender neck with his bare hands. And with that same horrific impulse, he saw that she was right to refuse him. No matter that he had lost everything important to him because of her. His priestly calling. The respect of Deogal. His honor. The fact remained that his love was not pure. Not good enough for her. For anyone.

But that was going to change. He had the key to the Elixir. Right here in his hand, that even now shook with the incredible significance of what it held.

It would render him perfect. In every way. All-knowing, all-powerful. He would rule Acre. Then Antioch, then Constantinople. All of Outremer and beyond. It might require a sea of blood, but in the end he would have the respect, nay, the obeisance, of the world. He would be the Beloved. Feared and adored by countless millions. Invincible. He would be like a god to them. Their god.

The God.

Chapter Twenty-Eight

Lucien opened his eyes. Where was he? What day was it? His head felt like a toadstool, big and fluffy; his limbs unwieldy, as though they belonged to someone else. He pushed himself up in bed and as pain shot through his arm from his hand, it all came back.

He looked at the bandage. Stained with blood, but not soaked. Better yet, nor did it stink. Kalle had done his work well. And Isidora had…ah. He shivered and smiled. Now that was something he could not possibly forget. He looked about. A faint glow shone from the eastern window of the solar. Dawn. Why was his lady not here with him?

Lucien put his bare legs over the edge of the bed into the cold air, waited a moment, then staggered to his feet. Just as soon as he found a pot to piss in, he would seek Isidora out and marry her.

Mauger, his head bloodied but not broken, had been laid out on a table in the hall. He had regained consciousness shortly, and Isidora sat with Rosamunde as the young woman tended him, dabbing at the lump on his head with a warm poultice.

It should have been a cold one, Isidora knew, but she hadn't the heart to correct her. And, Mauger did not seem to really need any tending, no thanks to Kalle. Or to Isidora herself. He certainly did not want it.

"My thanks, Rosamunde, but I am well enough, you may leave me be." He tried to sit up, but she leaned on his chest with her elbow, and for one awkward moment, Isidora feared the lass was about to kiss him.

"I want to help you," she purred.

"I need no help."

"Of course you do," Rosamunde insisted.

Isidora fought the urge to catch the girl by the hair and drag her off of Mauger. But he needed to fight his own battles when it came to this particular female. And, if the glint in his eye was any indication, Rosamunde needed to learn to heed certain warning signs.

Like a whale reaching the surface of the sea, Mauger heaved himself upright, an unstoppable force. Rosamunde, apparently not believing his defiance, did not shift her weight. Mauger shifted it for her and she slid with a bounce to the floor, landing on her rump amidst the rushes.

"Ow!"

"I beg your pardon, *mes demoiselles*." Mauger bowed, though it obviously pained him, and marched in dignity out of the hall.

Isidora held out a hand to Rosamunde to help her up. The girl churlishly refused and scrambled to her feet. "This is *your* fault, anyway! Half the men in the keep are wounded or gone!"

"You are right, lady," Isidora agreed quietly. Nothing Rosamunde said could make her feel any worse than she did already. Since last night's encounters, first with Lucien, then with Kalle, her shame and misery went bone-deep, almost paralyzing in their intensity.

She forced herself to function, for she was not one to lie abed and languish. But they rested like a thick pall over her, slowing her thoughts and her actions.

She heard a sound and turned. Lucien was on the stairs. What was he doing up? She was not ready for him, had no chance to flee. But she faced him, faced his inevitable discovery of her treachery, as a deer must face the hunter's fatal arrow.

He smiled at her. He did not know. She had to tell him herself; he should not find out any other way. But not here. She wanted to do it in private. No one else should have to witness his grief but her.

"My lord, shall we take the air for a while?"

"As you wish. Is…something wrong?"

Rosamunde gave her a daggered, gleeful smile, one that was not lost upon Lucien. He turned to the girl and inclined his beautiful head. She froze, with the smile still on her face.

Lucien approached her, paused, and drew the back of his forefinger along her rosebud cheek. With his touch, as if created by it, a tear trailed after his finger. He wiped it away with his thumb, but another took its place.

"Rosamunde," he said, his voice filled with velvet sorrow.

Isidora trembled, praying that he never used such a voice on her.

"This was all wrong," he continued. "It should never have been. I think it best that you go home to your parents now, deny any rumor about the sheet from my bed, and see if Mauger comes to speak to your father. Give him some room. If it is for the best, then it will happen. But I apologize to you, yet again."

Rosamunde swallowed, and sniffed, and rubbed one eye with a delicate knuckle. "No need, Lord Lucien. You have taught me…some—some things, as has Sir Mauger. And Isidora. I thank you all for that." She curtsied and drifted up the stairs.

Lucien threw his mantle over his shoulders and held out his hand to Isidora. "Let us see what else the day has in store, eh?"

She gave him her hand and a tentative smile. Oh, this was too hard! Through the anteroom and down the outer stair they went, the cold seeping up under Isidora's skirts. Immodest and impractical creature that she was, she had not put any leggings on. But that hardly mattered.

Built on a hill, from the upper bailey they could look out over the battlements, chest-high, to the valley below. The sky glowed pink and golden as the sun crested the horizon. Small dabs of gray dotted the land.

"The ewes will soon be lambing. Are you looking forward to that?" Lucien asked.

"Not being a ewe, I don't suppose I am."

He turned so his back was to the stone wall and pulled her before him. "What troubles you, Isidora? Is it something about last night?"

"I don't know why you are not still in bed. You cannot have recovered so quickly."

He shrugged. "I would prefer to be lying down, it is true. But one cannot always give in to such inclinations.

More's the pity." He drew her closer still, so they were thigh to thigh.

She touched his forehead with the back of her hand. As Kalle had done. "Your skin is damp. But cool. The fever has broken, thank God."

"I drank a whole cupful of that vile, disgusting potion, last night, you know, after...after ravishing you."

"It is a wonder you are conscious at all then."

"It is a greater wonder that I kept it down. But I do not want to talk about that. There is still something you are not telling me."

"Oh, Lucien. I hardly know where to begin."

"Just start. Anywhere. This is very uncomfortable. And soon you'll get a chill, if we are not careful."

Isidora took a deep breath. "Lucien..."

Coward that she was, she could not bring herself to tell him. Could not bring herself to spoil the fragile happiness they had shared.

Lucien waited, gazing at her. Then the sound of shod hooves on stone broke the quiet below. Isidora felt his attention shift, his body grow taut. Relief swept her that she might have time to think of a way to tell him that would not make him hate her.

"Pardon, my lady. I am not expecting anyone."

They got to their feet and looked below. The gate had been opened for the day. A riderless horse wandered into the courtyard.

Lucien's brow knit. "That is Larke's mare. What deviltry is this?" He turned and ran toward the stairs, then halted and spoke over his shoulder. "Get back into the hall, Isidora."

She ignored his command and followed him down, her

own heart pounding. What could have happened? A groom held the animal while Lucien examined it.

His brow was still furrowed, his hair fell across his cheeks as he crouched to feel the horse's legs. When he saw Isidora, he gave her a look of frustration and concern.

"There are no wounds, nothing missing or broken from the harness. She is not winded, but it looks as though she has been walking home for some time. See, the bits of grass on the bit? She's been grazing along the way. But where is Larke?"

He stood up and glowered at the groom. "Do you know anything about this? Did you saddle this beast for her?"

The young man shook his head emphatically. "Nay, my lord. I noticed it was missing, but Squire Wace's mount was gone, as well, so I thought they…" He faltered.

Lucien chewed his lip and stared at the youth. Isidora knew Lucien was not really seeing him, but the groom squirmed and fidgeted. At last Lucien spoke again. "Rouse Jager and get Caflice ready." He turned to Isidora. "What did I tell you? Larke is enough to drive even a saint mad. Let us hope she is indeed with Wace. And why are *you* still out here?"

"I cannot bear to sit by and watch. I can ride as well as anyone else. If the mare is not too tired, let me take her out with you. Or wait till my horse is readied."

"Aye, you have demonstrated all too well your propensity to ride out. But I cannot allow it. Kalle may be still in the area. I do not want you caught in any fighting."

"I will follow you anyway."

"Not if I have you confined."

"You would not dare!"

"What is to dare? All I have to do is tell Mauger, 'Keep her here.' And so help me, he will!" Lucien advanced upon her like a storm cloud, but instead of catching her arm or pushing her before him, he caught her up and carried her as though she were a child in his arms.

It was so unexpected Isidora did not struggle. Indeed she wrapped her own arms around Lucien's neck and relished his closeness, the power of his body…the fact that he cared enough to be angry.

He climbed the stairs, then shortened his strides as they neared the anteroom to the hall. In the shadow of the curtain he put her back on her feet.

"Isidora, do you not see? I need you here, to ease my mother's fears, to keep an eye on things. When I go, there is always the chance I will not return. In which case someone should deal with the *laboratorium,* make sure the elements are hidden or destroyed, and my books locked up. You still have the key. I won't take it from you. Guard the Work for me."

Isidora looked up at him. Lucien…person of light. "You ask a great deal of one who wishes the Work did not exist."

He drew her up against him and her knees nearly buckled. "I will make it up to you," he said.

Lucien was warm and solid and smelled of fragrant smoke and sandalwood. Isidora pulled together the last shreds of her resistance. "I will wait four marks of the hour candle. If you do not come back by then, I will ride after you. With Mauger or without him."

"I shall return in good time. Now, kiss me goodbye."

She stood up on her toes and put her lips to his in a tentative, delicate touch.

He gave her a wry smile. "You call that a kiss?"

Isidora let her feet go flat on the floor. "Come back, and I will try again."

Chapter Twenty-Nine

In the early morning light Larke trotted Faris's horse—formerly Lucien's—along the forest path, headed for home. She did not care if Wace or Sir Raymond didn't like it. In fact, she wanted to go even faster. As the path widened, she urged her mount into a canter.

Percy and Raymond had decided that to return the extremely valuable gray to Lucien would be a more convincing support to their story. To her surprise, Raymond joined her, his big courser's long, relaxed strides effortlessly keeping abreast of her.

At least the muck was not too slippery. They splashed along through muddy puddles, leaving Wace covered in brown splatters behind them. Raymond glanced back, then grinned at Larke. *Oh, my!* She felt herself blush to have such favor bestowed upon her by the legendary Raymond, and smiled shyly back. "Not far now," she said.

"Thank God," he replied.

They passed a group of crofters gleaning fallen branches from the forest floor, but Larke did not stop to greet them.

Lucien would be worried as it was, and furious, no doubt. She would be lucky if all he did was forbid her to leave the women's quarters for the next month.

But the hardest part would be to tell Isidora the lie about her brother. Wace, who had been given no reason not to believe Faris was dead, was still in the dark.

Larke worried that Isidora would try to get to the Cistercian abbey, to visit Faris's grave. Lies had such a way of complicating things!

The morning gave way to noon and Raymond turned his horse off the path. They cut across the fallow fields toward the castle, to rejoin the lane where it met the bridge. They slowed to a walk as they approached, for a group of riders was already halfway across it. Larke's heart leaped.

"Oy, Lucien!" Raymond called.

He was up, out and about! Had a miracle healed his hand? She hurried to meet him. "Lucien! You are well! Praise God!"

Lucien gave her a dark look, mixed with relief. "Larke, I swear, you deserve a hiding for causing so much worry! You can praise God and Kalle FitzMalheury, for he took care of my hand. By the way, my right one is in perfect health," Lucien added, loud enough for all to hear. "Fully capable of rendering your backside into a state of abject contrition."

Larke felt herself redden yet again, to be so chastised in front of not only her brother's men, but Wace and his lord. It was not like Lucien to be so harsh. "Oh, Lucien, you know I am sorry."

"I know you *should* be!"

Larke tried again. "I can explain, Lucien."

"I doubt that. Get yourself through the gates. Isidora is also worried for you. Greetings, Raymond. I am sorry you've been dragged into this. And you, Wace, I am grateful to you for returning her. But…" Lucien paled as Larke's mount pawed the ground. "That is the horse I gave… What does this mean?"

Raymond cleared his throat. "Your friend Faris was badly wounded. He barely made it to the abbey alive, and although Percy did what he could… We thought it best to bring you back the gray."

Larke marveled at Raymond's skilful avoidance of an outright lie. Of course it still was a falsehood, but by implication only. Then she saw the pain on Raymond's face, caused, she was certain, by that on Lucien's.

"How will I tell Isidora?" Lucien bunched his good hand into a fist against his thigh. "She cannot know. Not yet. Keep it to yourselves, please, for a time."

"Where is FitzMalheury?" Raymond asked.

"Gone. Now that Larke is safe, I can seek him. He has something of Isidora's that I would regain for her. And, since I am sure he is responsible for Faris's death, he owes wergild to Isidora, if not his life."

"Don't be hasty, Lucien. You should return to the hall with us and we'll talk about it first," Raymond said.

"I cannot lose Kalle now, it is imperative that I retrieve this thing. I swore an oath."

Raymond put a gauntleted hand upon Lucien's arm. "It is imperative that I speak to you before you leave. If you are meant to find Kalle, you will find him in good time. Please, listen to me, Lucien."

"All right. You ride with me and we will talk on the way."

Lucien glanced to Larke, as if to question why she remained. Reluctantly she reined her horse toward the gates.

Stranded between her and the party of armed men, Wace called to Raymond, "My lord, what would you have me do?"

"Escort Lady Larke the rest of the way in. Stay and help Mauger guard this place."

Wace nodded and brought his horse alongside Larke's as the others headed out. She saw the tightness of his jaw and his expression of annoyance—with her, no doubt.

"I am sorry you missed the riding, Wace."

He glanced at her, and with the swift cut of his eyes, tempered by understanding, the lean, determined look of his face, she realized Wace was no longer a boy. He was a man.

Ready for anything.

"Well, Larke, it is not as though Raymond is punishing me by having me stay here with you." Wace gave her a small quirk of his mouth and she felt more chastened by his remark than by Lucien's ire.

"I would like to see Isidora straight away, Wace."

"As you will, milady." He led the way across the bridge and to the gatehouse. Before entering the bailey, Larke looked back. In the distance, Lucien and Raymond rode side by side, the men-at-arms trailing after. She wondered if Raymond would tell Lucien the truth.

"Do not concern yourself. Your brother is more than capable of taking FitzMalheury. And with Sir Raymond along, there is no question of defeat."

Larke did not reply as they clattered into the courtyard. She abandoned her horse to Wace's care and ran up the stairs, through the hall and on up to Lucien's solar.

As she had expected, there stood Isidora, looking out the

narrow window toward where Lucien and Raymond were still just visible. Her hip-length, black hair flowed in loose waves down her back. Not for the first time, Larke envied Isidora her smooth, opaque complexion.

At the sight of Larke, Isidora ran to her and embraced her fiercely. "Thank God you are safe. I did not come down—it would have been that much harder to let them leave without me."

"Don't worry. Sir Raymond is with Lucien."

"Tell me what happened."

Larke hesitated. She had not thought of what to say, only of what not to say. "Em, well, Wace convinced me of the folly of my quest. My horse got frightened during our argument and fled. Then we were caught by a rain storm. Then we took shelter, in a…a barn and made our way home."

"But I saw you riding in."

"Oh, well, Wace is very resourceful. He managed to borrow a mount in a village along the way."

"I see."

Oh, God, she knows I am lying! And I told her I was good at it… Larke thought furiously how to distract her friend. "I was sent back in disgrace, Isidora. Lucien even threatened to beat me! Wace is staying, though, so I feel well protected, here. Perhaps too well protected."

"What do you mean?" Isidora drew Larke to sit with her on the bed.

"Wace looked at me…almost as though he *owned* me. Or as though he thought that to be a definite possibility. I am used to Lucien ordering me about, since our father died, God rest him, and because I love Lucien so much, I let him think he has control of me...but Wace...I have only ever thought of him as a boy.

"As of today I realize he is no longer that. And now I find him a bit frightening. He has not known me and loved me my whole life, as has Lucien. He is not thinking only of me and my welfare, as does Lucien. He wants something else, as well, a desire I have seen in the eyes of other men when they look at other women. I have even seen Lucien look at you that way, Isidora."

Isidora's cheeks turned a becoming pink. "Well, I suppose he might, considering how long..."

Larke smiled. "Uncle Conrad should be back soon with a priest, then we can get the formalities over with. You and Lucien, and Mauger and Rosamunde, I suppose."

"Lucien has sent Rosamunde home, Larke."

"How so? Not that I am over-sorry to see her leave."

"He feels it all was rather sudden, and that Mauger should have a chance to think upon the matter."

"Excellent. A relief, indeed," Larke said.

Isidora took Larke's hand in her own. "Milady, forgive me, but I know there is something you are withholding from me."

Larke swallowed. "Lucien has bade me keep silent until he returns. Please do not ask me to tell you anything more."

Isidora searched Larke's eyes. "Just tell me if you saw any sign of Faris. Can you say that much?"

"Nay. I can say nothing. I am sorry, Isidora. Perhaps I should go now."

Isidora sat up straighter. "I told Lucien he has four hours to return. Then I shall come after him. I have lost everyone who was dear to me in life. Nothing will get in my way this time to let it happen again."

Larke looked upon Isidora in wonderment. Women had vied for her brother's attention for as long as she could remember. But this was the first time she had seen a lady so protective of him. Or he of her.

"That is not much time for him to accomplish anything, Isidora. But on the other hand, a half a day's ride could put him leagues away in any direction."

Isidora stood, grave and beautiful. "Then I think that I should not try to follow Lucien, but Kalle. Lucien may indeed find him, but if I get there first, I may be able to avert a bloody fight."

"But Kalle is too dangerous—and besides, how do you know where he is?"

"He told me."

"What?" Larke exclaimed, disbelieving.

"It is true. He wants me to return to Acre with him."

Larke realized her mouth was open. "Kalle Fitz-Malheury desires this…but why? Is…is he in love with you?"

"He is in love with my mother, who has been dead for years, God keep her. Perhaps he believes I will provide some sort of link between him and her. And, I think, if he can take me away from Lucien, that would please him in some perverse way, which might keep him from doing worse things to Lucien, should he provoke Kalle. At this point I hardly know if Lucien would even mind my leaving, with or without Kalle."

"Of course he would mind!"

Isidora shook her head. "You say you allow him to believe he controls you, Larke. But in truth, he *does* control you. It is he who allows you to think you have a say in anything. He told me himself that this is the proper order of things, when it comes to men and women. So if he minds my going, I do not know if it is out of a sense of possessiveness or out of love."

Larke frowned. "I like this not at all!"

Isidora shrugged, a gesture which belied her intense tone. "Why do you think so many women go to convents? Would you not rather be subservient to God by your own choice, instead of being forced to do the will of an imperfect man?"

"Well…I see your meaning. But there must be some middle way…"

"It is rare to see it. Nor is it easy. Because when the woman loves the man, then she may choose to place herself at his mercy…and God help her, in that case."

Larke realized that Isidora was trembling. "You do love him."

Isidora met her gaze. "I wish I did not. Indeed, I wish that I had never met him."

"You can't mean that!"

"It may be you have not felt the pain I feel. And I hope you never do. But even as you have seen fit, out of your own goodness of heart to withhold something from me, Larke, so do I think it best not to share certain things with you."

"But you have to stay. You have to marry Lucien. Elsewise Mother will never be satisfied."

"Your mother needs to find out what she can do for herself, to make herself happy, instead of looking to Lucien to do it for her."

Larke, too, had felt that, but not dared voice it, for quite a while. Amelie…and Conrad. What if love of him was the source of her mother's misery, and not Lucien at all? How could they have been so blind? She bit her lip. "We have all encouraged her to behave this way, I trow."

Isidora looked down at her hands. "As I did my father, by ever doing his bidding instead of speaking my heart. It is not a loving act to allow people to destroy themselves unchallenged, however slowly or subtly."

"You must not go alone."

Isidora smiled grimly. "Familiar words, are they not?"

"Aye, but this is different."

"I do not wish to drag others into my sad tangle of events."

"It is too late, Isidora. We love you."

"You are right, it is too late, Larke. I have made my decision, and though one promise will be broken, another will be kept. If I can do no other service to Lucien, I will do this, though he will no doubt curse me for it."

Approaching footsteps sounded and Isidora jumped. She whirled about, to the formidable sight of Lucien standing in the doorway with a fair-haired, stern warrior at his side, and behind them, both Wace and Mauger.

"Isidora, this is Sir Raymond," Larke squeaked, and took a step backward.

Isidora nodded to Raymond, who inclined his head to her. *"Enchanté, demoiselle."*

"My lords?" she managed to ask. "How is it that you have returned so swiftly?"

Lucien, his hair in tangles and his cheeks shadowed, looked sorely in need of bed and board. "Isidora, I turned back from my pursuit of Kalle just now, because I thought you might provide me with a clue as to where he is, to save me time."

Isidora raised her chin. "Surely you do not need so many hands to bring me to heel, Lucien."

"Convince me otherwise, then."

She stood firm. "It is a matter of honor."

"Indeed, Isidora, what is there of importance that is *not* a matter of honor?"

"Pray tell me, then, Lucien—what has become of Faris? I think you know, and I must know, too." A lump formed in her throat, making it impossible to swallow.

Lucien looked down at his hands and began to ease the gauntlet from the wounded one. "He will not be coming back, Isidora." He glanced at Raymond, whose brilliant blue eyes flickered for an instant.

What are they hiding? Isidora thought, unwilling, unable to believe Lucien's words.

Raymond stepped forward and placed a large hand upon Isidora's shoulder. "When I left Faris, he looked not long for this world, *demoiselle*. But he was content. Indeed, he seemed happy."

Lucien stared at his friend.

Isidora shrugged free of the blond knight's hand and he moved back. "I must go to him!" She longed to flee the keep, to ride like the wind and find her brother.

"Nay. You must not." Lucien's voice was firm, his resolve upon the matter clear. "Let Faris go, Isidora. It was difficult enough for him to say goodbye once. Do not make him do it again."

Larke made a sound, as if she were weeping, and an

empty desperation filled Isidora. Nothing mattered now. She had lost too much, and too much of her loss was her own fault. She gazed at Lucien without blinking. "Then I will go to Kalle. And make him pay."

Lucien's fists clenched at his sides. "Don't be stupid!"

"I am no more stupid than you or any other man who would seek vengeance!"

"You are not me, nor are you a man."

"Aye, and I thank God for that every day!"

"Lucien." Raymond began to advance toward his friend.

"You're right. You will need my help to find Kalle," Isidora declared.

"What do you mean?" Lucien demanded.

"He is waiting for me." Isidora watched in dismay as Lucien's face drained of what little color it had.

"You…are close to him…in more than just enmity?"

"I made him a promise. I told you it was a matter of honor. That does not mean I cannot take my revenge, as well."

Raymond held up his hand. "As Lucien said, Kalle can pay wergild for Faris, you need not begin a blood feud."

"Gold does not satisfy such a debt!" Isidora bit her lip. Once Kalle had the Key, he would have all the gold he could ever want. An honor price would mean nothing to him.

"Isidora." Lucien's voice remained soft, but carried a core of iron. "You must tell me where Kalle is, and you must trust me to resolve this on your behalf, to act as your champion."

"I will show you, but I will not tell you."

Lucien moved to stand close before her, his presence warm and commanding. "Are you going to be my wife or are you not?"

Isidora wanted to run from him, to run from herself. He had not said it, but she knew that as far as he was concerned, to be his wife meant to give him her complete obedience. She could promise no such thing. "That is up to you, my lord, once this is finished."

"You have no preference on the matter?"

"My preference does not have any bearing upon it, in fact. If I wish to wed you, and you do not wish it, then my desire is of no account. But if you wish to wed me, and I do not wish it, you can still have me, if you so choose, and yet again—my desire is of no account. Is that not the way of the world, as you have described it to me and indeed, as I have experienced it? That the will of men is the will of all?"

"Nay, Isidora, you stubborn, stone-pated female! I want you. But I will not have you unless you want me, as well. That is the way of *my* world."

"You *want* me, Sir Lucien? You do not declare love nor ask for it in return? Perhaps the presence of your comrades prevents any such vulnerable admission. Or perhaps there is no such admission to be made, because of other things that consume your heart. Let me say this to you, then, Lord Lucien, before your friends and mine."

Isidora put her hand over her own heart. "I profess my love for you, Lucien de Griswold. You may accept it or reject it. Nothing you can do will change the way I feel. It remains to be seen if you feel the same about me. So do not tell me you love me, even if it be true. Say nothing until Kalle is gone from us, one way or another."

Lucien grabbed two fistfuls of air. "God in Heaven, Isidora, you weary me with your riddling and your convoluted logic and your cryptic words! I showed you full well that I loved you, the other night. What more proof do you need? Think you I share myself with just anyone who asks?"

Isidora could only stare up at him.

Raymond cleared his throat, but Mauger was the one who spoke. "Lucien, our Isidora is overwrought, as are you yourself. You need food and rest. There is no need to race off on the instant to look for FitzMalheury. Lady Isidora, think you Kalle is in a hurry to depart?"

"He awaits me, as I said. He will not leave until my business with him is done. Tomorrow is soon enough."

"There," Mauger said, his relief evident. "Sleep upon it, and on the morrow the proper course will be easier to discern."

"Aye." Lucien caught Isidora's arm. "We will have supper, and you will be spending the night with me, then, my lady. You love me? Well and good. I give you a new opportunity to demonstrate that as you see fit."

He marched her past his sister, Mauger, Sir Raymond and Wace. All of them stood red-faced and astonished except for Raymond, who looked the sort of man who would have done the same if in Lucien's place.

And, had she the least bit of pride left, she would have fought her way free and refused to cooperate with such a gesture of ownership. But she had none. For all she knew, these could be their last hours together, forevermore. She would take them, take whatever she could of him, to hold tight against the future.

The sun had set early. In the solar, with the door shut, Lucien cast off his clothes, throwing them to the floor as if challenging an opponent to some sort of combat. Isidora could only watch and marvel at what a beautiful creature he was. His sculpted face, his broad shoulders, his skin, golden in the firelight. He slid under the bed furs and sat with his muscular arms crossed, looking at her expectantly. "Well?"

What little composure she had, left her as self-consciousness spread. Her legs felt as though they could not hold her weight. "Please, Lucien, do not be cruel."

He closed his eyes and leaned back against the bolster. "Oh, Isidora. Just come here, I beg of you, and be with me."

"I can see that you are exhausted, my lord. But I will be with you." She clambered up, still fully clothed, and lay down beside him.

"Are you comfortable?" he asked, still with his eyes closed.

"Not particularly," she replied truthfully.

"Then make yourself thus."

"I don't know if that is possible."

"Take off your overgown, for a start. That would make *me* more comfortable, if I were you."

She did not allow her initial hesitation to gain a foothold, but undid her belt—then she froze. Isidora looked helplessly at Lucien. She wanted to feel free of pressure, free of guilt, free to live the moment, without thought of the past or what was to come.

Lucien said nothing, but handled her gently as he tugged off her overgown. Then he flung it out of reach, drew her close and covered her with the bed furs. He was warm and solid through the thin linen of her chemise.

"That's better," he murmured.

"What would you have me do now?" she whispered.

Lucien opened his eyes and slanted his blue gaze to her. He leaned down, cupped her face with his palm, and kissed her mouth as if she were still a virgin, still an innocent, as if he had an obligation to be careful with her. "Go to sleep, Isidora. Know that you are safe with me."

"I know," she said, a fresh tumult of conflicting feelings welling up inside. *I am safe, but my heart is not, for you are perilous fair, Lucien de Griswold.*

Chapter Thirty

Lucien woke to a moonbeam shining in his eyes from the solar's tall, narrow window. He sensed a warm presence at his side and remembered he was not alone. Isidora…dark and exquisite…outspoken and stubborn…brave and intelligent…she was here, now, her bare skin next to his, with nothing to stop him from kissing her awake.

Nothing but the certainty that she was, if not lying outright, withholding something from him. The knowledge Deogal had given her to deliver to him, for one. But beyond that, she withheld her trust. She did not trust him to use the knowledge wisely or judiciously. To guard against alchemy taking hold of his life, of his very being, the way it had her father.

He looked down at her, at the silver light spangling her hair. She breathed evenly; her breasts gently rose and fell. Then, as he watched, her eyelids fluttered, her brow knit and she began to push away some foe in her dreamworld.

"*La—la!! Effendi…*" she cried. *Nay, nay!! Learned One…*

"Shh, wake up, it is but a dream, Isidora." Lucien

stroked her hair back from her face and rubbed her arms. She stopped fighting and slowly opened her eyes. He pulled the furs up over her shoulders. "You've not been covered, you're cold."

"I had a nightmare."

"So I gathered. What was it?"

She squeezed her eyes closed. "Kalle. Kalle was there…I don't want to talk about it."

FitzMalheury again. Lucien made an effort to reply in a soothing voice. "Go back to sleep then."

To Lucien's surprise, Isidora turned to him and slid her soft arms around his middle. "I've slept long enough." She held him tight, her cheek to his, her eyelashes brushing his skin as she blinked.

She touched something within him that began to melt away his resistance and his anger, his sense of being trapped in his duty. "Isidora, I have not asked your permission to wed you, but I ask it now. Indeed, I should be on my knees before you, not lying here in your arms as if you were mine already."

When he started to sit up, she pushed him back. "But I am yours already." She made this profound statement, her voice soft, like the touch of an angel's wing. "I would—"

Lucien slid his hands through the skeins of her black hair and drew her face to his, capturing whatever she had been about to say in a kiss. A devouring hunger rose in him, as nothing he had ever felt before. A desire beyond possession, beyond the physical, one that simply burned for ultimate union on all levels.

If there was anyone in the world who could comprehend him, it was she. If anyone could challenge him and get away with it, she could. If anyone truly loved him—if no one else at all loved him—he hoped and he prayed that Isidora did.

He wrapped her in his arms, rolled her onto her back, and tried to show her how he felt before he himself was overcome. "Be at one with me," he breathed. "Let go of your fear."

"Lucien." She arched against him.

He slid her chemise up as her weight shifted, until her moist heat met his body, and he was lost in her.

The morning came all too soon for Isidora, and with it, the harsh reality of facing Kalle once again. Why could the night with Lucien not have lasted forever? Was she doomed to have only a few moments of happiness? She looked at him, and the soft, filtered light coming through the drawn bed curtains made him seem ethereal. Indeed, she had slept on the bosom of an angel, if ever there was one.

Her angel opened his eyes and slid his hand over hers. "What are you thinking, Isidora?"

She had to tell him the truth. Now. "First of all, let me say that…that anything I have done, is out of the love I bear for you. The other night it was necessary for Kalle to come to your aid. I made certain he did by promising him the Key."

Lucien's countenance darkened. "And what key might that be?"

"The…the thing my father sent me to deliver to you. The Key—to the Elixir. And the scrolls that I found that go with it."

"The Key," Lucien said slowly, as if in a daze. He stared at her. Then rubbed his brow. Then stared at her again. "Let me see if I understand what you just said. In return for my hand's recovery, you promised Kalle FitzMalheury the key to the saving of mankind from damnation? To wiping out famine and plague and war and ignorance for all time?" He sat up and brought her with him, catching hold of her arms, hard. "You've promised *him* the key to the divine power of the One God?"

Isidora could not breathe. Her heart felt as though it would burst. If she could escape Lucien's iron grip, she would run to the window and throw herself over the edge. What was he saying? *That the Elixir held the power of God?*

Her words tumbled out. "I thought it was a means to transmute base metal to gold. And, as you explained, to cure ills. I did not realize that—"

"You promised him this. Do not tell me you actually gave it to him, Isidora. Please." Lucien's voice was tight with quiet, desperate fury.

"I—I had to!" she sobbed, wishing the heavens would open and carry her away.

"You had to give it to him—but not to me. When?"

"Afterward— After we…oh, Lucien." Isidora's misery compounded. She had accepted Lucien's gift of himself, knowing that she had no right to such joy, because it had been an act of thievery on her part, as surely as was handing the Key over to Kalle.

His eyes full of pain, Lucien looked at her and did not speak.

"But, Lucien, what choice did I have? You were not with my father at the end. You did not have to mop up his flux and vomit and listen to his ravings. That was his ignoble death, my lord! Nothing sublime about it. And the Work was to blame—these operations you perform, the cooking of mercury and lead—it creates pure poison!

"How could I give those things to you? Send you rushing back into the greedy maw of the Work, with fresh, false hope? Your future, ours, your life and happiness, damned by the certainty of a horrible death!"

Lucien shook his head. "You had the scrolls even then, Isidora, did you not? Long before he died. You had no regular habit of visiting the bowels of Kalle's dungeons. You had them when you came for me. And yet you did not give them to Deogal?"

Isidora felt like a cornered animal. "I did not give them to him straight away. I did not know they were so important. I wanted him, for myself! Just once, I wanted my father to see *me,* Isidora—not Isidora who reminded him of Ayshka, or Isidora who prepared his food every day, or Isidora who was willing to sacrifice her life for him, because, after all, was that not what any dutiful daughter should do? I wanted him to ask me if I was happy and to tell me he loved me."

Lucien looked into her eyes for a long, long moment. She thought she might shatter beneath the intensity of his gaze.

He was a generous, noble soul. But no matter how well-mannered he was, he would not forgive her this. And she could not fault him.

"Lucien, I have one more thing to say… I see a great pity in this, a t-terrible irony. For you need nothing beyond what you already are. You are a fine man. Why do you want more than you have in yourself, more than is either reasonable or natural?" She bit her lip to mask the pain in her heart.

At last his hands relaxed and slid from her arms. "Isidora, it is not all for myself. It is too much for any one person to have such power. But it could have been guarded, until the time was right, the right kings and bishops and pope, men of intelligence and integrity. It is true, I had a selfish motive. I wanted to cure my mother of her melancholy, just as your father wanted to cure your mother. And just as he contributed to her condition, I was the cause of my mother's."

Isidora swallowed. "You mean, the death of your sister, Estelle? But that was not anything you could help."

Lucien ground his fist into his forehead. "It was my fault. I should tell you, I suppose, so you know the truth, before you hear some other version of it. She fancied a young man, you see. Robert de Clairvaux. One of my foster brothers. He was my best friend. My parents sent him away when they suspected her attachment. I was so angry with them. And with her. But she begged me to take her to meet him. Just once more. I could refuse her nothing. Nor him. She knew this, of course."

He took a ragged breath, drew up his knees and hugged his legs. "We rendezvoused near an abandoned cottage. A landmark we all knew. But we did not know a band of outlaws had taken shelter there. I should have considered that possibility, taken it into account. I was the eldest, if only by a few moments. But I was too worried about my father's wrath to think clearly.

"They came at us like wild animals. They took Estelle. Robert and I became separated as we fought. There were three or four of them attacking him at once. And others already had her—had her down… I was forced to choose. Him or her. Both of them were screaming my name. Each begging me to save the other."

His voice had dropped to a whisper and he looked down at his hands, crossed before him. "I hesitated. For an instant. Then…I left Robert to his fate and went for Estelle. But it was too late. *I* was too late."

Lucien raised his head and Isidora had never before seen anything so terrifying as the fierceness in his gaze.

"So I killed those men. Every last one. I cut off their heads and planted them in a circle, stuck on their own lances. I left them staring at each other's ugly faces. Then I rode home, with Estelle and Robert."

"How old were you?" Isidora asked, Lucien's pain making her own voice barely audible.

"We all had fifteen winters. My father sent me away after that. As far as he could. I spent the next six years in France. From there I went to Outremer. And in Acre, the farthest place I had ever been save Jerusalem, I found you."

Lucien still sat on the bed, his powerful arms now resting across his knees. He gazed at Isidora, who knelt beside him, and took a deep breath. "So, my lady, who am I to question anyone else's judgment? All I know is, a single mistake can grow into a huge calamity. I have made such a mistake already in this life. I cannot afford another. And you wonder why I seek perfection?"

She looked at him, her eyes stinging. "Oh, Lucien. No one else expects it of you."

"But there have been those with such expectations of me. And the Work demands it."

A spark of anger flared within Isidora at the unfairness of this, at the burden it placed on lives that might otherwise be spent loving others instead of alchemy.

"Then, my lord, the Work is futile! There is no such

thing as perfection, outside of God. Who are you to insist you are capable of it, when no one else is?"

Lucien's gaze softened and she felt as though he had touched her in kindness, even though he still sat by himself.

"Who are you, Isidora, to insist that I, or you, or anyone else, is outside of God? Is that not what we seek? Not just union with the Divine, but a reunion? Have you considered that perfection might be there all along, hidden, and we catch glimpses of it from time to time? Even within ourselves?"

Isidora's heart caught yet again, but this time in yearning. *This is the kind of thing he and my father must have spent hours and days and nights on end discussing. Apart from me.* "But to look for it by torturing metal, Lucien?"

"If it is in one thing, then it is in all. But metal can be worked. Flesh cannot. Mortification is not the way."

She sighed and shivered as a breath of chill morning air passed through the open bed curtain. "Then, neither is guilt."

Lucien was silent for a long breath, then opened his knees and held out one arm. "Come. You're cold."

How could this be, when she had torn from him his life's goal? "The saving grace of the world," he'd said. Why did he not throw her down in anger, as even a reasonable man might?

But such an invitation from him might not come again. Isidora crept into the warm circle of his embrace and he enveloped her in the thick folds of the bed furs, with her back to his chest. "Isidora, listen to me." Lucien put his cheek to hers and together the skin heated between them.

She knew she did not want to hear whatever he was about to say. She wanted the moment to last, just the way they were, with her surrounded by his strength and solidity. But he continued, as she knew he would.

"Kalle cannot be allowed to return with the Key to Acre."

His words struck like a hammer blow to her heart. "Nay, Lucien, how can you? He would kill to keep it, or die before giving it up. Either way—"

"It must be retrieved. Or he must be stopped. One way or another."

"I do not see how it can be done! He—" She fell silent as her mind came to a point of clarity and remembered the strange ring her mother had sent with Faris to give her. Ayshka had told him Isidora would know what to do with it when the time was right.

She thought back to Kalle's hands, in the *laboratorium*. He, too, had a ring. One that had looked curiously incomplete. And now she knew what she must attempt.

Lucien spoke again. "You must understand, Isidora, that while it is true I want this Key, I would not try to take it from him were he a man of sound principles. As it is, he is much too dangerous to have such power."

"But how can you do this? If something should happen to you…I will feel responsible…and I could not bear your loss…"

"You made a choice, the best you knew how to make in the moment. Now I am making my own. What I choose is not your responsibility. And if 'something,' as you put it, happens to me, then that is God's choice. But I have to try."

Isidora refused to think about what his effort might entail. "How does your hand fare now?"

"It pains me. But it is better. Kalle is full of surprises. Indeed, I wish he was not my enemy."

"I wish he had never darkened our door. He brought nothing but suffering to my father's house. What are you going to do now?"

"I ask that you tell me where to find Kalle."

"I cannot. I am sorry, Lucien. You sound calm, but I know I have made you angry. And I will not put you in harm's way."

"You *will* tell me. I command you in this."

"But don't you understand? Now that he has the Key, he will go back to Acre and leave you alone, leave *us* alone."

Lucien drew her from his embrace, turned her about and caught her by the hands. "Isidora, consider what is at stake. Think you Kalle will be content to sit by, concocting batches of the Elixir? Think you he will sell it as medicine in vials at the *souk?* Nay, he will *use* it himself, to become as powerful as any one man could ever be on this earth. He will try and rule the world, Isidora. And if he is determined enough, he can succeed. If that happens, then God help us all."

Isidora felt faint, as though she might keel over. "I am the ruin of the world, then?"

"Nay. You can help me get it back. You *must.*"

Isidora nodded, her defeat complete. "It seems I have no choice. But I will take you there, I will not merely tell you. I want to face him one last time, for Faris's sake. Do you understand, Lucien?"

"Aye, I do."

She rubbed one of his hard, taut thighs. "Lucien?"

He raised an eyebrow.

"Will it ever be again, as it was with us last night? Or has that been lost, along with the Elixir?"

"I do not know, Isidora. Only God knows what lies in store for us."

At these words of little hope, her tears flowed at last. She turned away from Lucien, knowing how awful she must look, red-eyed and red-nosed, and despising herself for even caring at such a time.

Chapter Thirty-One

In a secluded spot across the river, Kalle's encampment lay shrouded in mist. The day was cold and gray, and his horses stood with their heads low as his men readied them for departure. He emerged from his pavilion as Lucien and Isidora approached, his fur-lined mantle hanging loose about his shoulders.

Isidora stood before him, her heart hammering her ribs, with Lucien at her side.

"You came," Kalle said to her. "But not alone. Will the Lord of Ainsley act as your champion, then? Does he plan to try to best me?"

"To reason with you," Lucien replied. "We have an exchange to make."

"I made no bargain with you! It is Isidora to whom I swore, no one else."

"But you owe me a debt of honor, Kalle."

"So satisfy that later, instead of hiding behind a woman's business with me now!"

"There is more to it than that."

"*Oui.* More than you know."

Isidora turned to Lucien. "Please, my lord. Allow me to speak to Kalle first, in private, before you do anything further."

"What have you to say to him that cannot be said to me?"

She clasped her hands before her. "Lucien, I ask this of you now, do not make me beg."

He grimaced, as if her words pained him, and stepped back. "Very well."

Isidora walked to Kalle, her limbs trembling. "Ayshka—" she began.

Kalle's gaze sharpened. "What about her?"

"Faris brought me something of hers, which she gave to him before she died. I think you may want to see it."

Slowly, as if he was being bled, Kalle's face turned white. He wrapped his mantle closer about himself. "*Non*…I have no wish to see anything."

"I believe it is something you gifted her with."

"I gifted her with nothing. And if I had, how dare you use it—a piece of my heart—against me? What kind of woman are you? A conniving one, just like every other woman, I suppose!"

"You have a heart, Kalle? I thought you prided yourself on going without," Isidora said.

"Your only interest is that it might be a place you could stab."

She reached into a pouch at her waist and withdrew a small object. "Here, Kalle. See for yourself."

Kalle's eyes narrowed, as if what she held in her palm emitted a bright light. "That could be any bauble. Why should I look at it?"

"You know what it is," she insisted. "I wager it fits the ring on your own finger, curve to curve. Do you not see? Her keeping it proves that my mother cared enough about you to guard your gift, even beyond death. It meant something to her. *You* meant something to her…"

Kalle's jaw twitched. "And you would sell it to me, for the Key?"

"Aye," Isidora admitted, hating to degrade her mother's offering in this manner, and ashamed to be throwing the one decent part of Kalle back into his face.

"I should simply take it from you. I can, you know."

"I know. But I tell you this—Ayshka Binte Amir is watching us from Heaven, right now. And she will either smile upon you, or curse you, according to the choice you make."

Kalle stared at the ring a moment longer, then looked away. "I am already cursed. Take it. Take this." He wrenched the matching ring off of his own finger and stuffed it into Isidora's hand. "Lucien! Let us finish."

Lucien strode over to stand between Isidora and Kalle. "Keep the scrolls, Kalle, for they came from your own abode. But as Deogal was my master, you will give me the Key and return Ayshka's image to Isidora. It is not right to have taken them the way you did. Indeed, to have procured them in such a dark manner can only produce your ultimate downfall, should you use them for ill."

Kalle laughed. "You forget Deogal was my master, as well! But the scrolls are useless without the Key."

"I have sworn to retrieve these things from you. I am prepared to give you what you paid for them."

Kalle smiled without humor. "First your hand? And then your life?"

Lucien replied without hesitation. "Aye."

Isidora felt unsteady, as if the earth had shifted beneath her feet, as it had on occasion in the Holy Land. "Oh! Please, nay!"

Kalle looked at her. "You see to what foolish lengths men in love will go?"

"Women in love can be just as foolish," Lucien said.

Isidora looked from Lucien to Kalle. "There is nothing foolish about love. But what Lucien proposes is not about love, it is about pride."

"It is about honor!" protested Lucien.

"And why is your honor of more import than mine? Why can it not be my choice to give up what I will, to help you? Can you not accept that help graciously? Is it because you do not consider me your equal?"

Lucien and Kalle both stared at her in silence. Then at each other.

"Kalle and I are equals. We must fight it out," said Lucien, and Kalle nodded his agreement.

"But what are you fighting over?" Isidora nearly shrieked.

"The victor will take all," Kalle replied.

"All," confirmed Lucien, his gaze devouring her.

"What do you mean? Including…me?"

Kalle snarled, "Of course, including you. One or the other of us will be dead, so whoever is left must take you in hand. Now get out of the way!"

"But—this was about the Key. The Elixir. Not me!"

"It is now."

"I'll have neither of you, in any case!"

"It is not up to you."

Isidora could not believe Lucien had made such a bald statement. She turned around and began to run toward the river, leaving them both behind.

"What are you doing?" Kalle bellowed. *"Beteuse!"*

She flung the words over her shoulder. "I will give to the river what you claim you do not want!"

They pursued her and raced each other. Isidora dared glance behind her but once. Kalle had tossed away his mantle and was surprisingly nimble, Lucien was the younger and faster, but she saw that neither of them would catch her before she reached the river.

She teetered at the brink of the embankment. The water ran dark and swift before her. She held the two halves of the ring over her head, one in each hand. "This is your choice, Kalle. Do you wish to have these back, and with them your chance at redemption? Or will you have me cast what is left of your heart into these depths?"

"You witch! Give them to me!" Kalle roared and lunged toward her. She staggered backward, and Lucien charged. The men met like stags and Lucien's head butted Kalle's chest, knocking his breath from him.

Isidora took a step to regain her balance, her foot met with a slimy stone and she fell from the edge into the rushing torrent.

Chapter Thirty-Two

She bobbed and floundered in the icy water. Her clothing wrapped around her legs, as if she had been bundled in a rug and tossed into the sea like a harem girl who had committed some crime.

"Isidora!"

Lucien's voice, wild with rage and grief. But she could not call out, for the cold robbed her of speech. She struggled to keep her head above the roiling surface as she tumbled along, scraping rocks and tree limbs. Then there was no sound but the river, no sight but the gray sky and the turbulence surrounding her.

A small hill of water rushed toward her. Before she had a chance to decide what it was, she was swept up and over it, of no more consequence than a twig to the surging flow. She took a last gasp of air, then dropped. Her downstream journey ended as the water sucked her deeper. It churned around her, tossing her body. Captured by the water's strength, she was in a hole at the base of a huge boulder hidden below the surface.

Isidora caught a glimpse of a hoof, an antler…she was not the only one to have been trapped here. Her lungs ached with the need to draw breath. A prayer flashed through her mind, for Lucien to enjoy a long and happy life…and for she herself to be with her mother again at last, bringing her Kalle's ring….

Lucien plowed through the icy water. He knew this river, knew its moods and fury and awesome power. The water tried to overwhelm him, and was close to succeeding. He fought its weight, its speed, and his own inability to breathe it.

The great stone lay before him. In summer it reared up like a sea monster sunning itself. He willed himself to reach it, to reach Isidora before the current swept him past. Kalle was carried nearer, fighting his own battle with the river's spirit. The fool! It was obvious he could not swim.

The deceptive, smooth hump of water that marked the boulder's presence was just ahead. Lucien prayed for strength. For a miracle. He had only an instant to find something to hang on to before he rushed past the rock. He clawed his way closer, deeper. His fingers caught a submerged jutting of wood, he kicked hard and the back of one knee met with a snag.

Pain screamed through his leg. But using the branch as an anchor, he plunged his upper body farther into the river and reached blindly down. The cascade of water caught him, battered his head against the stone. Dazed, he reached again.

Something brushed his fingertips. A hand. She was here! Hope and joy lent Lucien renewed strength. He grabbed it and pulled. But it was not Isidora's face that emerged, but Kalle's.

The knight must have gone straight over the top of the stone and under, just as Isidora had. In the ensuing wave of disappointment, Lucien wanted to release his enemy's hand. Let the water sweep Kalle away. Be rid of him. But a small voice within bade him hold on.

Kalle caught Lucien's right arm and exerted a huge force, as if trying to pull Lucien from his precarious, agonizing leghold. Lucien resisted, his body at the brink of exhaustion, his lungs about to inhale whatever they could, even if water was all that was to be had.

Then Kalle brought his other hand up from the depths. In his fist was a skein of black hair…still attached to Isidora. Kalle held Lucien's wrist, wrapped the hair around it, and let go.

He vanished.

Lucien hauled Isidora upward with his arms, and himself back with the excruciating leverage provided by his leg around the tree limb.

He boosted her until her face was clear of the water. Her head lolled to one side. Her lips were blue, her eyes closed. He had her, but he could do nothing except hold on to her. He gasped for breath and became aware once again of the frigid water pounding his body, of the pain in his leg. It would not take long before he, too, would have to let go…

"Oy, Lucien!"

He turned his head, tried to focus. Raymond stood on the bank, with Wace and Mauger and Kalle's man… Raymond launched a spear. It sailed through the air, a rope trailing behind it. Lucien's hope faltered as it fell short and the current carried it off. But then Raymond mounted his horse and hurled a second lance as Wace reeled in the first.

This time Raymond's aim was true and the lance sailed overhead, upstream. The line slapped the water and when it reached him, Lucien wrapped the rough, blessed rope around his arm. He fumbled for his dagger and cut the lance free.

"Ready!" he shouted, and prayed through the numbing cold that he could hold on long enough. He clasped Isidora around the ribs with one arm and put himself beneath her, to shield her head and back from the stones.

He made ready to launch free of the snag. But his leg was in agony. It was stuck. Indeed, at last he understood how he had not been swept away. His leg was not merely hooked around the tree limb. A broken branch impaled his calf, by his own weight and the force of the water tugging at him.

With a final effort, Lucien pushed with his other foot and freed himself. Once he had shoved off, the river washed them farther downstream. But when the line grew taut, the team of men ashore acted as a pivot, and Lucien and Isidora swung closer and closer to the shallows. At last an eddy swept them into a calmer spot and Lucien was able to struggle far enough out of the water that he might collapse upon a bed of pebbles.

He lay for a moment, to breathe, with Isidora draped over his chest. He had got her, thanks in no small part to Kalle…but what was the use of having his own life, if she had lost hers? He heaved himself upright, cradling her body in his lap.

A clatter of feet and hooves met his ears above the rush of the river and the wail of misery rising in his own heart. He looked down at her. Strands of wet hair drizzled across her cold, white face, and a hank of it remained entangled about his wrist.

Raymond jumped down from his horse. "Is she…?"

Lucien met Raymond's gaze and saw his own anguish reflected in his friend's eyes. "I'm taking her home." Lucien struggled to his feet, lifting Isidora as he came. His wounded leg threatened to buckle, but he forced it straight. Then the weary muscles in his arms quivered and, fearing he might drop his lady, he slung her over his shoulder.

Her head flopped against his back. Dead weight. Dead…*dead!* Just like Estelle, just like Robert…

Then…her body spasmed. She coughed and warm water splashed. Lucien staggered with her off the rocky strand and lay her on the grass. She gasped, choked and gasped again.

"Isidora…" He stroked her face, chafed her arms and refrained from shaking her by the shoulders for being so rash. "Are you all right?"

After a final bout of coughing she opened her eyes, her lashes in wet, black clumps. "I—I think so…"

"You're shivering." Lucien's own teeth chattered as he accepted Raymond's mantle and picked up Isidora once more, wrapping her securely in its folds. He had nearly lost her…he would not let her go again.

She stirred and whispered, "I'm sorry for causing this trouble, Lucien. I thank you for saving me…and enemy or no, I would thank Kalle, as well, though I lost his ring."

Lucien kissed her cheeks and forehead. "Think upon it no more. But, Kalle…is gone."

To his dismay, Isidora stared at him dumbly, then began to weep. He looked to Raymond, who shrugged and murmured in an aside, "Who knows what goes on in their minds?" Then, more loudly, "I will send men to search the banks, milady. But, Lucien, you both need warming and we must see to your leg. Let us return to Ainsley."

"What is wrong with his leg?" Isidora demanded through her tears.

Lucien gave her a squeeze. "Shh, woman. 'Tis of no import. Be still."

She buried her face against his chest and was silent.

At the hall once more, with Isidora in the care of Larke, Amelie and Ceridwen's cousins, Lucien sat before the fire with Raymond, Wace, Mauger and Kalle's man, Earm.

Lucien's leg throbbed and had swollen to the point where to stand upon it made him clench his teeth so he could not speak. His head ached, he felt sleepy and could not remember much of what anyone had been saying. But he remained in the hall, though he longed to go upstairs to his solar. "Where did you find the rope, Raymond?"

Raymond looked in the direction of the dark knight. "Earm, here. His quick wits provided it from Kalle's horses' picket line."

Lucien inclined his head in a solemn nod. "Glad am I of your strong arm, Raymond. And, Earm, I will gift you with anything you desire, be it in my power to bestow."

The knight shifted and glanced from Lucien to Raymond and back. "I would only ask leave to remain, to try to find Lord Kalle's body. But I fear his people in Acre will not believe me when I tell them he drowned by accident."

Lucien rubbed his brow. "If we find him, he will need to be buried here, and we will give him the honor he is due.

We'll provide you with letters, and put our seals upon them as witnesses to what happened. None can fault you, Earm. Indeed, if you wish to stay, I can always use a good man."

Earm shook his head. "Many thanks, but I feel I must return. Someone awaits me in Acre. I will make a fresh start there…"

"There is news of another's death that should be delivered to his kinsmen." Lucien stared at the red glow of the coals.

"Em, Lucien," Raymond began. "I should tell you, it is not certain that Faris is dead. He asked us to allow you and his sister to think so, to keep Kalle from going after the Cistercians to find him. I am not convinced Kalle would have bothered, but the risk…"

Lucien swung his head around—regretted the sudden movement—and glared at Raymond. "You approved this? You partook of this lie, and created such suffering in Isidora's heart, as well as mine? And you allowed Larke to further it?"

"It seemed the lesser evil at the time, Lucien, and could well be the truth. But I humbly beg your pardon."

"Go beg it of Isidora!"

Raymond stood, his gaze even. "Right. So will I do. But she'll have more courtesy than thee, I trow."

Lucien realized he had gone too far. He got to his feet, as well, though only one leg bore his weight. "Raymond, please, forgive me. Take your rest here for as long as you will. I do not doubt your good intentions."

"Aye. Sit down before you fall down, Lucien." Slowly, Raymond retook his own seat. "But Wace and I should be heading home soon. We have some horses awaiting us, up the vale."

Lucien settled back into his chair with relief. "When you reach Rookhaven, tell Lady Ceridwen to make ready to attend a wedding."

Raymond raised an eyebrow. "Indeed? You'd best ask the bride before you make any further plans, Lucien. These things are not so simple as you seem to think."

"And a few things are more simple than you know, Beauchamp. Help me upstairs, will you?"

Isidora woke, but darkness surrounded her. Too much like the suffocating darkness of the cold, churning water. She shivered, then felt the reassuring warmth of a body at her back. A familiar, comforting hand slid down her arm, hugging it against her chest from behind.

"Lucien…where are Larke and the others?"

"I sent them away. Are you feeling better?"

She hurt all over, but her heart ached the most. "Aye."

"What is the matter, Isidora?"

She swallowed against the tightness in her throat. "I feel that I have been the death of Kalle. Taunting him like that…it was wrong."

Lucien sighed. "No one forced him to jump into the river when he could not swim."

"You offer little comfort, Lucien."

"I seemed to be running afoul of everyone this night."

Isidora turned in his embrace and felt his forehead. It was hot and damp. "I've caused you to suffer, as well. You have fever. Would that Kalle were here to attend your leg!"

"I thank God he is not. I am fine. I'll go to the monastery tomorrow, for Faris may live yet, Raymond says."

Brilliant, unexpected hope leaped in Isidora's breast. "Oh…I pray it is true! I will accompany you. And so will Larke. Make no attempt to stop us, Lucien."

"Heaven forbid that I even try! Raymond's brother there has some skill with wounds. He saw to Faris's, so I understand."

She turned back around, so Lucien was melded against her once more. "Good. He can see to yours, as well, then."

He gave her a little squeeze. "Isidora…I am…tired. I have been harsh with you. I—"

"Lucien, you are only trying to do your duty. Do not apologize for that. I understand."

"You understand…but do you want *me,* and all that I entail?"

"You mean, your pursuit of the Elixir?"

"Aye."

Isidora shrank inside. "I cannot compete with the lure of alchemy, Lucien. No woman can, unless she herself is part of the process."

"Earm has handed over the Key and the scrolls to me. He confessed that Kalle told him he would be cursed if he tried to steal them or profit from them."

"You did not even hear what I just said."

"I did. You cannot compete. But you need not, Isidora. I am returning the Key and scrolls to you, to do with as you see fit."

She could not believe she had heard a-right. "You are?"

"My wedding gifts to you."

"Your what?"

"You know what I said."

"Oh. Were I standing, I'd need to lie down!"

He murmured into her ear, "Well, you are not, and of that I am glad. The question remains…will you have me?"

She could not suppress a small wriggle of pleasure, which produced a groan from Lucien. She smiled. "Indeed, my lord, that I will."

Epilogue

The pure, clear voices of the Cistercian monks soared into the night, the song carrying with it their love of God. Isidora breathed in deep to savor the beauty of the sound, and held the Key and scrolls in a tight bundle as Brother Percy approached.

"My lady, you have summoned me?"

"I have something to give you in trust, brother. I cannot bring myself to destroy these ancient things, yet I want them kept in secret." She explained to him what she understood the power of the Key and scrolls to be and how she feared them, for Lucien's sake.

Percy listened in silence. "A heavy burden, indeed. The Elixir, a panacea for mankind, or the power to rule the world…no wonder Kalle was so sorely tempted by it."

"Not only him, but my father…and Lucien, as well."

Percy smiled charmingly. "But not you? You have no desire to be an empress?"

"Why, indeed not!"

"And Faris al-Rashid, who has become my good friend,

has no claim upon this legacy? I would not want to see him suffer any further loss."

Isidora frowned. "Faris, now that he is on the mend, will no doubt seek fresh glory in battle, not by mixing metals."

"Ah, so there is some good to be seen in conflict."

"Brother Parsifal, you confuse me."

"I mean only to say that should the world be made a perfect place, it would cease to exist. An excellent reason to keep such an Elixir out of the hands of those who wish to do good with it, as well as those who would do evil. So why keep it at all?"

"Because it has been so dearly bought. My father's life and more…"

"Very well. Give it to me, then, and you will have seen the last of it. I will be its guardian."

Isidora placed the bundle into his hands and breathed her relief. "Many thanks, my lord."

Percy bowed to her. "This abbey is home to many treasures."

"You are chief among them, I trow," she said sincerely.

Percy laughed out loud at this. "Go to your husband, lass."

Husband. Warmth spread through her at the thought of Lucien. They were wed. Informally, but wed nevertheless. Although Conrad had still not returned with a priest of his own choosing, the Cistercian abbot had given them his blessing in the meantime.

She turned, to see Lucien leaning in the doorway, carved stone kings on either side of him and ancient knights above. He smiled, though he was pale and, she knew, in pain.

"You should not be using that leg in such a manner, my lord."

"If not for this, then what would you have me do with it?"

She went to him, close, but not touching. "It should be in bed."

"Ah, would that it could, and me along with it. But it is time to depart for Ainsley. Larke is anxious to get Faris back to where she can keep a close watch upon him."

"And what will Wace think of that?"

"Wace is herding horses with Raymond, there is nothing he can do, except get wounded himself, to gain her sympathy. Besides, he is much too young."

"He is a stout lad and Faris is not about to allow Larke's fantasies to get the better of her. Or him. But she should be wed sooner rather than later," Isidora added.

"Well, it will have to be later, because I have not yet chosen a husband for her."

"If you do not make certain it is a man to her liking— she will do it for you, one way or another."

"At least my mother is pleased with the choice I made in you."

"And if she had not been?"

"Then she would have had a long time to regret not appreciating my wisdom."

"You are not wise, Lucien."

"Nay. I am a besotted fool." He caught her in his arms and put his lips to hers.

A monk walked in, saw them, and hurriedly turned around and fled.

Isidora squirmed. "We are being improper in this place."

"Nay, this is but the remainder of the kiss of God the

abbott bade me bestow upon you. In fact, there is a good deal more of it left. Indeed it may take the rest of my life to deliver the whole of it to you, in divine increments…"

"Oh, well, I thank you for being so thorough."

"Aye, I intend to be."

She pulled back. "Lucien, I—I have given the Key to Sir Parsifal, I mean, Brother Percy, for safekeeping. But if you—"

"That is good."

"You are not angry?"

He searched her eyes. "Isidora, have you no idea of the truth of the matter?"

"What truth?"

He put his hand to her face, cupping her cheek. "That *you* are the true Elixir. You are the touchstone. All fire and innocence. Devotion and love. Nothing more perfect exists for me."

"Oh, Lucien. You please me beyond words…."

His mouth hovered above hers and he smiled. "Then stop using them, Isidora."

* * * * *

Don't miss the next exciting volume in
MEDIEVAL LORDS & LADIES
COLLECTION,
Exotic East.
Available in November 2007 from M&B™.